THE LAST LORD OF GOWER

THE LAST LORD OF GOWER

PART TWO

A THORN IN FLESH

---

by

DEREK W. DRAISEY

DRAISEY PUBLISHING

DRAISEY PUBLISHING
73 CONWAY ROAD
PENLAN
SWANSEA, SA5 7AU

First published in 2007 by Draisey Publishing
Copyright © Derek Draisey 2007

ISBN 978-0-9546544-4-3

Set in Times New Roman by Logaston Press, HR3 6QH
and printed in Great Britain by
Bell & Bain Ltd., Glasgow

To the memory of my father

ACKNOWLEDGMENTS

Special thanks to Christine Eynon for providing the cover;
to Ron Shoesmith FSA for presenting the text and the maps as they
appear; and to Andy Johnson of Logaston Press, whose willing assistance
made this publication possible.

In **1116** – *he* (Gruffudd ap Rhys) *sent his companions to make an attack
and a raid upon a castle that was situated near Abertawe.
And that belonged to an earl called Henry Beaumont.
And after burning the outer castle and after the keepers had saved
the tower and some of his men had been killed, he turned back again.*

That same year – *a castle that was in Gower he* (Gruffudd ap Rhys)
*burnt outright, and slew many men in it.
And then William de Londres for fear of him left his castle
and all his cattle and all his precious wealth.*

Brut y Tywysogion (The Chronicle of The Princes)

CONTENTS

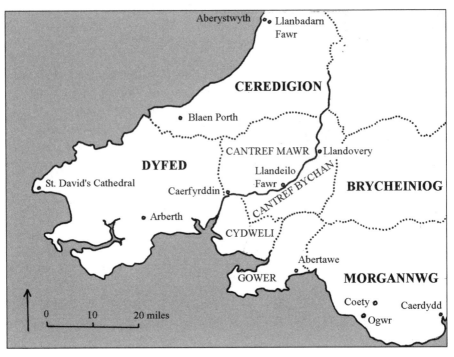

"The Southern Lands"

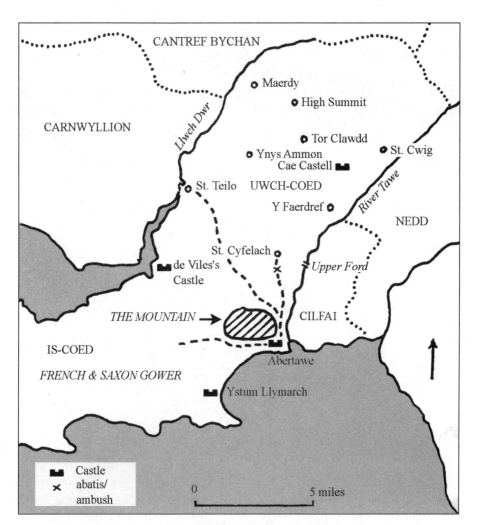

CANTREF BYCHAN

CARNWYLLION

Maerdy

High Summit

Tor Clawdd

Ynys Ammon
Cae Castell

St. Cwig

Llwch Dwr

St. Teilo UWCH-COED

Y Faerdref

River Tawe

NEDD

St. Cyfelach

de Viles's
Castle

Upper Ford

THE MOUNTAIN →

CILFAI

IS-COED

Abertawe

FRENCH & SAXON GOWER

Ystum Llymarch

Castle
abatis/
ambush

0   5 miles

"The Lordship of Gower"

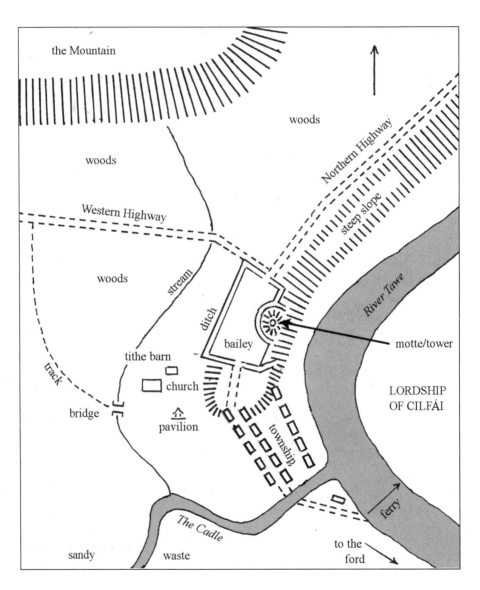

the Mountain

woods

woods

Western Highway

woods

stream

ditch

track

tithe barn

church

bridge

pavilion

bailey

woods

Northern Highway

steep slope

River Tawe

motte/tower

LORDSHIP
OF CILFÁI

township

ferry

The Cadle

sandy

waste

to the
ford

Abertawe

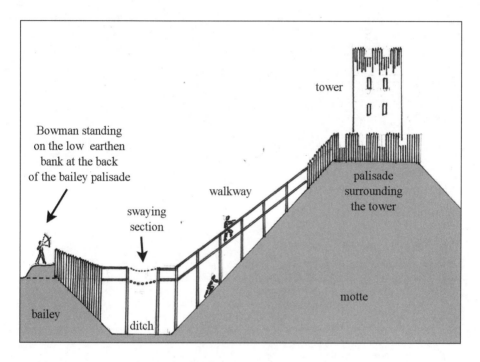

'The Walkway at Abertawe"

PROLOGUE

HOMAGE

On the open ground north of the castle at Abertawe the Frenchman, Henry de Beaumont, sat in a chair, observing the barbarian who made towards him. Unkempt, thick moustached, the man was typical of his kind: a Countryman whom the Saxons called Welsh, whom his own kind labelled a barbarian simply because he lived beyond the pale of French influence. The man could be seen for what he was, proud and intractable with a swarthy, raw-boned face that suggested he did not take kindly to paying homage to anyone.

But pay homage he would: Beaumont would settle for no less, not when Henry, King of England, had granted him the right to march on Gower and demand submission from the two chieftains who held sway. The older chieftain had been slain in the fighting, but this one, Rhydderch ap Cadifor, had proved a wily adversary from the start, finally routing the French and Saxon soldiers sent against him, a hundred and twenty of whom had been taken as prisoners to be used as counters for more favourable terms of submission.

When the barbarian came to a halt, Beaumont observed that his clothes were colourless, his woollen cloak the worse for wear; his left hand rested upon a sword hilt and his face, close up, bespoke intelligence, even hinted at humour. '*A pity,*' Beaumont thought, '*that he doesn't speak French. We could have talked, man to man. I would have like that.*'

"On your knee, Countryman," the Marcher lord, William de Londres, ground out in the Countryman's tongue.

The eyes of the barbarian narrowed disdainfully; it did not go unnoticed by Beaumont. His advisors were right: the man would rebel at the first opportunity. Nevertheless, a bargain was a bargain, terms had been agreed upon. If the peace held till winter it would suffice. As the barbarian dropped to one knee Beaumont took note of his hair, in particular the style: cut round to the eyes and ears at the front, then falling to the neck at the back, a fashion peculiar to both the men and women of his kind.

"Your hands," the Marcher lord spat, "place them between the Earl's."

The barbarian complied; Beaumont took the man's hands in his. Now he had him at his mercy. One word from him and the Marcher lord would cut the barbarian down – but what would that profit him when, a bowshot away, there were over two hundred barbarians, and ranged on their knees in front of them were the prisoners who, likewise, would be cut down, after which battle would begin and he, Henry de Beaumont, Earl of Warwick, would be caught in the thick of it. Far better to settle for terms.

"Do you wish to be the Earl's man?" the Marcher lord demanded.

"I wish it," replied the barbarian, his gaze fixed on Beaumont.

"Then repeat after me, I am your man of life and limb and hereby swear fealty."

No response was forthcoming; in the silence that followed, Beaumont empathized with the barbarian, seeing both his limitations and his forte. True, the man had done well in defence of his homeland, but to have fought on would have resulted in the annihilation of his people, either by the sword, or as a result of starvation. His strength was not so much his ability to outwit, but that his remarkable success could spark off a general uprising among barbarians everywhere; that made him dangerous.

"Why the delay?" the Marcher lord growled. "Didn't you understand what I said?"

"I understood perfectly," the barbarian retorted; he fixed his gaze on Beaumont. "I am your man of life and limb – and hereby swear fealty."

Beaumont brought the barbarian's hands close to his lips, then sealed the ceremony with a kiss. It was a moment in which, close up, each looked the other in the eye; both knew exactly what the other had been thinking. Beaumont indicated for the man to rise, satisfied that the ceremony had passed without incident; conscious, too, that it would not have been so had his right-hand man, Henry de Viles, been present. Poor Henry! To have suffered ignominious defeat at the hand of a barbarian, to have been taken prisoner, then ransomed, was more than the man could contain.

The question was, what to do with Henry? To take him back to Warwick was out of the question: the man had become increasingly deranged due to a blow to the head; he was now an embarrassment. On the other hand, to entrust him with a castle here, in Gower, would surely lead to trouble, for no matter how much he cautioned him, Henry de Viles would have but one goal: to avenge himself against the barbarian, Rhydderch ap Cadifor.

. . . . . .

PRAYER OF THE DAMNED

NINE AND HALF YEARS AFTER THE SUBMISSION CEREMONY

At his castle on the Llwch Dwr – the River of Shining Water – the Frenchman, Henry de Viles, sat in his fire-lit hall, watching his unexpected visitor leave. Only when the man had gone did he rise and, with two bloodhounds at his heels, make for the chamber at one end of the hall.

He pushed open a door, his eyes roving. A semi-darkness prevailed, but from a narrow window a beam of dust-laden light lit up a wall that displayed a cross, beneath which was a prayer stool. He made for the stool; as he knelt, staring at the cross, one of the bloodhounds slobbered his face. Dispassionately, he shoved the dog aside, made the sign of the cross, then crouched on the stool.

Eyes closed, hands together, fingers almost touching his lips, he prayed, his opening words taken from a psalm. "*Lord, Thou hast known my reproach, my shame and my dishonour* – for lo – ten years have I craved to avenge myself against the barbarian, Rhydderch ap Cadifor – yes, craved to be stood over him while his blood staineth the soil at my feet. And it will be so – for, Lord, I have learned that to be worthy of Thine assistance I must suffer – and suffer I have. Each time I have taken steps to bring about his downfall I have been thwarted – but Thou – *Thou art He that took me out of the womb; Thou didst make me hope when I was upon my mother's breasts* – and today – today, You have answered my prayers. Today, You sent unto me a man willing to betray his lord, a Judas who, for the price of gold, is prepared to deliver him into my hands. For this I thank You, Lord – and yet there is one thing more I must ask of You. Give unto me the life of the unbeliever, Maredudd Goch – and let Rhydderch ap Cadifor see him die – afore I destroy him too."

CHAPTER 1

FLIRTING WITH DEATH

On the eighth of February the hinds were in season. That same day, in a clearing where on all sides naked branches were a plexus against a leaden sky, a dozen horsemen milled about over withered grass when, suddenly, Maredudd spurred, distancing himself from two deer-hounds, one of which recoiled from the snapping jaws of the other. To stimulate their hunting instincts the hounds had been thrown pieces of raw flesh; hence the savagery of the pack.

Maredudd circled, a breeze ruffling his red hair. *Whomph, whomph, whomph* – a five-foot throwing spear he held at arm's length, twirling it between the fingers of his right hand. He was restless to be away, the delay due to the huntsman, Huw, moving about in woods. "Huw, what's keeping you?" he shouted. "You told me you'd seen a herd here this morning."

"So it's dropped back into the woods," Huw retorted, "and until I find tracks you'd be as well to shut your mouth, you thieving swine!"

"D'you have to vex him?" Rhydderch asked.

A grin distorted Maredudd's short, red beard as he turned to his foster-brother, Rhydderch ap Cadifor, Lord of the Commote of Gower Uwch-coed, to whom he was captain of guard. "Afore you turned up we were at knucklebone. And d'you know what? I took five pence from him – five pence! You'd think it was a fortune."

"Your bones, were they? Some say they're charmed, got a will all of their own."

"They can say what they like," Maredudd threw out. "I throw a good hand, that's all – not like some. And you, you caught up with that soothsayer yet?"

Rhydderch shook his head. "She can't be found; could be dead for all we know."

"Na, wherever she is, she'll be back. This is 1116, another *year with a cursed six as a last number – one in which death may walk at will.*"

"I wouldn't make light of it if I were you," said Rhydderch.

"I'm not, I firmly believe there'll be trouble – which reminds me, is there any word of that rebel, Gruffudd ap Rhys?"

"The King of England," said Rhydderch, stroking the neck of his white stallion, "he's ordered several lords of these Southern Lands to hunt Gruffudd down."

"They'll not catch him. I reckon he'll go on, stirring things up so we can settle with the French, more so with that pig, Henry de Viles."

The huntsman emerged from woods, a leather cap framing his rugged, unshaven face. "North it is, lads. Just remember what I said about dismounting in them woods, there's wild pig everywhere." Placing a foot in one stirrup, Huw hauled himself into the saddle. "One more thing. Afore you use your bows make sure no one's about to pass in front of you. We want no accidents on our first day out." Wheeling, he entered the woods, head down, following tracks and droppings.

Rhydderch led off; among those who kept station on him were his two youthful sons. Caleb, the eldest, was seventeen, somewhat tall like his father, his handsome features inherited from his mother. His inborn dignity of manner made him a haughty youth, dominant among the young men who, as a band of armed youths, were part of his father's retinue. The other son, Owain, a year younger, was more inclined to reach for a harp than a sword, but would not suffer the overbearing attitude of his older brother. There was always discord between them.

Ducking beneath a branch, Owain peered ahead. Moving in the ground cover were long-legged deer-hounds with thick, ragged coats that were mostly blue-grey. He whistled to the one called Giff; she bounded to his side, then leapt up at him.

"You ruin that bitch," Caleb sneered. "She should be with the pack, not fawning at your heels."

"Giff will give a good account of herself," Owain bit back, "you'll see."

"She didn't fare well against Arthog back there, when we were throwing meat."

"Arthog's bigger than her, all mouth like you."

Caleb snatched the reins of Owain's horse. "You never learn, d'you?"

"Not from you; now let go!"

"That's enough, you two; now separate!" Rhydderch waited for his sons to disengage. "Has it never occurred to you that I spend my days fostering good will among the lords of these Southern Lands, only to find that, like you who are brothers, they're more concerned about harbouring differences? Now let this be an end to your squabbling."

Caleb moved off, saying, in a subdued tone, "I'll settle with you later."

Owain opened his mouth, but his father's expression discouraged him from retort. He averted his gaze, spurring in the wake of his brother, resentment smouldering within.

The huntsman, suspecting that the herd had gone to ground, sent the dogs to quarter and suddenly the woods were alive as barking broke out, echoing among the trees; at the same time red deer were moving off with stiff-legged jerks, bouncing on all fours. A horn blew. Shouts resounded. Horses were spurred. The chase took off, but the hunters soon encountered difficulties: a fallen tree lay, obstructing their path; thickets forced them to turn aside; boggy ground had them swearing as their horses floundered in ooze. They became dispersed as the faint-hearted fell behind.

The baying of hounds carried over a clearing as, head down, Maredudd rode out of the woods, twigs giving way to his passing. Thundering over withered grass, the hooves of his bay sending sods tumbling in the air, he viewed hounds hard on the heels of swift-moving deer. None of the dogs set their teeth to flesh, but kept the herd moving towards the opposing tree-line.

On Maredudd's left, Rhydderch galloped, cloak billowing over the back of his white stallion. Rightwards, the huntsman set the pace, Caleb hard by, riding recklessly in a bid to take the lead. Maredudd snatched a glance over his shoulder – there was no sign of the yellow tunic worn by the younger brother. That Owain may have suffered a fall had occurred to Rhydderch also, it showed in his face; he reined hard, snatching a backward glance as he did so. Maredudd did the same. Someone thundered by almost colliding with Maredudd's bay.

Far out to the right, Owain appeared to view, a youth hard on his heels, when suddenly he slowed to negotiate a waterlogged hollow. Too close, the accompanying youth attempted to rein aside, but his horse collapsed, throwing him to the ground. A thump coupled with a loud neigh prompted Owain to turn his head and witness the horse down, its legs kicking air, the rider lost to view. He reined about, cantering towards the fallen horse and, without a thought to the huntsman's warning, quickly set his feet to the ground.

A rustle arose from nearby shrub. A boar stuck its head out from beneath the brush, its black eyes fixed on Owain. As it emerged, tusks projecting beyond fleshy lips, it proved a powerful brute with bristly hair.

Knelt beside the fallen youth, Owain was unaware of the danger. It was in his mind to go for help when, rising to his feet, he caught sight of the boar. Fear gripped him; he dithered over whether to stand or run. "God, no!" he muttered, feeling weak at the knees. "What am I to do?" Fumbling an arrow, he quickly laid it to his bow; at the same time the boar charged, its black bulk ploughing a swath through withered grass. Owain let loose; the arrow carried over the boar's head. Panic seized him, he started to recede. Dropping his bow, he made for his horse, but it bolted, taking the reins beyond his reach. A cry escaped his lips as, arms outstretched, he raced beside the horse; it soon showed him its hind quarters.

Not daring to look back, he kept going, pumping his arms as if by doing so he could impart speed to his strangely leaden legs. At any moment he expected to be knocked off his feet. '*God, no,*' he cried within, '*I don't want to die. Save me.*' Then a lengthy growl erupted into savagery, causing him to glance back.

Giff, having rushed the boar, had succeeded in warding off the attack; now the boar charged her while she, fangs exposed, repeatedly leapt aside, desperate to avoid those murderous tusks. The boar turned sharply as it came in low again. Giff was hit, tossed and landed in the grass, yelping pitifully.

The rumble of hooves grew louder, causing Owain to turn as Maredudd, leaning precariously to the right, closed with the boar, hurling a spear at the beast's hind quarters. The wild pig squealed, its anguish made manifest by the violence of its turnabouts. A second horseman drew close and, as Owain faltered, his father caught him, carrying him out of harm's way.

Reining about, Maredudd spurred. A second spear poised, he came in low again. The boar, still squealing, made to charge, dragging its lamed leg. Maredudd let loose, his spear embedding in the boar's side, but the wild pig continued forward until, passing beneath the horse, flying hooves cracked its skull. As the horse stumbled, Maredudd pitched over the high frame of his saddle. More by luck than management both he and the horse remained as one.

Drawing rein, Rhydderch lowered Owain to the ground. Both witnessed Maredudd leap from his horse and, with his skene, fall upon the boar, driving the eight-inch blade into its neck. Only when Maredudd appeared to relax did they progress towards him, the father riding, the son running until, falling upon his knees, he embosomed Giff's shaggy head. "No, Giff, don't die. You can't...."

"Let's take a look at her," said Rhydderch, kneeling. Probing the dog's flanks, he parted bloodstained hair. Giff raised her head from Owain's lap, her affecting eyes following his every move.

"Will she live, father?"

"I'd say so – she's got grit."

"And I haven't. I've never been so fearful in my life."

"That's nothing to be ashamed of."

"But I'm your son. One day I might be called upon to lead an attack."

"Just because you're my son doesn't mean I expect you to be fearless. When I was your age it wasn't a boar I faced, but a Saxon and, believe me, I was trembling just like you are now."

"Then – then you're not ashamed of me?"

"No, all I ask is that you think afore doing anything rash."

Maredudd's voice carried. "Come, Dewi," he called to the fallen youth, "on your feet." The youth rose unsteadily. Although dazed he was none the worse for his fall; nor was his horse, having moved some distance away.

Others arrived on the scene, voicing concern and commenting on the size of the boar. Caleb was among the last, jubilant about being in at the death of two hinds, one of which he had brought down with his own bow. In an outpouring to act he had ripped out intestines and thrown them to the dogs. His hands were still bloody when, reining in, he sneered. "Hunting boar out of season, brother? I'll wager you were afraid."

Owain looked askance at his father who quietly shook his head. "Not me. What's it to you anyway?"

"Come, admit it," Caleb persisted, "you were afraid."

"Caleb," said Maredudd, "go, make a bier for the dog."

"Why me? That's work for others."

"It's work for all," Rhydderch cut in. "One day soon you might need one for a companion. And I'll tell you this, Caleb. If you're unwilling to set an example, then you're unfit to lead."

A long moment passed before Caleb returned, "Very well, anything to oblige." He jerked his head, indicating to two youths to join him, then rode off, voicing derision. No one expected him to put his hands to work.

. . . . . .

At a hunting lodge that evening, Rhydderch sat at a trestle table, carousing with members of the hunting party. Despite good cheer his gaze drifted to the floor where Owain cared for his faithful hound – an affecting scene, for not only did it remind him of how close he had come to losing one of his beloved sons, but it made him mindful that what had happened was but a taste of what must be.

Flirting with death – there could be no escape: the land had long been cursed, though no one had been aware of it until that fateful day, ten years ago, when, in an oak grove to the north, he stumbled upon a rude shelter of branches and mud. He recalled a woman sat in the doorway, staring intently through smoke from a fire; her words rang in his ears. '*Know this. For these lands this year is cursed. Like all years with a cursed six as its last number, it is one in which Death may walk at will. Sometimes Death is impatient, so he comes afore his allotted time. Sometimes he chooses to come late, even unto the following year – but he comes nonetheless.*'

Her words proved true: with many men the Frenchman, Henry de Beaumont, Earl of Warwick, came to Gower against the sons of Caradog ap Rhydderch ab Iestin, and won the more fertile parts from them, where he built several castles. And he brought Saxons from Somerset there, where they obtained lands, and the greatest usurpation of any Frenchman was *his* in the Commote of Gower Is-coed.

Distracted by Maredudd's laugh, he heard him say, "No, Caleb, we're a people subject to French rule and nothing short of an uprising throughout these Southern Lands will change anything."

While he listened, Rhydderch became mindful of Maredudd's ability to relate to young people, a quality that served him well as captain of guard: it did not conflict with the way he commanded respect from the most obstreperous of youths, nor did it make him a liability, for in company Maredudd was careful not to say too much when speaking in the Countryman's tongue. Caleb, on the other hand, could be less than discreet: ousting the French was his favourite subject, one that might prove incriminating if what he said was passed on to the foreign administrators at Beaumont's castle at Abertawe.

"Yes, I understand that," Caleb returned, "and I also understand that we need someone like Gruffudd ap Rhys to unite us all under the one banner. I mean, he's a prince by right and his activities, they could start a revolt."

"What activities?" Maredudd asked. "All he's done is make pointless attacks on foreign abodes in Dyfed and Ceredigion. Then he melts away into the wilds of Cantref Mawr, a place so forested that no Frenchman would dare follow after him. No, Gruffudd will have to do better than that if he's to gain a following."

"Wait till he attacks a castle," Caleb persisted, "then we'll see his warband grow."

"Hotheads, no doubt, will join him by the score, but he's going to need the support of men like your father if he's to be taken seriously, only no lord is going to...."

"Look," Owain called from the floor. "Giff has gained her feet."

"Who cares?" Caleb returned. "We've important things to discuss."

"Important to you, you mean," Owain bit back. "Well, Giff is important to me and I'm indebted to Iorwerth for giving her to me."

"Iorwerth is a traitor," Caleb sneered, "but that never seems to bother you."

"Why should it? I'd rather him than you."

"That's enough, you two," said Rhydderch. "None of us care for your wrangling."

"Well, it's more than I can stomach," Caleb returned, "to have a brother who favours someone who took sides with the French against his own kind."

"Correction. Your brother uses Iorwerth to get at you. As for Iorwerth...." Rhydderch paused, then continued in French, "*I've told you afore, his close ties with the French are of use to us because, one, he enlightens us on how they think and, two, he has much to say about what goes on among Frenchmen far and wide.*"

"Well, I don't trust him," said Caleb.

"No more do I," said Rhydderch, "but to ignore him is to live in ignorance."

Caleb declined comment and, to ease the situation, Maredudd threw out, "I think a little entertainment is called for; now me, I've been piecing together some verse...."

"We don't want to hear your damn verse," the huntsman growled. "Let's have a song, only not by you."

"Very well, a song it is," said Maredudd, grinning. "Owain, let's have that one in which a mother sings of her husband to her young son."

As Owain rose in search of his harp, Rhydderch caught the disdain on Caleb's face. He bit his lip: no words could reconcile them to the fact that they were brothers who would soon have to take up in arms. Even to relate that he and his uncle, Rhys ap Caradog, the last native lord of all Gower, had been at loggerheads for five years, to be reconciled only five days before Lord Rhys's death had long proved a waste of words. Bad blood ran in the family, for Rhydderch ap Caradog – another of his father's brothers – had been slain by a cousin, Meirchion, the father of Iorwerth who had marched beside the French against his own kind.

That Iorwerth was perfidious Rhydderch could overlook, if only because it suited him, but one thing troubled him about cousin Iorwerth. Following the death of Lord Rhys, Rhys's son, Cadwgan, had been lord of what remained Countryman's land in the lowland areas until he met his death in a hunting accident. Such deaths were regarded with suspicion – and suspicion there was because Cadwgan had met his death while hunting *with* Iorwerth *on* Iorwerth's land.

What made matters worse was that Iorwerth's reaction had been to inform the French. Thus with impunity the French had marched on Cadwgan's court, taken hostages and annexed Cadwgan's Commote of Gower Is-coed. Iorwerth, of course, had benefited from the take-over, and while it had never been made convincingly clear why Cadwgan had been hunting with one he openly despised, there was no hard evidence to prove that Iorwerth had been involved in murder.

Owain's voice broke into his thoughts as, harp in hand, he sang,

"Dinogad's speckled tunic was made from the skins of a speckled stoat.
Whip, whip, whipalong, eight times we'll sing this song.
When your father goes a-hunting with his spear on his shoulder
and provisions in his hand, he calls for his dogs,
'Giff, Gaff, fetch it, catch it!'
And they would seldom fail to make a catch.
In his coracle he will slay fish as a lion does its prey.
When your father is on the moors he brings back stags, fawns or boars,
spotted grouse from the mountains,
fish from the falls at Old Oak Fountain.
Whatever your father strikes with his spear:
otters, wild cats, foxes in their lair –
unless it has wings it never gets far."

A round of applause petered out with the entry of Bledri, the court blacksmith, a short, burly man who approached the table, saying, "We've received some alarming news, my lord. It's to do with that rebel, Gruffudd ap Rhys."

"They've not caught him, have they?" said Caleb, rising from the bench.

"No, he's attacked Arberth Castle – took the garrison by surprise."

"Arberth," Caleb exclaimed. "That's in Dyfed, isn't it? I knew it, didn't I say he'd attack a castle?"

"So you did," said Maredudd and, to Rhydderch in French, *"Looks like Gruffudd has set his mind on bigger things. So why don't I go roaming early this year?"*

"So you can join with Gruffudd?" Rhydderch replied, also in French. *"No, let's see what develops first."*

"Why wait?" said Caleb in the Countryman's tongue. "Gruffudd has made the first move, let's join him."

"I said no," Rhydderch countered, then continued, in French, *"And if you've got to speak of rebellion, then do so in the Frenchman's tongue and I don't care whether you loath the tongue or not."*

Silence reigned until the blacksmith said, "My lord, will you be returning to court?"

"No."

"Well, how long will you be staying here?"

"A day, maybe two," said Rhydderch, reluctant as always to proclaim either his whereabouts or how long he would be away from court. Where the blacksmith was concerned he felt it necessary to be on his guard: the man had only recently taken up the appointment; moreover, he asked too many questions.

"I was wondering," said Bledri, "if I might join the hunt, my lord. There's not much to be done at the forge."

"Of course. I see you've brought your bow."

. . . . . .

The following morning, the ground covered by a light fall of snow, the hunting party headed south to where, the blacksmith claimed, good hunting was assured. When they entered a large clearing they spread out, searching the snow for hoof prints and droppings – signs that would indicate that a herd of hinds had been there at dawn, grazing hurriedly before returning to the safety of woods to regurgitate their food and chew properly.

Four of the hunters were out in the open, heading towards the opposite side of the clearing. The half-frozen grass crunched beneath their horses' hooves; their breath vaporized in the cold air. Then flatulence ripped from a saddle.

"Who the hell was that?" Maredudd asked.

"You," said Rhydderch. "Your horse is the only one that's steaming."

Caleb veered away. "Saints preserve us! That's the worst yet."

"I'll say," said the youth, Morgan. "It's worse than rotting flesh."

They continued to trot, three of them forging ahead while, left on his own, Maredudd chuckled. "Ale and venison don't mix."

Unbeknown to them, on the wooded hillside to which they were heading, they were observed by several men, one of whom, a Saxon, had climbed to a cleft in a tree. "I see four of them, monsieur," the Saxon said in broken French, "coming this way. Aye, and one rides a white stallion."

"Rhydderch ap Cadifor," said a young horseman, "it has to be."

"You're right, Wilfred," ground out a second horseman, twenty years older than the first. "*The wicked is snared in the work of his own hands. Selah.*" He looked up, saying, to the Saxon, "Ethelgar, take your men and go quietly down through the woods and *make ready thine arrows upon the strings against the face of them* – and I, I will circumvent, then fall upon them in their confusion."

"Is it wise, monsieur? We are but five and the woods are bare, they'll see us."

"No, they hunt; therefore, they *will have set their eyes bowing down to the earth.* Wilfred, my mace and shield, give them to me." As the Frenchman led off, heading down the reverse side of the hill, he was mindful of his ill-starred *anabasis* ten year ago. "This," he growled, "is where I avenge myself against the barbarian for his cowardly stratagem at Crow Wood – and it was cowardly, Wilfred. Did I not tell you how, with Satan's aid, he lured my war dogs from a clearing like that down there? Yes, lured them into woods where his men savaged them mercilessly; now *his mischief will return upon his own head. Selah.*"

Below, Caleb had entered the woods on foot to investigate tracks. Rhydderch and Maredudd looked on. The youth, Morgan, had ridden off, skirting the tree-line, and was now beckoning them from afar.

"Looks like Morgan has found tracks," said Rhydderch.

"I doubt it," said Maredudd. "We're wasting our time here. So much for our blacksmith knowing all the best places – and close to the border with you-know-who." He pricked up his ears. "Hear that? Someone's coming down through the woods."

"I heard. Caleb, come out of there now!"

Caleb, having heard sounds himself, came out in a hurry; no sooner had he mounted his grey than Maredudd said, "There they are, three of them at least. Let's go." They rode off, skirting the tree-line, Rhydderch blowing on his horn. Close to where Morgan had last been seen they wheeled to see three men, armed with bows, spilling from the woods; they all had long hair. "Saxons," Maredudd bawled as bows were raised. He spurred, head down, breaching the tree-line to be confronted by a morass bordering a stream. Dismounting, he shouted, "Come. When they see Huw and the others they'll head back the way they came. Let's cut them off." As he took to the slope he caught the approach of a horseman – on the far side of the stream – forcing his way through thickets. He turned sharply, expecting to see Morgan, riding a chestnut, but the horse proved to be a heavy bay and the rider, a mace poised, had his left side almost concealed by a kite-shaped shield. "By St. Teilo! It's de Viles."

Caleb, having dismounted, was the first to respond, loosing an arrow that embedded in de Viles's shield. Maredudd turned back, intending to hurl a spear, by which time de Viles's horse had sunk, knee-deep in ooze.

"Hold off, you two," Rhydderch shouted, "let him be."

"Like hell I will," Maredudd countered. "He's brought this on himself."

"No, there's too much at stake to go killing that madman! Caleb, I said hold off! There's more at stake than you realize!"

Rhydderch's words were all but drowned out by de Viles, ranting, now that his horse had sunk almost to its breast, "*Save me, O God, for I sink in deep mire. Let not the waterflood overflow me, neither let the deep swallow me up.*" Behind him two bloodhounds howled as they pranced at the edge of the morass; a retainer reined beside them, to whom he bawled, "Wilfred, spear the barbarian, the one on horseback."

Rhydderch raised a spear, shouting, in French, "Hold off, Wilfred, it's you we'll target first. Then we'll settle with your master at will."

"Don't listen to him," de Viles rasped. "Obey me. Kill him!"

Wilfred remained hesitant, spear poised: he had no clear throw, nor did he care to be shot at by Caleb. "I dare not, monsieur," he said. "They will kill *you*!"

"Never mind me," de Viles spat. "Hurl your spear, you Saxon whelp."

"You've been warned, Wilfred. Maredudd, go, check on the Saxons."

As Maredudd turned so the youth, Morgan, entered the woods, a bow at the ready. Maredudd looked beyond Morgan to the clearing. "All's well," he shouted. "Huw and the others are coming this way."

"Right, let's get the horses out," said Rhydderch. "Morgan, stay with Caleb and watch that retainer. Don't shoot unless you have to."

De Viles, meanwhile, had lowered his shield to expose the white bonnet which, tied beneath his jutting jaw, encircled his hot, flushed face, making his hollow, hate-filled eyes conspicuous. His breath vaporized as he snarled, "That's right, *depart from me, all ye workers of iniquity, for the Lord hath heard the voice of my weeping.*"

"Damn psalm-singer," Maredudd spat as, with a slap, he drove Caleb's horse from the woods. "No wonder they call you *the Bishop*, you mad bastard. I should have killed you long ago when I had the chance."

"*Why boasteth thou thyself, O mighty man?*" de Viles chanted. "*For the Lord shall cut off all tongues that speaketh proud things* – and I, I shall not die, but live, while you, *ye shall fall by the sword; ye shall be a portion to foxes.*"

De Viles's psalm-singing could still be heard, echoing in the woods, when, with the withdrawal complete, Maredudd mounted his bay, saying, "This is Bledri's doing, it was his idea to come here. I think it time we had a word with him."

"About what, treachery?" said Rhydderch, spurring towards Huw and the others. "No, if it had been a trap, then de Viles would have come at us with more men than he did. As for Bledri, he's not the only one to be regarded with suspicion. Think on who beckoned us to that part of the woods, then went missing." He jerked his head rearward to where Caleb rode in the company of a dark-haired youth. "Morgan," he mouthed.

. . . . . .

That afternoon, when the hunters were closing for a kill, an arrow came close to hitting Rhydderch. No one seemed to know where the arrow came from, no one claimed it was his. The incident passed as yet another misadventure.

CHAPTER 2

MORGAN'S WEDDING

Handsome with dark, curly hair, Morgan was a brash seventeen-year-old, one of Caleb's chosen companions. Early one morning, some three weeks after the hunting party had returned to court, he accompanied Caleb to the bathhouse down by the river. "For St. Teilo's sake, Caleb," he grumbled, "do I have to go through with this?"

"We agreed," said Caleb, "I gave you my clothes so you'd be married in style and *you* – you got the filth off you."

They entered a longhouse where steam wreathed from a cauldron, enveloping a pot hanger until it became lost to view in the shadows of a thatched roof. A woman in ragged clothes stood, back bent, poking a log fire, which spat out sparks as flames rose, licking the sides of the cauldron. After removing his clothes, Morgan had one foot in a wooden tub when, looking at what appeared to be scum, he remarked, "Someone's used this water. Oy! You, woman, who used this water afore me?"

"Some bard who turned up late last night."

"What, another one? There's a lot of bards been turning up here lately."

Caleb smirked. "My father may be a patron of bards, but I reckon he uses them to exchange messages with the lords of these Southern Lands – messages to do with that attack on Llandovery Castle, but don't you go telling anyone that, just keep it to yourself."

"You can trust me," said Morgan. "Which reminds me, your father's bard, what's his fee for attending a wedding?"

"Twenty-four pence. As to the fee paid to my father for the protection he affords to women...."

"Yes, yes, two kine, only it's Banwen's kin pays for that, and what with her being an only child I got myself a generous marriage portion."

"So you keep saying. Yet when it comes to Banwen you've little to say about her."

"I told you, she's a second cousin of mine on the distaff side and – well, you know what they say, marry within the clan and fight the feud with the stranger; that keeps the marriage portion in the clan and the marriage portion is all that matters to me." Morgan watched Caleb lather a foot while he,

15

fearing to lose his protective body oils, did nothing more than bluster about forthcoming revelry until, finally, he asked, "I take it your brother *is* coming?"

"Seems so. I believe he wants to meet that sister you're always bragging about. And I'll tell you something else, Maredudd wouldn't mind meeting her."

"Saints preserve us! You'd best warn your brother not to mention Maredudd in front of my father, he'll have a bloody fit if he does."

"I'd like to know what your father has against Maredudd. I heard it said he gave up being my father's doorward because the two of them were always at odds."

Morgan shrugged. "My father always said he gave up the appointment so he could work the lands of our *resting-place*; that's good enough for me because I don't have to see him every day, bastard that he is. I tell you, my father hates me – says I've been nothing but trouble since the day I was born. And that fight with Gronw yesteryear, that was the last straw."

Morgan lay back in the tub, reflecting on the brawl that had led to his father practically disowning him. It was all Gronw's fault, that detestable youth from across the valley. Even as boys they hated one other and not simply because they were of neighbouring clans. Then having to serve together in their lord's bodyguard proved more than they could contain. In the last of their frequent brawls, Gronw had come off worse with an ear bitten off. They had both been fined twelve kine for violent disturbance; to make matters worse, Gronw had claimed compensation: two kine for the loss of an ear and two shillings for the blood shed in anger – payments that his father swore he would deduct from his inheritance.

'*What matter,*' he thought. '*If I keep in with Caleb, I could do well for myself when he's lord of these lands – but that won't be till his father's dead.*' Then he laughed to himself, thinking, '*Maybe that madman, de Viles, will be the death of him.*'

. . . . . .

After traversing moorland the bridegroom's party drew rein. They were six in number: Morgan, his two cousins, Elidir and Guto, the brothers Caleb and Owain, and the Old One, Merfyn, the court bard.

"This is it," Morgan shouted into the wind, "my kindred's *resting-place*. Here it's pasture, but once we go down through the woods you'll see the corn land and, further down, the meadows. I tell you, my kin may have lost their lands in the Peninsula, but all this was wasteland till they got to work on it. One day I'll have my share, but not afore I've a taste of other things first."

"You'll never settle," Caleb shouted. "It'll be too much like hard work."

"Na, I'll have slaves to do all that, just like my kin did afore the French drove us from our *resting-place* above St. Illtud's Bay. I tell you, we must have had a dozen slaves at least, to say nothing of churls to work our corn lands and...."

"Yes, yes," said Caleb, placing a hand over his mouth as if yawning, "we've all heard it a hundred times or more."

Morgan bit his lip, then spurred, saying, "Let's go down, this bloody wind is cold."

They zigzagged in their descent between trees which, being bare, afforded a view of wild woodland falling steeply to the valley floor, from where it rose sharply to the opposing ridgetop. Halfway down the hillside they skirted terraced fields within the woodland and continued their descent to Ynys Ammon – the island clearing of Morgan's father.

Morgan's kin, including those from outlying homesteads, were there to greet them, full of warmth, offering to take charge of the horses while, in front of the hall, the six handed their weapons over for safekeeping, as a sign of peaceful intent. All six accepted the offer of having their feet washed, thereby signifying they would be staying the night.

While maidens entertained with conversation, poetry and song, Owain sat on a tree stump, smoothing his faithful hound, when a long-haired, barefooted youth approached, carrying a pitcher. The youth knelt to untie the thongs around Owain's untanned leather boots. He seemed unsure of himself, kept his head down.

"And who might you be?" Owain asked.

"Cadog," the youth stuttered.

"So you're Morgan's brother, yes?" Owain was surprised when, nodding, the youth looked up. Cadog was not at all like Morgan: his face bore no sign of aggression – if anything, it had the look of innocence. "I'm Owain; this is Giff."

Cadog leaned towards the dog, smoothing her as she rolled to make the most of his attention. "M-mercy! Look at the scars. W-what happened to her?"

"She got hit by a boar, trying to save me."

Cadog continued to smooth Giff, stuttering, "I got two dogs, best there are for any herdsman. That's what I do, herd cattle, my kindred's as well as my fathers."

"But not today, eh?"

"No, not any m-more. I've been c-commended to serve your f-father."

"Ah! Yes, you're fourteen tomorrow. You looking forward to coming back with us?"

Cadog shrugged. "S-seven years is a l-long time to be away."

"You'll soon settle. Tomorrow you'll have your hair cut to show you're a man. Then Caleb will give you his usual talk about, *whilst you remain at Y Faerdref you will forget the teachings of your mother and will learn from me courtesy and the etiquette of court.* He goes on a bit, but you needn't worry about him, it's Maredudd you take – notice of." Owain looked around to see if Morgan's father had overheard him mention Maredudd's name; Ammon showed no sign of having heard. "In the evenings you'll serve at my father's table, or my mothers...."

Two youths stood over them. "This is my brother, Cadog," said Morgan.

"Good day, Cadog," said Caleb. "No, don't rise, just finish washing my brother's feet – but tell me, is it true your only ambition is to work the lands round here?"

"W-what's wrong with that?"

"Come now, you don't want to step in dung all your life. I mean, out there is adventure and you, you're a free man, you can go wherever you please."

"Well, say something," Morgan ground out, keen to promote himself as Caleb's crony. He drove a foot at Cadog, toppling him so that he ended up sprawled, submission written across his face. Caleb grinned; Morgan guffawed.

"Why don't you leave him alone?" said Owain, rising, at which point he caught the approach of Morgan's sister, Anona. For some time he had been watching her as she moved about, cheerfully chatting to all but himself. Now that she was close he could see that, despite a limp, she was as comely as her brother had claimed. He bowed to the introduction, then stared: arms folded, her fingers clutching her mantle, her face framed by a white, turban-like headdress, she seemed confident in a charming sort of way. She reminded him of someone; he could not think who.

"My brother," said Anona, "looks like a nobleman in those clothes, don't you think?"

"Yes – yes, he does." Owain ran his eye over Anona's thin face and the eyes that seemed to laugh in accord with her mouth. Then he realized who she reminded him of – his mother.

"The clothes are Caleb's," said Morgan, preening himself. "He gave them to me."

Anona turned to Caleb who, because it made him feel superior, stood with one foot on the tree stump, an arm resting upon his raised knee. "Bribery," he explained. "It was the only way I could get him to take a bath."

"Well, now that he's well attired," Anona threw in, "maybe marriage will be the making of him as a man."

"At fifteen it's time you were married," Morgan countered and, to Caleb, "My father has tried for three years to find her a husband, only *she's* refused them all."

"Yes, and I'll refuse anyone who's not to my liking."

"Will you, now?" Morgan made to grab Anona's headdress.

She drew away, pushing aside his arm, saying, sharply, "Don't do that."

"Well, you shouldn't be so stupid. You should marry someone who can afford you a slave. Isn't that right, Caleb?"

"There's nothing to compare with good breeding," said Caleb, "but in your case – well, it's simply a matter of getting your hands on a marriage portion, isn't it?"

"No – no, I just said...."

"Don't excuse yourself, Morgan," said Anona, "we all know how you think, only the marriage portion will remain Banwen's property for the next seven years, and *you* – you'll add to it by gifting her six steers."

"Shut up," Morgan snapped, irked that his sister should dare to correct him. He was displeased with Caleb, too, for making public his designs. "Who the hell d'you think you're looking at?" he said, turning on Cadog.

"Go on," said Owain, "pick on someone else, but dare anyone find fault in you."

"What's it to do with you? They're my kin, I can say what I like."

"Yes, stay out of it," said Caleb, "it's no concern of yours."

Owain faced his brother. "This is your doing. You stir things up, then you get donkey, here, to do the rest, only he can't see it."

"Who are you calling a donkey?" Morgan spat. He made as if to set to; Anona got in his way.

"Leave him, Morgan," said Caleb, removing his foot from the tree stump, "I'll see to him." He approached Owain, jabbing a finger in his chest. "Don't spoil for a fight with him, it's his wedding day."

"It's not *me* who's spoiling for a fight, it's *you*."

Caleb spread his arms, palms facing out. "Not me, brother."

"You forget I've seen you play this game afore." Even as he spoke, Owain knew that Caleb would not throw the first punch because everyone would blame him for starting a fight. No, the plan was to provoke until he retaliated. He determined to hold his peace.

Caleb pushed him. "Enough of this nonsense, brother." Caleb pushed him again.

His fists clenched, Owain attempted to hold his ground.

"Listen," Cadog stuttered, "horns. Morgan, your bride's coming down the hillside."

"So what?" Morgan spat.

"So you'll be on your best behaviour," said Anona.

"I'll be what I want."

"Not here you won't," Ammon ground out as he approached. For a Countryman he was of exceptionally heavy build, his demeanour sufficiently intimidating to make even the stout-hearted think twice about disagreeing with him. "And after tomorrow I don't want to see you ever again. That's why I arranged with Lord Rhydderch for you to have a hall near his court, and if you," – his eyes roved till they came to rest momentarily on Caleb – "or anyone else spoil things here, then he'll answer to me and I won't give a damn about the consequences."

. . . . . .

The interior of Ammon's hall was gloomy, the lower half full of puddles in which a man could sink to his ankles in ooze, a mire littered with boughs which the cattle had stripped bare. In the upper part of the hall, which served as the living quarters, there remained little straw full of dust and fleas, for the cattle had eaten most of it. It was here that everyone gathered, including Banwen, a plump, unattractive twelve-year-old. She looked so small beside Morgan, so unsure of herself because he had so far said little to her, being more concerned, like everyone else, in her marriage portion: cattle had come under the scrutiny of older men; women had examined every moveable provided by her father. She felt left out: no one had scrutinized her.

A hush settled on the gathering as her father, a lean-faced, balding man, said, "Morgan ab Ammon, you and I are of kin because your mother, Hawys, was of the Clan of Eirig Mawr – but kinship bonded our ancestors long afore the union of your father and mother, for there was a time when our ancestors were as one. Then ten years ago the French drove your kinsmen from the Peninsula. So they came here, they transformed this side of the valley into a prosperous *resting-place*. And more, they were affiliated into the Clan of Eirig Mawr, thereby reuniting our people as one. Today the ties of kinship are about to be forged yet again, for I ask you, Morgan ab Ammon, will you take my maiden daughter, Banwen, to wife? To honour her and the terms of this union so long as she has issue?"

"I will," Morgan replied, "so help me, God."

"And will you, my daughter, honour Morgan by being faithful to him? Never to commit adultery, nor kiss or caress another man? Will you avoid at all times the use of contemptuous or insulting words towards him? Will you never be wasteful with whatever you may jointly own? Will you never leave him, except for leprosy, impotency or bad breath?"

"Yes, I will," said Banwen timorously, "so help me, God."

"Then may the ties of kinship be drawn closer by this union."

Hands were clasped by all to seal the agreement; it was time for the wedding feast to begin. In honour of the trinity everyone sat on the floor in groups of three, the women separate from the men. Owain and Caleb sat with the Old One, Merfyn, their father's bard, who had been their teacher and companion for as long as they could remember. As honoured guests they were among the first to be waited upon.

Ammon stood by, rubbing his hands, while Anona set before them a bowl of stew. Owain feigned indifference: with Anona so close and Caleb apparently watching him he deemed it wise to avoid making known his interest in her. After she had moved away, Merfyn was the first to partake in the stew. The bowl, then, passed to Caleb and, while Caleb ate, Owain followed Anona out of the corner of his eye.

"D'you want this, brother?" said Caleb, offering the bowl. "Or d'you prefer to feast your eyes rather than your stomach?"

"Just looking round, that's all."

"At whom, Anona? It is Anona, isn't it?"

"What's it to you?"

"Well, she's comely enough, though she doesn't appear to have any breasts yet."

"Why don't you keep your foul mouth shut?"

"That is enough, you two," said Merfyn sternly.

"Well, what d'you expect?" Caleb countered. "If I say anything to him, it's always *you're picking on me*."

"Well, you are, only you make out you're not."

"I said *that* is enough. I sometimes wonder if my efforts to make you worthy of your father have been wasted. Now let this be an end to your unlordly ways, Caleb. And you, Owain, perhaps you will bridle your tongue so that we may eat in peace."

After several courses had been served, the old bard arose. He appeared odd with his long hair coiled like a horse's tail and the grey strands of his lengthy beard reflective in the firelight. A loose, tartan vestment reached his sandalled feet; he wore a small cap with a peak. Harp in hand, he soothed all with a love song. His voice reverberated when, with a second song, he gave majestic descriptions of their homeland; turning to humour, he sang lively verse to the accompaniment of the pear-shaped, string instrument that was his *crwth*. Everyone clapped to his music, everyone sang to his songs. Then came the dancing as couples moved, hands on hips, legs kicking, across the earthen floor.

Owain managed but one dance with Anona. Despite her limp she was overwhelmed by admirers. Their insistence forced him to retire to a side-aisle where Cadog joined him.

"I've b-been listening to your b-brother, he's a lot to say ab-about fighting and that."

"It's all he ever talks about lately."

"Aren't you of the s-same mind?"

"No, there's more to life than fighting. I enjoy good company, though I often ride alone. And you, you must spend most of your time alone when you're out there with the herd."

"Yes, and b-because of that I find it hard to talk, b-but with you it's n-not so hard."

"Tell me something, why does your sister limp?"

"An a-accident – happened y-years ago. We were c-climbing trees. Morgan dared her to c-climb higher. Then he shook the b-branch and she fell."

"Mindless loud-mouth! Doesn't he ever stop to consider what he's doing?"

Cadog refrained from comment. Then a voice, a feminine voice, distracted them. "Not dancing, Owain?"

Owain was caught off guard. A flutter like the wings of a bird rose in his chest. His face reddened. He tried to appear calm when he said, "No, but I'd be happy to dance with you again if you so wish."

"Do you mind if we don't? Not for a while, that is?"

"Not at all. I'd be happy to just talk."

"Caleb said you would."

"If I know Caleb, he'll have said more than that, you know what brothers are like." Owain turned to witness both Caleb and Morgan drain their drinking horns. "And your brother, he'll be drunk afore the night is through and *that* means trouble."

Chapter 3

Trouble

By the early hours everyone had settled down in the low-roofed side-aisles where wicker screens partitioned the aisles into cubicles. In one cubicle Morgan and his bride consummated their marriage. In another cubicle, shared with two other men, Owain slept, wrapped in his cloak, until insufficient straw made him restless. Quietly, he made for the fire and, using his skene, peeled back the overlaying turf to feel warmth on his face.

With Giff at his side he thought of Anona, recalling the time when the younger element had drifted into the surrounding woods. There were steep slopes out there, in some places almost vertical drops. In the dark he had lost his footing, the brink crumbling beneath his feet as he tumbled to the bottom of a slope. After a few words of concern, Anona had called out directions that enabled him to ascend to the brink where she reached for his hand, an act that put an end to any reserve.

A stir carried as Morgan came out of a cubicle, naked, staggering towards the door, mouthing obscenity. Owain kept still, hoping that, in his drunken state, Morgan would not seek out his company. He sensed him pass by, heard the door creak open, then swing shut, and wondered why Cadog was so unlike his brother. Cadog was easy company. The same could be said of Anona – but no, she was delightful, more beautiful than any maiden he had ever met.

Feeling a draught at his back, he turned to see the door ajar, swinging on its leather hinges, then remembered that Morgan had not returned. '*What matter?*' he thought, but on reflection he ventured out into the cold, starry night to find Morgan sprawled, face down, near the tree stump. Straddling Morgan's back, he searched for a hold under cold, sweaty armpits. "Oh! No, he's been sick – Giff get away!"

He struggled to get Morgan to his feet, then shouldered him into the hall. By the fire he let him crumple and would have left him had not his conscience bothered him. With a sigh he raised Morgan to a sitting position and, removing his cloak, placed it about Morgan's shoulders. Morgan belched. As his head came up he tried to focus, almost toppling sideways.

"Ah! I'ss you. Agh! My leg – it 'urts."

Taking a rushlight from a nearby roof tree, Owain held it close to Morgan's left knee, upon which was a dark stain. "Blood," he said, fingering the stain.

"Blood! Well, a man can es-spect that when 'ee's lain wiv a maiden."

"I mean on your knee. You must have cut yourself when you fell."

"Ah! I'ss nuffing. Hey! I 'ad my way thrice back there. Could you do that, eh? Na, there's nuffing in you, you don't know what life's about." He laughed, his chin dropping to his chest. As he eyed his naked form his laughter faded. "Hey! There's no blood on me, no blood on my man'ood. I should be covered in it."

"No, you shouldn't – proves you're all mouth as usual."

Morgan grabbed Owain by the tunic. "No, I'm not. If that bitch was...."

"Get your hand off me."

Ignoring the demand, Morgan attempted to pull himself up, but when the rushlight touched his arm he let out a howl and fell back, yelling. In struggling up a second time he heard a growl erupt into savagery as Giff sprang at his leg. "Yaaa! Get 'er away from me. For Christ's sake...." Knowing only that he had been bitten twice and that Owain had repeatedly stepped on him, Morgan was unconscious of the difficulty that Owain had in pulling Giff away. Fearful of further attack, he looked up to see Owain stood over him, rushlight in hand. "I'll get you for this, you...."

"Try it. And you do anything to Banwen and I'll set Giff on you again. You understand?" Owain awaited a response, then kicked Morgan hard. "I said d'you understand?" Morgan had no intention of submitting, if only to save face, for the shadows rang with the voices of men disturbed by the tussle. Ammon, the first to appear in the tawny light, ground out, "What's going on? Morgan, what's the meaning of this disturbance?"

"It's 'im, 'ee burnt my bloody arm, then set 'is dog on me."

"And what did you do to deserve that, eh?"

"Nuffing. It's that bitch's fault. It is, I tell you. She was given to me as a maiden bride, only a maiden she was not – there's no blood on me. If you don't believe me, ask 'er yourself. Go on, ask 'er."

Ammon gestured for the rush candle. "Come here, girl. Come, my son won't harm you, I'll see to that."

Banwen's white shift appeared to view. As she drew closer, head bowed like a child expecting to be chastised, Morgan made towards her, but his father grabbed him by the neck, bellowing, in his ear, "Leave her; now get your tunic on."

Propelled by his father, Morgan staggered off, mouthing obscenity. Banwen, meanwhile, sought her father's arms, sobbing pitifully while he demanded an explanation for Morgan's conduct. She heard Ammon give a brief but apologetic answer.

Everyone crowded round, not just men, but women and children also, their voices thrummed in her ears. "What's wrong?" they asked. "What's going on? Is Morgan causing trouble again?" If any comfort could be derived from their ill will towards Morgan, it was marred by the thought that soon she would be called upon to explain. What could she say? Should she confess that she had experienced what could only be done once? Or should she tell them the truth, that a kinsman had forced himself upon her? No – how could she when the man was her father's crippled brother?

A thought came to mind. She could say the incubus was to blame, that demon who, like the men of her father's household, crept upon the women in the dark, only the incubus did it without so much as a whisper to wake anyone, including the woman herself. Yes, she would say the incubus was to blame. Her father would believe her. She sensed Morgan at her back, heard him rave, "I want the truth from you. Were you a maiden bride, or not?" She cringed, her fingers curling in her father's tunic. "Answer me!"

"Answer him, my child, he has a right to know." She sobbed, heart-rendering sobs that racked her body. Her father eased her away. "Say what must be said, my child. You must." She shook her head, then closed with her father again.

"See," Morgan yelled, "s-she doesn't deny it," and to her father, "Did you know she'd lost 'er maiden'ood?"

"No, I did not!"

Then s-swear to it."

"I swear, by the blood of our Lord, I did not know she'd lost her maidenhood."

"Then you agree to what must be done?"

She knew her father to be crying when he replied, "I have no choice."

"Light the candles," Morgan shouted. "Elidir, Guto, fetch a year-old steer. Cadog, get grease, as much as you can hold in one hand."

A voice rang out. "No, Morgan, what you intend is wrong."

"I'ss the custom, Old One."

"It is a degrading custom," retorted the bard. "I urge you, let it be."

"No, i'ss what she deserves. Gruffudd, gimme your skene."

Banwen drew closer to her father, turning him so that he shielded her from Morgan. Her father hugged her, saying, "My child, no matter what, I love you. Remember that. May it give you strength."

Morgan's left hand fell upon her shoulder, yanking her from her father's arms. The same hand drew taut the skirt of her shift. The blade in his right hand flashed before her eyes as he plunged, piercing the linen fibres of her shift; pulling her round, he cut until her shift had been slashed in two, the top half in tatters about her waist, leaving her naked from the hips down. He paused, panting, while she cringed, fearing that there was more to come. His left hand fell upon her again; he was about to propel her towards the door when Ammon moved to obstruct.

"The Old One is right, this is a degrading custom, and I'll not have you make it more unpleasant for the girl than it already is."

"She's my wife," Morgan spat, threatening his father with the skene. "I've a right to see this through."

"The skene," Ammon demanded, "give it to me."

Morgan held his stance, but his father moved quicker than his besotted mind could think. A huge right hand closed over his wrist, while an equally large hand wrenched the skene from his grasp.

"You've done all you've a right to do; now watch, same as everyone else."

While the distraught twelve-year-old sobbed, Anona moved to console her, reassuring her that Morgan would not touch her again, then said, "Those six steers my brother gave you, you still have a chance to keep one of them."

"No – no, I don't want any of them."

"Banwen, listen to me. You're going to have to stand up to my brother, or he'll treat you like a slave for the rest of your life."

"No – no, I couldn't, I'd be afraid."

"You must, believe me, you really must; now come with me to the door."

Banwen allowed herself to be led. The gathering gave way so that tawny, half-shadowed faces flanked the girls as they progressed towards the door. Unbeknown to Banwen, Morgan's cousins had taken a year-old steer outside. The door was now barred and, between the osiers, a length of tail protruded. Cadog faced the door, greasing the tail. The Old One stood close by, holding a rushlight.

The girls stopped beside Cadog who, with his back to the gathering, had his head turned towards his sister. Anona could not see his face, but could tell, by the way he held the tail between his spaced hands, that he had done what she had asked of him. She cast a glance over her shoulder; in the forefront of a now silent gathering Morgan lowered at her. "Listen," she whispered in Banwen's ear, "Cadog will have greased only part of the tail. All you've got to do is put your hands between his and hold on."

"No – please – I don't want to."

"You must. Come, take hold of the tail. That's it; now put your foot to the door." Anona raised a hand. "Are you ready?"

Banwen shook her head, pleading with her expression. Cadog withdrew.

"Now hold on." Anona rattled the door.

Outside, one of her cousins relinquished his hold on the steer, tapping it with a stick. As the bullock moved so Banwen felt herself drawn towards the door; panicking, she raised the other foot, slamming it against the door. The steer took fright, bellowing as it slipped in mire. Banwen hung on; like a child pulling at a clump of grass she raised her feet to the bar.

A murmur arose. A woman shouted, "Hold on, Banwen," and the encouragement was taken up by almost all. Outside, the steer grew frantic, stumbling and slipping as one cousin goaded it while the other restrained it. The bar bent under the strain; the door-frame shook. Still Banwen hung on, teeth clenched, straining every muscle. The bar pained her bare feet, her back ached; she knew she could not take much more.

"Enough," Ammon shouted. "I declare she keeps the steer."

The greased switch of the tail slid through Banwen's hands as she fell back into the arms of those ready to catch her. They set her upon her feet. She was robed, congratulated; her father embraced her.

Morgan remained aloof, suspicion flittering through his besotted mind. He visualized a tail that Cadog had failed to grease; a steer which, had it been goaded by his cousins, would surely have got away. His suspicion, then, turned to Anona. '*It would have been just like her.*' he thought '*to get that stupid brother of mine, my cousins too, to fall short in what they were supposed to do. Bitch! She's had time enough to....*' "The tail," he slurred, "let me see the bloody tail."

Ammon seized him from behind, throwing him against a wicker screen. His face worked to sudden strain as his father grappled his throat. He gasped, his breathing quickening, becoming deeper as he struggled to be free. His strained face turned livid with congestion, he became confused. Voices rang in his ears. Someone bellowed, "For St. David's sake, Ammon, let him go."

Shadows wavered on the walls as five men struggled with Ammon, three at his back, tugging at his neck and hair, while the other two yanked on his hairy arms. Only when those behind him had managed to arch his back was it possible for the others to break his hold on Morgan's throat.

Morgan crumpled to the floor. Someone shouted, "Stand back, let him breath," while a woman slapped his face repeatedly. Questions ran amok in his half-conscious mind. '*What's happening? My throat – what – my father – the tail?*' He sensed being lifted; suddenly he was struggling to be free. "Let me go! You're all against me! You always were!" He lurched. "The tail," he croaked, staggering towards the open door. "I gotta see for myself."

Spread-eagled in the doorway, he saw, in the moonlight, Cadog and his cousins beside the steer, apparently amused. He made for Cadog, pushing his fat cousin, Guto, out of the way; that prompted the older cousin, Elidir, a tall, lanky youth, into pushing Morgan hard, saying, "Don't do that, or you'll get my fist; now, if you want to see the tail, go and look."

"Yes, go and look," said Guto, emboldened by Elidir's aggressive stance – and, knowing that Cadog had re-greased the tail, added, "You'll find it is just as it should be."

. . . . . .

In groups, tired guests stood outside the hall, all set to leave, listening to Merfyn say, to Morgan, "An honourable man would never have disgraced his wife the way you did. Why – why did you do it? Are six steers that important to you? And the brooch, the gift you gave Banwen in exchange for her body, is that important too? I tell you, if you are not man enough to treat her with respect, then you do not deserve to have her as your wife."

"She was given to me as a maiden bride! If she hadn't tried to deceive me...!"

"Deceive! What are you talking about? I bid you, you tell me what difference it makes to you that she has experienced what can only be done once? Nothing, absolutely nothing, because she is as yet incapable of carrying a child. And I will tell you something else, if she had sworn on oath that she was a maiden bride, and had been backed up by the oaths of five of her kindred whom, I dare say, knew nothing of her loss, then that would have been the end of it – but no, she did not lie. Now give her the gifts that should have been hers, even if it is only the brooch."

"No, I promised her the brooch because I thought she was a virgin!"

Merfyn stared Morgan into silence while he considered ways in which he might force the youth's hand. He had it within him to do just that. Everyone respected him, his every word was given due consideration by all who exercised authority. To some extent he was feared, too, because of his great learning and his affinity to legendary men such as Arthur's Merlin, and beyond to an age when the words of men comparable to himself were considered law.

No one knew his age, where he came from, or if Merfyn was his real name. Such things he kept to himself. All that could be said of him was that he had made a name for himself as the warrior-poet of Lord Rhys ap Caradog. Then, for reasons known only to him, he became the bard of Rhydderch ap Cadifor. The only blemish on his otherwise untarnished reputation was that someone claimed to identify him with a bard accused of betraying his lord. He, of course, denied it, and the fact that, a few days later, his accuser had a fit of apoplexy only added to the belief that he had strange powers – powers that made men wary of him.

All this Morgan knew. It made him cringe within, but for the sake of his pride he stood, feet apart, staring into the hollowed eyes of the Old One, who might easily have been mistaken for a ghost were it not for a zephyr blowing loose strands of his beard – but it was the eyes of the Old One that held him, they seemed to numb his brain.

Around him no one moved, no one spoke. The only sounds to be heard were the caw of rooks in the surrounding woods, the occasional snorts of restless steeds, the otherwise awesome silence – a silence broken by Owain, saying, "Give her the brooch, Morgan."

Morgan made to utter a refusal, but found himself flustered by Cadog stuttering a similar request. He glared at his brother, only to be taken aback by what his youngest cousin had to say, then the older one, Elidir, saying, "I say so too; that makes five of us."

"What say you, Caleb?" Owain asked. "Should he give her the brooch?"

"No, the laws say, a morning gift is meant to compensate a bride for her loss of maidenhood, and if she'd already lost it, then I see no reason why he should be the one to compensate her for losing it to someone else."

"You would say that," Owain retorted. "Goes to show that all Merfyn has said about conciliation has, for you, fallen on deaf ears."

Caleb assumed an air of indifference until Merfyn caught his eye. "Oh! Very well. Morgan, give her the damn brooch and be done with it. Well, go on, I gave you my clothes, didn't I?"

Morgan was cut to the quick: Caleb was the last person he would have expected to turn on him – Caleb, the only one he could call a friend. Without him he would be bullied by older youths, something he did not relish; nor did he care to risk losing his standing with the one person who, in time, might change his lot for the better. He broke free of Merfyn's gaze and, turning on his heels, strode towards a knot of women, Banwen among them.

Observing his approach, Banwen became increasingly alarmed. She knew not his mood: no words had passed between them since he had demanded admission of her shame; what remained of her wedding night she had spent in the company of women. In fear she looked to her father, knowing that he would protect her now. She saw her father separate from the men and was about to run to him when Anona caught her arm, insisting that she stood firm. Even with her father only paces away she still quivered irrepressibly; she cowered when Morgan stopped short in front of her.

"Last night I was drunk," Morgan growled, unclasping the brooch. "Here, you can have this; now let's be gone from here."

Banwen made to follow him, but Anona held her back, saying, "Let him wait."

"No – please – I must – I...."

A hefty woman silenced Banwen with the words, "Don't worry about him, child. Just remember, if he oppresses you, then you have the right to appeal to us. We'll get our men to deal with him."

Banwen looked about at the hardy women whom, she knew, were a support to one another. She agreed with everything they said, not caring to upset them, yet knowing that she would never stand up to Morgan. A hand touched her arm.

"Don't be afraid," said Anona. "If you need someone to turn to, then go to the Old One, he's sure to help you all he can. And there's Owain, he'll watch out for you."

Owain, meanwhile, deliberated on whether Anona's oblique looks had been directed at him. Earlier, in the hall, she had singled him out, her friendliness linked perhaps to the fact that Cadog had been present at his side. Yet he felt sure that, time and again, he had caught her glancing at him because he had rarely taken his eyes of her. Whether there was anything meaningful in her looks, he determined, now that he had met her he was not going to forget her.

CHAPTER 4

GATHERING CLOUDS

Near the estuary of the Llwch Dwr, Henry de Viles looked down over a palisade to view the ditch that surrounded his ring-work castle. He was pleased with recent improvements to the ditch; pleased, too, with what lay beyond. A huge, rectangular area, once the interior of a Roman fort, was bounded on all sides by surviving ramparts, surmounted now by stout paling. Most of the enclosure lay vacant – a pen for sheep – but just beyond his castle ditch thatched houses lined a dusty thoroughfare.

Ramshackle though they were, the houses formed the embryo of what would one day be a bustling township. The potential was there: the enclosure commanded a tidal ford, a link in the coastal highway; there was access to the sea as well. Even now a ship lay at anchor, the crew loading wool destined for Bristol. As the township grew and prospered so his coffer would fill.

Unabashed by a domestic throwing rubbish into the ditch, he chanted, as he looked at the houses, *"Blessed is the Lord – who subdueth these people unto me – that they may prepare a city for habitation. Selah."*

Beyond the enclosure all the land that lay round about he held as a fief. It could never be enough; he needed to expand. Thumbs hooked in his belt, he paced beside his ring-work palisade, looking south over the narrow waters that separated him from the Is-coed Peninsula. On the southern shores of that Peninsula were men-at-arms with fiefs similar to his own. He visualized them, his peers, superimposed on the skyline, gathered together, shaking their fists as they railed at him. They were as much his enemies as were the barbarians.

"Call yourselves Frenchmen?" he spat at the imagery. *"I will not be afraid of ten thousands of people that have set themselves against me.* All that prevents me from taking what's yours is that the Earl forbade me to expand southwards."

In turning back he looked westwards. On the far side of the estuary lay the Commote of Carnwyllion. It should have been his, but one William de Londres, Lord of Ogwr, had subdued it and the neighbouring Commote of Cydweli on behalf of the Bishop of Salisbury. And God damn it! The man now administered those commotes as though they were part of his *own* domain.

"Why boasteth thou thyself, O mighty man?" he railed as if William de Londres could hear him. "You who boasted of your conquest of Gower on behalf of the Earl, *the Lord shall laugh at you, for He seeth that your day is coming."* His eyes rolled skywards. *"Let his days be few,* O Lord, *and let another take his office –* me!"

Chest expanded, he continued pacing. To the north lay the commote that belonged to Rhydderch ap Cadifor, a wilderness of woods and mountains. Ten years ago he had led an expedition into that wilderness to bring Rhydderch ap Cadifor to heel, but it was not to be, not because, with the Devil's aid, the barbarian had managed to steal French horses, but because his own men had turned on him, adamant that, without horses, there was no recourse but to return to the coast. Fools! Had they listened to him they would never have been taken prisoner and then ransomed. No matter: one day soon those northern lands would be his; it was where he was destined to expand.

Something caught his eye. Below, on the dusty thoroughfare between buildings, an archer by the name of Ethelgar, escorted a priest towards the castle. That the priest's head was concealed beneath a hood was reason for him to exclaim, "The Lord be praised, it is my informer, he must have seen the sign I left for him."

Something else caught his attention. Two horsemen had ridden in through the gateway of the enclosure. The identity of one, a retainer, he dismissed as of no import, but the leading horseman, in full chain-mail, he identified as a man-at-arms by the pattern on his kite-shaped shield. They rode past the houses, kicking up dust, forcing Ethelgar and the priest to turn aside.

"A thousand curses! It's that unruly swine, de la Mere!" Drawing his sword, de Viles made for the castle gateway where he stood, feet apart, louring at the horsemen as the hooves of their mounts clattered on the drawbridge.

The man-at-arms reined in, a derisory expression of his face that not even the nasal on his helmet could conceal. "Monsieur, I see you're recovered from your encounter with Rhydderch ap Cadifor."

"That I have, *for the Lord brought me up out of an horrible pit, out of the mire, and set my feet upon a rock and established my goings."*

"Glad to hear it because, two days from now, you'll relieve me by commencing your forty-day castle guard at Abertawe."

"Not me, it's the time of that Saxon who masquerades as a Frenchmen."

"It's *your* turn," said de la Mere, resting a forearm on the high frame of his saddle. "With Elgar the Saxon sick the High Steward insists that you take his place, and you'd best be vigilant because you'll not have a full complement of men."

"What d'you mean? Explain?"

"The King, he's in need of foot soldiers. So the Earl wants seventy archers dispatched. They march out first thing tomorrow."

"What, when there's a pretender on the loose?"

De la Mere nodded. "Oh! And – er – there's no equestrians at Abertawe either, they're still in the Peninsula. Could be their continued presence there will forestall an uprising – at least, that's how the High Steward sees it."

"It's madness. What am I to guard Abertawe with?" De Viles paused, eyes bulging: de la Mere had turned his attention to the priest as he passed by. "Never mind him. I said what am I to guard Abertawe with?"

"You're getting above yourself again, monsieur. It's the constable's place to keep safe the castle, not yours. You only relieve him when he says so, and when you do you'll have forty-three archers at your disposal; now what about refreshment afore I journey back?"

"You'll get nothing from me, you insolent swine."

"Still smarting over Crow Wood, are we? You never could accept that Rhydderch ap Cadifor proved himself a better man than you."

"He did no such thing, *for it was not an enemy that reproached me; then I could have borne it. Neither was it he that hated me that did magnify himself against me; then I would have hid myself from him – but it was thou, a man almost my equal,* that brought about my shame. I'll not forget that."

"No more will I forget it was your stupidity that caused us to lose our horses, you damn psalm-singer."

De Viles turned to Ethelgar, snarling, *"make ready thine arrows upon thy strings against the face of them."* He levelled his blade. "Begone, de la Mere, afore I have my man shoot you down as you threatened me at Crow Wood. Begone, I say!"

De la Mere wheeled, countering, "One day you'll get what you deserve," and rode off, followed closely by his retainer.

Taking the priest's arm, de Viles led him away, between buildings, saying, in the Countryman's tongue, "You saw the sign I left for you, that's good; now what's new that can be said of Rhydderch ap Cadifor?"

"Nothing. I said I'd get back to you when I had something worthwhile."

"Must be something – something said. Has he gone anywhere? Anything?"

"He's not left Gower and, as you know, those who are close to him speak only in the Frenchman's tongue. My man can't – wait, there is something. There's many a stranger received his hospitality lately, most of them bards, but who knows what they talk about, it's all done behind closed doors. Then there's his officers, gone for days, same ones every time. It's like I said, all the good will he shares with others of his standing is nothing more than a cover up for conspiracy – been going on for years."

"What about the woman whose word he puts store by, have you killed her yet?"

"No, she can't be found."

"Fie! You disappoint me. All this, it's a waste of time."

"Yes, and whose fault is that? I told you to wait. Coming here is too damn risky."

His face twitching, de Viles stared, not at the priest's face – there was little of it to be seen – but at his right shoulder. He felt tempted to cleave the man for his insolence, but this he suppressed with the thought that the barbarian might still be of use to him. Swinging his sword underarm, he dug into the purse attached to his girdle. "Here," he growled, offering silver coins, "for your trouble. And if you need me, then two days from now I'll be at Abertawe – and that's where I'll be for forty days thereafter."

· · · · · ·

Later, on moorland several miles north of de Viles's castle, Maredudd reined in his bay, the wind ruffling his red hair, his cloak and the legs of his baggy breeches, as well as the hairs of his grey, wolfskin coat. He sat tall in the saddle to reposition his baldric from which hung a sword, raising the buckle to a point closer to his right shoulder. Then he reined hard, wheeling round to observe a dozen of his youngest youths labouring to catch up with him. The first to join him stooped, hands on hips, and threw out phlegm.

"Best get your second wind, Hywel," Maredudd advised. "We'll be off again when the others catch up."

"I'm finished," Hywel gasped

"Finished! If you think this hard going, you should have served under Lord Rhys as I did. Now there's a hard-nosed man if ever there was one – fought more battles than I care to mention; the last, as you know well, was ten years ago when he forced marched his men twelve miles, then had them fight a battle at the end of it. Didn't matter to him that he'd been wounded in a previous fight, or that his age was against him. No, he got down off his horse and fought to the very end. Now me, I'm not asking you to fight a battle and die, just run a few miles, that's all."

"Don't need a battle to die," gasped a second youth, falling to his knees. "This running will be the death of me."

Maredudd grinned, then caught sight of someone in the distance, riding north, a hood raised to conceal his face. "A priest, and if I'm not mistaken, he's the one we saw earlier. Didn't want to know us then, either, and he's not from these parts, not on a horse like that. Now me, I'd say he's had dealings with de Viles." Then he mimicked de Viles in French, *"Depart from me, all ye workers of iniquity, for the Lord hath heard the voice of my weeping."*

Hywel gaped. "You speak just like a Frenchman, my Lord Captain."

"Good enough to get by, but then, afore you joined us yesteryear, we had a priest with us for what, nine years – an Erging man, came all the way from Hereford, and all he ever did was insist we spoke in the Frenchman's tongue."

"Caleb said he was always correcting him when he got his words wrong."

"Aye, and yet Caleb was able to pick up them words better than the rest of us."

Several youths joined them; Maredudd looked on, recalling how, with a play with words, he had teased someone in French – his foster-brother's wife, Gwenllian. He missed her, always did when on progress among the poverty-stricken hamlets of churls. Were it not for the training that he imposed on his youths, then lodging with churls could be a humdrum existence: boredom and bad weather, his only company a doorward, a cook and upwards of a dozen youths. He missed carousing in his foster-brother's hall – but, no, it was Gwenllian he really missed.

He was distracted by the arrival on horseback of his appointed doorward, Owain Is-coed, so named because, like so many, he was an Is-coed man whom the French had expelled from the Peninsula. "It's been a hard run," said Owain Is-coed. "I'd say they've had enough."

"I'd say so too. Take them back to Maerdy when they've recovered. Oh! And – er – take this," Maredudd added, removing coins from his girdle. "If there's ale to be bought, then let them have their fill. Just make sure they don't get troublesome."

"So where are you off to?"

"Y Faerdref. I'll be back tomorrow with that newcomer, Cadog ab Ammon."

. . . . . .

In the dimly-lit chamber attached to Y Faerdref Hall, Gwenllian, thirty-two-year-old wife of Lord Rhydderch, laughed to herself at something Maredudd had said when, about midday, he made an unexpected appearance. She pictured him as he appeared near the doorway: tall and lithe, thirty-six years old, his strong, handsome face displaying a mischievous grin that distorted the neat lines of both his beard and his moustache. The grin invariably proceeded some mischievous remark, as it had when he sauntered towards her, arms open, his feet scuffing the straw-covered floor. Maredudd was so risible, so full of surprises; for as long as she could remember he had never been any different.

She recalled occasions when, as a handsome seventeen-year-old, he made visits to her father's homestead; pictured herself, a young woman, thirteen years old, so full of excitement when she saw him riding out from the woods to her father's hall. They were carefree days, walking with him, hand in hand, through fields and woods, listening to the things he said that made her laugh. Only God alone could have known her feelings when he put his arm around her, the magic of their first nervous kiss. At the time she had thought such bliss would never end – but it did the day her father announced that she would be given to Rhydderch as a gift of kin. She retrieved Maredudd's response, *'Over my dead body she will,'* and her father shouting, at him, *'Get out – out of my house.'* There had been tears in her eyes when she ran from her father's hall and, touching Maredudd's arm when she caught up with him, cried, *'Maredudd, it's my father's wish.'*

Why did she allow their love to end? If she had been then, as now, a woman with her own will, she would have made up her own mind as to which of the foster brothers she should marry, but because of her age and her confusion she had let her father decide.

"My lady," her doorward announced on entering the chamber, "Merfyn Hen, your husband's bard, has returned from his wandering in Is-coed and, in view of your husband's absence, seeks an audience with you."

"Merfyn," said Gwenllian, moving to embrace the Old One as, staff in hand, he made towards her, "we were wondering when you'd return. Come, sit yourself down on the settle. Can I offer you refreshment? A horn of bragget perhaps?" She nodded to her doorward for bragget to be brought, then guided the Old One to the settle where they sat down. "So what's news in Is-coed?"

"What is news, my lady, is that everyone talks of Gruffudd ap Rhys's attack on Llandovery Castle. They say your husband's kinsman, Maredudd ap Rhydderch, defended it manfully."

"Yes, he did, on behalf of his overlord, Richard fitzPons, though why he should put himself at risk for one who tried to take Cantref Bychan by force is beyond me."

"It's a sign of the times, my lady. These past twenty years or more have seen the whole of these Southern Lands become subject to foreign overlords, or to the King of England himself; now the rightful heir to these lands has made his presence known and the usurpers call upon our leaders to safeguard their interests."

Aware that those present were eavesdropping on their conversation, Gwenllian said, in French, *"Still, it's a shame that the man most loyal to*

Rhydderch's *cause should be the first* Countryman *to contend with* Gruffudd ap Rhys."

"A shame, yes, and difficult for many to accept. You would not believe the trouble that I have had, trying to convince my Is-coed patrons that Lord Maredudd had little choice in the matter other than to do what he did, or suffer the consequences." Distracted by the doorward, proffering a horn of bragget, Merfyn took the horn, then continued, in French, *"So how has* Llandovery *affected* Rhydderch?"

"Messengers come from all parts, some saying their lords want him to use his influence to have Gruffudd ap Rhys *accepted as their king. Trouble is my brother, Rhain, finally caught up with* Gruffudd *at his hideout in* Cantref Mawr. *He came back, saying that* Gruffudd *is not the man to take these* Southern Lands *to war. Then there's the soothsayer.* Awst *has been away, looking for her again, but we've had no word from him."*

"I see," said Merfyn, thoughtfully. "And today the French have summoned Rhydderch to Abertawe."

"Yes, to a council, something to do with safeguarding our borders."

Owain came in, his greetings somewhat reserved. "That's no way to greet Merfyn," Gwenllian corrected him.

"My apologies, Old One," said Owain. "It's just that I've got a lot on my mind."

"May I ask what troubles you?" Merfyn asked.

Owain was hesitant; Gwenllian explained, "He's been broody this past week and, according to Caleb, it's to do with Morgan's sister."

"Yes, I must confess that Caleb did say something to me about your interest in Anona ferch Ammon."

"He would; he's said as much to everyone else."

"So what about your betrothal to Elinor ferch Iorwerth ap Meirchion?"

"The betrothal is no more than a proposal, something my father asked me to consider; that means I have a choice; that's what my father told Iorwerth."

"That is as maybe, but you do realize, young man, that a refusal could put your father in a difficult position. I mean, Iorwerth could take offence, as much to the fact that you have a preference for someone with no impressive lineage."

"Lineage! My mother has no impressive lineage. Yet my father could never have found someone her equal, not even if he had married a king's daughter."

Gwenllian tried to conceal a smile with her hand. "He's just like his father; he has a way with words."

"Yes, my lady, he sometimes confounds me with what he says; now all we have to do is hear what all this is leading up to."

"It's a question of making the right decision, Old One," said Owain, "and for me to do that I must see Anona again."

"Ah! Yes," said Merfyn, raising an eyebrow as he turned to Gwenllian, his expression one that invited her to have the last word.

"Your father will be back afore nightfall," she said. "I suggest you seek his permission to go to Ynys Ammon; I'll see that you get it."

CHAPTER 5

LOVE AND LEPROSY

The following morning, Owain had no sooner left the hall than Cadi, his eleven-year-old sister, a seemingly innocent, but mischievous child, caught up with him. "Where are you going, Owain?"

"Never you mind. If I tell you, you'll only stir things up."

Owain passed through the gateway of Y Faerdref to find, outside the stripped-timber walls, Maredudd pacing behind a line of youths, saying, "For the benefit of Cadog, what you've got are bows similar to what the French use. They're stouter than anything we've used in the past, but to become good bowmen in the service of your Lord Rhydderch requires strong arms and that means practice. So – look to your front, lay an arrow to your strings and – yes, Owain, what is it you want?"

"An escort to Ynys Ammon."

"Look to your front, Cadog, this doesn't concern you. So it's Ynys Ammon, is it? Now why would you be going there, I wonder?"

"He wants to see Morgan's sister," Cadi volunteered.

"Is that so? Maybe I'd best come along, show you how wooing should be done."

"Don't vex me, Maredudd, I've taken enough off Caleb as it is. All I intend is to pay my respects, that's all."

"Aim! I said aim, Cadog; that means pointing your arrow upwards, same as everyone else. Now hold it there." A mischievous grin creased Maredudd's short, red beard as he continued, "So tell me, Owain, what's Anona like? Is she pretty?"

"Look, can I have Morgan's cousins and Cadog to accompany me?"

"Cadog! He's only been with us a week. Ah! I see it all now. You want to create an impression, right? That's good, I like that. Shoot!"

"It's not like that at all."

"No! What then? Cadog, what the hell – look where your arrow has landed."

"Maredudd, will you stop vexing me and give me a straight answer?"

But Maredudd had his eye on Caleb as he rode towards the gateway in the company of two companions with whom he had spent the previous day hawking. "Didn't you bag anything, Caleb?"

"Half a dozen red grouse," said Caleb, reining in. "We gave them to Dewi's father, which is where we spent the night. Isn't that right, Dewi?"

"He's been to Ynys Ammon," Cadi volunteered.

"Now, now, Cadi, " said Caleb, dismounting, "don't go stirring things up."

"He has," Cadi insisted. "I heard him talk to Morgan about it yesterday. Morgan said he wouldn't go because of his father."

"Is it true?" Owain demanded. "I'll find out, I'm going there myself."

"I wouldn't bother if I were you. Anona was all over me in the woods. By St. Teilo! She's a passionate wench when she's roused."

Caleb knew what to expect: the first punch he blocked easily enough; grinning, he danced backwards, parrying a second punch with as much ease. Then Owain went for him, head down, like a battering ram at his stomach. He fell back, gripping his brother's tunic, and landed on his back with Owain on top of him. Rolling, he toppled his brother and was coming to his feet when Owain came at him again, throwing a punch at his cheek, killing his enjoyment. He fell to grappling, determined to prevent Owain rising to his feet before he did. With his brother unable to match his strength he gained an advantage in height that enabled him to drive a fist at Owain's mouth. Seeing his brother momentarily stunned, though no less full of fight, he drew back his fist to deliver a more forceful blow when Maredudd caught him by the tunic, swinging him to the ground.

Owain sprang, intent on battering his brother while he was down, but Maredudd's raised boot brought him to his knees. Maredudd hustled him away, arms flailing, then turned sharply. "Stay," Maredudd warned, pointing at Caleb as though he were a dog.

Caleb brushed the dirt from his clothes and, to save face, laughed, "Better luck next time, brother," then walked off with his companions.

Cadi, meanwhile, winced at the sight of blood on Owain's lip. "I know how to get the better of him," she said, referring to Caleb.

"Don't bother, Cadi," said Owain. "I'll get him myself."

"Not today you won't," Maredudd threw out, "you'll go now afore your father gets to hear of this – and take Cadog and his cousins with you."

· · · · · ·

On the moorland above Ynys Ammon, Cadog parted company with his cousins as each made for his own family homestead. Then, leading a grey, he took Owain on a steep descent through woods. His boyish voice rang as, referring to former days, he pointed to trees and trails, to dangerous, almost vertical drops on one side of the track – the landmarks of his former world of loneliness.

The companionship he now shared with Owain was something that he had never experienced before – Owain, the first of several new-found friendships, the one who had explained to him that, along with forty-three other youths, he should consider himself part of an enlarged family, the head of which was Maredudd Goch who, with the aid of Caleb, would make him a fit and mettlesome warrior so that when the alarm sounded he would go forth, marching to battle, eager for the fray, loyal to his lord. It all seemed distantly heroic, especially when expressed in the language of bards, but prove himself he would, given the chance.

Where the woods opened out onto terraced fields he stuttered, excitedly, "This field is named after my grandfather, Cynon, and see that stone over there, that's where they buried him."

Cold and grey the day with hard, brown earth underfoot, Cadog hurried across the field sure-footed, to miss the stones that made Owain stumble. As he topped a baulk he saw the herd, grazing on stubble in the adjoining field. Dogs barked, two came bounding towards him. When they leapt up at him he evinced his affection for them.

Owain kept a wary eye on Giff while the dogs sniffed her to their satisfaction. Then he caught sight of Anona, staff in hand, as she came out from the herd and straightaway that odd, light-hearted feeling returned. He watched her as she hurried to embrace Cadog, to consider and comment on his hair, cut in the manner of a man. As she disengaged she questioned him about the bow and quiver at his back.

Owain stood back, observing that her woollen clothes were wanting: a grey mantle, frayed at the edges, fell from her shoulders; beneath this, a brown overtunic appeared much the same, the hemline of her shift ragged about her bare feet. Her headdress, too, had seen better days, but her face, thin and swarthy, displayed teeth white like ivory through frequent rubbing with a green hazel twig and a piece of cloth; when she smiled it was God's special gift to her.

"Good day to you, Owain," she said, smiling.

"Good day to you, Anona," he replied, bowing. He stared at her longer than intended. *'By St. Teilo,'* he thought, *'she's more beautiful that I realized.'*

"It's good to see you again. Your brother said you'd come."

"Did he!" Owain was surprised.

"How is Morgan? Is he treating Banwen right?"

"Oh! The first few days were – well, bearable. Then he and Banwen started arguing – got so bad that Maredudd had to intervene. They've not bothered with each other since."

"Morgan wanted a separation," Cadog stuttered. "If he'd had his way, he'd have sent her back to her father."

"What – didn't he know that Banwen is entitled to nine days grace afore separating?"

"There's more to it than that," said Owain. "Banwen claimed to be with child and Morgan argued that she couldn't possibly know that. Well, Maredudd didn't agree. He said, *'Who am I to judge? I don't know what you've been up to, do I? If she says she's with child, then that's it, she has a right to stay nine months,'* and like a fool Morgan argued about that too. So Maredudd had him keep pace while he cantered about the fields. You should have seen Morgan after that, he was on his knees."

While he spoke, Owain had been unaware that Cadog had gesticulated behind his back. Anona took the hint; slowly she moved away. Owain looked to Cadog, but he appeared to have resumed interest in the dogs. *'You're a true friend,* Cadog,' he thought, then took to following her.

Still pacing, her back straight, she faced him, observing his bruised lip. "So what do you do with your day?" she asked, her eye on the bow and quiver at his back. "Train for war?"

"It's expected of me, but I'm not that bothered. Caleb is the one for that. It's as well he is, really. He's the edling and, therefore, heir to my father's court."

"Does that mean you won't have a share in the patrimony?"

"That's right. My father says that to share these lands between brothers will only serve to weaken them, and I agree, it will."

"So what will become of you?"

"Caleb will be obliged to support me – unless I find land of my own."

"Still, you dress well," she said, admiring the embroidery on the hems and cuffs of his yellow tunic.

"What are clothes? It's what you are that matters. When I look at you I see a beautiful face and I believe you're just as beautiful in ways."

"Flatterer – and anyway, I limp."

"No one can hold that against you. As for me, Caleb reckons I'm the worst kind of brother he could have, but, really, that's his problem."

She laughed; he did so too. That pleased her and she was glad that he had not tried to impress her with worldly wealth. So many admirers came, telling her how much land they stood to inherit, how many cattle they had, when all she wanted to know was what kind of men they were. Owain was the younger son of Lord Rhydderch. Yet she could detect no arrogance in him. He seemed to be the kind of man who would accept a woman on equal terms.

"What is it?" she asked, seeing him scan the tree-line.

"I though I heard something," he said, reaching for his bow, "like a bell."

"No," she said, a hand raised to discourage him from arming himself. "It's probably Ceredig the Leper. He comes here for food sometimes. I'm expecting him today."

Owain shuddered at the thought of a leper being anywhere near her. "Does your father know about this?" he asked incredulously.

"Only that I bring food. He doesn't know that I speak to him. What happened to your lip?"

"Nothing – an accident."

She crossed in front of him to take a closer look at his bruised lip. When her eyes rose to meet his, his face reddened, his breathing quickened; he shifted his gaze to her lips and was sorely tempted to kiss her. She moved away, perceiving his embarrassment. At least with him she would not have to free herself from groping hands, or call the dogs as she had on one occasion. The fact that he did not force his attention on her made her wish that he would, at least, reach for her hand. A thought came to mind: *'If I kiss him, maybe he'll set his dog on me.'* She laughed to herself.

"Your brother was here yesterday."

"Yes, I know."

His tone made her wonder about the bruised lip. Had it been the result of a fight between brothers? That would not do; she resolved to put things right. "Your brother spent most of the time telling me about Y Faerdref and Maredudd – and where your father is concerned I gather he'd do anything to please him. Oh! Yes, and he told me about his ambition to set Gower free, but he's not my sort, though I've no wish to hurt his feelings."

She perceived that he understood, then wondered why someone like him, or his brother, should take an interest in her. When men of worth considered marriage, noble lineage was their first consideration. Due to pride in their ancestry they were desirous to marry into noble rather than rich families. What was she? The daughter of a man with no impressive lineage, one who, to some extent, lived in the past, claiming that his father and the forefathers of his kin had been wealthy until the French drove them from their ancestral *resting-place* near St. Illtud's Bay. Morgan could remember herds of fat cattle, rich corn lands, fine clothes and slaves, but for her all that was no more than a distant memory. Now, like the rest of his kinsmen, her father had to work hard to produce oats from a relatively infertile wilderness; that made her, in her ragged clothes, a poor catch for someone like Owain.

A bell sounded close. Then what appeared to be an old man, dressed in rags, came out of the woods. His hair white, his skin scaly and covered in sores, he moved painfully slow, supporting himself with a stout stick. Anona made towards him; with every step Owain became more alarmed. She was closing to within thirty paces of the leper when Owain gently took hold of her arm.

"Don't be afraid, this is as far as I go." She faced the leper. "Good day to you, Ceredig."

"Anona," Ceredig croaked, "move up wind, please – both of you."

No sooner had they begun to circle than Owain, through fear, moved to shield Anona and kept the circle wide. Calmly, she said, looking past his head, "Ceredig, I want you to meet a friend of mine – Owain ap Rhydderch ap Cadifor."

"Good day to you – good day to you both," Ceredig faltered; he motioned for them to continue round until the wind was at their backs.

While he circled, Owain recognized the leper as one who often appeared on the outskirts of Y Faerdref estate. At the sound of a bell someone would be sent to place food at a certain spot, to pour milk into a leather vessel belonging to the leper. Owain had never spoken to him: like everyone else he kept well away.

"Owain is the younger son of our Lord Rhydderch," said Anona, kneeling to unfold a napkin, the contents of which she placed on the stump of a tree.

"Your father is an honourable man," said Ceredig. "I say this not for the sake of it, but because it's true. Not once have I been refused food at Y Faerdref."

Owain gave no reply, but Anona had plenty to say, cheerfully itemizing the food that she had laid out on the tree stump.

Ceredig waited patiently while she withdrew, his attention on the young man shielding her with every step. *'That young man cares for her,'* he thought. *'Ah! Mother of mercy! If only I'd not been stricken with this terrible affliction, then I, too, would have found someone to care for – someone to have been part of my life.'*

Tears welled in his eyes. Yet he could not deny that, in times of despair, he had found companionship with the One who had made him. Whenever he felt lonely, as he so often did, he listened to an inner voice. Through a presence, sometimes a faint whisper, he found the courage to cope with his predicament; it kept him sane.

At a distance, Anona sat down in the stubble. That Owain did not follow suit was reason for her to look up at him. Clearly, he was ill at ease, more for her sake than his own.

All this Ceredig perceived; he sought to put Owain's mind at ease. "Young man, when I was your age I travelled far. That's how I came to have this affliction. I did not sin, I swear it. If I'm guilty of anything, it's that when the blemishes first appeared I kept them hidden, but then, when I arrived home, my kin were so alarmed they had me appear afore a priest and it was he who declared that I was unclean. A funeral service followed, and I can remember my kin throwing earth at my feet. Then they went home to divide up my property. It was only to be expected – in their eyes I was already dead. Since then I have wandered for years – and then, when I came to these parts, I found that people were good to me, most of all Anona because she speaks to me, it's the one real pleasure I have in this life. Have no fear, Owain, I would not endanger anyone, certainly not someone as lovely as her."

A long moment passed before Owain faltered, "I understand. Forgive me if my caution has offended you. Truth is, I – well, because I have so much I sometimes forget that the simple things in life should not be denied to others less fortunate."

Anona reached up to him. He took her hand and, returning her smile, removed his bow and squat beside her.

"I took no offence," said Ceredig, lowering himself with difficulty onto the tree stump. "You did only what's to be expected. And now, if you'll permit me." He picked up a piece of oaten bread.

The couple watched him fumble with the food, not realizing that the bones in his fingers were too soft for him to take a firm grip; for a while all three went on talking, almost forgetting the sores that kept them apart. Ceredig told how, after becoming a sailor, he had joined a fleet of some two hundred ships, most of which had set sail from England to take part in the fight for the Holy Land. The way he told of his adventures and the long journey home was as if he had done so before. In fact he had recounted the stories many times, sometimes to himself, or to a squirrel if it stayed in the same place long enough. To relate to two young people was pleasure enough, but to hear one of them say, "Ceredig, tell Owain about...." was more pleasure than he had ever known.

Then a mist came down over the fields, prompting the couple to leave. As they walked back to the herd, Anona unexpectedly took hold of Owain's hand. He felt the warmth and tenderness of her skin and knew, then, that he loved her.

CHAPTER 6

HARBINGERS

Rhydderch's doorward entered the chamber attached to Y Faerdref Hall to announce, "My lord, your chief groom and personal arms-bearer, Awst, seeks an audience with you about the soothsayer."

A short, wiry man with dark, curly hair entered. "She's returned to her abode, my lord, of that I'm sure. We were making our way back from Brycheiniog when we decided to try the Oak Grove again, and it's as well we did. The hut showed signs she's living there now – a fire outside the door, moveables within, moveables that I know you gave her. Well, we waited a while, supposing she was out searching for food, but then, what with a mist coming down and it so close to dusk, I though it best we leave, otherwise we'd never have made our way here in the dark."

"That she's back is all I need to know. First thing tomorrow we'll pay her a visit; now let's talk until supper time."

. . . . . .

The horn that had summoned everyone to supper was now silent. The doorward had announced the arrival of all who had entered the hall – a longhouse, in the centre of which a log fire crackled between the arch formed by a pair of roof trees; spanning the gaps between the roof trees and the walls were the waist-high, wicker screens that divided the interior in two.

In the upper part of the hall with its slightly raised floor, Rhydderch sat in a chair near the end of a long, trestle table, his right hand to one of the wicker screens. Chaired officers ranged along the length of the table, talking, laughing, Caleb among them. On the other side of the screens, in the lower half of the hall, Maredudd sat at a similar table, his company comprising of the eldest youths who sat on wooden benches.

Servers passed to and fro in the dimly-lit hall. A candle-bearer stood beside Rhydderch to cast light upon him and the food that he ate. The flickering light of the fire reflected off the half-shadowed faces that ranged around the tables. Dogs snarled and fought as cast-off food was tossed to the straw-covered floor. The hum of conversation was frequently disrupted by a loud voice, by someone banging on a table, or by peels of laughter that carried far-off into the night.

Earlier, two itinerant bards had turned up at Y Faerdref. Both sat at Rhydderch's table and, when the meal was at an end, they were called upon to entertain. Men sat enthralled by the rise and fall of their rhythmic verse. Tawny in the lambent light they moved around the tables, dramatizing their words with gestures. The rich voice of the minstrel reverberated as, harp held to his breast, he sang the epics of old. In turn the jester brought on eruptions of raucous laughter. When the acclamation died down they were offered remuneration, whatever they so wished.

"My lord," said the minstrel, bowing, "our only wish is that we might speak."

"Then say what you will."

"My lord, gentlemen, you have all heard of Rhys ap Tewdwr, the last Countryman to rule these Southern Lands. Perhaps some of you did not approve of him, but whatever your views there can be no denying that, while he ruled, *we* were free from foreign rule. And when he died fighting to uphold that freedom it was the beginning of the end for all of us."

There were murmurs of agreement; the minstrel continued, "Rhys had many sons. Remember Cynon, that stout but valiant man who met his end not far from here? He was pursued so hard by his father's enemies he attempted a desperate escape through Crymlyn Bog where he drowned along with many of his men. I believe you've called the place Cynon's Pool ever since. Remember Gronw, the one taken by treachery and beheaded in London? And Hywel who, as a mere boy, was crippled by his gaolers at Castle Baldwin? Well, there was one son who escaped the wrath and cruelty of his father's enemies. You all know his name – Gruffudd ap Rhys. As a mere infant he had been taken to Ireland. Two years ago he returned and for a while wandered peaceably. At length he was accused to the King and it was represented that the minds of Countrymen were with him. For months they hunted Gruffudd like a wild animal, almost caught him on more than one occasion – but there comes a time when a stag turns at bay, and so it was with Gruffudd. When a band of hopefuls gathered at his side he turned to attack the foreigners in Dyfed and Ceredigion, and has since attacked the castles at Arberth and Llandovery. I tell you, there will be no stopping him now, not when he has captured the hearts of all who desire freedom from foreign rule."

The minstrel paused again, then said, to Rhydderch, "My lord, I know of the rivalry that exists between your kinsmen and those of Gruffudd, but you, you are a man who thinks in terms of unity. Gruffudd knows that and, having heard of your past exploits against the French, he now bids you, come, join him in rebellion."

A moment of stunned silence followed. Then, as everyone began talking at once, Caleb, who sat on Rhydderch's left, beyond the vacant chairs of the bards, got to his feet, saying, "This is what we've been waiting for, it's time to take up arms."

Stony-faced, Rhydderch nodded to his steward for silence. *Thud* – the steward struck the cross-beam that spanned the nearby roof trees. Voices were lowered; as they petered out, Rhydderch showed his annoyance by glaring at the minstrel. The man should have known better: he should have approached him earlier, in private, not publicly implicate him in rebellion – and it had to be now, afore he had had a chance to consult the soothsayer.

"So – Gruffudd bids that I join him. Why me? Why not his own kinsmen? He has an uncle who lords over part of Cantref Mawr, has he not? And kinsmen who lord over parts of Ceredigion? Why have they not joined him? Is it because they have no confidence in his ability to lead? I tell you, shortly after his attack on Llandovery Castle I sent someone to find out what kind of man your master is, and d'you know what he said on his return? He described Gruffudd as open-handed, quite able to win men to his cause, but he's too easily influenced by his companions over whom he has little control – and the fact that he'll do anything to keep them happy doesn't incline me to have confidence in him."

"*That* is but one man's opinion. *Mine* is that he has done well for himself."

"As a brigand, yes, plundering far and wide and with impunity. Then he melts away into the wilds of Cantref Mawr where no one can get at him – but the question *we* have to ask ourselves is whether *he* can command a host? A host made up of lords even more impatient of control than the hotheads who follow him now?"

"With respect, my lord, am I to assume that you'll not join him?"

"If you want an answer to that, then you'll have to wait till tomorrow."

"But, my lord, tomorrow may be too late."

"To late for what?" Rhydderch perceived the minstrel's hesitancy, the way he glanced at his companion. "Perhaps it's as well you don't answer that, not here, anyway. Wait for me outside my chamber door." He stood up. "Gentlemen, we've all had our fill of ale, too much, in my opinion, to be talking sense. I, therefore, bid you all goodnight." He cast a glance over the screen, nodding to Maredudd to join him. Then, escorted by his candle-bearer, he made to walk the length of the table.

"Father," said Caleb, almost blocking the candle-bearer's passage, "I want to hear what that minstrel has to say."

"No, Caleb, just make sure those young men of mine don't venture this side of the screens." In progressing further, Rhydderch met the gaze of his blacksmith, a dark-featured, unshaven man, the one officer whose loyalty was questionable; the blacksmith averted his eyes and left the table.

At the chamber door he dismissed his candle-bearer and, joined by the bards, watched his officers file past the fire. Maredudd approached. "Right," said Rhydderch, "let's not waste words. What did you mean when you said tomorrow may be too late?"

"It was no more than rhetoric, my lord," replied the jester, bowing. "Merely an excess of words."

"I think not. It's my guess Gruffudd is coming to these parts to attack the castle at Abertawe. I say this because, recently, two bards turned up at the court of my kinsman, Lord Maredudd, and while they didn't go so far as to solicit his aid, they did go about his courtiers, asking questions – questions to do with Llandovery Castle where they said they'd entertained the previous evening, all of which made Lord Maredudd suspicious, enough to be at the castle when it was attacked a few days later. Now there's no doubt in my mind that those two bards were you two gentlemen. So I'll ask you again, why is it that tomorrow may be too late?"

"We can't answer that," replied the minstrel.

"Indeed, no," said the jester, drawing a finger across his throat.

"Seems to me," said Maredudd, "you two gentlemen have second thoughts as to whether we can be trusted. Is that because my Lord Rhydderch's response has been less than enthusiastic? If it is, then...."

"It's not just that," the minstrel put in, "he questioned our master's ability to lead."

"That's right, I did," said Rhydderch, " and if you want to know why, then tell me, did you two take part in the attack on Llandovery Castle?"

"Yes-yes," said the jester, "we were there, scaling the walls at our master's bidding."

"Then I'm sure you'll agree that, while your master can claim success, burning the bailey, his action against the tower was mindless. According to my kinsman, Lord Maredudd, your master had his followers shoot at those up on the tower, a foolhardy move because both the garrison and Lord Maredudd's men had the more powerful bows and were, therefore, able to wreak havoc on those below, killing and wounding many of them. Then, when it became apparent that he's fouled up, your master allowed his followers to retreat in disarray."

"It was never our intention to take the tower," the jester interposed, "only to stir up rebellion."

"Action such as that won't drive out the French; nor is it likely to inspire the lords of our kind to take up arms. And that, gentlemen, is why I question your master's ability to lead; now let's get back to tomorrow. Is your master coming here, or not?"

"Come, loosen your tongues," said Maredudd. "If your master crosses our borders without our knowledge, he could be mistaken for a marauder – might lead to bloodshed, Countryman against Countryman. That won't do his cause any good."

The bards looked to one another. "Very well," said the minstrel. "He could be here within the next two days – depends on whether his men can pass through Cantref Bychan and Carnwyllion undetected. They'll come in small groups and meet up at Abertawe."

"Where they'll attack," said Rhydderch, "as at Llandovery."

"If you've a better stratagem, then I'm sure our master will heed what you say."

"I would expect no less and if you still want an answer as to whether I'll join him, then like I said you'll have to wait until tomorrow. Good night, gentlemen." No sooner were the bards out of earshot than Rhydderch said, to Maredudd, "Watch them, make sure they don't ride off. Come first light I want youths dispatched to summon the men of Uwch-coed to arms. All they need know is that there are forces at work that could cost these lands dearly."

"Bit vague, isn't it? And what about the men of Is-coed? Aren't you going to summon them?"

"No, I want to keep my options open. If the men in the Peninsula get to hear of this, they'll only take matters into their own hands. Oh! And inform the watch no one leaves this court tonight."

. . . . . .

The moment Rhydderch entered the chamber he directed his eye across the straw-covered floor to where a settle and calf-skin rugs surrounded a log fire. Bathed in the firelight, Gwenllian stood nearby, her handmaiden raising her gown so as to remove it over her head.

"You're early," said Gwenllian, shaking down her dark hair, her white chemise appearing grey in the poor light. "I would have thought those bards would have kept you entertained long into the night."

Rhydderch focused on her thin, swarthy face and the eyes that were made more alluring by the application of dark, powdered paint. She was to him more beautiful at thirty-two than when he knew her as a teenage bride.

"Did I speak?" she asked.

"The bards were full of surprises," he said, making for the settle, and continued, in French, *"They're the harbingers of* Gruffudd ap Rhys. *He*

50

wants me to join him when he comes here, to Gower, *either tomorrow or the day after, to attack the castle at* Abertawe."

Gwenllian stared, lips parted, while he sat down. As she made towards him, voices carried from the hall: his youths were making for the side-aisles where they would bed down; two of them, his page and candle-bearer, would soon enter the chamber to help him undress. She could rule out sharing this moment with him as she would have liked.

"Will that be all, my lady?" the handmaiden asked.

"Yes – yes, Arwena, you can retire." Gwenllian reached the settle, looking down at Rhydderch. "*So*," she said in French, "*the time has come. Well, it has hasn't it? You're hardly going to bar entry to the rebels, and if you stand aside and do nothing, you'll lose face.*"

"Gwen," he said in his mother tongue, inviting her to sit beside him, "I understand this isn't going to be easy for you."

"It's not that – and don't patronize, you know I don't like it."

"My mistake, but it's not all gloom."

"*No, you'll take the open country, it's true,*" she said in French, "*and you'll seize all the cattle you need to feed your men, but then you'll be storming or laying siege to castles, and the success – assuming other lords join you – well, now that depends on whether a host comes marching in from* England."

"*That's about the size of it, yes, but let's not forget that, one, the King is preparing to leave for France and, two, there's a mortality among the* Saxons in England, *making it difficult for him to raise foot soldiers, which is probably why seventy archers marched out from* Abertawe *this morning – two reasons why we can be confident that, for a while at least, there'll be no interference from beyond our borders. We've also got ourselves a prospective* pendragon – Gruffudd ap Rhys – *though whether we can use him remains to be seen.*"

"Use," she said, reverting to her mother tongue.

"Yes, use. If all he is, is a rabble-rouser, he could be more trouble than he's worth. On the other hand, if he's prepared to accept guidance, then we can still use him."

"And will you use God also?"

"Gwen, I haven't forgotten what God did for me in my darkest hour, and believe me, I really do understand that this isn't easy for you. It isn't easy for any of us."

"I know – I'm just voicing my thoughts. Nothing wrong with that, is there?"

"No – nothing at all."

Sat beside him she stared, unconcerned by the entry of two youths. *"What really bothers me is that somehow de Viles will be the death of* Caleb."

"Forget him," he said in the Countryman's tongue, "he's the least of our problems."

"I wish I could, only I keep recalling how he broke into a hall at Maerdy, a hall that was supposed to be our refuge, yet he broke in, killing anyone who got in his way. It's not so much what he tried to do to me, he nearly killed Caleb. I saw him raise his sword and – whatever you do, I don't want you to let Caleb out of your sight."

"Gwen, he's seventeen, I can't mother him. If it'll make you feel better, I'll arrange for your brother, Einion, to stick with him no matter what."

"Then see that you do."

"I will – for his sake and because I love you."

. . . . . .

Naked between blankets, Gwenllian lay with her head resting upon Rhydderch's shoulder. They had made love, each desirous to impart pleasure to the other until they reached a climax that made them forget, for a moment, their troubled world – but their lovemaking had not been followed by his usual tenderness, for he lay on his back, oblivious to all but his thoughts.

By the light of a taper she observed his solemn, rawboned face, a moustache shadowing his lips. He was not the most handsome of men and to be married to him was to be saddled with a fair share of anguish. Yet rather than acquiesce she had chosen to involve herself in his affairs.

In the early days, when they had lodged at his uncle's court, she had always been curious to know what happened while away on forays at his uncle's bidding, declaring, *'I want to know what happened – and why was it necessary to....'* There followed five years of comparative peace when, at twenty-one, he had opted to hold, as the means of his keep, the then insignificant manor of Y Faerdref where he raised horses. Then it had been a case of *'What's to be done with that mare? And when exactly will the ploughing start?'* Many a man would have told her to keep her station, but not Rhydderch: he had been glad to have her involved, Maredudd too, for they both knew that it was her way of asserting her place in the lives of two inseparable men.

But in the months leading up to the invasion, Rhydderch had changed to the point of ignoring her for the sake of preparing for war, him of whom it was said, *'Has not the makings of a man of war.'* He had pushed hard for his stratagem to be accepted, confident that he would smite the French, and smite them he had in the waters of two fords and in the woods surrounding his uncle's court.

Then things had taken a turn for the worse: his uncle was slain, resistance collapsed; he lost confidence in himself. Not only did she restore his confidence, she had sown the seed that led to him becoming a Christian; after that he proved indomitable: a speedy campaign in Cantref Bychan, a resounding victory over the French and he was able to settle for favourable terms.

The last ten years had been no less perilous: a second campaign in Cantref Bychan in support of his kinsman, Lord Maredudd, against the Frenchman, Richard fizPons; the never-ending discord with de Viles; above all the intrigue that accompanied his covert attempts to forge unity among the territorial lords of the Countrymen to which she had been a willing participant; now, with fruition at hand, she could count the cost with the lives of her loved ones.

Why? Why did she get so involved? Was it to prove that, being a woman, she was no less than a man? Perhaps, but like Rhydderch she believed in the survival of their way of life, knowing that to keep it, they would have to fight for it.

He stirred, hugging her as a reminder that she had not been passed over. She nestled closer, her free hand exploring his hairy chest; he kissed her hair. Was this the reason for her involvement? Was it all down to love?

CHAPTER 7

FAITH IN PERIL

By first light the majority of Rhydderch's youths had vacated the hall. Those who remained were erecting wicker screens in front of the side-aisles where they had slept. In the upper part of the hall, Caleb paced beside the chamber door until it opened. "Your decision, father, what's it to be?"

"Same as last night. I'll speak to the soothsayer."

"Speak to her about what? Gruffudd ap Rhys? It is Gruffudd, isn't it?"

As he made to walk the length of the hall Rhydderch ground out, in French, '*If you've something to say that's best said behind closed doors, then say it in the Frenchman's tongue.*"

"Very well. *We all heard the minstrel say,* Gruffudd *bids you join him and it's easy to reason why. He's coming here to attack the castle at* Abertawe."

"You're sharp, Caleb, and I commend you for it."

"*So tell me, why is it necessary to consult the soothsayer about* Gruffudd? *We know what he's about, he's the only man with courage to take on the French.*"

"*What we don't know is what he's capable of, or what the outcome will be if we rebel, whereas the soothsayer may have the answers, and I'd be a fool not to consult her when her prophecies, save one, have all come true.*"

"*But what if she speaks doom? Will you stand by and let* Gruffudd *go it alone?*"

"*Yes,*" said Rhydderch, ducking out the door, "*I'll not take these* Southern Lands *to war just for the sake of it.*"

"*But, father, we may never get a chance like this again. The garrison at* Abertawe *is down to two score men and....*"

"No, Caleb, you're not thinking straight – *the horsemen may have been recalled by now and there's still the townspeople and whatever seamen may be there; that could mean enough men to cause us grief.* So cool your heels and that's an end to it."

Caleb paled, then stalked off, leaving Rhydderch regretting his lack of tact.

"What's up with Caleb?" Maredudd asked.

"You know what's up. Are the horses ready yet?"

"No, you wanted youths to summon the men of Uwch-coed to arms. So I thought it best to get them out of the way first. And now, while we await our trusty steeds, a little arms practice won't go amiss. Swords and bucklers?"

"What, now?"

"Plenty of practice, we agreed. We've done little enough with me on circuit."

While blunt swords changed hands, Maredudd threw out, "The jester told me a riddle. Created afore the flood, a mighty creature without flesh, without bones. On land, on sea, it sees not, nor is not seen. Guess what it is?" When no response was forthcoming, Maredudd declared, "I said it was a fart."

"Let's get on with this, shall we?"

"Oh-oh! Someone's not in the best of moods." Crouching behind his buckler, Maredudd circled. "What's wrong? Gwenllian been giving you grief?"

"Leave her out of this, she's no concern of yours."

"She was once."

"Unfortunately for you she married me."

With that, Maredudd made the first move, a feint, which Rhydderch swept aside, followed through, then swung from the right, his blade striking hard the rim of Maredudd's buckler. With equal speed he swung at Maredudd's legs. Maredudd danced backwards, parrying Rhydderch's blade. When the onslaught slowed, both men circled, their swords held loosely in front of them, their breath vapourizing in the cold air.

"She married you because it was her father's wish."

"Still brooding about it, are we?"

A sudden move, followed by a succession of cuts and thrusts forced Rhydderch on the defensive. At one point he seized the opportunity to lunge. Maredudd swung down and out; blades rang as Rhydderch's sword was turned aside.

"Not fully awake yet, are we?" Maredudd taunted.

They circled yet again, the dust curling with the rapid movement of their feet. Then blades rang, sparks flew, shields resounded with forceful blows. A lunge by Rhydderch came dangerously close to drawing blood, causing onlookers to murmur. When their sword hilts locked briefly they each looked the other in the eye.

"Tired?" Maredudd jerked out. "Must have been good for you last ni...."

They pushed each other apart, then met more vigorously than before. Wood splintered off both shields. Blades clashed again and again, each an ear-splitting ring that threw out sparks. The positions of both men changed rapidly, the one giving ground until, circling, he drove the other back. Before their swinging swords bystanders gave way, sometimes scattering. Some muttered concern: this was not the usual swordplay they were accustomed to watching.

Then Rhydderch's steward stepped forward. "Gentlemen, I beg you, end this contest afore blood is drawn." When he realized that his words had fallen upon deaf ears the steward hurried to the hall where, in the porch, he met Gwenllian. "My lady, your husband and Maredudd fight like never afore. Come, put a stop to it."

"What are they fighting about?" Gwenllian asked, following the steward out into the courtyard.

"I don't know, except that you were several times mentioned."

'*It's not possible,*' she thought, finding it hard to believe that, after all these years, they could still contend over her. She hurried past bystanders whom the steward had hustled aside. All eyes were upon her when, coming to a halt, she shouted, "Enough of this. Put up your swords."

But Rhydderch continued to attack, swinging his sword overarm. Maredudd took the blow on his buckler, then executed his favourite move: a flick of the wrist brought his sword swinging upwards, the tip of the blade passing dangerously close to Rhydderch's forearm. Rhydderch drew back; Maredudd warned, "That's the last time I'll go easy on you."

One of the bystanders, a churl, held a pail of water which Gwenllian snatched from him, then advanced, shouting, "Rhydderch, Maredudd, you heard what I said, put up your swords. Right, that's it." She swung the pail, the water showering both contestants. Boldly, she moved too close for them to continue. "Enough; now put up your swords and act like responsible men!"

Maredudd tried to make light of it, but Gwenllian threatened him with the pail. She, then, faced Rhydderch. "So much for last night," she spat, throwing the pail to the ground; turning on her heels, she strode past bystanders, arms flailing, shouting, "Don't just stand there, find something to do," and they did.

"As for you," said Rhydderch, louring at Maredudd, "deputize for me while I'm away. And, Maredudd, no one leaves court without good reason, Caleb not at all."

. . . . . .

In the company of his arms-bearer and two youths, Rhydderch rode out, across fields, annoyed with himself, but apportioning blame elsewhere. "Damn, damn, damn it all!" he mouthed, thinking, '*That sword practice should never have taken place, but you, Maredudd, you had to press for it. The Devil's hoof! One of us could have been injured – yes, injured. And the taunting – I know it's to provoke so we cut and thrust like it's the real thing, but it shouldn't have happened. Damn it! You should have been on circuit. Yet you turn up unexpected and stay two days.'* He sighed, shaking his head. *'What am I thinking? It's not all your fault, Maredudd. After a restless night I'm never in the best of moods and, yes, I should have told you what to do with your damn practice.'*

Ascending a wooded hillside, he found himself haunted by his tactless exchange with Caleb. It was not that they lacked a sound relationship because Caleb made known his filial respect by the way he spoke to all newcomers in the bodyguard. Only a week ago he had overheard Caleb say, to one young man, *'Listen to me, Cadog, and I'll tell you one of the feats that made my father renowned. It happened soon after Is-coed had fallen to the French; that's when my father went on, harrying the invaders till they came against him. One hundred and sixty fighting men, led by the madman, de Viles, marched into these great woodlands, little realizing that that was what my father wanted them to do.*

'For a day and half my father hindered them by cutting down trees in their path. But , of course, the French had these war dogs – great, big mastiffs – which they let loose, foaming at the mouth, on anyone who tried to ambush them. Well, the dogs may have made thing difficult for my father that first day, but in the afternoon of the second day he lured the French into the Clearing at Crow Wood, where a score of our men came out of the woods to shower them with missiles.

'Then, when our men fell back into the woods, de Viles led his followers in, under the trees, to be confronted by a slope too steep for horses. While he dismounted, his war dogs raced up through the woods to be set upon by the Countrymen who were lying in wait for them. Yes, the dogs were slaughtered, and to make sure de Viles came on, our men mocked him by howling like the dogs they had just slain.

'Fool! While he struggled up through the woods my father was down below, stealing the horses. Aye, and without horses the madman had no recourse but to return to the coast, only my father had no intention of letting him succeed. When de Viles arrived at the Rock Face, dispirited and soaked by heavy rain, my father attacked, easily routing the foreigners, and the hundred and twenty he took as prisoners he used as counters for more favourable terms of submission.

'Now you may say, why did my father submit? Well, I'll tell you why. To have fought on against impossible odds our people would have suffered greatly. So my father chose that we should live to fight another day – and that day, I can assure you, Cadog, is not far off.'

Those words made it plain how much Caleb looked up to him. And he had no difficulty in empathizing with Caleb's desire to hitch himself to the rising star of Gruffudd ap Rhys. It was understandable: Caleb recognized the need for a pendragon, one who, because of his lineage, would be acceptable to most Countrymen, and who better than the son of Rhys ap Tewdwr, the last native king to rule these Southern Lands.

But what Caleb failed to grasp was what they were up against. There could be no repeat of former days, no luring the French into the mountains where woods and bog denied them their superiority in arms. On the contrary, *he* would have to attack their castles and see his own men suffer for it. Attack – there could be no easy alternative such as starving the garrisons into submission, not when a host might be raised and sent westwards, despite reports that the King had difficulty in raising a host for France due to a mortality among the Saxons in England.

And if the King came with a mighty host, then God knows he would have to retreat in the face of impossible odds, hoping that, by refusing battle, he would frustrate the King into giving up, like the King's brother, Rufus, had been forced to do almost twenty years ago. Even if the King stayed out of it for a while, and the rebellion seemed destined to succeed, it would take an exceptional leader to keep the discordant lords of the Countrymen as one, united in the face of the King's favourite ploys: bribery, threats and later an advance aimed at terrifying rebellious lords into submission, as happened only two years ago in lands to the north.

The question still was whether Gruffudd was fit to lead. If he proved unworthy, what then? What would be the cost? God only knows, but the alternative was to give up all thought of rebellion, to suffer foreign tyranny until Countrymen everywhere were reduced to a mere shadow of their former selves. No – no, the alternative was unthinkable: they were of Trojan descent, they believed in the prophecies of old, that one day they would re-establish the *Sovereignty of the Countrymen*, and *that* they would have to fight for, or slowly die of shame.

Between budding trees he impelled his mount upwards, conscious that there was another factor, too, in that the more resolute lords of the Countrymen were looking to *him* for a decision – and not only them: Caleb, like so many of his kind, especially the Is-coed tribesmen, looked to *him* as the man who would one day set them free; it put pressure on him to act. "But it's a hell of a responsibility," he mouthed as his horse floundered at the foot of a muddy slope.

He looked up, searching for assurance in an overcast sky, but perceived no ray of hope, no hint of a silver lining. "Where are You?" he mouthed as, compelled by him, his horse struggled to gain a foothold in ooze. He exhaled his frustration, thinking, *'God, You ask too much of me. You test my faith, You make things appear as if it's now or never, and yet my instincts tell me something's wrong, something I don't know about. If I'd still been an unbeliever, I'd have found strength in myself to do whatever needs to be done, but all that's gone now that I'm dependant on You – and yes, yes, my faith is wanting. Why else would I seek the soothsayer? But seek her I will.'*

He gained the muddy slope, confident that his strength of character had returned, saw himself as a man able to fend for himself, a man with a reputation second to none – only his resurgent spirit proved short-lived, waning with an emptiness of heart that stemmed from knowing that his faith was in peril. Yet he rode on, spurring to gallop over bleak, waterlogged moorland.

. . . . . .

"Left, my lord, go left at the stone!"

Startled, Rhydderch twisted round in the saddle. "Take the left fork," his arms-bearer called, "then carry on till you reach the stream."

Beyond running water, Rhydderch came upon the hollow remains of a dead tree, the skull of a ram fixed to its bark; as he passed it by, leading through rustling drifts of dead leaves, he sensed that uneasy feeling return. Thick, gnarled oaks stood like ancients: silent, watchful, resenting his intrusion. Manoeuvring round huge roots that spread as if to hinder hooves, he passed beneath ivy-clad branches that seemed to twist and turn for the purpose of ensnaring the unwary and snatching away their souls. Daunting too were the *mementoes mori*: skulls of sheep, strings of bones, strange marks on fissured bark – and a silence, a deathly silence made all the more foreboding by a feeling that someone was watching him.

The woods gave way to a glade where, facing him, stood a low crag, its weathered surface fissured – and there, at the brink, stood a rude shelter of branches and mud. Reining in, he stared at the darkened doorway, expecting the soothsayer to appear. "Woman, come out! It is I, Rhydderch ap Cadifor, Lord of Gower Uwch-coed!"

Nothing: not a sound, not the slightest movement in the doorway. He waited awhile before ascending the crag, on foot, by way of a gully to one side. Before a fire topped with turf he knelt to feel the turf warm. Rising to his feet, he placed a hand on the overhang of boughs and sods to peer into the pitch-black interior. "Woman, if you're in there, come out. You've nothing to fear, you know I'll not harm you."

Still nothing, so he turned to his arms-bearer, an overly superstitious man who knew the woman's habits better than anyone. "Awst, where would she have gone?"

"Searching for food. May even have gone begging at the Church of St. Cwig."

"Then we'll wait. Put what gifts you've brought inside the hut." Rhydderch made to descend when a disturbance in the woods alarmed his youths into adopting a defensive stance, bows raised.

"Easy, easy," said Awst gruffly, "it's only goats." With the youths so edgy, Awst had to stow the gifts himself, for which he chided the youths repeatedly. To alleviate their fear he, then, challenged them to a game of knucklebone.

Rhydderch, meanwhile, stood with his back to a tree and, facing the crag, he pictured the woman as she had been the first time that he saw her. She had sat up there, between the doorway and the fire, staring through smoke that did little to conceal her witch-like appearance.

He recalled her warning about the coming of French troops, the advice she gave about avoiding pitched battles like the one in which his uncle had been slain, and then, as he was about to leave, how she had cried out, *'You – and the one who is your foster-brother – you will be as a thorn in flesh – until the day one of you sees – the other die.'*

'Of whom did she speak?' he wondered. *'Me? Maredudd? No – no, she was wrong, we survived to forge unity among the lords of these Southern Lands.'*

It had not been easy: each lord had to be sounded out and for that he had used bards; now, ten years later, he could not claim the success that he would have liked. Some lords, like his kinsman, Iorwerth, could not be trusted, most were sympathetic if circumspect; few could be regarded as resolute. The best that he could hope for was that the initiative of the resolute would embolden the waverers to follow suit; that, of course, would depend upon initial successes. There was also the question of co-ordination: command not by a council of cohorts, but by a pendragon, the obvious choice being Gruffudd ap Rhys. What he needed was confirmation that the man was up to the task. *'But Lord,'* he thought, *'the longer I'm here the less likely I'll be around when the rebels come marching in. The outcome could be chaos.'* His reasoning made him impatient to be away.

Having failed to notice that a mist had crept into the grove, an awareness of being cut off came to him when the voice of a youth carried, echoing as if suspended in the damp air. Then a twig snapped nearby.

"How much longer do we wait, my lord?" said Awst. "I mean, if this mist thickens, were not going to find our way out of here."

"You're right, let's go."

At Awst's command the youths scooted for the horses, leaving Rhydderch searching the ground cover for two sticks and a piece of ivy with which he made a cross, embedded it into the ground and placed a bracelet over it. "A sign for the woman," he said to satisfy Awst's curiosity. "By this she'll know I've been and where I've gone."

. . . . . .

The Church of St. Cwig was not far away. When Rhydderch came within sight of an ancient yew, which stood out in the mist, visibility had dropped to within one hundred paces. As he drew closer to the low, rubble wall that surrounded both the church and the yew, the church became more discernable; made of the usual wattle and daub, it stood in an east to west alignment, no more than eight lengthy paces long by half as wide.

Stooped, he entered the church by a low porch in the south wall. It was dark inside and, although he could not see it, a wooden screen divided the interior in two. A veil covered a narrow doorway on one side of the screen, beyond which was the holy of holies where only a priest could go. He knelt, made the sign of the Cross and prayed, "Lord, what can I say? I know that by coming here I've put more store by the woman's words than my faith in You, but I have to know if Gruffudd ap Rhys is fit to lead and, yes, I have to know if the time to rebel is right, there's too many lives depend on it."

He paused, his mind vacant until remembrances of Crow Wood and the Rock Face prompted him to say, "Men say I'm a match for any Frenchman, but You and I, we both know that it's not true. Anything I've achieved is because of You. You were there, right beside me. I don't know why You concerned Yourself with me, seeing as I would have nothing to do with You, but You did and for that I am grateful; now I ask You, suffer my lack of faith and be with me again." A voice caught his attention. He went outside to find himself face to face with a gaunt figure in a grey cassock.

"Your companions tell me you've come in search of the woman of the Grove, my lord, and that you've left a sign for her to come here."

"That's right, father. I'd be obliged if we could wait here till she comes."

"A wise decision. As for the woman, she does come here for food sometimes – a pagan, I fear, though I've come to realize there's nothing unusual about that in these hills. Come, you're welcome to the small comforts of my abode."

Confined to a hut, Rhydderch proved poor company, preferring the seclusion of his thoughts. Anxiously and repeatedly he prayed that the mist might clear, but each time he looked out the door he perceived that conditions were worsening. Feeling trapped, he became increasingly restless, venting his frustration on his overlord, Henry de Beaumont, and the King for granting him right of conquest.

At length, when he could contain himself no longer, he cried, within, *'Lord, am I nothing to You? I ask for Your help. For months I've prayed to You, You know my dilemma. Now I'm forced to seek the advice of the woman. I need to know about Gruffudd ap Rhys. I need to know so that I can decide whether to rebel.'*

The voice of his conscience answered, *'That is not true. You made up your mind to rebel long afore coming here.'*

'So I did. Is that so wrong?'

He held his breath, anticipating an answer, and the words of his wife's priest came to him: *'He who rebels against authority rebels against what God has set up.'*

'No! What right has any Frenchman to lord over these lands? And Beaumont, he had no need of Gower. The number of times he's come here I can count of one hand.'

Again his conscience pricked him: *'Did not your forefathers usurp these lands from someone else? And not once, but several times? And in doing so were they not party to a massacre of one hundred and forty men from the North?'*

'Yes-yes, but my forefathers left things as they were. Not Beaumont. No, it wasn't enough to have his followers lord over what he claimed to have won, he had to bring Saxons over from Somerset so that, in the end, the greatest usurpation of any Frenchman was his in Gower Is-coed.'

'What is that to you?'

'Everything. I feel for those Countrymen who died fighting for what was rightfully theirs. And the survivors, those who had to stand back and watch their lands being usurped by those land-grabbing Frenchmen – I swear, if there's a chance to set things right, then, so help me, I'll do it. I will, d'you hear me?'

'Did not you, like your uncle's son, Cadwgan, strike a bargain with Beaumont that, in exchange for your loyalty, he would leave you in peace to carry on in the old ways?'

'So Beaumont kept his word, but he's a sick man. When he dies his followers will be free to grab more land, regardless of the grief it causes us Countrymen. Aye, and the first to satisfy his greed will be that madman, de Viles. So what do I do? Stand back while he takes what's mine? No, far better that I strike first.'

'Right now you are in no position to strike at anyone.'

Angrily, he hammered his fist against a post and was immediately aware that all eyes were upon him. He made for the door, then went out, slamming the door behind him. For a while he stood beneath the ancient yew, staring into the mist, thicker now with visibility down to twenty paces. It was deathly quiet, so cold and damp that he dropped his chin to his chest, drawing his cloak tightly around him.

Suddenly his senses were alert: a hooded shape appeared out of the mist, coming towards him. Instinctively, he reached for his sword and, ducking, darted out from beneath the tree. The hooded shape gave a start; he assumed that it was a woman. He levelled his blade at her chest. "Don't move, just speak your name."

The woman kept silent, her face shrouded in the hood of her mantle. His blade touched her chest. "Your name?"

"My name is no concern of yours."

He recognized the voice. "You, you're the soothsayer."

"*That* is what they call me; now what troubles you this time, Rhydderch ap Cadifor ap Caradog ap Rhydderch ab Iestin?"

He lowered his sword. "I've received word that a man of princely birth is coming here, to Gower, to attack the castle at Abertawe. What I want to know is whether he's best suited to be our pendragon? And if so, should I join him in his attack on Abertawe?"

The woman gave no answer, but as she tilted her head back he saw her face. She was by no means as old as he had thought – if anything, she was a few years younger than himself. He considered her eyes; glazed, they seemed to stare beyond him. Her lips moved; she muttered strange, unintelligible words. Then she began to speak more clearly.

"This prince you speak of – he has already crossed your border. Even now he marches on a great tower. Many have joined him. Fools! In vain will they scramble, in death will they fall, in rebellion will they falter. Their only glory will be the ravens that feast on their gore – for fate has decreed the rebellion will fail not many months from now – and you – it will mean trouble for you. Aye – and sorrow too because someone close to *you* – will die."

"Who? My foster-brother?" She gave no answer; he gripped her arm. "Tell me, woman, who it is will die?"

"You fool," she spat, staring him in the eye, "the vision is gone."

"You said someone close to me will die. You said as much afore, but you were wrong – my foster-brother and I are still alive."

"No – no, I'm not wrong. One of you will see the other die – but first – first someone close to *you* – will die; now unhand me!"

Releasing his grip, he pointed a finger at her. "Prophesy, prophesy again, only this time tell me who it is will die."

"No – no," she said, backing away as though fearful of others.

He glanced over his shoulder. Awst and the priest were close; the youths hung back, bows raised. As he focused on the woman again she spat, "Here, your bracelet, I have no need of it. Give me goats like you've done afore." Throwing the bracelet to the ground, she continued to recede, her form fading into the mist until she was gone.

"Awst, get the horses – quickly."

"No, wait," said the priest, restraining Awst. "My lord, you can't go now, it's too dangerous. You could be swallowed up in a bog out there."

"I'll have to take that chance. Awst, the horses, let's go."

Chapter 8

Chaos

While Rhydderch had been waiting at the Grove, a score of men had gathered at the gates of Y Faerdref, most of them tribesmen from the surrounding area, the first to answer the call to arms. Maredudd stood among them, he in the company of the bards who were the harbingers of Gruffudd ap Rhys. Both bards, along with Gwenllian's brother, Einion, had spent the night as guests in Maredudd's hall where, for a while, they had talked. The bards had given an account of how the assault on Llandovery Castle had been carried out, whereas Maredudd and Einion had tried to impress upon them how a better form of attack might be employed at Abertawe.

All four had risen early, and shortly after Rhydderch's departure, Maredudd had dispatched Einion to the neighbouring Commote of Carnwyllion, hoping that he would make contact with the rebels in their march on Gower; now, looking across fields, Maredudd observed a rider galloping towards the court. "Could be Einion," he said to the bards. "We'd best go, meet him out of earshot of these men here."

In distancing himself from those gathered at the gates, Maredudd identified the rider as Gwenllian's thirty-year-old brother by his bald head. Like many men, Einion had his head shaved so as not to suffer the fate of Absalom, nor risk an opponent grabbing him by the hair. Einion was often referred to as '*the Axeman*' due to his proficiency with a battle-axe – an axe that Maredudd observed, jouncing at his side.

Reining in, Einion jerked out, "Is Rhydderch back? I've got some alarming news."

"No," Maredudd replied, "he's not back. So what's this news?"

"I ran into five of Gruffudd's rebels in Carnwyllion, one of them an Uwch-coed man. He told me that Gruffudd would cross the Llwch Dwr sometime this afternoon – and more, he said most of Gruffudd's men are expected to be at Abertawe by then, where they'll surround both the castle and the town in readiness for his arrival."

Maredudd shook his head. "So there'll be no taking the castle by surprise?"

"No, and it gets worse. Two of the five were Is-coed men and, as harbingers, it falls to them to rally the men of Is-coed to come, join the attack."

"The Devil's hoof!" said Maredudd, turning to face the bards. "Did you know this was Gruffudd's stratagem?"

"No," the jester replied, "but if every man in Gower turns up at Abertawe, we'll overwhelm the garrison by weight of numbers."

"That," said Maredudd, "is something my Lord Rhydderch will never agree to; nor will the men of Is-coed if they've any sense. Question is, what are *we* to do about it?"

"There's nothing we can do," said Einion, "except wait for Rhydderch."

"Until when?" Maredudd asked. "Look at the mist on the high ground. You must have had trouble finding your way over the high moorlands."

"Yes, I did, but I made it. So what are you saying?"

"Rhydderch should be back by now. That he isn't makes me think he made it to the Grove only to find the soothsayer not there. So he waits, and the longer he waits the less chance he'll have finding his way back here. So it's down to us to do something in his stead?"

"Then let's all go to Abertawe," the minstrel suggested. "I'm sure we can get my Lord Gruffudd to put off any attack until your Lord Rhydderch turns up."

"That," said Einion, "is to assume your master will listen to what we have to say."

"He'll listen," the minstrel retorted. "He's always open to suggestions."

"Oh! Yes," Einion retaliated, "but will he act on what we say? I tell you, my brother was at your master's camp a while back, and d'you know what he said on his return? He said your master is no leader because it's not him who makes the decisions, it's his leading men, and he described them as unruly hotheads."

"That's his opinion," the minstrel bit back, "and in that he's entirely wrong."

"Let's not argue over this," Maredudd interposed. "We've no recourse but to go to Abertawe. So let's saddle up; you too, Einion, you'll need a fresh horse. And pick up your bow as well. I'll meet you back in the courtyard." Maredudd moved off, shouting, to a youth, "Meurig, get over to the stables and saddle my horse."

Before reaching the gateway, Maredudd was accosted by his clan chieftain, Rhodri Gadno, a thick-set, hoary man in his late fifties. Rhodri demanded to be told what had been said and why his son, Einion, was preparing to leave. Maredudd gave Rhodri a brief update, then advised him not to say too much to the tribesmen nearby.

As he approached his hall, Maredudd was thronged by four youths, Caleb saying, "It's Gruffudd ap Rhys, he's on the way, and you, you're going to meet him at Abertawe. Am I right?"

"If you say so. Morgan, get over to the stables and make ready a packhorse."

"Look, Maredudd," said Caleb, "if it's Abertawe you're going to, then we could go as part of your retinue."

"I think not. Your father left instructions – no one leaves this court without good reason, you not at all." Maredudd ducked into the porchway of his hall.

Caleb followed him in, saying, "Well, you're leaving."

"Yes, but I've got good reason; you haven't."

"No, but we'll do anything you say."

"Then go, pick up my buckler, a couple of darts and four French shields."

The doorway darkened with the entry of Rhydderch's steward, Sulien, a lantern-jawed man with an unusually weathered face for someone who rarely left court. Sulien came in, saying, "What's this I hear, Maredudd, you leaving for Abertawe?"

"Can't fart round here without everyone knowing about it."

"That's as maybe, but I need to know what you're about so I can inform Rhydderch when he gets back."

Maredudd motioned the youths to the chamber that served as an armoury, saying, "Go, get them weapons; this doesn't concern you." While he donned his cloak, Maredudd related what Einion had said, then explained why he was going to Abertawe, adding, "And now, Sulien, a favour. I want axes, candles and rope."

"What for?"

"So I can make ladders for a dawn attack."

Sulien eyed Maredudd suspiciously as he made for the side-aisle where he kept his cist. "You do realize that Rhydderch could come back with some reason for not getting involved with that rabble-rouser, Gruffudd ap Rhys?"

"I think it unlikely," said Maredudd, throwing back the lid of his cist. "So what's the problem?"

"*You*. As I see it, the attack will take place with, or without Rhydderch. And if I know you, you'll take part in it no matter what. Well, think on. If you're seen at Abertawe and the attack fails, what then, eh?"

"I've already thought of that." Maredudd removed from his cist a *tawlbardd* – a square game board – and the bag of counters that went with it, his symbol of office: Rhydderch had given him the *tawlbardd* the day he had been appointed captain of guard. He offered it to Sulien. "Give this to Rhydderch when he gets back. There'll be less trouble for him if I'm no longer one of his household. Oh! And when he asks you what I'm about, the first thing you tell him is that I've taken leave of my senses; that I've gone to Abertawe to parley with Gruffudd ap Rhys. You got that?"

"Yes, and I know why you've said it, but what I want to know is, whether your leaving is a temporary thing, or not?"

"Depends," said Maredudd, aware of Caleb's approach.

"Depends! Depends on what? I mean, why would you want to leave...."

Maredudd shook his head and made for the door. Sulien and three youths followed him out into the courtyard. Caleb appeared at his side.

"You're not really leaving my father, are you?"

"Hell! No, when your father and I first came here I'd go off for a month of two, looking for excitement, but I always came back; now – stables, wait for me there. No, no buts. Sulien, that favour, let me have four wood axes, half a dozen rushlight candles and plenty of rope."

"The axes are down at the forge – had them taken there for sharpening."

"Tewdrig," Maredudd shouted, "give those two shields to your companions, then go, tell our blacksmith I want four sharp axes."

Sulien cleared his throat. "Bledri's not there, he came to me last night, said his brother had been taken ill – you know, the one who's a priest."

"The Devil's hoof! And you let him ride off just like that?"

"Now hold on, Maredudd. I know what you're thinking, but Bledri is a kinsman of mine. I'd stake my life on him being trustworthy. And what about Caleb? It's bad enough you being irresponsible, but taking Caleb – if something...."

"Watch him," Maredudd cut in, "make sure he doesn't slope off. I don't want him turning up at Abertawe; now there's nothing to be done about Bledri. So let's get back to what I asked for – oh! And a day's rations for four."

"Ah-ah! It's not for me to go, handing out such things."

Maredudd slid an arm across Sulien's shoulders. "I've noticed you're getting along well with the new baking woman. Well, why not when your wife is away, eh?"

"Now hold on, Maredudd, anything I've got to do with her is strictly in accordance with our responsibilities."

"Ah! Sulien, it's me you're taking to. We're old friends, remember? I'd be the last man to let slip what's going on. Why, if I were to pass your father-in-law's hall on my way south, would I say, *'Hey! Olwen, have you heard what Sulien has been up to?'* Na, not me."

Sulien threw off Maredudd's arm. "Oh! Yes, you would, you bastard. You might not say it straight out, but you'd drop enough hints to get Olwen thinking." He curled a finger at approaching youths. "Come with me, all of you."

Meanwhile, outside the stables, Caleb conversed with Morgan and Meurig, the one holding the reins of Maredudd's bay, the other having charge of a packhorse.

"So that's it," Morgan grumbled, "we're not going to Abertawe."

"Oh! Yes, we are," said Caleb. "Just one problem. If I know Maredudd, he'll have told Sulien to keep an eye on me. Now you, Meurig, everyone says you and I look alike, right. So we change clothes; so Sulien's watching you, not me. As for you two," said Caleb, facing Morgan and Dewi, "you get all the other youths together for a wrestling contest. Then, when everyone is watching, we go over the wall."

. . . . . .

His eyes roving over the courtyard, Maredudd made for the stables where three men sat astride their horses, ready to ride to Abertawe.

"You look as if you'll miss this place," the minstrel, Elfed, called out.

Maredudd observed that Elfed had dispensed with his long, tartan vestment to reveal clothes more suitable for a fight. Yet there could be no mistaking the man's bardic vocation: his jet-black beard fell to his chest while his hair, brushed flat to the back of his head, had been twisted into a stiff coil. Elfed was no more than twenty-five, swarthy and as carefree as Maredudd himself. They had had established a rapport. The previous evening, when they had talked of storming castles, they had spoken, too, of themselves, with the result that Maredudd had recognized in Elfed something of himself, for behind the jokes he perceived, in Elfed, the embers of an unrequited love – the woman being the wife of the pretender, Gruffudd ap Rhys.

"They say it's carousing in the hall that does it," Elfed continued, "makes a man feel he belongs."

"Na," said Maredudd, taking charge of his bay, "there's other things that take root in a man's heart."

Elfed caught Gwenllian's approach and perceived her distress. "Something tells me we'd best leave you, my friend. We'll wait for you outside the gates."

As the three men moved off so Maredudd turned to witness that, in her approach, Gwenllian had her hands concealed in the hanging cuffs of her green overtunic, that she wore no headdress, something he admired about her. His attention, drawn by the dark ointment on her eyelids, centred on her eyes; they showed not her usual verve, rather they hinted at sadness, as did the expression on her thin, swarthy face – but for all that she was no less beautiful, no less the woman of his dreams. He would have loved to have taken her in his arms, told her that he still cared.

"I'm told you're leaving. Why, Maredudd? Surely it's not over of that sword contest."

"It's nothing to do with that. Didn't Sulien tell you that Gruffudd ap Rhys has to be dissuaded from his mindless intentions at Abertawe?"

"Yes, and he also told me you've relinquished your appointment. Does that mean you intend to throw in your lot with Gruffudd?"

"Hell, no! You know me, I get the urge for a little excitement and off I go."

"No, that's how it used to be. You've got responsibilities now. So why not dissuade Gruffudd from his intentions, then wait for Rhydderch to join you?"

"Gwen, there's no telling when Rhydderch will get back," said Maredudd, leading her away from nearby youths. "Now me, I'll do what I can to get Gruffudd to agree to a dawn attack, but with or without Rhydderch an attack will take place because I'm in no position to put a stop to it; that being so, I intend to be right there in the thick of it."

"No, don't – you could be killed, you and Einion."

"Einion has a mind of his own. Me, I've waited ten years for something like this."

"No, not just you – you and Rhydderch, you're as one."

"That's as maybe, but what exists between him and me is not the only reason I've hung around all these years?"

"Yes, I realize that, and yes, I know it's not been easy for you. And I know that when we first came here you'd ride off for a month or two because you couldn't bear to see Rhydderch and me as one, but it's not like that any more."

"Isn't it?" he asked, drawing to a standstill to face her.

She let her gaze fall rather than allow him to discern how she felt. It was all so anomalous when parting with him had always been a joyful affair, a time for farewell laughs and promises of return.

"Remember when you gave me this?" he said, removing a ring. "My symbol of office."

Her eyes flickered from side to side as they searched his. That ring may have solemnized his appointment as captain of guard, but it also symbolized that, for her, a love once cherished had not been entirely forgotten; now, with the return of the ring, she feared that he might not be coming back. "If you go, I'll fear for you."

"Will you? How much, Gwen?"

She did not answer, but let her gaze fall again, thinking, *'Don't press me, Maredudd, not when you already know the answer.'* She saw his feet move as he made to mount up. "Maredudd," she said tearfully.

"What? Hell! I'm sorry, I shouldn't have said what I did. I only meant...."

She raised herself up on her toes, kissed him, then withdrew, her eyes meeting his. "Maredudd, keep the ring."

He kissed his fingers and transferred the kiss to her lips. "Take care, Gwen."

"And you – for my sake, if not yours." She watched him put one foot in a stirrup, then said, "I'll pray for you."

"Yes," he said, hauling himself into the saddle, "yes, you do that."

. . . . . .

In the company of Einion and the two bards, Maredudd rode out over the surrounding fields, recalling a time when he had just turned seventeen. He pictured himself and Rhydderch, riding through September woods, on their way to pay their respects to the newly-elected head of their clan, death having laid claim to the previous one, their father, whom they had buried under a pile of stones, high up on a windswept mountain to the north.

At a place never to be forgotten they had chanced upon a maiden, sat beside a stream. He recalled, saying, to Rhydderch, *'That maiden, isn't she beautiful?'*

'They're all beautiful to you,' Rhydderch had returned, *'but yes, you're right, she's more beautiful than most.'*

Even now, after twenty years, he could relive the moment when he had stood over her, a hand resting upon the bole of a tree. *'Good day to you, fair one,'* he had said and, knowing full well the direction, added, *'Might I enquire of you the way to the hall of Rhodri Gadno?'*

The maiden, whom he reckoned to be thirteen, had stood up, eyeing both himself and Rhydderch, to reply, *'The man you seek is my father.'*

Such a sweet-sounding voice, and as he stared, transfixed by her face, she had turned away; with the spell broken he had followed her, making several attempts at humour. Soon he had her laughing, and she was to laugh so many times in the months that were to follow – but there had been tears in her eyes when, one day, she followed him out of her father's hall and, touching his arm when she caught up with him, cried, *'Maredudd, it's my father's wish.'*

"She's a beautiful woman," said Elfed, intruding on Maredudd's thoughts.

"How d'you know what I was thinking?"

"Last night, when we talked, I knew you'd seen through me. Well, my friend, back there in the courtyard I saw through you, and like I said she's a beautiful woman."

"Yes – yes, she is. She's the most desirable woman I've ever known."

. . . . . .

The wrestling contest was underway when Caleb, dressed in another youth's clothes, sloped off to where three youths awaited him with bows and quivers. One by one, his companions followed him, climbing over the palisade to leap beyond a shallow ditch. Dewi, the last to hit the ground, came down awkwardly and had to be shouldered across the fields. When they reached the surrounding woods they caught the approach of horses.

"Down," Caleb hissed and, from the base of a tree, he glimpsed four horsemen. Recognizing one of them, he scrambled up to obstruct their passage. "Owain – Owain, stop! You'll never guess what's happened."

Owain reined in, as much surprised by his brother's sudden appearance as seeing him in clothes that were obviously not his. "If it's about the call to arms, then, yes, I ran into Bedwyn earlier and he told me – said something about Gruffudd ap Rhys, though none of that made sense."

"It will when I tell you he's coming here to attack the castle at Abertawe."

"Aye, and we're off to join him," said Morgan as he passed by to confer with Cadog and his cousins.

"What's he on about? And where does our father stand in all this?"

"Our father has gone in search of the soothsayer," Caleb replied, "and Maredudd, he's on his way to Abertawe."

"And you've just come over the wall, right? Well, it won't be long afore you'll have several officers after you."

"So what? If we share the horses, we'll be way ahead of them."

"No, Caleb, this is not what our father would want."

"Yes, but your father will turn up anyway," said Tewdrig, joining the group.

"That's right," said Caleb. "Why else would he have called everyone to arms?"

"You do what you want," said Owain, moving off. "I'll have no part in it."

"What about the others?" said Caleb, seizing the reins. "Elidir, what say you?"

"We've just been talking about it," the lanky Elidir returned. "I think we should decide for ourselves. Me, I'm all for it."

"Me too," said fat Guto.

"What about you, Cadog?" Morgan demanded. "You with us?"

"I'm for Owain, I'll g-go with him."

"You gotta come," Morgan blustered, "we're Is-coed men. If we can take that castle, we can retake our lands in the Peninsula."

"Let him be," Owain snapped. "He's made his decision."

"Stay out of this," Morgan bit back, "he's my brother. Cadog, never mind what he says. Just be a man and come with us." He kept up the pressure, knowing that he would soon browbeat Cadog into submission.

Caleb, meanwhile, said, to Owain, "Look, I didn't get to say this, but Maredudd has gone to make arrangements with Gruffudd ap Rhys in readiness for when our father joins him. Now you and I, we've never been companions. So why don't we do this together?"

The to-do at his back caused Owain to turn and witness Morgan swearing at Cadog as he tried to pull him off his horse. Giff went for Morgan, forcing him to recoil, drawing his skene.

"No, not the dog," Caleb snapped, darting forward to stay Morgan's hand. He restrained Giff, then addressed Cadog. "You with us, or not?"

Cadog looked shamefaced at Owain: it was obvious that Morgan had made him change his mind. "I think m-maybe we should g-go. I w-will, anyway."

"That's settled then," said Caleb. He approached Owain, offering a hand in friendship. "No hard feelings?"

Owain regarded his brother, thankful that he had saved Giff, yet suspicious of his show of friendship. If it was the horse Caleb was after, then his demonstrative approach had failed. On second thoughts there was Cadog to be considered: in Morgan's company he would be too compliant for his own good. "If I come," he said to Caleb as he turned away, "I don't want you ordering me around and you keep *donkey* in his place."

"Fair enough," said Caleb, then spat, "Shut up, Morgan." He looked Owain in the eye. "I'm just glad to have you along. Let's go."

"What about Dewi?" said Tewdrig. "His ankle is swollen."

Caleb left the track to find Dewi sat beside a tree. "How bad is it?" he asked.

"By St. Teilo! It hurts," Dewi replied, rotating his foot. "You'd best go, Caleb. I'll stay here for as long as I can."

"You sure?"

"Yes, you go – and kill a few Frenchmen for me."

Returning to the others, Caleb gained a rearward position on Owain's horse. "We're brothers-in-arms now; that means we're in this together, come what may."

CHAPTER 9

ABERTAWE

Ejected from the kitchen, two Saxon waifs, a boy and his sister, stole into the hall at Abertawe, the only place where they could satisfy their hunger. The moment they eased open the door the smell of greasy meat and stale wine carried to their nostrils, compelling them, mouths watering, to make straight for the nearest table. Scrambling onto a bench, they were no sooner stuffing scraps into their mouths than they heard a familiar voice outside. They froze, the girl the more fearful of the two.

Expelling food as well as sound, the boy sputtered, "Quick, Elfrida, behind the sacks."

Elfrida did not move until, pulled by her brother, she fell from the bench as it toppled to the floor. Her brother struggled to get her to her feet, then dragged her, stumbling and strewing the straw with the scraps that fell from her mouth. When they reached the sacks the boy compelled her to the floor, pushing her into a gap between sacks and a dry-stone wall. In a state of panic she crawled into the gap until, faced by a wicker screen, she could go no further. The boy, having following at her heels, whispered, "Keep quiet, Elfrida, and he won't know we're here."

Elfrida held her breath. For a moment daylight flooded the hall as, framed in the doorway, Henry de Viles waited for his two bloodhounds to pad past him. He came in, slamming the door behind him, plunging the hall into semidarkness, the only light coming from narrow windows. While he cast his eye about the interior, both bloodhounds made for the nearest table, sniffing the straw as they progressed. Neither dared to climb onto the table. The smaller of the two confined its activities around the upturned bench; the other veered away. The boy watched it come, head down, sniffing the straw, pausing only to gobble the scraps that had fallen from Elfrida's mouth. Near the sacks it raised its wrinkled head, its hooded, solemn eyes fixed on the boy. It let out a woof, causing the boy to quail, then gave tongue to several resonant barks.

In terror the boy looked up to see, illuminated by a beam of dust-laden light, de Viles towering above him. He searched the Frenchman's face for pity, but two hollow, hate-filled eyes and a jutting jaw made de Viles's face more like a mask than the visage of a human being, its shape defined by a white bonnet that, tied beneath his jutting jaw, emphasized his pronounced, dimpled chin.

"Ah-ha! *You cry, but there is none to aid you, even unto the Lord, but He answers you not.* You Saxon scum! D'you think I didn't see you come in here?"

Daylight flooded the hall again as the captain of archers stuck his head inside the door. "Monsieur...." The hound nearest the table bounded towards the door, which slammed shut.

"*Au pied, Brutus,*" de Viles roared at the dog, "*Au pied.*"

While the hound continued to nose at the door, de Viles strode to the nearest table, stepped over the upturned bench and sent the table crashing to the floor. Both bloodhounds fell upon the grizzly remains of a pig's carcass, tugging at it until the larger of the two drove the other away.

"You can come in now!"

The door opened slightly; through the gap the captain of archers called, "There's a priest to see you, monsieur."

"What does he want?"

"Don't know. He speaks only in the Countryman's tongue. And he's got a brooch. Maybe that means something to you."

De Viles had no sooner opened the door than the captain recoiled, fearful of the dogs, his sword half-drawn. Close by, a priest stood, head bowed beneath the hood of his cassock, hands buried in the sleeves. "Return to you duties," de Viles growled at the captain, then motioned the priest inside. As the priest passed through the doorway, de Viles said, to him, in the Countryman's tongue, "I trust you've got something worthwhile this time." He was about to shut the door when the priest grabbed his arm.

"Come eventide this castle will be attacked by Gruffudd ap Rhys. It's true, believe me. I was there, at the Church of St. Teilo, when five of his harbingers crossed the river, saying they'd come to herald his approach."

Without waiting to hear more, de Viles hurried out the door, calling, to the captain in French, "*De Chalus, call out the guard. Inform the townspeople we expect an attack by the pretender*, Gruffudd ap Rhys, *he'll be here by eventide. And inform Monsieur la Steward as well. You'll find him in the Tavern of the Town.*" He re-entered the hall, saying, in the Countryman's tongue, as he led the priest towards the table that remained upright, "No need to worry about the dogs. Just don't make any sudden moves." On the far side of the table he sat upon the end of a bench, an arm resting upon the table. "You've done well. What else have you to say?"

"Those five harbingers I spoke of, they were annoyed that Lord Rhydderch wasn't there to receive them."

At the mention of Lord Rhydderch, de Viles's expression became more intense, his eyes widening. "Are you telling me they were free in offering you this information?"

"Yes, one of them was a kinsman of mine. I told him, all I knew was that, last night, two bards invited Lord Rhydderch to join the rebels, only he wouldn't commit himself. Then, first thing this morning, Lord Rhydderch sent youths to summon the men of Uwch-coed to arms."

"So that's it, he's involved, my sworn enemy is involved, right?"

"No-no, we can't be sure of that. The reason given for the call to arms is that there are forces at work that could cost these lands dearly."

"Bit vague, isn't it?" de Viles spat, but the priest was more attentive to the peal of a bell. "Never mind what's going on out there. I said the call to arms, it's a bit vague, isn't it? And if it went out first thing this morning, why is it that you've left it till now to come here?"

"Couldn't be helped. I was at the Church of St. Teilo since early this morning, so I knew nothing of the call until some men came by, saying they'd tried to reach Y Faerdref by way of the high moorlands...."

"Y Faerdref! Is that where they're mustering?"

"Yes, only those men were turned back by mist, and when they said they were going to circumvent by way of the Lliw Valley I told them I'd follow as soon as I got saddled up, but then those five harbingers forded the river and I couldn't just ride off. You see, there were two other men at the church, and the harbingers wanted to press on to Y Faerdref. So we all travelled in company until such time as I made out my horse was lame. Then I came straight here."

"Yes – well, I can't fault you for that, but Y Faerdref, if that's where the men of Uwch-coed are mustering, then that's where they'll be told what's expected of them. So you, you go to Y Faerdref and find out what's happening."

"No-no, I dare not. There's men in the woods out there. I saw them as I rode past and they're sure to have seen me. They'll have heard that bell too."

"Then you can help defend this castle."

"No! My agreement with you goes no further than words; now give me my due."

De Viles looked long and hard at the priest as he took from his girdle a purse, the running cord of which he loosened to let coins spill onto the table. *"Les trente pieces d'argent, Judas."*

"What did you say?"

"I was merely saying your words are well worth these coins; now count them to your satisfaction."

De Viles stared while the priest reached for the coins. Then his eyes narrowed as he cast his mind back ten years to his ill-fated *anabasis* when, with eight score fighting men, he had advanced on the Monastery of St. Cyfelach. There had been a Countryman there, claiming to be an abbot; that tonsured imposter had clung to his horse, demanding that *he* leave. Fool! He had only to raise his mace; one fell swing and the would-be abbot had crumpled, head bloodied, into a pool of rainwater.

His face wried, his nostrils widened; he was sure he could smell blood as he relived, inside that so-called church, taking part in the massacre of thirty men, women and children until the head of his mace was covered in blood and bits of hair. *'It had to be done,'* he reasoned. *'It was the Lord's wish that the children of the damned be laid low.'*

The priest, meanwhile, had sat on the bench opposite to count coins. De Viles looked on, his jaw fixed as he continued to ruminate on his ill-fated *anabasis*. *'If only my men had been perfect of heart – like me – I would have severed the head of the barbarian,* Rhydderch ap Cadifor *– but, no, my men were base creatures and because of them the Lord turned His back on me, leaving the Devil free to aid the barbarian in slaughtering my war dogs and stealing the damn horses.'* His face twitched. "Damn him," he mouthed, slamming a fist on the table.

The priest gave a start; a coin fell to the floor. The priest pushed back the bench to search for the lost coin.

'The ignominy of all,' de Viles thought, *'to be forced to retreat by the scum under my command. Well, the scum suffered when they were attacked and routed, but the Lord, He favoured me, for I alone made good my escape.'* When the priest's face re-appeared above the table, de Viles ignored the man until he caught his hand moving towards the purse.

"D'you want this?" the priest asked.

"Take it," de Viles spat, then snarled, in French, *"I would have lost my pursuers had I not tarried in that hall, that den of iniquity, wherein was a woman who, unbeknown to me, was the whore of* Rhydderch ap Cadifor. *For that the Lord put me to the test; for that the Lord had me measure my strength against the miscreant,* Maredudd Goch."

The priest, who had been taken aback by the outburst, was now less fearful, having come to realize that the tirade had not been directed at him, as de Viles had his head inclined towards the rafters. He picked up several coins, depositing them into the purse.

"Were it not for me being tired," de Viles continued, *"I would have won that sword fight.* His eyes widened, his jaw sagged – It was if, having been

laid on his back, he was looking up at Maredudd Goch who, sword poised, was about to deliver a mortal blow. *"Twas the Devil that gave him strength to do unto me what he did, but the Lord, out of the goodness of His heart, spared me, for didn't the Lord stay the hand of Maredudd Goch? And didn't the Lord set myself and my men free?"*

He rose suddenly, the bench toppling back and, leaning on the table, blurted out, *"Ten years have I to repent, ten years in which my soul waiteth for the Lord more than they that watch for the morning. And now – now the Lord God shall let me see my desire upon mine enemies. Only remember, Lord, let me first avenge myself against the unbeliever,* Maredudd Goch *– and let* Rhydderch ap Cadifor *see him die – afore I destroy him too."*

The door burst open and Wilfred, de Viles's retainer, stood in the doorway, saying, "Monsieur, the High Steward is calling for you."

"Wait here," de Viles said to the priest, "while I explain things to the High Steward." He made for the door.

The priest followed. "I've changed my mind. Give me an escort across the river and I'll make my way to Y Faerdref from there."

"Consider it done." De Viles opened the door. "Brutus, Savage, out!"

Believing himself to be alone, the priest looked up, saying, "Great Lord! He's mad, utterly mad, and the sooner I'm away from here the better." A whimper reached his ears and, between sacks and a dry-stone wall, he caught the face of a child. "Out – out, I say!"

The boy did as he was bid. "We meant no harm, father," he said in the Saxon tongue, "honest. We were hungry, that's all."

The priest understood not a word, nor was he listening. What held his attention was the whimpering. He gestured to the boy to bring out the child still in hiding.

"Elfrida, all is well, de Viles is gone. There's only a priest here now. Come, Elfrida, you'll be safe with him."

The girl backed out from between the sacks. She, then, threw herself at the priest, gripping his cassock and sobbing a profusion of words. The priest drew back, tugging his cassock, but the girl hung on, following him on her knees. Not only did she continue blubbering, but the boy tried to explain something. All that the priest could make out was de Viles's name. Then all three fell silent. The bell had ceased to clang, but orders and the sound of hurried footsteps could still be heard.

"We must go, father," said the boy, raising his sister to her feet. "Come, Elfrida, hurry."

The priest followed the children to the door, but made no attempt to stop them leaving. As they ran out, through the porch, someone shouted, at them,

"On your way, you filthy brats." A moment later, de Viles stood, silhouetted against the incoming light. "Come," he said, "the High Steward wants a word with you. After that, I'll see to it you're escorted across the river."

. . . . . .

In woods north of the castle, seven youths had settled down in a hollow to await the arrival of Gruffudd ap Rhys. None of them were aware that men were approaching; it was not until three men appeared above the rim of the hollow that the youths caught sight of them. Caleb was the first to get to his feet.

"Stay where you are," said Maredudd, plunging into the hollow. Of the two men with him, Huw, the huntsman, cut a diagonal descent to the right, intending to cut off any attempt at escape. The other man, the jester, circled to the left. Then Einion the Axeman appeared on the far side of the hollow.

"Maredudd," Caleb exclaimed, "how d'you know we were here?"

"Easy," said Maredudd, slackening pace. "Once Sulien realized you'd gone, he sent Huw to inform me – and finding you wasn't difficult. I've told you afore about keeping your voices down."

"So what now?"

"You'll return to Y Faerdref."

"Ah! Come on, Maredudd, my father will be coming here once he gets back from the Oak Grove. So what's the point...."

"We don't know if he'll make it back from the Grove; more to the point, we don't know if he'll have a mind to come here. You know the reservations he has about Gruffudd ap Rhys."

"So why are you here? And don't tell me it's to parley with Gruffudd like you told Sulien."

"Ah! But there's truth in what I told Sulien. You see, Gruffudd's rebels are coming here to surround the castle and the town so he can turn up later like a king. Then his men will attack while it's still light, like they did at Llandovery. Me, I'm here to persuade him to go for a dawn attack because, one, it'll give your father more time to get here and, two, there'll be less loss to the Is-coed men who'll turn up as a result of Gruffudd's harbingers."

"So what happens if my father don't turn up? Are you still going to take part in the attack?"

"Yes, that's my choice. You don't have a choice."

"Ah! Come on, Maredudd, if you're taking part, why not us?"

"Because if anything were to happen to you, your father would never forgive me. Same goes for the rest of you."

"My father wouldn't give a damn," said Morgan, "nor would he shed a tear...."

The peal of a bell captured the attention of all. Caleb was the first to revert to the issue. "None of this is fair. We've trained for the day when we'd storm castles...."

"I'm not here to argue with you, Caleb. You leave and that's it."

"Ah! Come on, Maredudd, you can put us in the rear troop. There'll be no heroics, I swear – we'll all swear to it, and I'll make sure everyone here stands by their oath."

Four youths added weight to Caleb's words. Maredudd understood: he had only himself to blame for their enthusiasm. There were, however, two youths who showed little enthusiasm. Maredudd said, to one of them, "What about you, Owain? I can't imagine you wanting to be involved in all this."

"I'm here now. If I leave, it won't look good for me."

"Cadog?"

"Same g-goes for me too."

Maredudd shook his head. "No – no, it can't be done. I can't lead and keep an eye on you lot."

Huw cleared his throat. "I wouldn't mind having a go at that castle and, if I did – well, I could keep and eye on some of them."

"And if some of them were with me," said Einion, "you'd be free to lead us all the way up to the tower."

Maredudd frowned. "You're a great help, the pair of you."

It was then that the minstrel's voice carried. "Maredudd! Maredudd!"

"Over here, we're in a hollow! What's up?"

"It's the French, they're preparing for attack! I'll wager it was that damn priest I saw earlier who warned them."

CHAPTER 10

DEATH'S DITCH

In the grey light of dawn, Caleb picked his way to the edge of woods, eager for a glimpse of the castle. Despite the poor light he could make out, silhouetted on the brow of a low ridge, the pudding-shape of the motte, a wooden tower crowning the summit. Smoke made him cough, reason for him to recall the township on the far side of the motte, how, with the arrival of thirty of Gruffudd's rebels, he had run down to the estuary, setting fire to more than a dozen halls and numerous outbuildings.

The arrival of that first group of rebels the previous afternoon had been followed by the arrival of other groups until, eventually, more than two hundred rebels had assembled north of the castle. Then, in the eventide, Gruffudd ap Rhys had turned up. It was easy to see why men looked to Gruffudd for leadership: at twenty-five the man had charisma, a flamboyant charm that bonded with his strange accent, the result of living most of his life in Ireland. Meeting the man had been a memorable experience in that he witnessed Maredudd persuade Gruffudd and leading rebels to agree to a dawn attack and to making ladders according to his specifications.

Other reflections to enthuse him were the successive arrivals of men from the Peninsula. That some of those Is-coed men had marched many miles at night to get here was reason for him to anticipate his father's arrival. He was thinking, *'Even now he could still turn up.'* when voices snatched him from his reverie.

Four men had emerged from the woods, one of them holding a rushlight. He identified each of them in turn: Maredudd; Einion the Axeman, his mother's brother; Huw, his father's huntsman; and the minstrel, Elfed. What struck him about the last named stranger-in-their-midst was that Elfed had chosen to remain with them because of the rapport he now shared with Maredudd; it was as if the two of them had known one another all their lives.

"Looks daunting," said one of two shadowy figures, referring to the tower.

Caleb recognized the voice as that of his brother. The other person he presumed to be Cadog. "We'll soon torch it, you'll see," he said to attract Owain's attention. "Sounds like I'm sure of myself, doesn't it? Truth is, I'm not, and d'you know what bothers me most? Our father – can't help thinking I've done him wrong."

"So you admit to that, do you?" said Owain.

"Yes, and there's something else. Tewdrig and I, we've been talking and he said you and I should settle our differences. I mean, we're brothers, and let's face it, either one of us could get killed in the attack." Caleb awaited a response. "Look, I know I've always picked on you, but give me a chance and I'll put things right."

"So you've said – several times as I remember."

"You don't believe me, do you?"

"You lied to me, you led me to believe that our father was coming here."

"So I was wrong. What more can I say?"

Before he could reply, Owain was distracted by the approach of several youths, one of them, rushlight in hand, saying. "Owain – Owain, is that you?"

"I don't believe it," said Caleb, "it's cousin Rhys. So what's he doing here?"

"Same as you," said Rhys, drawing closer.

"Huh! I find it hard to believe," Caleb sneered, "that you, the son of Iorwerth ap Meirchion, should have the nerve to show your face here."

Ignoring Caleb, Rhys clapped a hand on Owain's shoulder. "Owain," he said amiably, "they told me you were here."

"Good to see you, Rhys," said Owain, returning the gesture. "Is your father here?"

"Lord, no! I heard what was going on and slipped away without him knowing."

"Did you, now?" Caleb sneered. "Well, what d'you want with us?"

"We're of kin, aren't we? So let's be brothers-in-arms."

"With you, no. Your father has too many dealings with the French for my liking. I'm surprised he's not up there, taking part in the defence."

"Huh! There's no way my father would help de Viles defend that castle."

Caleb was taken aback. "What d'you mean, de Viles? I thought...."

"Elgar the Saxon fell sick," Rhys cut in. "So de Viles took his place."

"By St. Teilo," Caleb exclaimed. "Maredudd, did you hear that? De Viles is up there, in that castle."

"I heard," Maredudd returned, making towards them, rushlight in hand. "Rhys, how did you know what was going on? Was it the town burning?"

"That, and you know my father, there's little goes on without him knowing about it."

"Well, you're welcome to stay with us," said Maredudd.

"No," Caleb blurted out, "let him attach himself to others."

"Caleb, he's one of us. He can stay, if that's what he wants."

"I'm obliged to you, Maredudd," said Rhys. "I wasn't sure I'd be accepted, but my companions said I had nothing to fear on that score." Rhys turned to Caleb. "D'you know why they said that? They know me, they know I have no love for the French."

"Well said," said Maredudd.

Caleb bit his lip, irked that Rhys had the better of him. Maredudd led him away.

"Right, lads, gather round," said Maredudd, turning to face the men of Gower.

Despite ribaldry, which Maredudd countered tit for tat, the men closed in, leaving Caleb wondering whether he would ever assume command with such apparent ease. He fully accepted that Maredudd had earned the respect of most Is-coed men because he often rode about the Peninsula, encouraging groups of men to prepare for the day when they would storm castles; nor was that the extent of his covert activities, for whenever Maredudd took Y Faerdref youths roaming during the summer months, he was invariably joined by the offspring of prominent Is-coed men. These youths from all over Gower he took to remote places where he had them practise storming improvised defense works. Little wonder that Maredudd was here to see his ideas and his efforts put to the test.

"Off with your cloaks and plaids," Maredudd continued, "and listen to me. Last night we talked things out – nothing new, most of you have heard it afore, or you've practised it, but for the benefit of those who turned up later we'll go over it again. When we go forward we keep a steady pace. No shouting – we don't want to draw attention to ourselves. First thing we come up against is the bailey ditch."

Maredudd paused: everyone knew the bailey to be a huge, rectangular enclosure on an escarpment overlooking the River Tawe. A massive ditch defended the bailey on three sides; the motte and a steep slope to the riverside protected the bailey on the east. A palisade enclosed the bailey interior, behind which, it was assumed, the garrison stood to in readiness for an attack from the north.

"There'll be two troops. Those of you with bows will be in the troop led by this man, Einion the Axeman. Einion, as most of you know, is an accomplished bowman; he's usually been with me when I've roamed the Peninsula, trying to persuade you Is-coed men to make use of stout bows. Now, when you bowmen reach the edge of the ditch, you await Einion's command to let fly your arrows at any Frenchmen behind the palisade. Do it well, lads, or we'll all suffer for it. The rest of you will be in my troop and we'll be carrying three ladders."

The ladders that were to be used by the Gower men lay behind Maredudd. Two of them were wide enough for two men to climb side by side. The third ladder could accommodate three men side by side; it lay between the two narrower ones.

"Once we've reached the ditch we drop down over the edge – not much of a drop, about the height of two tall men, and the sides slope. We got to get the ladders over to the far side of the ditch, then scale them. And once we're in the bailey, then, and only then, will the men in Einion's troop follow on." Maredudd paused, placing a hand on Caleb's shoulder. "I'll leave the rest to you."

"If the French can't hold the bailey," Caleb shouted, "they'll withdraw to the tower, up there on the motte. The easiest way up to the tower is by a walkway on poles. It's the walkway we got to go for if we're to carry the day. To your places, men, and may God be with you all."

At first there was confusion as to who went where. Maredudd got things sorted out. Then, kneeling beside the butt-end of the central ladder, he ordered that all rushlights be extinguished. In the grey light of dawn the torches of Gruffudd ap Rhys's rebels still flickered on the left.

Maredudd pondered: whatever misgivings he had about the involvement of seven youths, small comfort could be gleaned from the fact that he had placed four of them at the tail-end of the ladder at which he knelt, the brothers, Caleb and Owain, each carrying one of the French shields that he had brought with him. He had also arranged for the Gower men to hold a position on the right flank; hence they were furthest away from the walkway where, he knew, the worst of the fighting would take place. The rest he could only leave to chance; that bothered him. He caught someone's approach. "Cadog, is that you? I told you to stay with Einion."

"I just w-want to speak to Owain, th-that's all."

"He's back there. A few words, no more."

Cadog made his way to the rear. "Owain – Owain, w-where are you?"

"Here. What is it you want?"

Cadog dropped to one knee. "I d-didn't understand w-what Maredudd said."

"Then stay close to Elidir and Guto, they know exactly what to do."

"They will?"

"Yes. Remember what I said about Cae-castell? My father built it so we could practise storming a castle. That's how Elidir and Guto know what to do."

"Yes, but they've g-got bows. Me, all I've g-got is my s-sling."

Owain declined comment, knowing that Maredudd had relieved Cadog of his bow, giving it to someone who knew how to use it; that, as he recalled, had prompted Morgan to sneer about how they would all live longer now that Cadog no longer had a bow. He felt sorry for Cadog, but the moment passed when long, war horns blared, the sound carrying in the misty, morning air.

. . . . . .

"Men of Gower," Maredudd barked, "let's go. Lift – up."

Grunts followed as ladders were raised. With untrammelled missile men taking the lead a long, ragged line of rebels moved off, some shouting, "For God and Gruffudd ap Rhys," until the words were drowned out by the grim utterances of the unruly.

Onward, towards the north ditch some three hundred rebels marched – and with a sling dangling from his right hand, Cadog stumbled through withered grass to join Einion's bowmen. He wished that he taken the trouble to relieve himself. He had intended to do just that when, instead, he had knelt beside Owain. As he passed Maredudd by he glanced back at the ladder crew. Owain he could not discern, being hidden among the shadowy shapes that seemed to move as one. '*He'll be safe back there,*' he thought, '*and he's got a shield, but me, I could be....*'

"Mother of God!" he stuttered, panicking. "Elidir, Guto, where are you? Wait for me." Stumbling rightwards, he searched his surroundings, hoping to identify his lanky cousin, Elidir. It was fat Guto that he recognized first. Quickening his steps, he trailed behind his fat cousin; from then on that was where he stayed.

A chant rose. "Death to the French! Death to the French!"

Desperate to withhold his wee, Cadog stuttered the words, then remembered that Maredudd had said, *Don't shout – we don't want to draw attention to ourselves.* '*Maredudd,*' he thought, '*must know what he's about.*' Yet it seemed strange that the men of Gower spoke only in subdued tones while, further left, more than two hundred rebels volleyed hate. It made him feel that he was part of a well-practiced troop.

Gradually, the dawn light surrendered to view the more chilling aspects of the castle: the motte loomed, the tower on its summit appeared daunting; ahead, the outline of buildings within the bailey became discernible. Suddenly, above the clangour of long, war horns, a roar erupted as, en masse, Gruffudd's rebels surged, the advance falling into disarray as missiles men raced ahead, leaving the ladder crews lumbering behind.

Unnerved, his urine flowing free, Cadog made to run, kicking the heels of Guto whose response was sharp. Cadog dropped back a few paces, wondering why the men of Gower had not surged. Then it dawned on him that Guto was going forward with his back bent, an arrow notched on his bowstring. *'We must be close,'* he thought, imitating Guto's posture. He scrabbled in his satchel for a stone, only to drop it.

The crescendo on his left compelled Cadog to look that way. *'Those men over there must have reached the ditch,'* he thought and, hearing a scream, stuttered, "Mother of God! They're being shot at." Facing frontward, he saw Guto drop to one knee. He followed suit, realizing that those round about had done the same. Edging forward, he touched Guto's back. "Guto, w-what's happening? W-why are...?"

"Shh!" Guto spat, clapping a hand over Cadog's mouth.

Cadog froze, eyes wide open, staring ahead at the dark outline of the palisade. Suddenly his ears rang with the shouts of the men around him. The game was up; their presence was known. Cadog rose, moving leftwards to let loose a stone. As far as he could tell there were few defenders directly in front of him; now their shadowy shapes where no longer to be seen, but they were still there, sheltering behind the palisade. Expecting their reappearance, Cadog had no sooner reloaded his sling than Maredudd shouted, "Out of the way." Instinctively he ducked, the ladder passing over his head.

Behind the cover of a French shield, the butt-end of the ladder resting upon his left shoulder, Maredudd moved forward, using his feet to locate a branch, one of many that had been placed near the outer edge of the ditch during the early hours. He was in high spirits, his blustering an inspiration to all.

"Keep going, lads! We've got the bastards worried now!"

Having pushed the ladder leftwards, a string of curses reached his ears. The voice he recognized as that of the minstrel. Whatever Elfed's misfortune, the curses kindled Maredudd's sick humour, but his amusement passed when, pushed from the far side, the ladder struck him in the face. He staggered sideways. Shouting, "Elfed, you bastard, I'll get you for this," he became aware that his right foot had touched a branch. "Down with this end, down! Elfed, for St. Teilo's sake, lower your end!"

The ladder inclined, the butt-end hitting the edge of the ditch hard. Maredudd dropped down, over the edge, shouting, "Into the ditch, lads, push." Pushed from above and pulled by those descending the slope, the ladder soon found its own momentum, sliding over withered grass. When it came to a standstill, Maredudd shouted, "Get a hold of the ladder, lads. Twelve paces should do it. Ready. Lift – up. One, two...."

At a slant, the top end bumping down the slope, a score of men hauled the ladder across the ditch. On the count of twelve the leading men thrust the butt-end into the mire. Everyone crowded round, raising the ladder, then pushing it so that the top arced until it jarred against the palisade. A shout went up. A scramble ensued. Between two men, Maredudd scrambled up the vibrant rungs, knowing that he would no longer have the support of Einion's bowmen. Peering beyond the rim of his shield, he saw, above the sharp points of the palisade, a shadowy shape appear against the dawn sky. *Whoosh*! An arrow sang past his outstretched arm to lodge, quivering, in the rung beside his knee. He swore; the archer withdrew to recharge his bow.

Knowing that it was now a race against time, Maredudd galvanized himself into climbing faster. To his left Elfed held the lead and, climbing crosswise, he obstructed Maredudd's ascent. Maredudd attempted to climb rightwards, only to be blocked by the man on that side of the ladder. He never heard the twang of a bowstring. The only thing he witnessed was Elfed tilting back like a falling tree. The man upon whom Elfed fell, yelled, as did others lower down.

Pausing on the uppermost rungs, Maredudd jerked his spear higher, intending to use it as a stick should an opportunity arise. He waited for what seemed an age, ignoring the plight of the man on his right as he battled with an enemy spearman. The archer reappeared. Maredudd swung, his spearhead striking the archer's forehead; the man fell back from the wall.

"Got you, you bastard!" Shield raised, Maredudd topped the ladder and leapt into the bailey, landing awkwardly on the leg of a fallen defender. He toppled sideways, dropping his spear. As he struggled up, searching for movement in the darkness around him, he became aware that others of his troop were dropping down beside him, all of them landing on the low, earthen bank that served as a wall-walk on the inner face of the palisade. None were meeting opposition. Confident that the defenders had abandoned the palisade in his sector, he moved forward, kicking his spear as he did so, to drop down off the earthen bank. As he bent to retrieve his spear the shadowy shape of an archer appeared directly in front of him.

The archer came at him with a sword, but with his vision impaired by blood from a head wound the man misjudged his swing, the hilt of his sword striking the rim of Maredudd's shield. Maredudd whipped out his skene, thrusting the blade into the archer's midriff. The man agonized, falling upon Maredudd's shield, gripping the rim, expelling the words, "*Je t'aurai, Breton*," as he tried to raise his blade.

Maredudd thrust harder, jerking the blade upwards. "Die, you bastard, die!" His hand warmed and, straining, he shoved his shield sideways, withdrawing his skene. The archer slid to the ground.

Maredudd retrieved his spear and, moving forward, barked, over his shoulder, "Form a half-circle. Everyone, form a half-circle." To his left the noise made it plain that Gruffudd ap Rhys's rebels were swarming over the palisade. "Huw – Huw, can you hear me? Have you got your four lads with you?"

"Huw's not here, Maredudd," Caleb returned from some point in the defensive half-circle. "He went down afore we dropped into the ditch. And Morgan, last I heard of him was in the ditch."

"Then get over here with Owain and Tewdrig and stay close to me!"

Shouting, "Countrymen," Maredudd headed for the end wall of a building. It was in his mind to circumvent the fighting near the palisade and the adjacent buildings, and make his way round to the walkway where the garrison would retreat. Somewhere along the way he hoped to settle an old score, for coming to grips with Henry de Viles was something that he had set his heart on.

As he rounded a corner he met with a mass of moving shapes, a cacophony of sounds: pigs squealed, one charging his legs; chickens clucked, flapping their wings; cattle mooed – all panicked by the sounds of conflict. He had expected to encounter livestock, but not in such utter confusion. As he made his way past the terrified beasts, careful to avoid horns, he had to accept that there would be no speedy advance on the walkway, that the chances were de Viles was already dead.

But between buildings de Viles was still alive. Retreating behind the cover of his shield, his retainer, Wilfred, behind him, he volleyed orders at his panic-stricken men, but they, fearing that they might be cut down by one of their own, were shouting their racial identity. Even Wilfred had difficulty in catching the commands due to the baying of a surviving bloodhound. De Viles gave up shouting when several men hurried past, leaving him faced with the prospect of being isolated

No sooner had he backed beyond the corner of a building than two rebels rushed him. One recoiled, fending off the bloodhound; the other came at him, jabbing furiously at his shoulder-to-knee-length shield. He backed away, almost bowling Wilfred over, at which point the rebel lunged at his legs, missing them by a hand's breadth. It was a chance to retaliate and retaliate he did, his mace striking his opponent's forehead. He drew back, bellowing, "*Au pied, Brutus, au pied*," but he failed to detect her rabid howling.

Head snapping left and right, he retreated, ready to strike anyone who came near him. On all sides his men were retreating to the walkway that, on piles, spanned a ditch and continued up the steep slope of the motte. At the foot of the walkway it was every man for himself, though a hoarse voice suggested that someone conducted himself manfully. That someone, flanked by two supporters, was a Dane, Olaf of Leicester, the castle constable, a stubborn man if ever there was one.

"Wilfred, a spear," de Viles bellowed, thrusting his mace into his belt, "give me a spear."

Guided by the hoarse voice, he moved sideways until he closed with Olaf's left flanker, a bailiff, so that, in line, they would be a support to one another. As they backed towards the walkway, spears projecting beyond their shields, they were besieged by a clamorous mass of struggling shapes. In the poor light it was difficult to tell friend from foe – not that de Viles gave a thought to who was in front of him. He thrust, piercing a man's thigh. The man fell, screaming in the Saxon tongue, then crawled to claw the leg of the bailiff, who recoiled.

"Back," de Viles snarled, shouldering the bailiff, "onto the walkway."

De Viles and Olaf closed ranks, but the retainer on the Dane's right failed to respond quickly; a rebel assailed him. By the time Olaf realized his retainer's plight he was himself harried by other rebels, who came at him, shouting and jabbing at him with their spears.

"You're next, Wilfred," de Viles barked. "Get on the walkway!"

Wilfred disengaged, squeezing between a post and his master's back, losing his shield in the process. Then Olaf started to recede, spear still levelled at the rebels who harried him. One rebel rushed de Viles, knocking aside his spear and swinging an axe, the blade embedding in his shield. He fell back, onto the walkway, and would have lost balance had it not been for Wilfred at this back. An over-the-shoulder spear thrust by Olaf gashed the axeman's neck, bringing the man to his knees, time for de Viles to regain himself and retreat a few paces so that, flanked by paling, his spear and that of the Dane were sufficient to keep the leading rebels at bay. Slowly, one step at a time, he retreated along the walkway, below which was a four-meter drop to the bottom of the ditch.

Crowding first the paling, then handrails, the rebels kept pace, intent on following de Viles all the way up to the tower. He shouted, at them, *"How long shall ye imagine mischief against a man? Ye shall be slain, all of you, for I am fearfully and wonderfully made."*

Shouting and stamping their feet, the rebels continued to keep pace; that suited de Viles. Behind him was a section of walkway known to as the *swaying section* – suspended, in part, by ropes serving as handrails, and by ropes lashed to either end of its base. The moment that he backed onto the rope-bound planks he felt the section sway, but with Wilfred at his back he managed to maintain balance.

"Wilfred, are there men standing by to cut the ropes?"

"I dunno – I think so, monsieur."

Aided by Wilfred's steadying hands, de Viles continued his precarious retreat; he was halfway across the *swaying section* when the leading rebel stepped onto the rope-bound planks. "Come, you fool. Come, follow me to your death." At his rear was a platform where, under normal circumstances, men passed one another by on their way to and from the tower. As he backed onto the platform he passed two men, both cutting ropes. The *swaying section* tilted sharply, throwing the leading rebels into panic, their shouts turning to screams when the section suddenly fell away from the platform, sending rebels plummeting to the ditch below. For a moment a hush reigned over the rebels crowding that part of the walkway that remained intact.

De Viles laughed, at them, "*I have wounded them that they are not able to rise; they are fallen under my feet. Depart from me, therefore....*" An arrow thudded into his shield. He roared with laughter again as, head lowered behind his shield, he retreated towards the tower.

At the top of the walkway he entered within a palisade, then stood back while a gate was shut and barred. Wilfred approached to relieve him of his weaponry. "Are you hurt, monsieur?"

"Cuts to my legs – my right arm."

"I'll get a torch so I can bind your wounds."

"No, Wilfred, not now, the day is far from over. Just go, replenish the men's arrows, for *happy is the man that hath his quiver full of them.*" Summoning his remaining strength, de Viles made to walk upright between the men manning the palisade and those leaning against the wooden walls of the tower. "Face your front. Regain your strength. You're going to need a steady hand for when they come again. *Therefore, shalt thou make them turn their backs when thou shalt make ready thine arrows upon thy strings against the face of them.* Then *they shall fall and perish at thy presence* – and they will, for *the children of Ephraim, being armed and carrying bows, turned back on the day of battle.*"

As he passed by, an archer said, to the bailiff, "He's mad, you know that?"

"That's as maybe," the bailiff returned, "but because of him we're still alive."

Chapter 11

The Tower

Maredudd observed the throng at the foot of the walkway. The confusion had worsened with the arrival of latecomers, all of them confounded by the angry men who were turning back from the walkway. More latecomers were approaching when he recognized the voice of one of them. "Einion, over here!"

"Maredudd, is that you? What's going on?"

"Can't say, but I'll soon find out." Maredudd buttonholed a man about to pass him by. "What's up? Where's everyone going?"

"Back for the ditch," the man replied. "We're going to make our way round to the north side of the motte and attack the tower from there."

"I take it," said Einion after the man had moved on, "we won't be doing that."

"No, we'll get below the walkway," said Maredudd, "and attack from under there."

"I'm all for that," said Caleb.

"I don't think so," said Maredudd. "From now on you'll be a support to the rest of us, as is expected of you."

"But why? We've come this far with no more than scratches."

"Huw didn't," said Einion. "I came upon him afore I dropped down into the ditch – said some Is-coed youth had jabbed a spear in his shoulder."

Maredudd nodded. "You didn't come across Elfed in the ditch, did you?"

"Na, couldn't see a damn thing down there. Why, is he...?"

"Dunno, I just saw him fall from the ladder. Send some of your troop to look for him and anyone else who didn't make it this far."

While Einion singled out the men nearest, Caleb reverted to what concerned him. "Look, Maredudd, we've done everything you...."

"I said no. It's getting light and from hereon the harder and more bloodier it's going to be." Maredudd moved onto the walkway where paling prevented him from descending into the ditch. He retraced his steps to the bailey palisade, looking for a place to breach it. "Einion, can you use your axe to cut through this paling? Only you'll have to do it quickly if we're to gain a place under the walkway."

While Einion got to work, Owain looked on, thinking of Giff. His last recollection of her was in the ditch, romping about his legs until he scrambled up the ladder. '*Must be still down there,*' he thought, and recalled Cadog saying that, in the ditch, she had fussed around his legs as well. He shook his head: what surprised him about Cadog was his enthusiasm for battle. When Einion had caught up with the ladder troop Cadog had singled him out, stuttering, '*Owain, guess what? I was the first in Einion's troop to make it into the ditch and the first to climb a ladder.*'

Morgan spoke; whatever he said Owain ignored.

"I said it smells like someone's shit himself. Not you, is it?"

"Sod off, Morgan. Find someone else to pick on."

"There's no one else, just you, you think you're better than the rest of us, but my sister wouldn't think much of you if she could see you now."

"Nor would she you," said Tewdrig, approaching.

Morgan spun round. "What's that supposed to mean?"

"You," said Tewdrig, "you weren't with us when we formed a half-circle and you didn't show up till Einion's troop caught up with us."

"Not my fault. Someone fell on me in the ditch, nearly broke my back."

"Always got some excuse," said Tewdrig, grabbing Morgan by the tunic; he shoved him hard. "Now go, get out of my sight."

"Agh! To hell with you. I'm going for a piss."

While Tewdrig hurled back a few choice words, Owain had time to consider that, at twenty, the son of a prominent Is-coed man, Tewdrig was more suited as Caleb's companion than Morgan would ever be, but why he should take sides against Morgan was not altogether clear. "So where's Caleb?" Owain asked.

"Back there," said Tewdrig, "awaiting Maredudd's orders. That's why I'm here. He told me to watch out for you."

"Did he, now?"

"Yes, he really wants to put things right. You should meet him half way."

"I know, it's just that I can't trust him."

"You can take it from me he means what he says; he wants to put things right."

They were distracted by some of Gruffudd's men as they passed by, one of them saying, "Talhaearn, we got what we wanted from the drawbridge." The rebels carried heavy beams to bridge the gap in the walkway. Owain and Tewdrig barely had time to remark that an advance up the walkway, in view of French archers, was madness when foul language had them turn to witness Morgan directing his urine at castle ravens, three of them pecking at the gore of a dead man. They witnessed, too, the return of those sent to find the minstrel, one of whom approached Morgan.

"M-Morgan guess w-what? Elidir had his leg g-grazed by an arrow."

"So what d'you want me to do?"

"W-well, aren't you c-concerned?"

"Piss off," Morgan spat, pulling up his breeches.

Cadog turned away, making for the palisade where Maredudd directed Einion to align his bowmen so as to shoot at those up on the tower. Believing his sling to be of no further use, Cadog approached Maredudd, stuttering, "If I find myself a spear and shield, can I be with Owain?"

Under pressure to get things moving, Maredudd dismissed Cadog with the words, "Yes, yes, only make sure you stay with Owain. Caleb, I'm relying on you to do what I said. So don't let me down. Right, my troop, through the gap – let's go."

Caleb stood by the gap in the palisade while Maredudd and a score of men descended into the ditch. Several times Caleb called the names of companions who had been with him at the tail end of the ladder crew. When they responded he drew them to one side of the gap.

"What is it?" Owain asked. "What's going on?"

"Maredudd wants us to stay here with Einion's troop and shoot at those bastards up there, on the tower."

"So we're at the back again," Morgan grumbled. "It's not fair. Maredudd doesn't object to those Is-coed youths being in the forefront."

"You ignoramus," Tewdrig spat, "that's because he's not responsible for them like he is us."

"Well, I'm not staying here," Morgan countered. "I'm going down into the ditch."

"You're going nowhere," Caleb snapped, grabbing Morgan by the tunic. "You'll stay here because I say so; now get yourself ready to shoot at the tower."

In his heart Owain wanted to say, '*That's right, Caleb, you keep donkey in his place,*' but rooted mistrust made him hesitate, allowing Morgan time to complain about the way Caleb had manhandled him. Owain threw down his French shield and ascended a low bank to take his place at the palisade. He had no sooner laid an arrow to his bow than Caleb appeared at his side.

"Have you seen Cadog?" Owain asked.

"Last I saw of him," Caleb replied, "was when he went looking for a spear and shield. He's probably with Guto right now."

Meanwhile, in the ditch, Maredudd moved between the piles that carried the walkway, picking his way through mud and castle refuse. As he approached the foot of the motte someone cried, "Watch out, for God's sake, my ankle's broken." That the man had fallen from the *swaying section* made him mindful of the rebels on the walkway above him, whom he could hear talking in subdued tones. Cautiously, he ascended the lower slope of the motte until he could make out, in the growing light, the palisade that surrounded the tower. Kneeling beside a pile, he focused on the embrasures in the palisade where archers stood ready to loose their arrows at anyone who appeared out of the darkness of the ditch.

'*So close,*' he thought, '*they'll not fail to cause us grief. And there'll be more of them up on the tower.*'

He continued to observe, taking comfort from the thought that, because the palisade continued round in a circle, only a few embrasures actually overlooked the walkway; he felt confident, too, that Einion's bowmen were sure to inflict casualties on those who opposed them. His thoughts turned to seven youths; he question the wisdom of allowing them to take part in the attack, even though they would have been called upon to fight had Rhydderch turned up. At least the seven had not been dispersed in the confusion, as had the Is-coed men, half of whom were probably with Gruffudd's rebels on the north side of the motte. He looked up, anxious about the increasing light, and wondered how much longer it would take for Gruffudd's rebel to form up; he was sure he could hear some of them in the ditch to his left. Then a voice carried from the tower.

"*Destroy, O Lord, and divide their tongues, for I have seen violence and strife in the city! Day and night they go about the walls thereof; deceit and guile depart not from her streets!*"

"It's that damn psalm-singer," someone whispered, "he's still alive."

Horns blared. A cheer went up as Countrymen advanced on the tower. Beneath the walkway, Maredudd resumed his uphill advance, counting, "One, two," while his men following behind in silence. Then a rabid command rent the air; the sting of death shot out of the embrasures. To his left he caught two rebels agonize, clutching feathered shafts; ahead, he witnessed an archer fall back from an embrasure – a victim of Einion's bowmen – and another archer appeared in his place.

"Five, six," Maredudd panted, blotting reality from his mind. A scream carried from above, a handrail snapped; a man fell from the walkway. "Seven, eight...." He slipped, swearing as he hit wet grass. As he struggled up, shouts told him that the men on the walkway were in retreat.

"Nine, ten...." An arrow thudded into the wooden pile beside him. "Devil's hoof! Eleven, twelve – this is it; here I go." With the walkway too low to proceed further, he ducked out, into the open, his French shield held aslant above his head. Slipping, swearing, clutching at wet grass, he vigorously sought footholds until, panting, he threw himself against the palisade. Others joined him, one of them gasping, "For St. Cadog's sake, Maredudd, what now?"

Craning his neck, Maredudd peered beyond the rim of his shield. Directly above him an archer appeared to be leaning against the side of an embrasure. '*He's going to let fly*,' he thought. Then it struck him that he had got it wrong, that the archer, a hand to his throat, had been pinned by an arrow to the palisade.

"Quick," he said to the man nearest to him, "give me a leg up!" Placing a foot in the man's cupped hands, he jerked himself upwards and, with the aid of two other men, rose to see the archer being torn from his impalement and the embrasure sealed off by a kite-shaped shield. He no sooner swore than a rabid laugh carried from behind the shield. A spear was then thrust towards him, which he managed to deflect; then it swung rightwards, hitting him in the ribs, the sustained pressure unbalancing him. He toppled sideways, expecting spears to pierce his back, but found his fall broken by the men upon whom he collapsed.

In a muddle of arms and legs he tumbled down the slope, coming to rest with someone's leg across his chest. He struggled up, turning to face the tower, only to be bowled over by a downhill rush that had him rolling almost to the foot of the motte where, in the shadows of the ditch, men bustled about in confusion.

Meanwhile, in the bailey, Einion shouted, "Hold off shooting. Save your arrows." Separating from the palisade, he dropped down off a bank to walk behind a line of bowmen, repeatedly asking whether anyone had suffered injury. At the end of the line he checked on Caleb, Owain, Tewdrig and Morgan.

"We're all unhurt," said Caleb, "but Guto and Cadog – they're not with us so I can't account for them."

"Guto was with me," said Einion, "but Cadog – I've not seen him. I'll check again."

"Cadog can't be hurt," said Caleb, "otherwise someone would have...."

"Shh!" Owain cut in. "Hear that? It's Giff, I know her bark." He moved closer to the gap in the palisade to whistle and shout, "Giff, here, come on," several times.

With Guto at his heels, Einion returned, saying, "Cadog is not among us."

Then Giff's shaggy form appeared to view as she struggled up the inner face of the ditch. When she reached the gap in the palisade, Owain tried to smooth her head, but she turned, barking, and retraced her steps to the ditch.

"She's trying to tell you something," said Caleb.

"Cadog," said Owain, "it's got to be Cadog. He must be down there, in the ditch." He passed through the gap to slide down the steep slope, shouting, "Giff, come back." At the bottom of the slope he had no sooner gained his feet than Morgan came upon him from behind, pushing him so that he fell in ooze.

On the far side of the ditch, Maredudd had been calling his troop together when he was accosted by two Is-coed men, complaining that a kinsman of theirs was missing. Aware of Giff's barks, he then caught Morgan's shadowy shape as he passed by, swearing, to ascend the lower slope of the motte. Moments later he heard Owain rave, "Let go, let go, I gotta find Cadog myself."

"No, you'll get yourself killed," Caleb countered. "I can't let you do it."

Maredudd moved to intervene.

"It's Cadog," said Caleb, "we think he's up there on the motte."

"He *is* up there," Owain insisted. "He's not with Einion's troop. I know because Einion said so. And Giff – she came to me barking, trying to get me to follow her; that's why I know he's up there on the motte."

"Caleb," said Maredudd, "I thought I told you to stand by the gap and call the names of your companions."

"And that's what I did," Caleb returned, "only you never said anything about Cadog. So he must have passed by and followed you down into the ditch."

Maredudd detailed two men to go among the men, calling Cadog's name.

"He's not among them," Owain interposed. "He's up there; that's where Giff went; that's where Morgan went too."

Maredudd looked to the motte. On the lower slope he could make out the shadowy shapes of men moving about in search of fallen companions. None were being shot at, reason for him to presume the French were reserving their arrows against further attack. "So which way did Morgan go?"

"That way," said Owain, "over to the left. See, there's someone kneeling. It's probably Morgan."

"Right, you stay here. I'll go, see for myself."

"My Lord Captain," said Tewdrig, proffering a French shield, "take this."

"Good lad." Stooped and peering over the rim of the shield, Maredudd ascended the lower slope of the motte. Keeping a wary eye on the embrasures from which French archers hurled abuse, he made his way towards the shadowy shape of someone who appeared to be knelt, keening over a body. As he drew closer he realized that it was Morgan. He no sooner knelt beside the youth than Giff got in his way, whining and nuzzling his face. "Yes, Giff, I know," he said, pushing the dog aside. Morgan turned to him, inviting him to see the cause of his distress. Cadog lay on his back, mouth open, his grey-white tunic stained by a dark mass oozing from around the broken arrow lodged in his chest; he was still breathing.

"Do something," Morgan wailed. "Take the arrow out, anything, just...."

"Can't do that, not here, it's too risky. Here, take this shield and keep it raised." Maredudd slid his hands under Cadog's back and legs; lifting him gently, he rose. "Steady me, Morgan. Get a hold on my back and keep that shield up."

Although slippery, the lower slope was not so steep as to make it impossible for Maredudd to remain upright. When he reached the foot of the motte four youths thronged him, Guto crying, all of them wanting to know whether or not Cadog was dead. Maredudd continued northwards, squelching through mud to merge with dispirited rebels withdrawing from the north side of the motte, where they had failed in their assault on the tower. Such was the confusion that he was compelled to move slowly; thus he had time to consider Cadog, a picture of innocence, a boy really, whose head and limbs dangled, apparently lifeless, the broken arrow still in his chest.

That arrow told a story: the fact that it was broken suggested that Cadog had rolled from higher up the slope and may, therefore, have been in the forefront of the assault. And what had he stuttered near the gap in the bailey palisade? *'If I find myself a spear and shield, can I be with Owain?'* Could it be that he thought permission to *be with Owain* put him among those who were to assail the tower? The Devil's hoof! Owain had been transferred to Einion's troop, but Cadog would have known nothing about that. He must, therefore, have found a spear and attached himself to those who passed through the gap, thinking that Owain was among them. What then? Did he lose his way in the dark? Did he go forward with rebels who were strangers to him? If all those assumptions were correct, then Cadog had proved himself a fit and mettlesome warrior.

"Hurry up," Morgan rasped at the rebels in front of him, "my brother has got an arrow in his chest."

"So what?" a rebel retorted. "He'll be dead soon enough."

"No, he won't," Morgan countered; he turned to Maredudd. "We'll get the arrow out, won't we?"

"We'll see," Maredudd returned, rather than state the truth, that if the arrow was lodged deep, then taking it out would only speed Cadog's death. Moving on amongst the throng, he wondered how he would get Cadog out of the bailey ditch, but the problem was solved when several youths secured a ladder; with men occupying every rung Cadog passed from the ditch into the bailey where Einion laid him down near a building. Morgan knelt while others crowded round.

"He's dead," Owain faltered, his voice full of anguish. "Cadog is dead, I know he is." He stared, tight-lipped, at Morgan's back. All his pent-up emotions, everything he despised about Morgan, the fact that in the ditch Morgan had pushed him to his knees, consumed him with rage. "Did you hear what I said, donkey? He's dead and it's all your fault, you damn loud-mouth. If you hadn't got him to come here...." He grabbed Morgan's tunic, intending to pull him back, but Morgan, still on his knees, lashed out, striking his cheek; that was the last straw. He drove a foot at Morgan's side. Morgan toppled sideways and rolled, too stupefied to protect himself when Owain fell upon him, raining blows upon his face.

"That's enough," said Maredudd, pulling Owain off. "Can't you see there's no fight in him? Let him grieve his brother."

Panting, Owain watched Morgan crawl to lament his brother. Then he turned away to weep against the eaves of a building.

CHAPTER 12

SEPARATE WAYS

Caleb hurried across the bailey drawbridge, eager to distance himself from the buildings that crackled to the fierce tongues of flame. He was one of several youths who had carried out the task gleefully, but his joy faded when he focused on Gruffudd ap Rhys's rebels as they marched westwards, a rabble laden with loot, cattle swelling their ranks. It was down to those rebels that the attack had been called off. Not even Gruffudd could get them to change their minds; that had exasperated the men of Is-coed as they hated the foreigners more than anyone else. The wrangling abated when it was suggested, to the rebels, that loot could be had for the taking if they assailed a castle only five miles away, one that had only a small garrison. The compromise, to which the rebels agreed, had been approved by the Gower men because the castle belonged to one William de Londres, Lord of Ogwr, the man credited with the conquest of Is-coed on the Earl of Warwick's behalf.

Some distance from the bailey, Caleb approached Owain, panting, "Come with us. Ystum Llymarch will be easy compared with that castle back there."

"Get wise after the event, Caleb. Gruffudd didn't take part in the attack himself, so why risk your life for him again?"

"Not for him, for *us*. We want the French out, don't we? Or are you holding back because of me?"

Owain put a hand on Caleb's shoulder. "Look, I know you've tried to make amends and I've not made things easy for you, but all that's behind us now and...." He laughed. "You know, you really don't look the edling in those clothes. Here, you'd best take my cloak, my horse as well. You'll need them."

They fell to an embrace. "I'll bring them back, I promise."

"Just make sure *you* come back. I mean it, Caleb."

"Do something for me," said Caleb, separating. "Explain to our father that all this is important to me. And yes, I understand that he has to weight up the odds, but me, I have to be doing something; that's why I'm here, that's why all these men are here."

"I'll explain, you can count on it."

Owain fell to a farewell embrace with, first, Tewdrig and then cousin Rhys. Rhys outstretched an arm towards Caleb, inviting him, as a kinsman, to join them. Caleb responded, his differences with cousin Rhys forgotten.

After separating, Owain caught sight of Morgan as he checked the ropes that held Cadog's body to a horse. Since his brother's death Morgan had been unbelievably quiet. Caleb went to him, but Owain held back, observing the congealed blood on Morgan's face, satisfied that his fist had been the cause of it.

"Right, lads," Maredudd shouted, "we've some catching up to do." He manoeuvred his bay close to Owain. "We're being watched. So you'd best trail behind till we're out of sight in them woods, then head north for the monastery. Oh! And – er – give your father my regards – your mother too. Tell them I'll not let Caleb out my sight." He offered a hand in friendship. "Till we meet again."

Trailing behind the men of Gower, Owain led a horse upon which the huntsman, Huw, slumped, his left arm in a sling. Guto followed with two horses in tow, one carrying his injured cousin, Elidir, the other an Is-coed youth who had been wounded in the attack, and whose kinsmen had insisted that he should be placed in the care of monks. Morgan brought up the rear, two horses in his train, the saddles of both swaying, one with Cadog's body, the other with Elfed's corpse.

Labouring through mud on the western highway, Owain experienced a riptide of mixed emotions. On the one hand, Cadog's passing was never far from mind, each heartfelt reflection coming to him like a surge of sea water over wet sand until it retreated as backwash, leaving his mind swamped by remembrances of the morning's events – and they came at him, wave after wave, eddying his conscious thoughts like driftwood.

His thoughts turned to the assault on the tower: it had been a shamefaced failure, for it transpired that, in the dark, a large number of Is-coed men had ended up on the north side of the motte, where they joined Gruffudd's rebels in storming the motte on that side. The assault had come to nought because Gruffudd's men wavered in the onset. Consequently, a fracas had broken out in the ditch between the men of Is-coed and Gruffudd's followers, and this had led to further dissention in the bailey.

In a depression, unobservable to the French, Owain left the highway, waving farewell as he cut across a deforested verge, heading for the surrounding woods. Following a track, he pushed in, under the trees, and immediately felt isolated, burdened with the responsibility of getting five traumatized men to safety. He experienced, too, the emptiness of heart that follows an emotive separation. Where his brother was concerned he had warmed to his friendliness; he would miss him.

He recalled the dangers they had encountered, and one incident stood out in relief. After Cadog's death, when he had wept beside a building, Caleb had approached at a time when foreign women and children stumbled into view, being kicked and pushed by several of Gruffudd's followers who, whilst looting, had found them in the bailey hall. One woman appeared to have been raped; another, no more than a child, had stumbled to her knees, and a boy, possibly her brother, had gone to her aid only to be floored by a rebel leader.

'*What's to be done with them?*' Caleb had asked.

'*There's only one thing to be done with them,*' the rebel leader had ground out. '*Slaughter them in full view of those bastards up on the tower.*' The rebel leader had grabbed the girl by the hair and the boy, who tried to intervene a second time, was shoved so hard that he fell against a wall. Owain recalled something about the boy that reminded him of Cadog, but what really held his attention at the time was the expression on the boy's face as the rebel leader raised a spear. It was the boy's eyes, the way they pleaded, *Do something, please, he's going to kill me,* that prompted Owain to rush the rebel leader, pushing him off balance.

Caleb had made to join in, but Giff beat him to it, her snapping jaws driving the rebel leader to a wall. As to the two rebels who had rushed to their leader's aid, one pitched over Maredudd's raised boot, the other found himself threatened by cousin Rhys, who levelled a spear at the man's chest. Then, drawing his sword, Maredudd had roared, '*Men of Gower, form a half-circle.*'

Women and children scattered, screaming, as men closed on Maredudd to form a united front. The speed at which everyone moved, the fact that three rebels were held hostage, may have cautioned nearby rebels, but it did not stop them summoning aid from further afield; in a situation such as that it required only one man to let loose a missile and the result would have been a blood bath.

The situation had been defused by the intervention of Gruffudd ap Rhys, who came on the scene hot under the collar, having just mediated in a fracas between his followers and disaffected Is-coed tribesmen. Gruffudd proved himself to be the voice of reason, but without Maredudd's humorous rejoinder he would have been seen as an ineffectual leader.

Owain warmed when he relived how both Caleb and Rhys had stood by him, arguing that the women and children should be spared, to which Gruffudd had agreed. Yet he sensed the affair would mean trouble for those he knew, as it was perilous enough that they would be taking part in another attack, but to do so when certain rebels might be harbouring a grudge posed a more sinister threat. Hopefully, they would all be on their guard.

101

Turning to encourage the huntsman's horse uphill, Owain glimpsed Morgan, ducking beneath a branch, and became mindful of his ill will towards him. Since separating from the others he had expected Morgan to bluster, '*Oy! You, what d'you think you're doing, taking us through all this mud and shit?*' That Morgan had kept silent made no difference: he still damned him for Cadog's death.

Cadog – the very thought of him brought tears to his eyes. He visualized his face, a picture of innocence, recalling his excitement when he stuttered, '*Guess what? I was the first in Einion's troop to make it into the ditch.*' His recall was swamped by an image in which Cadog appeared limp, his face deathly pale, in sharp contrast to the dark mass that spread from the broken arrow in his chest.

He stumbled on, wiping tears from his cheeks, not caring about the offshoots that snapped at his passing. Yet beyond the gloom of Cadog's death there appeared a faint light in the imaginative distance. Beyond windswept moorlands he visualized a steep, wooded hillside where, on terraced fields, someone waited with a welcoming smile. '*Good day to you, Owain. Where's Cadog?*'

God, no! How could he tell Anona that Cadog was no longer with them? His heart pained as he envisaged her response: eyes expressive of horror, her mouth open as realization sank in. God! What would she do? Would she meet him so that they might mingle their tears? Or would she turn away, holding him responsible for her brother's death? There could be no pointing a finger at Morgan: accusing a blood relative would get him nowhere. He could only hope against hope that she would not turn away, for to see her again had influenced his decision to return.

"Owain, look, the highway," said Guto. "I thought we'd never make it."

"I'll go ahead, see if it's safe!" Owain picked his way to the edge of the woods. The open space that lay beyond appeared as a broad strip, separating him from the opposing tree-line. The northern highway, which divided the open space in two, was hidden by withered grass and tree stumps, the trees cut down by the French to reduce the risk of ambush. To his right the deforestation ran south; there was no sign of the castle, just poor visibility, fading into mist. It was quite save for the *caw, caw, caw*, of rooks, rebounding in the open space. He doubled back to the others, then led them out of the woods. On his approach to the highway he caught the rumble of hooves to the north. His first thoughts were of danger, that French reinforcements were bearing down on him.

"Back," Guto shouted, "back to the woods, quick, afore we're seen."

Owain spun round to see Guto turning his two horses towards the tree-line. Morgan, on the other hand, made no such move. His gaze fell upon the Is-coed youth slumped in the saddle; there was no fight in him. Then Huw caught his eye, as if expecting him to take flight. He determined to stand firm. "Stay, Guto, we'll never make it, not with injured men!"

But Guto pursued his intention to flee, only to be caught in a heated exchange with his injured cousin, Elidir, who contested with him for the reins. Then, turning to lay an arrow to his bow, Owain saw horsemen appearing out of the mist. *'Never run from horsemen,'* he recalled Maredudd saying. *'Form line and they'll think twice about a frontal attack.'* "Guto, Morgan, to me," he shouted over his shoulder. "Form line; look to your bows."

He fixed his gaze on the approaching horsemen, about a dozen of them in column. Hoof beats drew his attention to Elidir as he reined in on his left. Then he heard Guto, still voicing objection until Huw bellowed, at him, "Shut up and get in line, or, so help me, I'll lay my spear across your back. You too, Morgan, and show some resolve, damn you."

"I'll target the leading horseman," Owain shouted. "Elidir, you aim at the one to his left. Tell Guto to go for someone to the rear." He turned to Morgan as he appeared on his right. "You heard what Huw said, show some resolve, you spineless loud mouth. Target someone to the rear of the leading horseman. Now await my command to aim."

"Wait," Huw barked. "Owain, that first horseman, it's your father."

Owain stared. It was a moment before realization struck him: a white horse and, yes, it really was his father. Relief flooded through him, soon to give way to consternation when, barking orders, his father trotted towards him, hooves thumping the ground.

Rhydderch reined in, staring at Owain, his horse snorting profusely. "I need not ask if Abertawe has been attacked. And you, I'd have expected better of you."

Owain bit his lip: to answer back was to invite further rebuke, a view shared by his companions as they, too, held their peace, whereas Rhydderch regarded, in turn, the two corpses to their rear. "Where's Caleb?"

"He's in one piece, father; so is Maredudd and Einion."

"So where are they?"

"Gone to attack the castle at Ystum Llymarch."

Rhydderch appeared not to be listening, having moved closer to Huw. "Bad is it?" he asked.

Huw nodded, groaning about his shoulder, his spear falling from his grasp. Owain gaped: Huw's condition appeared to have taken a turn for the worse. *'You crotchety, old devil,'* Owain thought, *'you're putting that on.'*

Rhydderch detailed several of his men to escort the wounded to a nearby monastery. Then he turned to Owain, saying, "Get yourself a horse, you're coming with me. You can tell me about Abertawe along the way."

"You mean you're going to join Gruffudd ap Rhys?"

"No. According to the soothsayer the rebellion will fail."

"Then it's Caleb you're after."

"Caleb and anyone else who's subject to me."

"Then you'd best think on, father, because if you're seen near Ystum Llymarch, it'll be assumed you're with the rebels."

"You have me there, but to do nothing may cost your brother his life and I wouldn't want that."

"No more would I. Caleb and I have patched up our differences, though it's more his doing than mine."

For a long moment Rhydderch regarded his son, the expression on his rawboned face losing its severity. "Rhain," he said, turning to a bard, "make haste for Ystum Llymarch and tell everyone what the soothsayer told me. And if Maredudd won't be persuaded, then impress on him that I want Caleb back. Awst, get back to Y Faerdref and tell everyone who answered the call to arms they can go home. If they want to know about Abertawe, as I'm sure they will, then play it down. I don't want anyone else spoiling for a fight while my back is turned."

Dismounting, Rhydderch approached Owain with open arms. "Come, my son," he said, inviting Owain to an embrace, "let me show you that I'm glad you're still alive."

. . . . . .

"Open the gate," de Viles coughed, his eyes smarting as a result of smoke.

Followed by a dozen men he passed through the gateway, dropping down off the walkway to descend into the ditch where, mace in hand, he picked his way through mud and refuse until, in the northern ditch, he approached a makeshift ladder that enabled him to ascend from the ditch. Feeling the heat, his face blackened by smoke, he circumvented the still smouldering bailey to arrive at a place overlooking both the burnt-out township and the estuary.

"Monsieur," said his retainer, pointing to two boats, "you were right, it's Iorwerth ap Meirchion."

"Yes, Wilfred, Iorwerth and his cutthroats, come to see if there's any of us left."

De Viles descended to where women and children huddled together on the slope above the burnt-out township. Several men passed him by, eager to make contact with loved ones. As he drew near the gathering, unaffected by joyful reunions, he demanded, "Did anyone here recognize any of the rebels?" He looked about, anticipating a response, then ground out, "I said, did anyone here recognize any rebels? What about Lord Rhydderch ap Cadifor, anyone see him?"

A few women shook their heads. Then an old hag croaked, in the Saxon tongue, "E wasn't 'ere, I'd 'ave recognized 'im if 'e was – but I recognized someone else."

De Viles stood over the old woman whom he knew to be Bertha, a kitchen assistant who sat alone, dirty and in rags. "So who was it you recognized?"

Bertha thrust out her hand, palm facing upwards. De Viles dug into his girdle and, finding no purse, turned to the castle constable. "Olaf, a penny. You'll have it back."

"This had better be good," Olaf growled as he threw a silver penny.

Bertha snatched the coin from the grass. "A tall, red-'aired man," she croaked, revealing her almost toothless gums. She fingered her chin. "Short beard, I've seen 'im 'ere afore, many times."

"Maredudd Goch!"

"That's 'im. Saved our lives, 'e did."

"And you should be grateful, you old hag," a woman spat, separating from her husband. "Now be silent."

"Grateful," de Viles snapped. "To a barbarian?" In moving towards the woman de Viles found himself threatened by the husband, a townsman. Two more townsmen came forward, hurling abuse. De Viles checked himself, his eyes rolling from one man to the next until he turned, growling, at Bertha, "Pay no heed to these fools. Just tell me who else you saw."

Bertha held out her hand again until another coin landed beside her. "There was a young man with the red-'aired one. 'E wore fine clothes, 'e did – probably the son of a rich man. I'm sure I'd recognize 'im if I saw 'im again. You see, if it wasn't for 'im, we'd all be dead."

"I'll speak to you again, Bertha. Olaf, see to it that no one intimidates this witness." De Viles turned and stomped downhill, intending to meet the boatmen who were coming ashore. There were two boats – skin-covered curraghs, propelled by oars, each carrying four men, and there were four horses in tow. By the time he reached the mud that had been exposed by an ebb tide the boatmen were floundering in ooze, bringing their curraghs and their horses with them. Rhydderch's kinsman, Iorwerth ap Meirchion, Lord of Cilfái, a short, reddish-haired, wiry fellow, led ashore. "So you've decided to join us now the fighting is done."

"I've nothing to say to you, you damn psalm-singer," Iorwerth retorted in perfect French. "I'll speak to Monsieur la Steward."

"You'll speak to me, you insolent cur, and I'll remind you that a bailiff was sent to summon you here yesterday – only you didn't come. That makes you spineless."

"I don't have to answer to you, madman." Iorwerth made to pass by, but when de Viles started for him he spun round, spear at the ready.

"Stay where you are, both of you," Olaf barked, moving between them, facing de Viles. "This is not what Monsieur la Steward wants."

"I have my orders," de Viles countered. "Now get out of my way."

"I know what your orders are, monsieur. I suggest you carry them out."

"And what are his orders?" Iorwerth demanded.

"That he came down here to meet you," Olaf replied, not daring to turn his back on de Viles, "that he makes contact with the equestrians in the Peninsula and that he does so with your help."

"I don't need help from a man who should have been here yesterday."

"Yesterday I was hunting," Iorwerth bit back, "and I didn't receive Monsieur la Steward's bailiff till it was too late. By then the rebels had set fire to the township and there were hundreds of them, more than I could match. So I did the only thing I could do. I sent the bailiff to summon help from the Lordships of Ogwr and Coety."

"We've only your word for that; now hand those horses over to me."

"Never!"

"It's what Monsieur la Steward wants."

"The answer is still no, madman."

De Viles attempted to push past, but the Dane retreated, a hand extended as if to stop him. "Wait," Olaf snapped. "I propose a compromise. I propose that each of you have two horses and an equal number of men, and that you both go forth into the Peninsula."

"I'll agree to that," said Iorwerth. "I might even see him dead should an opportunity arise."

"Well, monsieur," said Olaf, "what's it to be?"

"It never ceases to amaze me how you, a Dane, and that gutless barbarian can accommodate one another."

"Tolerance is what it takes," said Olaf. "Now what's it to be, monsieur?"

"Very well. I'll take my retainer and six archers. Wilfred, lay hold of two horses and bring them here."

. . . . . .

It was some time later that de Viles approached Ystum Llymarch. On the slope below a burning castle he found survivors, sitting on the grass, too shattered to get to their feet. "Where's the keeper of this castle?" he demanded in the Saxon tongue.

"Dead like a lot of other men," an archer retorted. "So where are you from – Abertawe? Thought so. We saw the smoke, it put us on our guard. Not that it made much difference. The Welsh had the better of us by their trickery."

"You mean you didn't put up much of a fight."

"No, I mean they tricked us into thinking they would attack from the south because there were more than a hundred of them coming at us from that direction. Then they stopped while a few of them came on to direct fire arrows at buildings. Well, half of us had to leave the palisade to put the fires out. Then another troop of Welsh came over the palisade on the north side, and did so under cover of the smoke."

"And that's when you yielded without a fight," de Viles ground out.

"No, we fought, but half the men here are serfs; they know nothing about fighting."

"That's right," another man ground out. "Me, I'm a reeve not a man-at-arms, and if we'd fought on, the Welsh would have killed the lot of us, every man, woman and child. Could be they would have killed us anyway, only someone warned them that French horse were heading this way. So they left in a hurry."

"So where are they now, these French horsemen?"

The reeve shrugged. "Who knows, they didn't come. The only reason we know about them is because of that woman over there – she's Welsh, she overheard what her kind had to say."

De Viles cast a glance at the woman, then stared at Iorwerth with whom the woman spoke. "You," he said to the archer, "did you recognize any of the Welsh? What about a tall, red-haired man, short beard, wolfskin coat?"

"I don't recall anyone wearing a wolfskin coat," the archer replied, "but there was a tall, red-haired man among them, one of their leaders. It's down to him we're still alive."

"Would you recognize him if you saw him again? You would?" De Viles turned to the reeve and three other men to become increasingly animated each time one of them told him what he wanted to hear. "What about a well-attired youth?"

The archer shook his head. "Na, there were some youths in attendance upon the red-haired man, but none of them were well-attired."

De Viles turned to his retainer. "You hear that, Wilfred? Maredudd Goch, he was here. I'll see him hang for his part in all this."

Wilfred nodded, drawing his master's attention to Iorwerth's approach.

"There's a woman over there," said Iorwerth, "who says French horse were seen on the high ground yonder, though where they are at this moment is unknown. We'd best move, we're wasting time here."

De Viles wheeled, saying, "Then move out, let's go."

"What are you doing?" the reeve demand, grabbing de Viles's surcoat. "You can't just leave us here like this."

"What d'you expect me to do? Bathe your wounds? If you want help, make your way over to the Bishop's manor in the next valley; now unhand me, if you know what's good for you."

CHAPTER 13

BITTER BURIAL

After a night spent in an abandoned hut, Morgan journeyed on until he led the horse laden with Cadog's body into the clearing where his father's homestead stood. Ammon, spear in hand, and the rest of the family were gathered at the entrance to a hurdle enclosure, which came as no surprise to Morgan: the dogs had forewarned of his approach. He cudgelled his tired brain, wondering what he should say, when his stepmother suddenly broke ranks and rushed towards him. Anona and her younger brother and sister followed, as did the dogs, but Ammon, after embedding his spear in the ground, progressed grim-faced like a giant with a purpose. Morgan watched him come, not knowing what he might do. Trepidation gripped him, he felt weak, wanting to plead that he had no stomach for a confrontation, not with Cadog dead.

"You bastard," his stepmother spat. "You killed him, you troublesome bastard!"

Morgan was taken aback. "Na-na, it wasn't me, it was the French, I swear it!"

"Don't give me that, you no-good swine!" Teeth clenched, his stepmother went for him, arms flailing, intending to claw his face. "You got him to go to Abertawe, I know you did, you mindless son of a bitch!" Morgan recoiled, causing the horse to turn, bringing Cadog's body closer to her. She cried out, then tried to take possession of the body, little realizing that it was bound by ropes to a saddle strap.

Anona did her best to restrain her mother, but met with flailing arms and abuse, the children got in her way and the dogs were that frantic they frightened the horse. "Morgan, don't just stand there, do something, please!"

But Morgan had his hands full, trying to calm the horse. Feeling threatened, he turned, expecting his father to roar until he lost control. His father's course of action took him completely by surprise.

"Leave her, Anona!" Ammon hauled his wife away from the horse, imprisoning her in his left arm. Then, drawing his skene, he sliced through the securing ropes. "Enough, woman! Let me carry him to the hall!" With Cadog's body in his arms he led the way, wife and youngest daughter keening at his side. His eight-year-old son fell over, trying to keep up. Anona picked the boy up, then turned to Morgan.

"Come," she said, wiping tears from her cheeks.

"What for? You saw them, they hate me, they always have – and I didn't kill Cadog, it was the French."

"I know – but when our father was at Y Faerdref he heard from some youth who'd injured his ankle that you persuaded Cadog to go with you. He swore, then, that if anything happened to Cadog, he'd hold you responsible."

Morgan closed his eyes, then blurted out, "He's right, I am responsible." He looked heavenwards, fists clenched, his expression one of remorse. "Great Lord! What have I done? I know I picked on him, but he was still my brother.""

"Oh! Morgan – Morgan, I've known all along that you're not what you try to make out – ever since that day you shook me out of that tree. You cried then, fussed over me for days. It helped to take away the pain. Come – come into the hall."

Shaking his head, Morgan allowed himself to be led. "What's the point, Anona? They hate me, you know that. Ah! I can understand our mother – I'm not one of hers like the rest of you, but our father, he's never treated me like a son. It's always been harsh words and the rod. Great Lord! I've got marks on my back like a slave. Why, Anona, why? If he'd treated me right, I swear I'd never been the way I am."

"I know, I know." She fell silent, not knowing what to say until they passed through the hurdle enclosure. "Owain, is he...?"

"Na-na, he's in one piece – and Guto, only Elidir had his leg grazed by an arrow."

"And Cadog, what happened to him?"

"Took an arrow in the chest. We were attacking a tower – the French were shooting at us. Wasn't till it was all over that we found him." He buried his face in his hands.

Anona drew closer. "Thank God you weren't killed too."

He broke away. "Na-na, I wish, to God, I had. I wish, to God, it had been me, not Cadog."

On reaching the hall, Anona had to plead and pull to get him inside the porch from where he glimpsed, in a side-aisle, his family lamenting over Cadog. She faced him. "You look awful – and your clothes, they're wet. When did you last eat?"

"Dunno. Yesterday, maybe."

"I'll get you something."

"Never mind him," Ammon snarled, "the cattle need feeding more than he does. Get them to pasture and take that mindless bastard with you." He rose, threateningly. "Go, or, so help me, I'll...."

Anona bundled Morgan out the porch, only to find that he took exception to her rough handling; thrusting her aside, he swore vehemently, then railed, "See what I mean, always threats, nothing but bloody threats. I swear, to God, one day I'll...."

"Don't swear so," she pleaded, fearing her father would react. "Help me, please, I'm late. There were wolves about last night. Our father wouldn't let me take the cattle till he'd checked that the woods were safe. Then you turned up. You've got to come with me, I can't face being on my own."

She coaxed him to help get the cattle moving and, stick in hand, drove them out, across the clearing, glancing at him frequently, fearing that in his present mood he might turn back. At length, when the cattle were moving up through the woods, she said, to him, "We can't go on this way. Say something, please."

"What's there to say? Cadog is dead, isn't he?"

"I know, I know, but – maybe it's the way God wanted it to be."

"Then tell me why, Anona? Go on, tell me why?"

"I don't know. Maybe it's the only way He can make you see the error of your ways."

"Don't say that. It's not right that Cadog had to die for me."

A long moment passed before she returned, "You do believe he's gone to heaven, don't you?"

"Yes, where else would someone like Cadog go?"

There was silence again until she said, "Owain, are you sure he's in one piece? You didn't just say that because...?"

"He's in one piece. I said so, didn't I?"

His reply had been abrupt. Yet it had nothing to do with disdain for Caleb's brother. Even the thought of Owain bloodying his nose did not matter. Nothing mattered, nothing except Cadog's death – and Anona. He considered her, conscious of her concern for Owain, the thought of which brought privileges to mind. It struck him that her lack of finery was not simply due to the French driving them from their lands in the Peninsula; it was, to some extent, his doing: his troublesome ways had cost his father dearly. And the limp, that was definitely his doing. Yet there was something about his sister that made her special, good enough for the Owains of this world. "You care about him, don't you?"

"Yes, I care. What I don't understand is why he took part in the attack."

"Caleb lied to get him to go." He fell silent, moving ahead with comparative ease in spite of the slope being steeper, but he could not detach himself from his sister for long, for she alone had stood by him; he was conscious of that above all else. He turned back, offering his hand while she struggled, ankle-deep in ooze. Hand in hand, they continued, too breathless for further words, until they reached the terraced fields.

"Morgan."

"What?"

"How is Banwen?"

He bit his lip, not wanting to discuss yet another of his failings.

"I'm told there's bitterness between you. Oh! Morgan, don't be so hard on her. You of all people should know what it's like. Our father has always been hard on you."

"He never loved me, not like Cadog."

"They say there was always bitterness between him and your mother. Maybe that bitterness got passed on to you. Don't make the same mistake. Give Banwen a chance to prove her worth."

"It's too late for that now."

"It's never too late. Go back to her. Just don't be so demanding, or everyone will say you're just like your father."

. . . . . .

Later, Morgan returned to the hall, intent on telling his father that he was genuinely sorry about Cadog's death, for all the trouble he had caused over the years, that somehow he would make amends, but as he neared the porch he heard women wailing and knew then that kindred from outlying homesteads had arrived to pay their respects. The moment he passed through the doorway two women rebuked him, one of them spat in his face. Fearing that his father might explode, he let it pass, circulating among the men, only to find that they would have little to do with him. It made him feel ill at ease, to put off declaring his remorse.

When the men – but not Ammon – went out to cut wood for a bier, Morgan followed: any excuse to leave the hall was good enough for him. In the woods one of the men asked about the attack. They all listened to what he had to say, but none gave ear to his self-reproach. Exasperated, he shouted, at them, "I know I've caused my father pain, but, Great Lord! Can't you see, I'm grieving too? So why ignore me? Come on, tell me why, for St. Teilo's sake?"

"You, you're nothing but trouble," one man retorted. "You've been that way ever since we settled here. Whenever something got damaged we all knew you were to blame."

"Aye," said another, "and there were always complaints from Cingualan's kinsman. We only had to see them coming across the valley to know it was because of you."

"So I'm trouble, I don't deny that, but Cadog is dead and it's my fault – mine, and it grieves me more than you'll ever know. So why can't you accept that? Why d'you have to be like my father, always shutting me out?"

The men turned away, murmuring among themselves, but Guto's father, a talkative man, said, "You think we're hard on you? You think your father is hard on you? I tell you, until you became of age the law could not touch you, but your father still had to pay damages and fines. The way you are reminds us of your mother's brother, Iago Du."

Morgan bit his lip: until yesterday he would have laughed at being paralleled with the likes of Iago Du, but not now, not while he was full of remorse.

"Iago was trouble just like you," Guto's father continued, "at least, he was till he fell foul with Cingualan's kinsmen."

"What's that got to do with losing a brother, eh?"

"Nothing, but it's got a lot to do with loss, with a man seeing the error of his ways and doing something about it."

"I dunno what you're talking about."

"Iago, he had a grudge against one of Cingualan's kinsmen, a man named Gruffudd Goch, right? Well, one day Gruffudd's barn went up in smoke. No one actually saw Iago do it, only Gruffudd swore it was him on account that he'd been seen only a mile away. Iago, of course, denied having anything to do with it, but the court ruled that he should compensate Gruffudd Goch for damage *and* pay seven pounds to redeem himself. Well, Iago had little in the way of wealth – he'd lost most of it in fines. So he went around his kinsmen, looking for assistance, only they'd all had enough. Aye, and when Gruffudd got it into his head he'd get no compensation he was furious, so were his kinsmen. I tell you, things were looking pretty bad between the two clans. Then the strangest thing happened. According to Iago, someone gave him the means to put things right – only Iago never did say who it was."

"So what's that got to do with me? I asked you to accept that I'm sorry and all you've done is give me a load of shit about something that happened years ago."

"Ten to be exact, just afore the French came. Anyway, the point I'm trying to make is this. After the fighting – and I'll say this for him, he fought well – Iago earned himself respect, became a changed man, even took up certain vows."

"So what are you saying? That I should become a priest? Not me, I got no time for any of that."

The other men were about to leave. Guto's father made to follow, his last words being, "Who said anything about becoming a priest? I said he took up certain vows, he's certainly no priest."

. . . . . .

It drizzled the day they took Cadog's body for burial; for a quarter of a mile the men of Morgan's *resting-place* slipped and struggled, taking it in turns to carry the bier up through the woods. Behind them, led by their clan chieftain, the men of affiliated *resting-places* – those who claimed descent from Eirig Mawr, the founder of their clan, the most prominent in Uwch-coed – made their ascent in silence. At the rear, amongst wailing women and children, Anona stayed close to her mother, helping her to negotiate the steep, muddy track.

It grieved her that Cadog was no longer with them, that everything about him was now no more than a memory – like eventide, when she would remove hurdles in readiness for his return. To see his smiling, boyish face as he entered the clearing, herding cattle, had been such a joy. And to hear him stutter, *'Anona, guess what....'*

Her heart pained, she sobbed bitterly, and once she had moved out from beneath the trees she peered through the drizzle to where woods bordered the top end of a field. Somewhere up there, shrouded by mizzle, stood Cynon's stone, the burial site of her grandfather, the man who had been the acknowledged head of her kindred group, the same who had been credited with creating their *resting-place*: acres of woods, fields and rough pasture shared by kinsmen who, like her father, had established their homesteads in island clearings. Near that un-hewn stone they would bury Cadog among the graves of Cynon's people, many of whom had been no more than children when they died.

She stumbled on, arms about her mother, looking up now and then to stare tearfully at the men in front of her. In a desultory way she thought of Morgan, shunned by all except herself and Guto and, to some extent, Guto's father. She wondered how he felt, knowing that his kinsmen were unhappy about having him as a bearer. She wondered about her father, too, why he had not exploded. For days everyone had been wary, expecting him to lose control.

She was halfway up the field when it dawned on her that, close to where she knew the stone to be, upwards of a dozen youths were observing their approach; reasoning that they were the young men commended to serve in their lord's bodyguard, she wondered whether Owain was among them. *'He must be,'* she thought, *'Cadog was his companion.'* Her mother let out a wail, almost collapsing, reminding her of the occasion. How could she think about

Owain at a time like this? '*Oh! God, forgive me,*' she thought, trying to support her mother, '*I must put him out of my mind.*'

Several women closed in to take charge of her mother, leaving her free – once she had moved aside – to catch sight of a lone horse. Then, believing the horse to be Owain's and that he had led those youths here, she warmed to him, only her mother's hysteria reminded her of the occasion again. She tried, unsuccessfully, to dispel all thought of Owain, telling herself that it was unthinkable that he should have any heartfelt interest in her. He was their lord's son, destined to marry someone of noble birth, not a tribesman's daughter.

Close to the stone she stumbled to one side of a hole flanked by spoil. While her mother continued to wail she stood, shivering, teeth chattering, her bare feet numb with the cold. Her eyes travelled over the men gathered on the far side of the hole. She despaired: Owain she could not discern, only men wrapped in drab, woollen cloaks, hoods covering their heads. '*He's not come,*' she thought. '*I can't see his green cloak.*'

A priest spoke, loud and clear, reminding everyone of the life Cadog had led, a herdsman, obedient to his father, loved by all, a little warrior who fell, going forward in the attack. The keening grew more intense, the mother more hysterical; while Anona did her best to console her younger sister, four men set about lowering Cadog's body into the hole. As the shrouded corpse disappeared to view a voice sounded:

> "*This grave the rain makes wet and sleek,*
> *no more, to us, will Cadog speak.*
> *Now past, now hid, the life he led;*
> *Uwch-coed's soil now roofs his head.*"

It took the combined effort of several women to get an hysterical mother past the grave. Anona followed, scooping a handful of wet soil. *Plop, plop, plop* – soil from her hand and from the men who passed by on the other side spattered the muddy water that almost covered the shrouded corpse. She stumbled on, horrified by the sight, losing her sense of direction. Someone steadied her, a man in a grey, woollen cloak. She glimpsed his face, wet with tears and rain. When she realized that it was Owain she buried her face in his cloak. "Is that it?" she sobbed. "Is that to be his grave, a hole full of dirty water? Oh, my God, he'll bloat!"

He held her tightly. "No, only his body, not his soul." He led her away, then distanced himself a little.

She knew they must part, that he must resume his place with the men, but was relieved to hear him say, "I'll be back a few days from now – if that's what you want."

"Yes, yes, come, please. Oh, God! I shouldn't be saying...."

"No, that's exactly what I'd hoped you'd say."

. . . . . .

That evening, when supper was about to be served, the men of Morgan's *resting-place* sat on the floor in groups of three, Morgan and Guto being the odd ones out. Morgan felt ill at ease: his father, who sat nearby with two other men, had still not spoken to him since the day he had arrived home. Only Guto, and occasionally Guto's father, had made the evenings in the hall bearable, which was why, during daylight hours, he spent his time with Anona up on the terraced fields. She alone showed real concern, a calming influence, though never slow to correct him for his mindless talk.

A bowl of broth was placed before Morgan who gestured for Guto to eat first. He knew that his father had his eye on him; it made him cringe. When the broth passed to him he had no sooner put a spoonful to his lips than his father ground out, "I want the truth from you. Did you press Cadog into going to Abertawe?"

Everyone fell silent. Morgan tried to appear calm when, choosing his words carefully, he replied, "Yes – yes, I did. And for that I'm sorry. I know I've been trouble, but believe me, when I leave our lord's bodyguard I want to return here to work the land as Cadog would have done."

Ammon took a deep breath, expelling air slowly. He could hear Hawys, his first wife, laughing. He pictured her lying in the long grass with another man, and she – she was betrothed to him. Yet she had been unfaithful to him. Damn her! And the man, it was he who was to blame. It mattered not that the man denied all knowledge of their betrothal: he was womanizer, the bane of his life. Damn his soul! And Morgan, he was not his son, he was not like Cadog.

Morgan, meanwhile, had let his gaze fall, knowing that, in his present mood, his father might explode. He decided to sit tight, but no sooner had the spoon passed to his mouth that Ammon snarled, "You work the land! There's no work in you, you're far more concerned in damning us all with your troublesome ways. Well, I can't stop you claiming your share of this *resting-place*, but I'm damned if I'll have you remain under *my* roof. I want you gone by first light tomorrow."

Ammon rose; a number of men did likewise, intending to dissuade him from doing anything rash. "Leave me," he growled at them, "afore I kill someone – and kill I will, so help me." He went out, slamming the door behind him.

CHAPTER 14

DE TURBERVILLE

Rhydderch rode to Abertawe with a mind full of nagging thoughts. Not only did he fear for Caleb's safety, but the involvement of members of his household with rebels, coupled with the fact that someone was keeping de Viles informed of his affairs, promised trouble as the soothsayer had foretold.

As to Caleb, twice he had sent Rhain, his bardic brother-in-law, to secure his return as well as the three men who were with him. On the first occasion, Rhain had caught up with them as they approached the castle of Ystum Llymarch. None were prepared to leave the rebels. Rather, they persuaded Rhain to take part in an attack that, under Maredudd's direction, had resulted in the castle being burnt outright and many men therein slain. Rhain had returned to report that the rebels had left Ystum Llymarch because French horse had been seen on a nearby hill.

On the morrow, when he dispatched Rhain a second time, he had been shadowing the rebels as they retreated north, laden with loot, but again Rhain failed to secure Caleb's return, although he did report that most of the Is-coed men had left the rebels of their own accord. He caught the approach of a horseman. "You," he exclaimed when Maredudd drew abreast of him. "You've got a damn nerve. And where's Caleb?"

Maredudd shrugged. "Well on the way to Cantref Mawr by now."

"Then why didn't you stay with him? You know what he's like."

"Way things are, I'd say Caleb is the better for what he's been through – uses his head more."

"He could still get killed. Rhain must have told you what the soothsayer prophesied, that someone close to me will die."

"Ten years ago she prophesied that one of us would see the other die, but here we are, looking at one another, and what a sight it is from this end."

"Never mind the jokes, I'm not in the mood; now let's talk about Caleb."

"Look, he's nigh on eighteen, and you, you can't go on shielding him for ever."

"He's impulsive, he won't listen to reason and...."

"*Was*, you mean. I tell you, after Abertawe I'd say he's the better for it. He listens to reason, does what he's told, he put things right with Owain and, in my opinion, he's all that I'd expect of an edling. Aye, and if that's not good enough, then I can assure you Einion won't let him out his sight."

Rhydderch shook his head. "So what brought you back?"

"Rhain said there'll be trouble for you. So I thought you could do with some help."

"From you? It's you who's caused the trouble."

"If you say so. So where are we heading – Abertawe?"

"Not *you*. I've had a message from Iorwerth ap Meirchion, saying you were seen at Abertawe and Ystum Llymarch at the time the attacks took place."

"Na, not me, I'd have gone unnoticed."

"You never go anywhere *unnoticed*, and the fact that you *were* seen only confirms what I've said. So you can stay out of sight till I find out what's afoot. Try St. Cyfelach's over there."

"What, stay at a monastery? You must be joking."

"Far from it. Piro is there in retreat. Get him to hide you in one of the huts, then bar yourself in till I get back."

Maredudd shook his head. "I wonder if everyone else will be as glad to see me as you."

"I know someone who won't – Ammon."

"Young Cadog, eh?"

"They're burying him today and it's been said that Ammon has a score to settle with you. You'd best be on your guard. Ammon is a dangerous man."

"I'll bear it in mind." Maredudd reined towards the monastery; when Rhydderch called after him he replied, "What? If it's about my appointment, you know what you can do with it."

"Suit yourself. I was just going to say I'm glad you're back in one piece, though I'm sure to regret it."

· · · · · ·

On his approach to Abertawe from the north, Rhydderch observed that men were at work restoring the burnt-out bailey. On the open ground outside the bailey's northern drawbridge, tents had been erected on either side of the highway. Not far from the tents several groups of men congregated near a trestle table, at which sat Beaumont's High Steward, Payn de Turberville, a greasy, corpulent man whose origin was that of a Breton from northern France.

Rhydderch knew de Turberville to be a calculating man. It was said of him that, when the lowlands of Morgannwg fell to the French, Payn – Pagan to many – had been given men and told to establish a border lordship of his own; whereupon he had marched into the wooded foothills of Coety. Morgan ap Meurig, the native Lord of Coety, had met him, proposing that, instead of battle, he should marry his daughter, Sybil, or fight to the death in single combat. Payn settled for marriage and became Lord of Coety without a fight. That Payn was an experienced administrator, that he spoke fluently in the Countryman's tongue, and that he was well-acquainted with the customs and laws of Countrymen, were reasons why Henry de Beaumont, Earl of Warwick, had entrusted him with the administration of the Gower Lordship.

Rhydderch dismounted, his attention not on de Turberville, but on Henry de Viles who stood near the table, easily identified by his close-fitting, white bonnet. A retainer came forward to usher Rhydderch to a position in front of the table where, amongst several prominent Countrymen from the Peninsula, stood his kinsman, Iorwerth ap Meirchion, Lord of Cilfái. Rhydderch bowed, acknowledging de Turberville who wasted no time in coming straight to the point.

"Gentlemen, I have summoned you here to find out if any of you, or your people, were involved in rebellion against the King's will. If you are innocent, but have knowledge of anyone else's involvement, then I demand that you declare it, even if it means informing on members of your own households. Naturally, the declaration will be made under oath and, for that purpose, a finger bone of St. Teilo, one of your most celebrated saints, has been brought here from the church at Llandeilo Ferwallt. Let us start with you, Monsieur de Cilfái. Were you involved in this unsettling affair? Answer in French so these men-at-arms who surround me may understand."

A monk moved forward, holding a box containing the holy relic. Rhydderch watched as Iorwerth put a hand into the box and swore to his innocence. It came as no surprise to hear his kinsman also swear that he had no knowledge of anyone else's involvement: he never expected Iorwerth to inform on his own son, Rhys, nor on anyone else who, in retaliation, might do so in his stead.

De Turberville frowned, unconvinced by Iorwerth's denials. "Monsieur de Gower," he said, addressing Rhydderch by his French nomenclature, "were you in any way involved in this unsettling affair?"

Rhydderch put a hand into the box, his fingers touching a segment of bone. "I swear by this holy relic that I was *not* involved in rebellion against the King's will."

"Do you know of anyone who was?"

Hesitant, Rhydderch wondered how much de Turberville knew. Over the past few days he had considered several ready-prepared answers, though which one he should use....

"Why the delay, monsieur? You heard the question, answer it."

'*Lord,*' Rhydderch thought, '*there's only one thing I can do.*' He removed his hand from the box. "Monsieur la Steward, if any of my household, or my people, were involved in rebellion, then I suggest you level the accusations yourself. I will not."

De Viles unfolded his arms, ready to hurl objections, but de Turberville cut him short. "Hold your tongue, monsieur, I'll handle this." Payn fixed his gaze on Rhydderch. "I warn you, monsieur, do not presume that, because you and I have accommodated each other over the years, *you* can chance your arm in this matter. Now – after the attack on the tower here, at Abertawe, an affray took place in the bailey. It appears that certain rebels were intent on butchering defenseless women and children, while others were prepared to put a stop to it. We have descriptions of two of the rebels who intervened, one a dark-haired youth, sixteen or seventeen, dressed in a manner befitting the son of a nobleman; the other a tall, red-haired man with a short beard. The first description may be a little vague, but the second in most certainly that of your captain of guard. Is that not so, monsieur?"

"If you had said the man had been wearing a wolfskin coat, then, yes, I agree the description would fit...."

"Never mind the coat – he could have taken that off – and even if the description had been somewhat vague, I would still wonder why he's not here with you."

"Maredudd Goch is no longer my captain of guard, as you well know, monsieur."

"Whether I know is not an issue. What is an issue is that, if he's no longer your man, then it's reasonable to suppose he gave up his appointment so he could serve Gruffudd ap Rhys, and it, therefore, follows that he's with the rebels right now."

"Wrong. I spoke to Maredudd only a short while ago on my way here. And if you doubt that, I have enough to know and who'll swear to it."

"Oh! I'm sure you have, but *that* doesn't explain why he gave up his appointment in the first place."

"Then allow me to explain, monsieur. Four days ago I left my court to attend to certain matters. When I returned the first thing my steward told me was that my foster-brother had resigned his office, that he'd taken leave of his senses, and that he'd come here with some confused idea about parleying with Gruffudd ap Rhys."

"So you admit that he was here?"

"Yes, to parley with Gruffudd ap Rhys; what's more, my steward was adamant that he'd taken leave of his senses, and when I ran into Maredudd earlier his gibberish talk only confirms my steward's judgement."

"You insult me, monsieur, you take me for a fool to believe all that."

"You wanted an explanation, monsieur. I gave it."

"Then tell me where Maredudd Goch is right now?"

"In the company of monks where prayer may bring him back to his senses."

De Turberville laughed, shaking his head in disbelief. "You always find some way to amuse. You must bring your foster-brother here. I'm sure he'll amuse me more than you – when he stands trial for his part in rebellion against the King's will."

"With respect, Monsieur la Steward, Maredudd's gibberish renders him incapable of speaking in his defence and, according to our law, a man who has taken leave of his senses cannot be held accountable for his actions."

"I am aware of that – and since you've tried to confuse the issue with your own gibberish he can stand trial according to French Law, where truth and retribution rest in the hands of God. Now – we have a description of a youth who was with Maredudd. Could be anyone, but I want your eldest son, the one who speaks openly of rebellion, brought here with Maredudd Goch."

"I see, and will you be accusing my son of rebellion as well?"

"No, I just want to establish whether he was here. If he's not recognized as the youth in question, then he can walk free."

"And the witnesses, are they the women and children who were spared?"

"Yes, they described a youth dressed in a manner befitting a nobleman's son."

Rhydderch cudgelled his brains: Caleb had not been wearing his own clothes, but Owain had. Then realization struck him.

"Well, monsieur, have you nothing to say? I take it he didn't lose his senses and go missing like Maredudd Goch."

"He's perfectly sane, Monsieur la Steward, and you, of course, would recognize him if you saw him?"

"As your son, yes, I never forget a face."

"If you will permit me, Monsieur la Steward." With a bow Rhydderch withdrew to his escort to single out the youth, Meurig, still wearing Caleb's clothes. "Walk proud like Caleb," he whispered. Meurig came forward to stand contemptuously before the table. "You say, monsieur, you never forget a face. So who is this young man?"

De Turberville eyed them both questioningly until, turning to a boy in ragged clothes, he ground out, in the Saxon tongue, "*You*, approach that youth and take a good look at him. Then tell me if he is the one you spoke of."

The boy came forward, cap in hand, to stand, staring at Meurig's face. From various angles he vaguely recalled the face, being similar to that of another youth, although the clothes and the contempt with which Meurig viewed him seemed out of place – it was certainly not the face of the young man to whom he had pleaded, with his eyes, *Do something, please, he's going to kill me.* He turned to de Turberville, shaking his head, saying, in the Saxon tongue, "Tis not he, my lord, I swear it."

"I trust you have not said that because you feel you owe him your life?"

"No, my lord, may I be damned if I tell a lie." The boy looked at Meurig again. "If it were he, it would grieve me to point a finger at him, but it's not him, I swear it."

"Get out of my sight!" De Turberville turned to his constable. "Olaf, let's have that old hag, Bertha. She'll have no scruples about pointing a finger at anyone."

De Viles bent forward, whispering, "Why bother with witnesses? We know the eldest son was here, the priest said so. Order that he be brought here to be tried according to our law – and my mace, it'll be the instrument of God's truth."

"Enough of your rancour," said de Turberville, brushing de Viles aside. "Bertha, take a good look at that young man there and tell me if it's he you spoke of."

A toothless, old woman approached Meurig to look him up and down. "Na," she croaked, grimacing, "tis not him, arrogant young devil."

"Two witness," said Rhydderch when the woman had been dismissed, "and it's plain neither can identify my son as one who was here on the day of attack."

"There's still Maredudd Goch, the description I have of him is irrefutable. I want him here, tomorrow, to stand trial for his rebellious activities. And since you've raised doubts as to his motive for being here, he can stand trial according to French Law, where truth and justice rest in the hands of God."

Rhydderch stared, his face expressive of the contempt he had for the way Frenchmen put a man on trial when the evidence against him was inconclusive. For the unprivileged it was a sordid affair conducted by a priest. The accused might have an arm bound in linen cloth and plunged into boiling water; if no blisters appeared within three days, then he was declared innocent. Alternatively, his hands bandaged, the accused might be told to pick up a hot iron, the appearance, or non-appearance of blisters deciding his fate. Equally obnoxious was the cursed morsel, a piece of dry bread placed on the accused's tongue, which he was expected to swallow; with his mouth dry through fear it was likely that he would choke even when innocent. Maredudd, of course, would be spared such treatment: being privileged, he would fight his cause with a mace and shield, a form of combat that he was unfamiliar with, whereas someone like de Viles would have proficiency on his side.

"Have you nothing to say, monsieur?"

"Do wish me to express my contempt? Remind you that, according to our law, a man stands or falls by the testimony of men under oath?"

"Are you saying that the testimony of men is above divine intervention?"

"What I'm saying, monsieur, is that I will not have Maredudd subjected to...."

"Will not! Monsieur, if you do not bring him here to be tried by our law, then at the very least you risk forfeiture of your lands."

"The risk is yours, Monsieur la Steward. Take action against me and you play into the hands of Gruffudd ap Rhys. Then everything in this lordship that is French will be laid waste; it'll be an uprising that will spread throughout these Southern Lands."

"No," de Viles snarled, slamming a fist on the table. "*Thy tongue deviseth mischief, like a sharp razor, working deceitfully* – but you, you will be subdued just as the Lord subdued unto me all those who rose against me."

"Stay out of this, de Viles," de Turberville warned, "or, by the blood of Christ, I'll have you removed."

"I'll not be silent while he tries to confuse the issue, for *the Lord bringeth the council of the heathen to nought. He maketh the devices of the people to none effect*." At a signal from de Turberville two men in chain-mail closed with de Viles, each taking hold of an arm while he, pausing in his tirade, tried to shake them off.

"I'm warning you, de Viles," de Turberville ground out, "those two men have orders to remove you by what ever means is necessary."

"You have no right to remove me."

"I have every right. It is I who presides over this inquisition and I'll not have you flout my authority."

Both men stared, each trying to face the other down. "Monsieur la Steward," said Iorwerth, breaking the deadlock, "if I might be allowed to speak?"

Moments passed before de Turberville replied, "Very well, say what you will."

"Monsieur la Steward, no one can dispute that the depredation has proved costly enough, but think how much worse it would have been if Monsieur de Gower had thrown in his lot with the rebels. One word from him and every Countryman in this lordship would have been up in arms, eager to avenge their loss of ten years ago, and the fighting, would it not be going on right now? In short, monsieur, his loyalty to the Earl has spared this lordship unspeakable loss. Yet you seek to alienate him, you insist on a trial that will alienate every Countryman in this lordship."

"Yes, yes, monsieur, get to the point."

"The point, Monsieur la Steward, is that, if Maredudd Goch is guilty, then justice will prevail even if he's tried according to our law. It may take longer, but at least it'll avert a confrontation. Now you, monsieur, are quite capable of presiding over a suit according to our law. So why not settle this affair in a manner that will dispel further grievance among the Countrymen of this lordship?"

"It's not that simple. How can Maredudd Goch be called to account when Monsieur de Gower claims he's taken leave of his senses?"

"You're both shrewd men; I'm sure you'll come to some arrangement on that point."

De Viles appeared barely able to contain himself, whereas de Turberville, his gaze fixed on Rhydderch, did no more than ponder the proposal till he rose, saying, "There will be a recess while I consider the matter in private."

"No," de Viles spat, slamming a fist on the table. "The act of rebellion took place here, on French soil; therefore, you must convene according to French Law."

A man-at-arms seized de Viles from behind and hustled him away from the table. As he struggled free he recognized the man as Elgar the Saxon, one of his sworn enemies. His hand closed over his sword hilt; at the same time he heard, at his back, Olaf's blade scrape the inside of its scabbard. He no sooner witnessed Elgar recede, drawing his sword, than he caught the approach of a third man-at-arms. Three blades, the brands of men he loathed, caused him to stay his hand.

"You make too many enemies," said de Turberville. "Now d'you want Messieurs Elgar and de la Mere to run you through from the front? Or would you prefer my constable to cut you down from behind? Either way I'll not have you intimidate me."

De Viles thrust his half-drawn blade back into its scabbard. "The Earl will hear of this."

"I'm sure he will. In the meantime, I will decide what's to be done." De Turberville rose. "Monsieur de Gower, I will see you in my tent. Olaf will show you where it is."

De Turberville had no sooner moved away from the table than de Viles raved, "*They that sit in the gate speaketh against me,* but *God shall let me see my desire upon mine enemies.*" He made to follow de Turberville only to find his passage blocked by the three men who had drawn their swords.

Meanwhile, Iorwerth indicated for Rhydderch to move away from the table, saying, "If anyone has lost his senses, it's that madman." Then lowering his tone, he continued, "I trust that I did the right thing, speaking as I did?"

"I'm obliged to you as I am for the message you sent me – gave me a chance to prepare myself against de Turberville."

"My pleasure, cousin, and for what it's worth I suspect de Turberville was offering an easy way out for Maredudd, that of a trial by combat."

"How can that be when the witnesses who saw him here are women and children, none of whom are competent to bear witness against a man?"

"Ah! Yes, but what de Turberville hasn't said is that Maredudd was also seen at Ystum Llymarch, and by men. That's why I say, a trial by combat is the better option."

"No, Maredudd is no match for someone like de Viles, not with a mace and shield."

"He could improve his skills."

"In so short a time?"

"Perhaps not, but be warned, de Turberville knows more about this affair than he's letting on. And another thing, that priest who forewarned the garrison, he's been here again, yesterday, obviously to inform on your affairs; that makes him one of your people."

"How d'you arrive at that?"

"You know about my son's involvement, right? De Turberville does not. If he did, he'd have been calling for my son to be brought here. As it is, it's Maredudd he wants, though I dare say Caleb is by no means in the clear." Iorwerth glanced over his shoulder. "That's not Caleb back there, I know him too well to be fooled by a resemblance."

Rhydderch caught a signal from the High Steward's constable.

"Let Olaf wait," said Iorwerth. "The proposed betrothal of my Elinor to Owain, I was wondering if my priest might conduct the ceremony. He's been an invaluable officer to me and I'd be obliged if we were to consider him, instead of Father Piro."

"I'll get back to you on that; now you must excuse me – Olaf is getting anxious."

CHAPTER 15

COMPROMISE AND TROUBLE

Rhydderch entered a tent to find the High Steward stood near a table, a thumb hooked in his belt, over which his paunch sagged; below the belt his overtunic fell in loose folds to his knees. "Ah! Lord Rhydderch, come in, come in," de Turberville said in the Countryman's tongue. "You know, it would have been better all round if you'd agreed to Maredudd fighting his cause in a trial by combat."

"Against whom – Henry de Viles?"

"Why not? If Maredudd were to kill him, it would make life so much easier for both of us – but first things first." De Turberville signalled to a retainer to fill two goblets. "Have some wine; relax. I enjoy the company of a man I can do business with."

"You do me an honour, my Lord Steward."

"No more than you deserve. Your only shortcomings are, you failed to safeguard your borders and you failed to fall upon the rebels when they retreated north."

"I'm under no obligation to place my sword at the Earl's disposal. And I ask you, my Lord Steward, why didn't your own kind fall upon them? There were horsemen near Ystum Llymarch at the time of the attack, were there not?"

"That hasn't escaped my notice; now let's get down to business. I'll preside over a trial according to Countryman Law providing we agree to a few ground rules, and the first is that you forgo the claim that Maredudd Goch has taken leave of his senses. I mean, he *is* guilty – you know it, I know it, and for a trial to proceed there can be no such claim. In return, there will be no action taken against Maredudd for his involvement here, at Abertawe, because the witnesses are all women and children and are, therefore, not competent to give evidence against a man. That leaves Ystum Llymarch, where his presence there was observed by men. So he can stand trial for his involvement there according to Countryman Law, and the charge most fitting is what you call *treis* in that he did ferociously deprive William de Londres, Lord of Ogwr, of his castle, cattle and movables in the fief of Ystum Llymarch, and that he did molest, wound or kill Lord

William's men and tenants in the said fief. So tell me, are you in agreement with what I've said?"

"What you've said could be the basis of an agreement, my Lord Steward, but if Maredudd is to be charged with *treis*, am I right in assuming William de Londres will be the plaintiff?"

"Er – no, I'm afraid Lord William is away in the King's service. So I'll have to appoint someone to plead in his stead."

"With respect, my Lord Steward, that cannot be because, according to our law, only Lord William can file a plaint for the damages incurred."

"Yes, I know, but if I were to tell de Viles that you and I had come to an arrangement whereby he could represent Lord William in his absence, then it's a sure way of getting that madman to agree to a trial according to Countryman Law. Then, if a trial were to take place, Maredudd could object to de Viles acting on Lord William's behalf. So the trial would have to be postponed until Lord William returns. In the meantime, I'll have the pleasure of witnessing de Viles's frustration when I apply that law. Now afore you say *no* let me explain. I have to be seen upholding law and order. So I want Maredudd brought here tomorrow so I can give him time to find sureties and prepare his defence; after that we'll proceed slowly. I say slowly because there are many points in your law that allow postponement – sickness, a call to arms, pilgrimage. All that I'll leave to you, but the thing to remember is this – between us, we'll make sure the whole process is put off for as long as possible."

"And what good will that do? Maredudd will still have to stand trial eventually."

"Not necessarily. The Earl could grant him a pardon on my recommendation. That, of course, would take time in that I'll have to get a carefully-worded document to Warwick, and no doubt the Earl will need time to consider its contents, which is why I say we postpone Maredudd's trial for as long as possible. I'd say it's worth a try. I mean, you weren't involved, I know that, and Maredudd did save lives, both here and at Ystum Llymarch; now I can't be fairer than that, can I?"

"Ystum Llymarch is one thing, my Lord Steward, but I cannot image de Viles agreeing to no action being taken for what happened here, at Abertawe. What he'll do is go straight to Warwick and complain to the Earl."

"Hah! De Viles has upwards of thirty days castle guard to complete and I'll see to it he does just that. Of course, he could send a message to the Earl, but I doubt whether his words will carry more weight than mine. So, there you have it, my full support for a trial according to your law. Naturally, I'll want something in return."

"Naturally."

"What I'm concerned about is that Gower is not caught up in rebellion again. So I want you to safeguard your borders. If there's any incursion, I expect you to inform me immediately, which is what you should have done days ago. You must have known something was up, you called your tribesmen to arms. Yet you made no attempt to inform me."

"A priest come here, did he not?"

"What?"

"A priest, he came here long afore that township of yours was burnt."

"I wasn't aware the priest was your man."

"Come, my Lord Steward, you can hardly expect a man in my position to be seen as one who aids Frenchmen."

"Yes," said de Turberville, suspicion written all over his face, "I can understand that, but...."

"But what? Didn't the priest inform you that this castle was in danger of attack? And that I had called my tribesmen to arms? And was it not so, that much of what the priest had to say he said to de Viles?"

"Yes, that's more or less how it was, though I fail to see – no-no, I don't understand all this, you'll have to explain."

"Explain what? The priest's connection with de Viles? I'm afraid you'll have to trust me on that for the time being."

Suspicious still, de Turberville placed his goblet on the table. "You must excuse me, there's something I have to attend to."

"My Lord Steward, if you've a mind to confer with de Viles, then you can forget about doing business. I don't want anything I've said to go beyond this tent and I certainly don't want de Viles to have doubts about that priest."

"I wasn't going to confer with de Viles; I've something far more pressing to attend to." De Turberville turned to his retainer, growling, in French, *"Get me a pail, I need to relieve myself."* Then reverting to the Countryman's tongue, he continued, "Now there's something I want to make plain, though in view of what you've said it may seem unnecessary. I don't want your people getting mixed up in rebellion; I want *you* to keep them in check. It'll be in their own interest, I can assure you."

"You have my word, I will dissuade anyone from embracing the rebel cause."

"Good. I knew we could do business. We're two of a kind, you and I, and I can assure you that, where the Earl is concerned, I will speak most favourably for you."

"Thank you, my Lord Steward, and if the rebellion should get out of hand, then where Gruffudd ap Rhys is concerned, I will speak most favourably for you."

De Turberville frowned, then laughed, "You've a sense of humour, my friend. It's a pity some of my kind can't match it. De Viles, now he never makes me laugh. In fact it's common knowledge I loathe the swine." He shook his goblet. "More wine?"

. . . . . .

On his way to the monastery, Rhydderch pondered: de Turberville had done him no favours. The man had made capital out of Maredudd's recklessness, agreeing to a trial according to Countryman Law as a means of staying rebellion in the Lordship of Gower. The question was, until when would the trial be postponed? Until the rebellion failed *not many months from now*? He would not be surprised if de Turberville changed his stance once the prospect of further incursions had passed.

Nor could *he* overlook the fact that de Turberville had not questioned *him* about *his* whereabouts on the day the attacks took place. It would have been the natural thing to do. Yet the man had said nothing other than, '*you weren't involved, I know that*,' presumably because the priest had said as much when he turned up at the castle two days after the attack. Be that as it may, *he* now had confirmation that a priest had not only forewarned the garrison, but the same was in league with de Viles, though how long it would take de Turberville to discover the truth – that the priest was not *his man* – and how de Turberville would react remained to be seen.

On the other hand, the High Steward might remain oblivious to the truth, for while information had been given to de Viles, the sum of that information did not appear to have been passed on to de Turberville. Why? Could it be that, out of malice or mistrust, the madman was withholding information. unwilling to divulge the true nature of his involvement with a mysterious priest? There was definitely something lacking in that, had de Turberville been in full possession of the facts, then he would never have been tricked into thinking that the priest was '*his man*' and not de Viles's.

On the face of it, de Turberville had singled out Maredudd and Caleb for their involvement at Abertawe because both of them had allegedly been seen there. That may have been so with regard to Maredudd, who had also been seen at Ystum Llymarch, but the description of a well-attired youth, pointing to Caleb's involvement, did not add up. Caleb had been attired in another youth's clothes, whereas Owain had been wearing his own. Obviously, the well-attired youth had been Owain. Yet de Turberville had not mentioned him; nor had he said anything about the involvement of seven other Uwch-coed men, two of whom had accompanied Maredudd to Ystum Llymarch.

As to the mysterious priest – if, indeed, he was a priest – there was only one churchman who had intimate knowledge of his affairs – his wife's priest, Father Piro. To suspect him, a worthy scribe, was unthinkable. It was more likely that the priest was simply a messenger, that someone else – someone at court – must be providing the priest with information. If he were to point a finger at anyone, then the blacksmith was the most likely candidate, the only courtier known to have left court on the night the bards were at play. The man swore that he had received word that his brother – a priest residing at the Church of St. Teilo – had been stricken with St. Anthony's fire, as had several people who farmed the low ground beside the Llwch Dwr River. The reddish colour of the priest's skin, coupled with a kinsman's claim that he had been the bearer of ill-tidings, had since confirmed the blacksmith's story.

Be that as it may, there remained Maredudd's claim that he had twice seen, on the moorlands above St. Teilo's Church, a priest riding with his hood up? According to Owain, such a priest had forewarned the garrison at Abertawe. There were few priests who had use of a horse; only one, as far as he knew, habitually rode about the country with his hood up – the priest of his kinsman, Iorwerth ap Meirchion.

So what could be said of Iorwerth? That he was scheming? Untrustworthy? A man who had gained his lordship as a result of fighting alongside the French against his own kind? Iorwerth was all those thing and more – his position as Lord of Cilfái depended upon French backing. It was, therefore, in Iorwerth's interest to keep in with de Turberville, but if Iorwerth had sent his priest to warn the garrison, then the priest would have crossed the estuary by boat and not ridden in from the north.

Besides, Iorwerth hated de Viles, and for some strange reason he feared that, in the event of his death, and that of his son, his Lordship of Cilfái might pass to a Frenchman such as de Viles. Iorwerth had, therefore, proposed the marriage of his daughter to Owain so that, in the event of his death, and that of his son, Cilfái would pass through his daughter to Owain and no one else.

Rhydderch rode out onto terraced fields to glimpse, on a knoll partially obscured by trees, the Monastery of St. Cyfelach. His thoughts turned to when, ten years ago, de Viles had marched on St. Cyfelach's, burning it to the ground, leaving thirty men, women and children as corpses. Several of the victims the madman had battered to death with his mace while his men massacred the rest; now, rebuilt, the monastery was home to a new community of monks and their dependants.

On foot, Rhydderch had no sooner entered within the rubble-wall enclosure than he met his wife's priest, Father Piro, a dour, flaxen-haired man, who said, to him, "My lord, thank God you've come."

"Why? What's wrong?"

"It's Maredudd, he's barred the door to the ale house and we can't get him out."

Rhydderch made for the alehouse. Father Piro kept abreast of him, saying, "My lord, he's got his horse in there and God knows the damage it's doing."

The Abbot, a gaunt man with outrage written on his face, approached. "My lord, I must protest about Maredudd Goch. He's not only helping himself to our ale, he's bathing in it – and the songs he sings, they're blasphemous. I've a mind to have him excommunicated."

"I wouldn't bother, Lord Abbot, Maredudd was damned years ago."

The Abbot paced beside Rhydderch. "In all my years I've never known anything like it. He's disrupted two services to the point where none of us could concentrate on our prayers – and the ale, someone will have to pay for it."

"Yes, Lord Abbot, you'll be reimbursed. Just let me know how much and I'll see to it that Maredudd pays to the last penny."

At the ale house door were three monks and Rhydderch's steward, Sulien, who had been sent for in the hope of getting Maredudd out. They all gave way as Rhydderch approached the door, through which the slurred words of a psalm carried. "The Lord is my shepherd; I shall not want. He maketh me to lie down in a vat of ale. He leadeth me to wallow in fermented waters...."

Rhydderch rattled the door. "Maredudd, I want you out of there *now*!"

The psalm ended abruptly. "Rhyz-zerch, is zat you? 'Old on while I open up." A sloshing sound, like someone removing himself from a tub, preceded that of a bar being lifted from the door. Maredudd appeared, his clothes wet, a horn of ale poised. "Bar your-zelf in, you zed. So I did. D'you wana dwink?"

"No! Now let's have you out of there."

"Right – I'll get my 'orse."

Rhydderch's hand fell upon Maredudd. "Awst, get his horse out of there."

Rhydderch's arms-bearer entered while Maredudd was brought, still holding a horn of ale, face to face with the Abbot, who glared at him. "This is outrageous. I...."

A commotion within the alehouse began with a loud neigh. Then Awst came tumbling out the door, panting, "Sulien, you'd best give me a hand with the horse."

"Why, what's wrong with it?"

"Pissed, I'd say."

As Sulien made towards the door so Maredudd whistled. A bay appeared, head down, driving Awst and Sulien before it; it came to a standstill near Maredudd, snorting and scraping its hooves.

"Easy, easy," Maredudd slurred, stroking the horse's forehead.

"My apologies, Lord Abbot," said Rhydderch, grim-faced. "Like I said, I'll see you are reimbursed for any loss."

"That's as maybe, but I want that man to do penance for what he's done, or, by all that's holy...."

Maredudd, meanwhile, having lurched to the horse's left flank, attempted to place a foot in one stirrup. He misjudged the move and his leg peddled air. Grinning, he tried again, only to topple against the horse. The Abbot could take no more. He ordered his monks to disperse, then strode off.

"Damn you!" said Rhydderch. "You're well and truly pissed."

"Oo, me? Na – my legz maybe – but den, all dat ale'z gotta go zomewhere." Maredudd attempted to mount again.

Awst, Sulien," Rhydderch barked, "get him onto his horse and let's be gone from here afore we're all excommunicated."

It took considerable effort to get Maredudd into the saddle; had it not been for Father Piro he would have slid off on the far side. Once righted, Maredudd inadvertently spurred. The bay moved off and, with Maredudd hanging on for dear life, it sped towards the gateway.

· · · · · ·

In the chamber attached to Y Faerdref Hall, Gwenllian pricked up her ears: the sound of horses told of Rhydderch's return. She hurried from the chamber, intending to meet him as he entered the hall to ascertain if he had any update on her eldest son. She knew about Maredudd barring the door to the ale house: her priest had informed her when he came for Sulien; moreover, her priest had quoted Maredudd as saying, '*When I left the rebels, Caleb was in safe hands with Einion watching his every move,*' only the knowledge had done little to dispel her anxiety. Passing between the central roof trees, she saw, at the far end of the hall, the doorway darken as Rhydderch entered. "So Maredudd is back; now where's Caleb?"

"Have a care with what you say," he replied, unbuckling his sword belt, "or...."

"Don't use that tone with me, I won't have it!"

He threw his sword belt onto a trestle table. "Then be careful what you say, otherwise it'll go ill for Caleb."

"*Then answer my question,*" she countered in French. "*Where is he?*"

"Cantref Mawr. *He's alive and well and, according to* Maredudd*, he's not so impulsive – more inclined to heed advice, though I find that hard to believe.*"

"*I don't see why,* Owain *said as much.*"

"*Yes, it's just that I've never found him to be so.*"

"*You wouldn't. He's always heeded* Maredudd *more than you.*" She averted from him, regretting her sharp tongue. As he approached, saying, "Gwen, let's not...," she threw up her arms, preventing him from getting close. It was not just her anxiety over Caleb, or that the month was upon her, but those moments in the courtyard before Maredudd had left had rekindled embers which, until then, she believed to have been damped down; now, much as she reproached herself, she was forever venting her frustration on Rhydderch. She met his gaze. There was sadness in his eyes: yes, he knew how Maredudd's departure had affected her. Yet he had said nothing, not one word of reproach. "So where's Maredudd?"

"In his lodgings, out cold."

"Pissed, I suppose. We'll I'll soon sober him up." She made for the door.

"You'll be wasting your time. We were coming down through the woods when he fell asleep. Next thing we knew, he'd fallen from his horse. I just hope he gets the worst hangover in his life for all the trouble he's caused."

At the door she turned. "Damn Maredudd! It's my son I'm concerned about."

"Yes, and that's what I want to talk to you about. It's serious business, Gwen."

At the point of responding she sensed, at her back, someone in the doorway. She moved aside; Gerwyn, Rhydderch's page, entered, a hesitant, apologetic expression on his face. Like everyone else, Gerwyn had several times witnessed the strained relationship between herself and Rhydderch.

"Your attire, my lord, I...."

Rhydderch gestured for Gerwyn to approach, then said, in French, "Maredudd *was seen at* Abertawe *and* Ystum Llymarch *on the day the attacks were carried out. Fortunately for him, de Turberville has agreed that he should be tried according to our law. I say fortunately because at* Abertawe *the witnesses are either women or children. So there'll be no action taken against him on that score, but at* Ystum Llymarch *the witnesses are men. So he'll be tried for* treis *according to our law.*"

"*What has that do with* Caleb?"

"*It would appear that* Caleb *was also seen at* Abertawe, *but the truth is, it was* Owain *who was seen, not* Caleb; *now it's likely that the informer knows all this and passed it on to de Viles. And yet de Turberville doesn't seem to be aware of the mix up, though I dare say he'll get to know of it soon enough. Then he'll want* Owain *to appear afore him, and probably* Caleb *as well.*"

"*So what are you going to do about it?*"

"*Right now, I can only play it by ear.*"

"*I don't agree. Our first priority is to get* Caleb *back.*"

"*I'll send* Rhain *first thing in the morn....*"

"No! *You'll send him now.*"

"Gwen, *it'll be dusk soon.*"

"*I don't care. If you don't send him now, I will. He's not one of your officers, he's my brother, he'll do what whatever I ask of him.*"

"Very well." Rhydderch turned to his page who, with cloak and sword belt in his possession, was heading for the chamber. "Gerwyn, leave what you're doing and tell Rhain I want him." He faced Gwenllian, saying, in French, "*There's something else that needs to be said if only to allow you time to think about it.* Iorwerth *was at* Abertawe – *in fact, he spoke on my behalf – and he wants to know if his priest can conduct the betrothal ceremony.*"

"*I don't care what* Iorwerth *wants.*"

"*I can understand that. All I ask is that you think about it.*"

"*You think about it, and while we're on the subject, you do know that* Owain *has a fondness for* Ammon's *daughter?*"

"*I surmised as much, but he's said nothing of it to me.*"

"*No, he wouldn't, not when it puts you in a difficult position, and I don't care to see him in a similar situation to me. I – oh! You know what I mean.*"

"Yes – yes, I do. You've made that painfully obvious."

Her heart pained: she knew that she was being unreasonable, but how could she talk to him about the affect that Maredudd's leaving had on her? She could not tell him and yet she could hurl her frustration at him. Why? What did she want of him? An angry response so that she could let fly about how she felt? No, she could not throw it in his face; she must keep silent. '*Of course you can tell him,*' a thought urged. '*It's not as if he won't understand – he always has.*' She drove the thought from her mind, refusing to curb the bitchiness that held sway over her emotions.

At that moment her daughter, Cadi, entered the hall, making straight for Rhydderch, welcoming him with open arms. "Cadi," he said, responding to her approach so that they fell to an embrace.

"So what's my father been doing today?"

Gwenllian looked on, tight-lipped, wondering whether Cadi was demonstrating that she, at least, still cared for him. She fixed her gaze on Rhydderch, at a loss for all those years they had been as one, not simply as man and wife, but as companions. He was a man like no other, one prepared to share his thoughts, his aspirations, even his weaknesses, accepting her as she was, foibles and all; now her life with him seemed at an end.

She walked away, thinking, '*Maredudd, you've got a lot to answer for.*'

CHAPTER 16

MORGAN ACCUSED

At first light on the day following Maredudd's to-do at the monastery, Morgan left his father's hall with a mind never to return. Avoiding the mist on the high ground, he passed through the ancestral land of a man named Meurig, who had two sons, the younger of whom Morgan had injured in a fight the previous year.

Later, the sons turned up at Y Faerdref. The elder son, Caradog, surprised Morgan by standing a Cross in front of him, accused him of stealing jewellery belonging to his wife and demanded that the jewellery be returned. Morgan responded in no uncertain terms; whereupon, Caradog produced a holy relic from his local church and demanded that Morgan swore to his innocence, which Morgan did, knowing that, if he refused, it would be seen as testimony to his guilt. Caradog's response was to sneer, then demand that he be allowed to search Morgan's abode. Morgan reluctantly agreed, knowing that a refusal would be used as evidence against him. Meurig's sons virtually ransacked Morgan's abode, much to Banwen's dismay. She protested, she disputed with Morgan to stop them; to her horror, she even had to witness the younger son, Gronw, slyly spit wherever he failed to locate the missing jewellery. Then the sons left, making straight for the court of the *Rhaglaw*, where Caradog filed a plaint for the recovery of his wife's jewellery.

The *Rhaglaw* – the officer entrusted with the legal affairs of the commote – had at his disposal a small staff of bailiffs. The following day a bailiff arrived at Y Faerdref and, in the presence of witnesses, informed Morgan that he had to appear before the *Rhaglaw* in three days time. When the bailiff left, Maredudd – who had witnessed what had been said – dismissed everyone so he could speak to Morgan in private.

"Theft," he said, somewhat the worse for drink, "when it's done secretly, is the worst act a man can commit. It's lucky for you, you weren't caught with the jewellery in your possession, otherwise you'd be facing the death penalty."

"But my Lord Captain, I swear, to God, I stole nothing belonging to Caradog's wife. I admit I crossed his father's land, but I went nowhere near his father's hall. Great Lord! I'd have been asking for trouble if I had."

"For *which* we have only your word."

"But I didn't steal, I tell you. Believe me, Caradog is lying. He's using this to get back at me for biting his brother's ear off."

"*That* I can believe, only it's not going to help you. Caradog can have you convicted on mere suspicion and the only hope you have of clearing your name is by compurgation. So how are things between you and the men of your *resting-place*?"

Morgan shook his head. "My kin are all against me."

"You know," said Maredudd, putting a hand to his throbbing head, "when Caradog planted that Cross in front of you, it might have been better if you'd said you'd taken the jewellery. Then all he could have done was demand the jewellery be returned."

"But there's nothing to return! I haven't got the jewellery and whatever else I'm no bloody thief, never have been!"

"Fair enough, only don't shout, my head won't take it. Now me, I'm off to Abertawe. So you'd best have a word with Sulien about your defence."

. . . . . .

Not far from court, on land given to Morgan by Lord Rhydderch as a boon to Ammon for past services, stood a modest hall. A pig wandered into the porch, soiling the clean paving stones. When Banwen drove it out she caught Morgan's approach. He appeared as dejected as he had been the previous day when he returned from Ynys Ammon. It had come as a surprise to her to find that not only had he returned, complaining about his treatment at Ynys Ammon, but that he did not lounge about, blustering in his usual manner, nor did he follow her about to provoke upsetting arguments. There were still occasions when he snapped, but surprisingly he soon changed his tone, fumbling some sort of apology on more than one occasion.

What struck her most was that there seemed to be no fight in him, being overcome with remorse, at times struggling to hold back tears and, of course, she pitied him, the more so when, at nightfall, she went to where he lay and he cried in her arms. They never made love, which was as well, for Morgan's approaches had always been insensitive, almost brutal.

While Morgan had not actually said that he was prepared to make amends, and she certainly had her doubts as to how long this new situation would last, his return did give her hope for the future. She knew that if any good was to become of their reunion, then *she* would have to play her part, and it was the thought of meeting him halfway that prompted her to go to him. She walked slowly, wishing she were a little older, a little less plump and, yes, beautiful too, for *he* was handsome – if only he would smile.

They had almost converged when he grunted acknowledgement while she, after slowing to a standstill, did no more than turn and walk beside him. There was something about him that she construed as aggression. Yet she could detect nothing in his manner to suggest that he might be annoyed with her.

"What is it? What's wrong?"

"Caradog, bastard that he is, he's had the bailiff round like I said he would. I dunno what I'm going to do. Nothing, I suppose. There's nothing I can do."

"There must be something."

"Na, you don't understand, I've got to find twelve men who'll swear my denial is true. Now who's going to do that for me, eh? Not my kinsmen, that's for sure."

"You could at least ask them."

"What's the point? They've had it with me. Na, you're a woman, you don't understand, the only way I can redeem myself is to find seven pounds, only I haven't got seven pounds. So everything I own will be taken from me; I'll be banished from the commote with only a tunic on my back."

"No, you won't. Everything I own you can have. There's my marriage portion, my wedding gifts, my jewellery."

"What – you mean you'd give all that up for *me*?"

"Yes, I'm your wife, I want to help."

"Na-na, a week ago I'd have taken everything you've got, only not now."

"Why not? Between us we'll have enough."

"You must be bloody joking. I'll be expected to pay for the jewellery as well. Caradog reckons it's worth more than two pounds. That's more than nine pounds in all, it's too much. We'll have nothing left – not enough to live on, anyway."

"Well if you leave Uwch-coed, then so will I. They can't touch what's rightfully mine. Morgan, we could start afresh."

"What, without land?"

"We could enter into an agreement with someone who's got land to spare."

"Can't do that, we'd be no better off than bloody churls. I'd have no standing, I – na, it's no good, it's not worth thinking about."

They reached the hall where, with one hand, Morgan leaned against the porch. "Let's face it, I'm no bloody good. You'll be better off without me."

"No, we're in this together and I'll – I'll pray for you."

"Pray! What good will that do, you stupid bitch?"

"Don't shout at me! Shout at someone else, instead of moaning *it's no good, there's nothing can be done, I'm going to become a saleable thief.*"

"Shut up!"

"No, I won't. You're gutless, you are. You don't mind pushing me around, but when it comes to...." She paused, seeing his face work to sudden anger; he clenched a fist. "Go on – go on, hit me."

He slammed his fist against one of the porch uprights, then drew back, shaking his hand in pain.

"Serves you right, I hope it hurts." She entered the hall, leaving him hugging his hand and sucking the abrasions. Moments later she reappeared.

"You – you weren't the quiet one for long."

"What d'you expect? I've had to learn to stand up for myself."

He grimaced. "I'll get my things and go."

"No, you won't, you'll stay right here."

"What's the point?"

"I dunno, but you'll stay – you'll stay till I find out what's to be done."

. . . . . .

Old Merfyn, the court bard, looked beyond the young minstrels who sat before him to observe Banwen's approach. Seeing her hesitant, he gave instructions for his novices to continue their practice without him. "Banwen, my child," he said, meeting her with open arms.

"Can I speak with you?" she asked timorously.

"Of course. Did I not say whenever you so wished?"

She rushed into his arms, almost burying herself in the folds of his tartan vestment. "It's Morgan," she sobbed into his beard, "he's in trouble. The bailiff's been because someone says he's stolen jewelry, but he hasn't, I know he hasn't."

"Calm yourself, my child. I already know about the bailiff's visit."

"Tell me what's to be done?" she said, looking up at him. "Morgan won't do anything to defend himself."

"Well, first, we must find him a pleader, someone to speak for him. Rhain ap Rhodri is the best man I know. He is away at the moment, but he will be back soon enough." Merfyn led her towards the gates, an arm about her shoulders, while she continued to look up at him. "Next, we must find him a counsellor. I will be his counsellor. There, now already we have made a move in the right direction."

"Morgan said he'll need twelve men who'll swear his denial is true."

"And so he will. Since no one saw him steal, and the jewellery was not found in his possession, he will stand accused of theft absent – it will be Caradog's word against his. Now if he has twelve good men who will swear that, in their opinion, his denial is true, then the verdict will be in his favour."

"What about me? I know his denial is true."

"No, a woman cannot be a compurgator in a suit where a man is accused of theft. It has to be a man and a good one at that." He smiled. "Believe me, there are many such men in Gower Uwch-coed. So come, dry your eyes, all is not lost."

She wiped tears from her cheeks. "Finding those good men – won't it be hard?"

"I am afraid Morgan has only himself to blame for that, but *we will* find them. Come, let us walk. I will explain something to you."

Like a child she paced beside him, looking up at his grey, bearded face, attentive to his every word.

"As I said, twelve good men must be found. Six must be *nod men*; that is, men of distinction – high men such as your father, or court officers. One of the *nod men* must be a man of vows, a man who has sworn to abstain from women, horses and fine linen. The other six can be free men of lower status. His kinsmen, Elidir and Guto, will no doubt qualify." Merfyn came to a halt near the gateway, aware that horsemen were about to leave the court.

"Old One," said Maredudd, reining in, "I'm away to do penance at St. David's. I'll be gone about five days. So I'll be back in time for Morgan's *Day of Pleading*."

"Then I can look forward to five days of peace," said Merfyn, "five days in which I will not have to endure your endless gibberish and your atrocious verse."

Maredudd grinned, his eye on Banwen. "He'll miss my company, he just won't admit it. Now about Morgan, he'll need sureties. So tell him to have a word with Sulien." He tapped the side of his nose. "It's all been taken care of."

Maredudd had no sooner ridden off in the company of his doorward than Banwen turned to Merfyn. "What does he mean by sureties?"

"He means," Merfyn replied, "Morgan will have to find two men who are willing, on his behalf, to remain here, at court, while he attends to his defence. Should he abscond, then those same men will be obliged to hunt him down or pay a fine."

"Are there any who'll do that?"

"Maredudd has already said there are, though you can be sure that, when he taps the side of his nose, he's been up to no good."

Banwen shook her head, then made as if to bite her nails, at a loss for all that needed to be done.

"Banwen, my child, do not distress yourself over the difficulties. And I – I will speak to Sulien about sureties."

139

"Yes, but what about me? What am I to do?"

"Encourage Morgan. He is in need of your strength and courage."

"But I have none of those things to give."

"Oh! Yes, you have. I have witnessed you grow in stature since the day I first saw you. Now Morgan needs your strength, whereas you, you need someone who will be with you night and day. So I ask you, do you believe that God can help?"

"Oh! Yes – yes, I'll pray, I'll pray and pray for as long as I can."

"That, my child, will not be necessary. When it comes to prayer I say this – on their own, prayers are not enough, something else is needed. Now if you were to ask a friend for help, would you show your mistrust by repeating your supplication over and over again? No, having asked once, you would then take them at their word. Well, so it is with God. Once you have appealed for His help, then you, for your part, must cast all doubt aside. You appeal to Him just once, then believe that it is as good as done. Now go, my child, into the church and pray just once, then go on your way, believing."

. . . . . .

Three days later, Morgan made his appearance at the *Rhaglaw's* court. When he returned he told Banwen that he had been granted three days to procure sureties and prepare his defence. Morgan's reluctance to expand on what had been said, coupled with his negative, self-pitying attitude, prompted Banwen to seek the Old One, whom she found at his lodgings in Maredudd's hall. As she ventured in through the porch she heard him say, "So Caleb is alive and well. That is good news. His mother must have been overjoyed to hear you say that."

"She was, even though I didn't actually see him," said another man. "As I said, Gruffudd ap Rhys claims…." The man paused, then continued, in French, *"he's been sent on a quest that has to remain secret. So I spoke to some* Gower *men who were there at the rebel camp; they confirmed what their master had said."*

Banwen stood in the doorway to see the Old One sat upon a settle. In his company sat a much younger man, whose long hair, beard and tartan vestment gave her the impression that she had intruded on a conversation between father and son. She identified the younger man as Rhain, the brother of Lord Rhydderch's wife.

Merfyn caught sight of her. "Ah! Banwen, come in," he said, beckoning to her. "I take it Morgan has returned from the *Rhaglaw's* court."

She nodded, saying, as she made toward him, "He won't talk about it, he just keeps saying he didn't steal, but he has to suffer for Cadog's death. I've a mind to give him a good slap."

Merfyn chuckled. "Well afore you do," he said, inviting her to join them on the settle, "this is Rhain. He arrived back only a short while ago. So I have not had time to discuss Morgan's cause. Rhain, this is Banwen, Morgan's wife."

Rhain acknowledged Banwen while she took her place beside the Old One, his arm about her shoulders. She regarded Rhain with uncertainty, intimidated by his black beard and his plaited hair, but conceded that his greeting had been friendly. He looked tired, though, and his clothes were dirty, his boots caked in mud.

"Caradog ap Meurig has filed a plaint for theft absent against Morgan. Maredudd and I are of the opinion that Caradog has done this out of malice, sure in the belief that Morgan will never find twelve compurgators. I have elected to be Morgan's councillor, and Banwen and I, we were hoping you would be his pleader."

"It will be my pleasure," replied Rhain. "I've never liked Caradog."

Banwen warmed to Rhain, pleased that he had no love for Caradog.

"We already have sureties," said Merfyn, "our lord's huntsman being one of them."

"Huw," Rhain exclaimed. "That crotchety old devil hasn't stood surety for anyone in years."

"Well he has now – claims he has nothing better to do while his shoulder wound heels. And if you think that surprising, you will be all the more surprised when I tell you that our lord's steward has also agreed to stand surety."

"What, Sulien," exclaimed Rhain, "but he's of kin to Caradog. Why should he…?"

"Their procurement was Maredudd's doing. Need I say more?"

Rhain and Merfyn stared at one another, the words *bribery* and *coercion* in the minds. What they did not know were the details, that prior to his departure to do penance, Maredudd had bribed the tight-fisted Huw by reimbursing him several times over for any loss at knucklebone, assuring him that, if Morgan absconded, then *he* would pay the resulting fine. In the case of Sulien, Maredudd had coerced him into agreeing to stand surety as a result of catching him in an uncompromising situation with the baking woman.

"So what's the position with regard to compurgators?" Rhain asked.

"Not good," Merfyn replied, "which is why I have my suspicions about Caradog."

"I see," said Rhain, his eye on Banwen, "Well, right now, I'm tired after a two-day ride, but first thing tomorrow I will accompany Morgan to his *resting-place*, where we'll enlist the aid of kinsmen on the spear side. Then we'll try the distaff side, even if it means calling on all the men of Eirig Mawr.

. . . . . .

As she made her way over fields, Banwen focused on the two horses outside her abode, one of which she was sure belonged a kinsman. On entering the hall she found her cousin, Cadifor, talking to Morgan. Cadifor told her that her father had been taken ill and wished to see her, adding that he had brought a horse for her to ride. Although low in spirit, Morgan insisted that she visited her father, assuring her that he would be occupied with his defence. She told him about Rhain, what he intended to do on the morrow. Her last words before leaving were, "You will go, won't you?"

"Yes, yes," Morgan replied. "I said so, didn't I?"

When Banwen returned at eventide two days later she was dismayed to find Morgan not at home, nor at the court. She found him down by the river, his head buried in his hands. She had no need to enquire about his defence: the Old One had told her that Morgan had refused to speak to the men of his *resting-place*, with the result that, while he tarried with his sister on the terraced fields, Rhain had gone on alone, only to meet with hostility from Ammon, refusals from the other men; only Guto's father said he would think about it.

Nor had there been a positive response from among those related to Morgan through his mother, Hawys. The only thing that could be considered encouraging was that the Old One had told her that he had made Morgan see sense, persuaded him to forego the idea that he had to suffer for Cadog's death, as suffering would not bring Cadog back, nor would Cadog have wanted him to suffer. She questioned him about it – and yes, the Old One had made him see sense, as his reply had been a positive, "Yes, I understand that now."

As she sat beside him, telling him about the improvement in her father's health, Morgan put an arm around her, drawing her close. She did not resist, but drew comfort from their togetherness. Gone were her bitter recollections of their wedding night; gone, too, were the angry scenes. Something else had replaced those bitter memories: it was the knowledge that for her he cared.

CHAPTER 17

DAY OF PLEADING

The following day Owain made his way to court, travelling in the company of Morgan and his two supporters, Merfyn and Rhain, and also Maredudd, who had come simply because he wished to witness the proceedings. Owain's motive for journeying to court was that Anona might be there, as she had only to cross the valley. He thought of her constantly, reliving, more than anything, the last occasion they were together, three days after Cadog's burial, when he had tarried with her on the terraced fields. He had said nothing to her about his forthcoming betrothal to Iorwerth's daughter. How could he have told her that? How could he have made his feelings known? She was still heart-broken over Cadog's passing, anxious too about Morgan's fate. No, his visit had to be seen as that of a friend, not an admirer.

Maredudd dropped back to ride abreast of him. "Still brooding, eh? If I were you, I'd have it out with your father, tell him what he can do with the betrothal."

"It's not that simple, he's got troubles enough without me adding to them."

"You underestimate him. Me, I'm trouble to him every day."

A shout proved reason for Maredudd to ride forward, leaving Owain conscious that Maredudd was in good form even though he had troubles of his own. Paying for what he had done in the alehouse did not bother him. It had been said that, despite a hangover, Maredudd had gone to the monastery, put a hand in his girdle, pulled out coins, placed them on the Abbot's table and apologized for his misconduct; he even agreed to do penance without demur.

Owain had not the slightest doubt that the penance imposed had been his father's doing: two visits to the shrine of St. David's constituted a pilgrimage to Rome, reason for the High Steward to defer Maredudd's trial. Many viewed the episode as laughable, none more so than the High Steward who, according to his father, had *almost split his sides laughing* when told of the to-do in the alehouse. Equally laughable was his father's account of how Maredudd had stood in front of de Turberville's table, bleary-eyed, rocking on his feet, slurring between hiccups about how *rough* he felt until, finally, he had to be saved from falling flat on his back.

Not everyone saw the humour. The indignant Abbot, who had been present to confirm the penance imposed, had taken exception to de Turberville's response, only to be told, '*If I choose to laugh, then laugh I will,*' whereas de Viles had slammed a fist on the table, predicting that, when the Earl received his message, a writ would be sent so this travesty of justice would be put right.

Maredudd had since returned from his first pilgrimage. Whether or not he actually arrived at St. David's Cathedral was questionable, the consensus being that he had got no further than an alehouse somewhere along the way, for his description of both the shrine and the Bishop were considered vague.

. . . . . .

Towards midday, Morgan and his supporters entered a clearing where the theft had allegedly taken place. Maredudd led the way, his bay progressing at a leisurely pace. At his back, Banwen sat astride the crupper, leaning to the right to observe what lay ahead. On a rise at the northern end of the clearing some thirty men congregated on either side of what, she presumed, to be the *Rhaglaw's* chair. She had no need to be told that the men were all high men, owners of ancestral land, for they alone had the privilege of occupying such an exalted position.

Lower down, to the right of the *Rhaglaw's* chair, Caradog and his supporters were assembled. A swarthy, stocky man in his late twenties with an ugly scar above his left eye, Caradog stood, hands on hips, observing the approach of Morgan's company; sneering at his side, his brother, Gronw, a sly-looking fellow with unkempt hair and part of his right ear missing, appeared to relish Morgan's predicament. Banwen's recollections of when they ransacked her abode made her blood run cold.

Maredudd had no sooner reined in than Morgan helped Banwen to the ground and, for a moment, she regarded him, still unsure as to why he should be considerate. Perhaps his sister had something to do with it: Morgan had often alluded to things his sister had said. The Old One had certainly put an end to his self-pitying attitude, but what had become even more evident was a change in Morgan, which she perceived as an air of dignity; that had to be Maredudd's doing. The previous day, when Maredudd had returned from his first visit to St. David's Cathedral, he had spoken to Morgan in private, telling him that, if the worst came to the worst, he should at least hold his head up high, let no one, least of all Caradog, see him as anything less than a man who would give a good account of himself.

"Morgan, over here," Rhain called, "we're waiting for you."

Taking his place between Rhain and Merfyn, Morgan made towards a bailiff who stood below and to the left of the *Rhaglaw's* chair. All three walked tall like men who were about to do battle against the odds. The odds were definitely against them; that Banwen perceived when she considered Caradog and his eleven supporters. What dismayed her was that Caradog displayed the arrogance of a man sure to win; his sneering brother, Gronw, appeared to confirm it.

"I wouldn't worry about Caradog," said Maredudd, taking his place at Banwen's side. "The important thing is that Rhain gets the pleading right. One faulty word and he could lose Morgan's cause, but that won't happen. Rhain always gets his words right. Caradog – well, I've no doubt he'll plead for himself. Nasty piece of work, never did like him, nor that ferret-faced brother of his."

Banwen gazed in awe at Maredudd, glad that he was on Morgan's side. Her gaze fell to the hilt of Maredudd's sword – black-handled, the pommel and the quillon shiny through burnishing. It occurred to her that if he drew his sword, he could easily drive Caradog and his supporters from the field. A foolish thought, she knew. Yet she was grateful that he should have taken the trouble to be present.

Her attention drifted to the rise. The *Rhaglaw* had occupied his chair, his probing eyes seemingly fixed on her. She put her hands behind her back and resolved not to fidget lest her presence – the only woman on the field – should offend him.

"I wouldn't worry about him, either," said Maredudd as though he had read her thoughts. "The *Rhaglaw's* only purpose is to bring the parties together. It's those men around him who'll decide what's to be done. Isn't that right, Owain?"

"Huh! Oh! Yes – yes, and fairly. You see those men coming down from the rise, they've probably been told to leave on the ground of impartiality. They're kinsmen of Caradog; of Morgan too. Look, there's Ammon among them."

Banwen nodded, unsure as to where Owain's loyalty lay. He would have nothing to do with Morgan, nor did Morgan seek his company. The words of a bailiff snatched her from her thoughts.

"Silence! The *Rhaglaw* has risen! Whoever breaks the silence will be fined three kine!"

The *Rhaglaw* called upon Caradog to answer a series of questions; the same questions he put to Morgan. "Defendant, who are your sureties?"

Banwen tensed, fearing that Morgan's reply would be half-hearted, but his words carried when he answered, "Huw ap Gruffudd, out Lord Rhydderch's huntsman, and Sulien ap Maredudd, our Lord Rhydderch's steward. As both men are not here, I have with me four witnesses who will testify to this being true."

"Are the witnesses those four men who accompanied you here?"

"Yes."

"Then name your counsellor?"

"Merfyn Hen, our Lord Rhydderch's bard."

"And your pleader?"

"Rhain ap Rhodri, the brother of our Lady Gwenllian."

"Will you put to loss or gain by entrusting them with your cause?"

"I will, so help me, God."

"Merfyn Hen, Rhain ap Rhodri, will you stand by the defendant in what he entrusts to you?"

"We will, so help us, God."

"Then let the pleading begin."

A priest approached Caradog, holding the remains of a staff, believed to have been the property of the revered St. Teilo. Caradog drove his spear into the ground before kissing the staff. Then, with one hand on the holy relic, the other on his hip, he ground out, hoarsely, "I, Caradog ap Meurig, do swear by this holy relic that, on the ides of March in this year of our Lord, I was in the adjoining field, burning grass with my wife, Tanwen, and my brother, Gronw, when I was alerted to the barking of one of my dogs. Knowing there was no one at my father's hall, save my aged father, Meurig, and that one dog, I hastened to find out what was wrong. When I reached the hall, I found that my dog had been slain and that my father was distressed, but he, being feeble-minded, could not tell me what was wrong. If there's anyone who doubts the slaying of my dog, or my father's feeble mind, then I have enough supporters who'll swear that what I say is true.

"When my wife arrived on the scene she searched the hall and found her jewellery missing. If there's anyone who doubts that my wife owned such jewellery, then I have enough supporters who'll swear to it.

"I sounded my horn and my kinsmen came a-running. Two of them told me they'd seen you, Morgan ab Ammon, crossing their land by way of a track leading to Cwm Dulais. I knew then, because of the bad blood that exists between you and my father's household, that you, Morgan ab Ammon, had been the perpetrator of those evil deeds. Aye, and bad blood there is.

"Before you became of age there were many times when you caused damage to my father's property. If there's anyone who doubts this, then I have enough supporters who'll swear to it. Aye, and they'll swear to the bad blood I spoke of and to the malice that is in your heart."

Having dealt with his supporting testimony, Caradog paused, eyeballing Morgan as a prelude to stating the relevant part of his pleading. Then, pointing a finger, he ground out, "I now accuse you, Morgan ab Ammon, according to the Laws of Hywel Dda, of slaying my dog which, being a trained hunting dog, was valued at ten shillings and claim its worth. I also accuse you, Morgan ab Ammon, according to the Laws of Hywel Dda, of theft absent in that you surreptitiously took my wife's jewellery, valued at two pound and two shillings, and claim its return."

Banwen closed her eyes: everything that Caradog had said sounded so damning; not a word of it could be faulted. She was distracted from hearing the *Rhaglaw's* response by the low utterance of someone close by.

"I thought he'd never get to the end of it," Maredudd yawned, putting a hand to his mouth. He looked down at Banwen, whispering, "All wind. If Rhain does no more than deny it, it will still be one man's word against the other."

Banwen wanted to reply, 'Yes, but what about the old man? And that poor dog?' Her attention was diverted again by Rhain saying, in a stentorian voice, "I do solemnly swear by this holy relic, that Morgan ab Ammon is innocent of the accusations that *you*, Caradog ap Meurig, have levelled against him. While it is true that, on the ides of March, he rode south to avoid the mist on the high ground, he did not go anywhere near your father's hall, nor did he kill your dog, nor did he steal your wife's jewellery. To have done any of those things would have been foolhardy because, in your pleading, you spoke of the bad blood between him and your father's household, bad blood that stems from the long-standing enmity between your brother, Gronw, and Morgan, an enmity that made itself manifest last year in a fight that resulted in both men being fined for bloodying the soil. If there is anyone who doubts that enmity and the fine for bloodying the soil, then enough supporters can be brought here to verify it.

"As to the malice that *you* spoke of, if there had been malice in Morgan's heart that day, then why stop at killing a dog and stealing jewellery when he could have wreaked untold damage on your father's hall? I tell you, Morgan had other things than malice in his heart. He was grieving for his brother, Cadog, whom he had buried the previous day. If there is anyone who doubts that Morgan's brother, Cadog, had been buried the previous day, then enough supporters can be brought here to verify it."

Rhain levelled a finger at Caradog. "*You* may have supporters who will testify to having seen a dead dog, who will testify to your wife owning certain jewellery and, yes, two of them may well testify to having seen Morgan ride south through their land, but it is still your word against his that he did anything untoward. I therefore deny, on his behalf, that he slew your dog, which you claim to be valued at ten shillings, and I also deny, on his behalf, that he committed theft absent by surreptitiously taking your wife's jewellery, which you claim to be valued at two pounds and two shillings. I am, moreover, unimpressed by the number of your supporters because, according to the Law of Hywel Dda, Morgan's cause cannot be decided by what they say, only by the testimonies of twelve good men who will sweat that his pleading is true."

"What's he saying?" Banwen whispered. "We haven't got twelve men to support him."

"Don't worry, Rhain knows what he's doing. The important thing is that he got the pleading right. Couldn't have done better myself." Maredudd paused: the *Rhaglaw's* priest had already started to recite the relevant part of Caradog's pleading and, having no wish to hear it all again, he whispered, out of the corner of his mouth, "Owain, how many compurgators did Rhain say he had?"

"Two, Elidir and Guto, although Guto's father and Dewi said they'd think about it."

"Hmm! I'll have to do something about that."

"You'll be wasting your time. Rhain has petitioned everyone he could think of."

"Well, there's me, I'll do as a *nod man*."

"No, you won't because, right now, you're doing penance for...."

"Yes, yes, I knew you'd bring that up."

"So would Caradog and you know it."

Banwen, seeing that a bailiff had his eye on them, tugged at Maredudd's sword. Maredudd, who had already observed the bailiff's interest in him, responded with an affected grin, waving to the man in a manner that implied there would be no more talk. The priest, meanwhile, had no sooner begun to recite the relevant part of Morgan's denial than Maredudd spoke again, this time with a hand covering his mouth. "Owain, listen to me. If we were to find another youth, let's say, one willing to put aside his ill-will for the sake of someone he's fond of."

Owain casually turned, presenting his back to the bailiff. "Yes, Maredudd, I know, you're hinting at me. I'll have myself sworn in next Sunday."

"Good."

Banwen dropped back so that, behind Maredudd's back, she could catch Owain's eye. "You will?" she whispered gleefully.

Owain nodded. "Yes," he whispered, "for you I will."

"I would think," Maredudd said into his hand, "Anona will be pleased too."

"Shut up, Maredudd. If we're caught breaking the silence, you'll only lay the blame on me."

With the recital of Morgan's denial at an end, the *Rhaglaw* offered both parties the opportunity to amend their pleading to which both parties declined. The *Rhaglaw* then sat down and the atmosphere became more relaxed as twenty-three landowners began moving off to a location further afield, accompanied by the *Rhaglaw's* priest, to deliberate among themselves. Banwen looked up at Maredudd, bewilderment written all over her face.

"The *Rhaglaw's* done his bit," Maredudd explained now that he was free to talk. "He's brought the parties together; it's them landowners who'll do the judging from now on. One of them, whom they'll call *the Judge*, will be their spokesman. The *Rhaglaw's* priest will start off by praying for guidance, then you'll hear them all chant the paternoster. After that *the Judge* will recite the relevant part of both pleadings again, and *then* they'll decide what's to be done. You can take it from me, they'll not bother with Caradog's supporters, not when the charge is theft absent. No, what they'll go for is a trial by compurgation – which brings us back to twelve good men."

"Of which," said Owain, "Morgan has only three – five if Dewi and Guto's father decide to support him."

Maredudd affected a grin. "I'll soon talk those two round, don't you worry about that. Aye, and I might even find another seven."

"Says you. And where will you find someone who's sworn to abstain from horses, women and fine linen."

"I know just such a man," said Maredudd, "who'll be only too willing to help out."

"Who?" Owain asked.

Maredudd tapped the side of his nose. "You just leave it to me."

"Can I go, tell Morgan that?" Banwen asked.

"Yes, only don't say anything out loud. We don't want Caradog to hear."

Banwen ran off, making straight for Morgan who greeted her with an outstretched arm, a gesture that met with Merfyn's approval. Maredudd moved to join them, saying, to Owain, "Can't see Ammon about, can you?"

"He's gone. I saw him slope off when he separated from the judges."

"*Fie*! That's bad, not staying to give a son moral support."

"I want a word with you," said Merfyn, approaching; he led Maredudd aside. "What's this I hear, you finding twelve good men?"

"That's right, Old One, you leave it to me."

"Maredudd, I will remind you that every compurgator must have a character beyond reproach. Now how will you go about soliciting such men? Blackmail? A drinking bout with men who will get so drunk they will agree to anything? Or would it be a game of knucklebone with you setting the stakes and using your own precious bones?"

"Nothing wrong with my bones."

"No! They will do anything but float. I repeat, Maredudd, we need men of good character, men who will, with good heart, be sworn in, in church."

"And that's what you'll get. Ah! Listen, they're chanting the paternoster. Won't be long afore their deliberation is over."

When the twenty-three judges returned, the one designated *the Judge* announced, "We have deliberated and, according to the Laws of Hywel Dda, we cannot decide this suit on the pleadings alone. This suit will, therefore, be decided by the sworn testimonies of twelve compurgators. Morgan ab Ammon, you have the next two Sundays to procure the aid of twelve compurgators and have them sworn in, in church. You will, then, see to it that they assemble here for the *Day of Judgement* on the Monday following the second Sunday. Until then the court is adjourned."

"Right, that's it," said Maredudd, moving to the side of his bay, "I'm off." He raised himself into the saddle and, wheeling, said, to Owain, "See you back at Y Faerdref, about supper time if all goes well." Then, with a wave to Banwen, he spurred.

CHAPTER 18

AMMON

Using a long-handled wood-axe, Ammon hacked off a branch from a fallen tree, the branches of which blocked the track above the terraced fields. He needed to clear the obstruction and, with the aid of a horse and rope, he dragged the branch across the wooded margin that separated the track from a precipitous drop, below which was a quagmire known as the Abyss. His intention was to use the branch to reinforce the barrier above the precipice.

As he manhandled the branch into place he thought of Morgan. It was of no consequence to him that men closely related to Caradog had to forgo their place among the judges on the ground of partiality; nor did he consider it a slight that those same men had insisted that he, being Morgan's father, should also stand down on the ground that he would be bias towards his son. True, he had left the field of his own accord, and for that his conscience pricked him. It was unfortunate, but Morgan would only get what he deserved: he had been trouble enough in recent years; now he was responsible for Cadog's death and *that* was unforgivable.

On his way back to the fallen tree the sound of a bell caused him to look uphill. At the sight of a hooded figure he ground out, "The Devil's hoof! It's that bloody leper again. Hey! You, get off my land. I don't want you corrupting my daughter with your filthy sores; now clear off."

The leper had no sooner turned back than a horseman appeared to view. "God Almighty! I don't believe it – it's *him*!" Ammon hurried past the fallen tree, gabbing the axe to stand, feet apart, with the axe held menacingly in front of him. "That's it, come on, you bastard, I've got a score to settle with you!"

Maredudd reined in. "Ammon, listen to me, we've got to talk."

"All that's to be said is that because of you my son is dead – dead, d'you hear?"

"Yes, I know I should have sent Cadog back. I wish to God I had, only this thing between us goes deeper than that."

"Aye, you've been a thorn in my flesh for nigh on twenty years."

"Why – because of Hawys?"

"Hawys was betrothed to me and *you*, you had to have her."

151

"Hell! Ammon, I've told you afore I knew nothing about the betrothal."

"You must have known. And I – I caught you with her in the long grass."

"For St. Teilo's sake! Hawys was a loose woman. Even you must have known that."

"She was to be my wife, and not only did you violate her, you sacrificed my son in a mindless escapade. Well, I've thought of nothing but revenge these past few days, and by St. Cadog! I'm going to settle with you right now."

Seeing Ammon advance, axe poised, Maredudd raised a spear, ready to throw it at his opponent's chest. "I'm warning you, Ammon, pass that root and I'll spear you."

Ammon stopped short at the root. "God Almighty! If I could only get at you with my bare hands."

"You tried that afore, in the long grass, only you didn't fare too well then."

"You fought dirty, that's why."

"With you, yes. Even then you were big."

"Then fight me again, you gutless bastard!"

"If that's what you want, you can have it – after we've talked. Now get rid of the axe. When you've done that I'll throw down my spear and dismount. Agreed?"

Ammon swung the axe overarm, the bade embedding in a root.

"Don't take me for a fool. I meant throw it away."

Yanking the axe free, Ammon threw it into the underwood.

"Now move back. I don't want you jumping me while I dismount." Maredudd watched Ammon retreat, crab-like, his fists circling as he warmed for a fight. Only when he judged it safe did he cast his spear into the ground and dismount. "Right, let's talk about your son."

"My son is *dead*."

"It's Morgan we're going to talk about. He needs you and the men of this *resting-place* to support him."

"He's no good. For years he's plagued me with his troublesome ways."

"All he wanted was your attention. When you never gave it…."

"He got what he deserved; now enough of this, let's fight."

Ammon had no sooner moved forward than Maredudd put a hand to his sword. "I'm not finished yet."

"I've kept my part of the bargain. We've talked; now you won't fight."

"I'm not going to get through to you, am I?"

"That's right, you won't, you bastard!"

"Very well, get rid of that skene in your belt, then move back. Well, go on, do it and I'll put aside my sword."

Casting his skene into the woods, Ammon moved back, staring fixedly as, with one hand, Maredudd removed his cloak and threw it over thickets. Flexing his fingers, his arms raised, he watched Maredudd remove his baldric; as soon as that had been disposed of, he rushed forward, but Maredudd sidestepped off the track onto the sloping ground of the wooded verge. Ammon followed, arms outstretched, then leapt with the intention of bringing Maredudd down.

Catching Ammon by the tunic, Maredudd fell back and, with his knees, threw him in a somersault so that he landed downhill, snapping offshoots as he rolled. Maredudd followed and, as Ammon struggled up, he drove a foot into Ammon's face. Ammon reeled; Maredudd lost balance. As both men struggled up, Ammon lurched forward, seizing Maredudd by the tunic. Maredudd propelled himself, head first, so that, nose bloodied, Ammon fell back, pulling Maredudd with him.

Both men rolled downhill until, coming to a halt, they each strove to regain their feet. Maredudd knocked aside Ammon's left arm, but a huge right fist caught him on the cheek; he reeled. A second blow hit him full in the ribs. He doubled up; as he fell back he managed to roll further downhill. Ammon went after him, in his haste slipping on damp leaves; that gave Maredudd time to take refuge behind the bole of a tree.

Several times Ammon attempted to circle the tree from different directions, bellowing, as he did so, "Come out, you bastard – out where I can get at you."

Maredudd appeared to view, his foot swinging towards Ammon's groin. Ammon arched to avoid it, laying himself open to a punch to his mouth. Still he waded in and, with both hands, caught Maredudd by the tunic, pulling him closer, intending to butt him. Maredudd shifted his head quickly, his knee shooting up into Ammon's groin. Ammon groaned; like a bear he threw himself forward. Once again Maredudd fell back, throwing Ammon in a somersault. Ammon landed on his back, straddling the root of a tree, the wind knocked out of him.

Maredudd looked down at him, a hand resting against a tree and the other nursing his bruised ribs. "Sorry about the knee, Ammon," he jerked out, "my foot slipped."

"You always were a dirty fighter when it came to fists."

"You wanted the fight; now let's get back to where we were. Morgan needs your help. Whatever he's done he's still your son."

"What's he to you?"

"A young man who serves his lord, one that I believe is innocent of the charge brought against him."

"Nothing more?"

"What d'you mean?"

"Don't you know, he's your bastard?"

"You don't know that. It's just something you've let fester for years. He could be the offspring of half a dozen men I know."

"Na – he's yours, he's got your troublesome ways."

"Even if he is, I find it hard to believe that, after raising him, you never loved him as a son."

"What would you know about that? You've never raised a son."

"No, but my father fostered Rhydderch and I know, for a fact, he loved him just as much as he loved me."

"Aye – only he didn't have to raise someone who's no bloody good."

"Ammon, you're a pig-headed bastard. So I'll just leave you and go, speak to your kinsmen." Maredudd retraced his steps up the slope of the wooded margin.

Ammon rolled onto his side, shouting, "You'll be wasting your time. They're like me, they've had enough of Morgan."

His words went unheeded. So he took hold of a rock and, despite the pain in his back, struggled to his feet, then shambled upwards, taking a more direct route to the track where, leaning against a tree, he kept the rock hidden at the side of his leg.

Having retrieved his cloak and weapons, Maredudd led his bay around the fallen tree, then descended towards the track. "I'm warning you, Ammon, you try to stop me and it'll go ill for you."

Ammon waited until Maredudd had regained the track. Then, steeling himself against pain, he moved forward, hurling the rock as he did so. Maredudd swore, ducking as the rock shattered against a bough above his bay's head, the fragments showering both man and horse. The bay shied, dancing off the track to descend the slope of the wooded margin, taking Maredudd with it.

"Whoa," Maredudd shouted, pulling on reins, but the bay continued downhill, dragging him towards the barrier above the precipice. He hung on, several times digging his heels in wet soil, until he finally checked the bay's progress. Whilst calming the animal down he failed to catch Ammon's approach; when a bough struck his skull he reeled, collapsing at Ammon's feet.

How long he lay unconscious Maredudd did not know, but when he came to he found himself lying face down, aware that, at his back, Ammon was forcing his left hand towards his shoulder blade. Ammon gripped his hair, pulling his head back so that a rope secured to his left wrist could be put around his neck.

"You must be wondering why you're still alive," Ammon snarled, tying a knot close Maredudd's shoulder blade. "Bastard! If I kill you, an affiliated kinsman, I'll be banished from the commote." Ammon struggled up, still in pain. "Now *you* , you're a fine swordsman, but if you were to lose your right hand, what then, eh? You'd no longer be fit to be captain of guard."

Unable to comprehend what Ammon had said, Maredudd rolled, almost choking, onto his left side, using his right hand to support himself. Ammon placed a foot upon Maredudd's right arm, forcing it to the ground.

"So," Ammon growled, laying hold of the wood-axe, "I've decided that *you* – are going to lose your right hand."

Maredudd struggled to no avail. He heard Ammon growl, "Now watch, you bastard, while I chop it off." As the axe was raised he caught the approach of a young woman.

"No, father, don't, please, you can't do it!"

"Stay out of this," Ammon snarled, shoving Anona aside. "He's only getting what he deserves."

Anona rushed her father again, reaching for the axe. They struggled, shouting at each other until Ammon shoved her hard. She fell back, hitting a rotten bough, one of several that fenced off the precipice. The bough snapped; she fell, screaming, to the Abyss below.

"God Almighty! Anona, no!" Ammon made for the brink, relinquishing the axe, then dropped down over the edge.

Swearing as he struggled up, Maredudd fumbled with the rope around his left wrist. A bell tinkled, alerting him to the approach of a leper, at which point he caught sight of his skene beside a coil of rope. Kneeling, he picked up his skene and sliced through the rope around his neck. Ceredig, meanwhile, shuffled to the brink where he fell about, jabbering to God to be merciful. Maredudd joined him.

Below, at the base of a three-meter drop, Ammon moved out from a toe of displaced soil to flounder at the edge of a quagmire. Not far away, Anona, having rolled off a steep-sided buttress of brown, crumbly earth, lay on her side, her legs submerged in the quagmire. Ammon tried desperately to reach her outstretched hand, but having sunk, shin-deep in ooze, he could not get close enough.

"My lord," Ceredig cried, "please, I beg you, save Anona – quickly, afore it's too late."

Maredudd doubled back for the rope, returning to slide down the steep slope until he came to rest on the toe of displaced soil, close to Ammon's back. Hurriedly, he made a noose, shouting, at Ammon, "Don't go any further, you fool, you'll sink deeper; now get your damn head out of the way." Coiling part of the rope, he called, to Anona, "I'm going to throw this over your head. What you've got to do is get it under your arms. D'you understand?" The noose came down over Anona more or less as Maredudd had said. She worked it under her arms, the effort causing her to sink so that when Maredudd shouted, "Ready?" she had to raise her head to splutter a reply. Taking up the slack, Maredudd slid the rope around his back only to find that Ammon, anxious to play his part, had laid hold of the rope. "Leave it," Maredudd snapped. "I need a straight pull."

"Then pull hard, you bastard!"

"Leave it to me, fat man!" Maredudd dug his heels in the displaced soil and leaned back, straining until his feet slid from under him. He fell back, then struggled up.

"What's the matter with you?" Ammon spat. "Haven't you got strength?"

Edging to his left, Maredudd took up a position, which he hoped would prove firmer than the last. He took up the strain again and, leaning backwards, pulled hard until, sensing movement, he retreated two steps only to find one foot sinking where the soil had given way to ooze. He fell back, yanking his foot, minus a boot, from a mud-filled hole.

Ammon seized the rope and, to Maredudd's astonishment, used his muscular arms to haul Anona slowly towards him. Maredudd could only admire the man's strength and determination, for his groaning bespoke pain, whereas the effort caused him to sink deeper. By the time Anona had been dragged within reach, Ammon had sunk to his buttocks.

Maredudd took up the rope, pulling hard as he retreated in search of firmer footholds. At last he was able to retrace his steps and haul Anona bodily towards him until he fell back, gasping, onto the displaced soil with Anona's ooze-covered body covering his legs. He wished for nothing more than to rest.

"My father," Anona gasped, tugging at his coat, "we've got to get him out."

Maredudd raised his head to see that Ammon had sunk to his waist. "I don't see how," he said, tapping Anona to get her to move off his legs. "He's in too deep, and with his weight we'll never pull him out."

"But we can't just leave him. We must get help. I'll send Ceredig." Anona looked up at the bundle of rags crouched near the brink. "Ceredig – Ceredig, go to…"

"No," Ammon bawled, "there's no point to him going anywhere. By the time he reaches the nearest homestead I'll have gone under."

Anona looked to Maredudd, only to be told, "He's right. Even if the leper could ride my horse, it would make no difference."

"But we can't just watch him sink, he's my father."

"There's nothing can be done for me, Anona, it's the way it is. As for you, you bastard! Get her out of here so she doesn't have to witness my death."

"That I'll do, fat man," Maredudd returned, struggling to his feet. He took hold of the mud-covered rope and began coiling it. "Ceredig," he said, looking up, "have you any experience with horses?"

"As a boy, my lord. My father was chief groom to the Bishop of St. Davids."

"The Bishop, eh! I wonder if he's the same one who warned me, only a few days ago, about wallowing in anything but holy water." Maredudd stepped back until his feet sank in ooze. "Don't look so confused, my friend. I'm going to throw you this. Put it over my horse's head, only do it gently." He threw the rope, watching it uncoil until it cleared the brink. Ceredig had no sooner disappeared to view than Maredudd said, to Anona, "Wipe your hands on my coat, you'll have a better grip on the rope."

"You damn fool," Ammon snarled. "Anona could end up with his bloody sores."

"It's a chance we'll have to take if we're to get her out of here. And you, I don't understand why you've risked your life for her, and yet you'll do nothing for Morgan. I mean, if you hated him that much, why didn't you have him fostered out?"

"I've said all I'm going to say about *him*."

"You really are a pig-headed bastard, but I'll tell you this – once Anona is safe I'm going to get you out of there to where I stand. Then I'm off to have a word with the men of this *resting-place*. You never know, without you scowling at them, they might listen to reason. If they do, then maybe, just maybe, I'll tell them you could do with some help."

. . . . . .

When Maredudd arrived back at Y Faerdref, he went straight to his hall, which by custom he shared with Merfyn, the court bard. "Evening, Old One," he threw out, making for the side-aisle where he usually slept. "Anything happen while I was away? Something I should know about?"

The old bard considered Maredudd as he passed by: one boot missing, his clothes caked in mud, a raw bruise on his left cheek and his head bandaged. "Only that we have received word that Gruffudd ap Rhys continues to cause great depredation in Dyfed and Ceredigion. And judging by your present state *you* must have had a hand in it."

"Me! Na, I had other things to do." Maredudd embedded his spear in the ground.

"You mean you had a fight with Ammon. Well, I hope it was worth it."

"I hope so too," said Maredudd, rubbing his bruised ribs. He unfastened his cloak and threw it into the side-aisle. His baldric he let fall to the ground, which is where most of his belongings ended up. "Still, not to worry, we can count on another five compurgators."

"And not one of them a man of vows, am I right?"

Maredudd lay down in the side-aisle, still nursing his bruised ribs. "No, I didn't get around to that, but I will – tomorrow."

"Will you be up to it?"

"All it'll take is a few horns of ale with an old friend of mine."

"Iago Du, a man well known for his troublesome ways."

"That was afore he became a man of vows. So he can't be faulted for any of that. Enmity, yes, if it can be proved, but that's all."

"That's as maybe, but Rhain has already asked him and the answer was no."

"Yes, but Rhain doesn't know what you and I know, does he?"

"*You*," said Merfyn, shaking his head, "are without scruples. I sometimes wonder whether you give serious thought to anything." A horn sounded, prompting him to say, "Time to get up again, that is if you want supper, but I would suggest that you change first."

"Na, I think I'll stay here awhile."

"As you wish." Merfyn made for the door.

Maredudd called, after him, "Old One, I'd be obliged if you didn't say anything to Rhydderch about me. You know what he's been like after that affair at the monastery. It would be just like him to fine me twelve kine for bloodying the soil. Besides, I wouldn't want to upset him. A good belly laugh might ruin his appetite."

CHAPTER 19

QUESTIONABLE SUPPORT

On the day preceding the *Day of Judgement*, Owain went in search of his father, whom he found near the gates, talking to Awst. As he drew near he heard Awst say, "No, they'd gone there to kill her. She said she'd frightened them by throwing something into the fire. One of them ran off; the other tried to gain the crag while she swung at him with a stick. If he hadn't caught my approach, I dare say he'd have speared her."

"And you've no idea who those men were?" Rhydderch asked.

"Only that they were Countrymen. Well, I followed their tracks to the outskirts of the grove only to find they'd regained their horses and ridden off. So I went back to the woman and tried to get her to leave, but she would have none of it"

As Owain drew level with his father, Awst gave him a curt nod, causing Rhydderch to turn. "Can I speak with you, father?"

Awst had no sooner been dismissed than Rhydderch motioned Owain to walk with him, out through the gateway. "You heard all that, I take it?"

"Yes, the soothsayer, someone must have a grudge against her."

"Or de Viles put them up to it. He must know about my connection with her." Rhydderch walked on a few paces. "So what do you want to speak to me about?"

"My betrothal to Iorwerth's daughter – I've given it a lot of thought and, yes, I know it'll make things difficult for you, but now I find myself drawn to someone else."

"Ammon's daughter – you met her, what, seven weeks ago? Why didn't you speak to me about her then?"

"Because I wasn't sure about how I felt, how she felt about me, and since then there's been Abertawe, Caleb gone and – well, things haven't been right between you and my mother. I just didn't want to add to those troubles."

"I see – and have you spoken to Ammon's daughter about how *she* feels?"

"No. How could I when I'm to be betrothed to someone else?" In the silence that followed, Owain felt ill at ease, unsure how his father would react. It was not that his father had imposed the betrothal on him – it had been no more than a proposal – but to break off the betrothal now gave his father every right to reproach him. "As I said," he felt obliged to say, "I know this makes things difficult for you and, yes, I understand that if I were to marry Anona, it would be no benefit to you."

"I married a clan chieftain's daughter. Many said at the time the marriage was of benefit to both me and the Clan of Eirig Mawr, but really it was personal to me because I married someone I loved. So why should I deny you marriage to someone I presume *you* love?"

"But you don't know Anona, you don't know what she's like."

"Oh! Yes, I do," said Rhydderch, putting a hand on Owain's shoulder, "I took the trouble to find out. She's a fine woman, I'm told, very much like your mother."

Owain warmed to his father: he was free to declare his intentions – but a problem remained. "What about Iorwerth? He could take this as an insult."

"That's true, he could."

"Then I'll go, speak to him, get him to understand."

Rhydderch shook his head. "We'll go together because a betrothal is a family affair and it's tied up with inheritance; that being so, Iorwerth may make demands, whereas you, you're in no position to arrive at a settlement, which is why he'll want to speak to me. Not that there'll be a settlement. He's hedged about the betrothal himself. It's as if he's got something else up his sleeve, only he can't make up his mind which is the best option." Rhydderch drew to a standstill, a thumb hooked in his belt. "And now that's settled, there's something you can do for me. What with Caleb gone and Maredudd no longer captain of guard, Owain Is-coed has his hands full, trying to keep those young men of mine in line. So I want you to take Caleb's place as the edling."

"Why, you don't think Caleb is…?"

"No – no, I accept what Rhain said, that Gruffudd ap Rhys has entrusted him with a quest that has to be kept secret. It's my guess Caleb's doing exactly what he's been taught – know your enemy, watch him, study his defences – which means he's scouting the next castle to be attacked, probably Caerfyrddin."

"Makes sense, I suppose, though I never know how you work these things out."

"Simple – you think, long and hard," said Rhydderch, prompting Owain to walk on. "Now about taking Caleb's place. Some of my young men will be difficult to say the least. Maybe we should talk about that."

"Afore we do, there's something I have to say. Tomorrow I'm to vouch for Morgan's pleading, and since that means journeying westwards, I thought I might stay at Ynys Ammon. If I were to go now, I'd have time to talk to Anona up on the terraced fields."

"Then we'll talk about it when you get back. In the meanwhile, Awst will accompany you with an escort – at least as far as the moorlands above Ynys Ammon. Then tomorrow you'll return in the company of Morgan's supporters. It'll give your mother and I less to worry about."

"It's those men, isn't it? The ones who tried to kill the soothsayer?"

"Yes, which brings me to something else that bothers me, though I'd rather you don't speak about it to your mother. It's my guess de Turberville knows all about your involvement at Abertawe. The only reason he's not summoned you to appear afore him is that he seeks to avert further trouble here, in Gower, but if the rebellion fails, as the soothsayer said, then he's likely to change his stance, which is why, when you get back, we're going to have to consider your defence – Maredudd's too, if I can get him to take it seriously."

"Maredudd reckons he'll stand a better chance in a trial by combat."

"Well, yes, he would say that, but bludgeoning someone to death is no way to settle a charge of *treis*. It has to be done by law; that's what de Turberville and I agreed to; that's why I stand surety for Maredudd. And if I know him, he's out there somewhere, practising with a mace and shield, but it'll do him no good because he's no one to teach him the skills that go with that form of combat. De Viles, on the other hand, knows every dirty trick there is; he's also as strong as an ox."

"Yes, I understand what you say. What I don't understand is why, when Maredudd has caused so much trouble, you don't hold him to account."

"Why should I? We've known one another all our lives. And if there's one thing I can count on it's Maredudd's loyalty. He's no fool either; that's why he resigned his appointment – to keep me in the clear. I tell you, things would be pretty dull around here without Maredudd."

. . . . . .

A while later, Owain rode out through the gateway in the company of Awst and six youths. As he skirted the stripped-timbered walls surrounding the court, intending to head north, he caught sight of a priest, on horseback, approaching from the south.

"That's him," said Guto, pointing. "That's the priest I saw at Abertawe. Remember when we hid in the woods? Well, I caught a glimpse of him as he rode by. He had his hood up and he rode a bay just like that one."

"Iorwerth's priest," said Owain, "come to discuss the betrothal, I shouldn't wonder."

"D'you want to turn back?" Awst asked.

"No, anything I've got to say to Iorwerth I'll say to his face, not his priest."

. . . . . .

The following day, Owain left Ynys Ammon, reflecting on Ammon's appearance. Ammon had said nothing of his fight with Maredudd, but the marks on his face confirmed what he already knew: Anona, when they met on the terraced fields the previous day, had told him about the fight, recounting how the leper had come, warning her of the harsh words that had passed between her father and a red-haired man. She had also explained that she had not been present on the *Day of Pleading* because her father had insisted that it was her place to look after the herd. Ammon had since changed his stance; Anona had his permission to witness Morgan's *Day of Judgement*. She now sat side-saddle on Owain's horse, he leading his mount by the reins. He felt content, except for one thing, and when she looked down at him, smiling, his response was half-hearted.

"Something is wrong," she said. "What is it?"

"Remember what I said about my betrothal to cousin Elinor? Well, I realize now that, when her father's priest turned up yesterdays, I should have turned back instead of riding off the way I did."

Anona bit her lip, not daring to question why he should want to extricate himself from a betrothal to someone of noble birth. The fact that he had said, '*It's not what I want*,' gave no ground for her to suppose that he *wanted* her. Much as she anticipated his company, she considered it presumptuous to assume that, because he had visited her on three separate occasions, it had anything to do with heartfelt interest in her. He had been her brother's companion; to her he had shown himself to be no more than a friend, always courteous. Perhaps it was best that she accepted the status quo so there could be no fear of having read him wrong.

When they arrived at the clearing near the hall of Caradog's father, they found Guto – who had stayed overnight at his father's homestead – was already there, along with five men from his *resting-place*. Guto joined them for a while, but when he left to rejoin his kinsmen, Owain lay down his cloak so that he and Anona could sit and talk, which was what they had both come to anticipate.

"So Morgan really has changed," said Anona.

"Surprisingly enough, yes. I thought that once he'd got over Cadog's death he'd soon revert to his old ways, but he hasn't, not in the seventeen days since Caradog filed his plaint."

"Seventeen days," she said thoughtfully. "Tell me something. Why is it, when a man is accused of something like theft, everything moves so fast?"

"Because it's a crime, and the accused must be called to account in the lifetime of the lord in whose time the crime has been committed. You see, it's a breach of my father's peace, and if my father were to die afore judgement, then there'd be an amnesty and Morgan would walk free."

"And yet that is not how it is with Maredudd."

"Well, no, Maredudd has gained two postponements, the second to recover from the injuries your father gave him. Well, those injuries were certified by a priest, which means the High Steward has accepted that he's in no condition to ride let alone make his second pilgrimage to St. David's."

"So Maredudd won't be coming here?"

"He'll be here – there's nothing wrong with him, at least not with his body."

"But what if the High Steward finds out he's ridden here?"

"That won't bother Maredudd, it's the way he is."

"You really are attached to him, aren't you?"

Owain shrugged. "From the age of seven till we were fourteen, Caleb and I were in the care of the Old One, and since he lodges with Maredudd we more or less grew up with him. He really is good company, except when he chooses to have his *little joke* as he calls it."

While he spoke, Anona noticed his attention shift to where a party of seven had entered the clearing. "That's Morgan and his supporters, isn't it?" she said, rising to her knees. "Oh! Wait till he finds out that Guto and five men from our *resting-place* are here to support him."

When the seven drew near, Anona went straight to Morgan and Banwen, welcoming them with open arms. Owain, meanwhile, singled out Maredudd, enquiring, "What happened yesterday?"

"Yesterday," said Maredudd, scratching his bandaged head. "What about yesterday?"

"You know, Iorwerth's priest."

"Oh, that! Well, they talked about this and that – usual thing."

"And?"

"I wasn't present, I just happened to be passing a window and picked up a few words here and there."

"Maredudd, if I know *you*, you went to that window to eavesdrop on everything that was said. So did my father say anything about me not wanting to wed Elinor?"

"No."

"What d'you mean *no*?"

Maredudd caught Merfyn's approach and, nudging Owain, threw out, "He doesn't look too happy. I wonder what's bothering him."

"Maredudd, you haven't answered my question."

"Question – what question?"

"Oh! The Devil take you."

Owain walked off, leaving Maredudd grinning as Merfyn drew near. "Maredudd, we have a problem. That high man – what's his name?"

"Hywel Fychan."

"Yes, well, he has changed his mind about supporting Morgan."

"Has he, now?" Maredudd caught Hywel Fychan, a short, balding man, circulating and went after him. "Hywel, my friend, a word, if I may."

Hywel spun round, pointing a finger at Maredudd. "I want no argument from you. I've already explained to the Old One that I can't vouch for Morgan."

"That's not what you said when I called on you, what, nine days ago."

"Nine days ago I sympathized because of what *you* said."

"I got the impression you just wanted to be rid of me. Now why would that be, I wonder? Could it have had something to do with that man I saw in your bed? The one you said was drunk."

Grim-face, Hywel bit back, "He's no concern of *yours*."

"No? Correct me if I'm wrong. Some years ago your sister was violated by one Iestin, at least that's what *she* claimed, only Iestin was never convicted. So your brother cut off Iestin's manhood. Nasty, that."

"So my brother acted rashly, but Iestin got what he deserved."

"That's as maybe, but your brother ran off rather than abide by law, which put him outside the law."

"Maredudd," Merfyn interposed, "what has all this to do with Morgan?"

"Patience, Old One, all will be revealed." Maredudd put a hand on Hywel's shoulder, prompting him to move out of earshot. "Now if my suspicions are correct, that was your brother in bed – means you're harbouring an outlaw. Question is, do *you* want me to forget about it?"

"Are you trying to intimidate me?"

"Call it what you like, but if I were to ride to your hall right now I could find out for myself if he's your brother or not."

"You'd be wasting your time," Hywel spat, knocking aside Maredudd's arm. "He's not there."

"I think he is. I saw a blood-stained cloth near the bed. Got himself into trouble again, has he?"

"Enough of this," Merfyn interposed. "Maredudd, you are perverting the course of law."

"Wait," said Hywel, "if I agree to verify Morgan's pleading as true...."

"Then I'll forget about the man I saw in your bed."

"Very well, consider it done."

"Good," said Maredudd, leading Hywel back towards Morgan's supporters. "It's as well you were sworn in on the first Sunday, otherwise I'd have come for you sooner."

"This is not the way it should be," said Merfyn, obstructing Maredudd's progress.

"Old One, you don't want Morgan banished for something he didn't do, do you? Well, without Hywel here, that's exactly what'll happen."

"Maredudd, if this man so much as hesitated afore…."

"He won't. Isn't that right, Hywel? Come now, accept Hywel's offer of support. We need him to represent the distaff side."

"Very well, have it your way, you usually do, anyway."

Maredudd joined Morgan's supporters, taking his place beside Owain. "You're touchy this morning."

"Yes, and you know why."

"What's the problem? You can still see Anona."

"What, when I'm betrothed to someone else?"

"You know, the reason why your father didn't speak about *you*, was that Iorwerth's priest had the unenviable task of explaining that his master had changed his mind."

"I don't understand."

"Silence, the *Rhaglaw* has risen! Whoever breaks the silence will be fined three kine!"

"Maredudd," Owain whispered, "what are you talking about?"

"*Shh*! I don't want to be fined."

"I don't care about a fine. I want to know."

"Well, it's like this," Maredudd whispered into his hand. "Iorwerth has for some time been trying to betroth Elinor to the High Steward's son – and now that he's succeeded…." Seeing a bailiff had his eye on him, Maredudd folded his arms, affecting a wide smile. He waited for the bailiff to turn away, then continued, out of the corner of his mouth, "You're like me, your services are no longer required."

CHAPTER 20

JUDGEMENT

Owain could not believe his ears. While Maredudd strolled off, he cudgelled his brain, trying to reason why Iorwerth should have changed his mind when the whole point of the betrothal was to ensure that the Lordship of Cilfái would not escheat through Elinor to a Frenchman. It only made sense if he considered de Turberville – a Breton married to a Countrywoman – as a man well disposed to Countrymen's ways. And, of course, Iorwerth would be better placed to work hand in glove with the High Steward.

In turning round he saw, less than a stone's throw away, that Maredudd now stood with Anona and Banwen. Anona waved, warming his heart, prompting him to respond, though not so as to attract attention. Disregarding Maredudd's mimicry, he mused, '*It's just you and me, Anona – if that's what you want.*' In turning again to face the court, he envisaged a more meaningful relationship with Anona, one in which he would be free to make his feelings known as an admirer, not just a friend.

Unaware that the man designated *the Judge* had taken charge of the proceedings, he failed to hear him say, "Are the compurgators here on the field?"

Rhain's sonorous reply, "They are," snatched him from his reverie.

"What is the status of these men?" *the Judge* asked. "And their kinship to the defendant?"

"All are free Countrymen, residing in this commote. Six are nod men, one of whom is a man of vows, another an officer at our lord's court; the remaining four are all high men. As to the six of lower status, one is our Lord Rhydderch's son, two are married men from Morgan's *resting-place*, and the remaining three are youths, serving in our lord's bodyguard. As to their kinship to Morgan ab Ammon, eight are from the spear side and four from the distaff side."

"Will you," said *the Judge*, addressing the twelve, "abide by what is required of you?"

"We will," the twelve replied.

"Then may God prevent you from making a false oath." *The Judge* addressed Rhain again. "Let these men parade for all to see."

"Iago Du," said Rhain aloud, "a high man, sworn to abstain from women, horses and fine linen. His kinship to Morgan is on the distaff side."

As Iago, a dark-skinned, unshaven man with curly hair, stepped forward, Caradog called out, "God knows you are a peace-breaker and, if you deny it, I have enough supporters to swear that it is so."

"Why would I deny it?" Iago bit back. "You can't fault me for my past."

"That's as maybe, but I say you're here out of enmity towards me and my kinsmen, your peace-breaking ways were always directed at us."

"There *is* no enmity in me, and I can call upon compurgators of my own who'll swear to it, as many and as good as you'll ever call upon to say otherwise." Iago stared, grim-faced, awaiting a response. "Well," he demanded, "are you faulting me for enmity or not?"

Caradog sneered, dismissing Iago with a gesture; whereupon Iago approached the *Rhaglaw's* priest, then looked towards *the Judge*, who asked him, "What say you of Morgan's pleading – do you believe it to be true or false?"

"In the name of God," said Iago, kissing the remains of St. Teilo's staff, "I stand unbidden and unbought, without enmity, and do solemnly swear that I consider Morgan's pleading to be true."

The next man to be called, Owain Is-coed, Maredudd's doorward, found himself challenged for want of relationship to Morgan; whereupon he recited his lineage to one of his four great-grandfathers and was, therefore, able to establish his relationship to Morgan on the spear side through a common ancestor. He then found himself challenged for being a *yes-man*, only too willing to do Maredudd's bidding, in response to which he denied that he had come at anyone's bidding other than Morgan's. After supporting Morgan's denial as true, he was followed by Hywel Fychan, who approached the *Rhaglaw's* priest unchallenged. Two high men from Morgan's *resting-place* also paraded unchallenged. Then Guto's father, Cadwgan, stepped forward.

"You're here out of enmity," Caradog spat, "because you've a grievance against me, one you've harboured for the last two years, ever since you lost that land suit you brought against me."

"Not so," replied Cadwgan. "I gave sureties to abide by law, and if you've cause to complain, then I demand that you declare it."

Caradog curled his lip, dismissing Cadwgan, an act that should have been encouraging. Yet Banwen remained unsure as to whether everything was proceeding in Morgan's favour. Maredudd had told her that as none of the twelve could be faulted for being foreigners, clerics or for want of relationship to Morgan there was nothing for her to worry about – but worry she did, for not only had Caradog's venom unsettled her, but it was plain that he was trying to vex the compurgators, claiming two of them were here out of enmity towards him. '*What will happen,*' she wondered, '*if someone gets angry?*'

She stared at Morgan's back. He stood tall, and although at home he still had a rough side to his tongue, his manner towards her had definitely improved, the change having become more noticeable over the past few days due, she suspected, to Maredudd's involvement. Several times Maredudd had taken Morgan with him when riding about the countryside. Each time they had returned, Morgan had spoken at length of a man who showed more interest in him than his own father ever had.

Her gaze drifted to the hilt of Maredudd's sword. She wished that Maredudd would put an end to the proceedings – draw his blade and drive Caradog and his supporters from the field. She had no sooner dismissed the thought as futile than she became aware that a man from Morgan's *resting-place* had approached the *Rhaglaw's* priest unchallenged. Moments later another man stepped forward, a married man in his twenties, whom she knew as Arwel, Guto's elder brother.

"You," Caradog spat, "you, above all others, have a grievance against me on account of your wife, who claimed that I tried to violate her, only it was never proved."

"My wife agreed to abide by law," Arwel bit back, "and I supported her in that."

"That's as maybe," Caradog countered while his brother threw out phlegm, "but it's well known you've cursed me ever since."

"No more than I'd curse anyone else who's crossed me. It comes from being hot-tempered."

"Hot-tempered! Na, out of the abundance of a man's heart so his mouth speaks."

"In moments of anger we all make threats, but when that anger cools...." Arwel paused, taking a deep breath in order to suppress his growing anger.

"Yes, yes, say it," Caradog goaded him, "when that anger cools, he what – broods?"

"No! For some that may be so, but for others, when they've had time to reflect, they put it all behind them. They don't go around, burning and killing."

"Never said you did. It's all in your head, an unresolved insult to your wife's honour."

"It's no such thing!"

"I say it is. I say you hate me. I say you're here out of enmity."

"Then prove what you say. State the harm I've done you in the last three years."

Caradog ground his teeth. "Go," he said contemptuously, "take the oath."

Rhain called Morgan's cousin, Elidir, next and, as he came forward, so Owain wondered about Guto, the least experienced in court proceedings. Caradog had tried to fault both Guto's father and brother on grounds of enmity. The question now was whether Guto would be provoked into displaying ill-will: he had several times declared that he would be faulted for enmity because of the derogatory remarks that he had expressed in public about Caradog and his despicable brother, Gronw.

Once Elidir had taken the oath, Rhain called upon Dewi to parade. Dewi went unchallenged, but while he took the oath, Owain sensed Guto's nervousness. It had been agreed that he would parade last, so as to bolster Guto's confidence. "Remember," he whispered to Guto, "don't let him vex you."

"No," Guto whispered in response, "I can't do it."

"Yes, you can. Your father and your brother did it. So can you."

"Guto the Fat," Rhain called out. "His kinship to Morgan is on the spear side."

Startled, Guto stumbled forward to pause, expecting to be challenged, but Caradog said nothing; it was as if he had resigned himself to defeat. Guto looked to Owain who quietly waved him forward. While Guto took the oath, Owain considered Caradog's piggish face, noting the deep lines about his mouth, the result of a set jaw. He was thinking, '*You've lost and you know it*,' when he caught Gronw spitting in his direction.

"Owain ap Rhydderch, our Lord Rhydderch's youngest son! His kinship to Morgan is on the distaff side!"

Owain advanced, his cocky deportment intended to provoke a challenge, but Caradog did no more than match his gaze. As he kissed the remains of a staff realization struck him: soon he might be on trial himself for his part in rebellion. For a moment he felt vulnerable. Then he made his declaration, loud for all to hear. "In the name of God, I stand here, unbidden and unbought, without enmity, and do solemnly swear that I consider Morgan's pleading to be true."

The judges had no sooner retired to deliberate than Owain noticed that Caradog's supporters were in a sullen mood, whereas Morgan's supporters were buoyant, some going so far as to shake Morgan's hand. Owain held back, not caring to involve himself with someone he still disliked. Maredudd, meanwhile, had approached Iago Du and, while the two men shook hands, Owain edged closer to eavesdrop on their conversation, at which point Iago was sidetracked by two other men.

"About Iago," said Owain, "what did he mean by *any time, Maredudd, I owe you*?"

"A long story," Maredudd returned. "It wouldn't interest you."

"No? I've heard it said that Iago's beholden to you – goes back to the days when he was convicted of arson. What did you do – pay for his redemption?"

Maredudd glanced around, then led Owain away from the crowd. "Now where would I find seven pounds to pay for anyone's redemption?"

"Huh! Next to my father you must be the wealthiest man in the commote."

"Now perhaps, not ten years ago."

"Don't lie, you inherited a great deal from your father."

"If I did, I still wouldn't squander my inheritance."

"I didn't say you'd squandered anything, only that you paid for Iago's redemption, which explains why you've had a hold on him ever since."

"Well, thank you, it's nice to know you've such a low opinion of me."

"What d'you expect? You're devious, aren't you?"

Maredudd caught Owain by the ear, leading him further away from the crowd. "Let me enlighten you somewhat. If Iago had been a little less troublesome, I dare say his kinsmen would have supported his denial, same as Morgan was supported back there, but they didn't because they'd had enough of his troublesome ways, and being accused of setting fire to someone's barn was one trouble too many. You see, Caradog over there has a kinsman named Gruffudd Goch, and when Gruffudd's barn went up in smoke, it was Iago who got the blame for it. Well, it so happens Iago was able to raise nigh on six pounds towards his redemption, but what he couldn't do was raise another pound; nor could he compensate Gruffudd for the damage done. I tell you, once Gruffudd realized that he wouldn't be compensated for his barn he was furious. So were his kinsmen."

"For St. Teilo's sake, Maredudd, let go my ear."

"Not till I've finished. Now I'm not saying that Iago's inability to pay would have led to a feud, but things were pretty unpleasant between Gruffudd's clan and our own, and that at a time when the French were expected to come marching in. I tell you, there's not many of Gruffudd's kinsmen residing in this commote, but there's a lot of them in the neighbouring Commote of Carnwyllion, which is where many of Caradog's supporters have come from. Anyway, last thing anyone wanted was discord between our own kind. So I put it to your father that, if we covered the shortfall, or at lease gave the money to Iago, then everything would be resolved."

Owain broke free, his ear reddening. "I don't believe you. My father wouldn't have had anything to do with that."

"Ah! But he did. You see, just afore the French came, your father had enough to contend with, trying to get the men of Uwch-coed to fight his way; more than that, he was trying to get the men of Carnwyllion to join him. I tell you, the last thing your father wanted was more upset. So he agreed to go half with the shortfall. Aye, and not only that, we both put Iago back on his feet when the fighting was done. You, see, Iago gave a good account of himself, always in the forefront when it came to a fight. Look at him now – gets on with his life, rearing sheep, grazing them on everyone else's land, so their little black balls nourishes the fields. Done well for himself, he has – got the biggest flock this side of the Lwch Dwr."

"I'm surprised you didn't do it yourself."

"Na, I wouldn't be interested in sheep, but Iago – well, he's sworn to abstain from women. So it keeps him out of trouble. Now *you*, you owe me an apology."

"You won't get one."

"No? I think maybe I should have a word with Anona – tell her a few tales that you'd rather were left unsaid."

Maredudd had no sooner set off towards Anona than Owain caught his arm. "Wait, I take it back, I apologize."

"Should think so too." Maredudd made as if to cuff Owain's ear, then walked off, calling back, "And don't you go, repeating anything I've just said."

Anona approached Owain, looking perplexed. "What was all that about? And why was Maredudd pulling your ear?"

"It's his way of ensuring that no youth gets the better of him. I tell you, Anona, he's a miscreant."

"Surely not. I mean, it's down to him that my brother got his twelve compurgators, and if the judges rule in his favour, he's sure to walk free."

"He'll walk free, you can count on it, and it won't be a two-thirds majority of judges who'll rule in his favour. The ruling will be unanimous."

"You really think so?"

"Yes. Look – they've done with their deliberation, and so soon. It's a good sign." Owain clasped Anona's hand. "I'll have to go."

Somewhat bemused, she warmed to his touch. '*He's never done that afore,*' she mused, following his departure. '*What am I to make of it?*'

On his return *the Judge* called upon Caradog to name two sureties who would see to it that, after judgement had been passed, he would abide by law. When the names of the sureties had been given, *the Judge* reminded the two sureties that, as Caradog had been the one to file the plaint, they were liable to pay the judges' fee of twenty-four pence, should Caradog fail to do so. *The Judge* then addressed Morgan.

"Defendant, who are your sureties to abide by law?"

Rhain answered, on Morgan's behalf, "Maredudd Goch, a high man, and Merfyn Hen, our Lord Rhydderch's bard, both of whom are on the field."

"Then let it be known that we, the judges, have deliberated on the oaths of the twelve compurgators. We have, therefore, to a man, decided, according to the Laws of Hywel Dda, in favour of the defendant. Morgan ab Ammon, you are free to go."

CHAPTER 21

CARADOG'S WIFE

The verdict caused a stir among Morgan's supporters, almost all of them thronging Morgan to congratulate him. Owain alone held back, although he did embrace Anona as she made to join the throng – after which his attention centred on the opposition. A mood of despondency had taken hold of Caradog's supporters. Caradog looked on, grim faced, while his brother sneered and threw out phlegm.

"Away with you, get away from here!"

Owain turned to witness a bailiff shouting at a leper. "Anona," the leper croaked, "I must speak to Anona."

Owain hurried towards Morgan's supporters, shouting, "Anona, it's Ceredig, he wants to speak to you." As he led her from the throng he saw the bailiff hurl a stone, causing the leper to raise an arm before the missile struck him. "Idnerth," Owain shouted, "let him be."

"What, and have him corrupt us all with his bloody sores?"

"Calm yourself, Idnerth," Maredudd shouted. "Let the leper speak."

"Anona," Ceredig croaked, "for days I've been watching Caradog's hall and there's times when his wife goes into the woods over there. I've not gone there myself for fear of the dogs and – maybe I'm foolish, but I have my suspicions. Come, bring your companions and I'll show you where."

Anona followed Ceredig at a distance, as did Owain, Maredudd and those nearby. Close to the tree-line, Ceredig's approach was barred by a woman holding a stick. At her side a greyhound growled, baring its teeth. "Get away from here, leper," the woman cried, "or so help me, I'll hit you."

"Stand aside, Tanwen," said Maredudd. "Let the leper pass."

"No," Tanwen retorted, raising her stick, "this is my father-in-law's land; now clear off, all of you." She advanced threateningly, inciting the greyhound to dart towards Ceredig. Owain directed his deer-hound to attack. The two dogs met, snapping and snarling until, yelping, the greyhound ran off, its tail between its legs.

Caradog arrived on the scene, grabbing Maredudd's arm. Maredudd shook free, then directed the bony base of his hand at his opponent's face. Caradog staggered back, his nose bleeding. Maredudd drew his sword, directing the point at Caradog's neck. "The spear," Maredudd spat, his blade touching Caradog's throat, "drop it."

Tanwen called the names of kinsmen, screeching, "look what that son of bitch is doing to my husband. Stop him. Gronw, Gronw, get this leper away from me."

"Gronw," Caradog rasped, "get the leper. You're not answerable for what you do to someone who's already dead."

Acting on his brother's words, Gronw rushed forward, intending to spear Ceredig. As he drew level with Morgan's supporters, Owain directed a foot between his legs so that he pitched forward, falling to his knees. Owain sprang, intending to disarm him, but Gronw quickly regained himself and, drawing his skene, he lashed out, his blade arcing dangerously close to Owain's face. Owain recoiled, unsure whether Gronw intended to harm or frighten him – in either event he was in no position to counter Gronw's blade as it arced left and right before his very eyes.

Then Morgan leapt on Gronw's back, trying to gain a hold on his opponent's wrist, time for Owain to direct a foot at Gronw's groin, exactly as Maredudd instilled in him with the words '*You don't take chances with an armed man.*' Gronw agonized, his mouth open, at which point Morgan brought him to the ground. Even then Gronw still managed to ply his skene. Owain trod on Gronw's wrist, knelt and removed the blade from his grasp. In doing so he met Morgan's gaze.

Someone grabbed Morgan from behind, hauling him to his feet. "That's enough," spat Cingualan the Bald, the accepted leader of Gronw's *resting-place*, "or we'll end up with a free for all. Gronw, cool your heels. D'you hear me?" Cingualan made towards Maredudd, shouting, "Put up your sword and let my kinsman free."

"Ah! Cingualan," Maredudd returned, veiling his sword, "good of you to join us. Caradog, here, he's got something to show us in them woods."

"There's nothing in them woods," Caradog countered, "nothing but traps, you troublesome bastard."

"Well, I hope they're marked," said Maredudd, "because you're going in there first."

"He's going nowhere," Cingualan growled, moving closer. "And you, you're going to pay him his honour price for what you've done."

"Provocation," said Maredudd. "He grabbed my arm. And now, gentlemen, if you'll excuse me, I'm going to walk over to them woods."

"Stay where you are, I want a word with you!"

Maredudd turned to witness the approach of his clan chieftain, Rhodri Gadno, a thick-set, hoary man in his late fifties. "You," said Rhodri, his pockmarked face as baleful as it could be, "you were trouble enough as captain of guard; now you're ten times worse; now sheathe that sword."

"As you wish," said Maredudd, sheathing his blade. When he looked up he glimpsed the leper, a forlorn figure, apparently resigned to the fact that he could no longer pursue his intention. "Gentlemen, I've done as you wished; now hear me out. The leper claims there's something we should know about in them woods. Me, I'm quite prepared to pay Caradog his honour price; I'll even overlook Tanwen's tongue wound against my dead mother, but first I want them woods searched. If there's nothing there, then we can all go home. What say you, Caradog?"

"Go to hell! You're not sidetracking me with your talk, you damn peace-breaker."

Maredudd looked past Caradog, catching the eye of his doorward, Owain Is-coed, to whom he jerked his head in the direction of the woods.

"I saw that," said Cingualan the Bald.

"Saw what?"

"You nodding."

"You mean like this," said Maredudd, directing his gaze at two men from Morgan's *resting-place*, both of whom also made for the woods.

"Caradog, Gronw, Cingualan," Tanwen screamed, "Look, those men, they're making for the woods. Stop them."

Caradog bent to pick up his spear. Maredudd trod on the shaft. "Leave it, if you know what's good for you."

Caradog uttered a string of insults mingled with foul language. Rhodri Gadno expressed displeasure in no uncertain terms. Cingualan the Bald voiced his objection, as did several of his kinsmen, whereas Tanwen, exasperated by a lack of action, exclaimed, "Agh! You men, you're bloody useless." She rushed at Owain Is-coed, swinging her stick with such ferocity that he had to retreat, parrying her stick with his spear shaft.

"I think, Cingualan," said Maredudd, "you'd best do something about Tanwen, or we'll end up with a free for all like you said."

Cingualan the Bald glowered at Maredudd before moving off to restrain Tanwen, who had just switched her attack to one of Morgan's kinsmen. Amid a torrent of foul language and the clatter of a stick striking a spear shaft, Cingualan bellowed, "The stick, woman, give it to me." An instant later, Tanwen swung at him, striking him on the shoulder. He grabbed the stick and had no sooner wrenched it from her grasp than she clawed at his bald head. Most men laughed at Cingualan's misfortune, but the bald one's kinsmen were outraged to the extent that it led to a heated exchange with Morgan's supporters.

"See what you've done," Rhodri Gadno ground out, jabbing a finger close to Maredudd's face. "And you, you're supposed to be suffering from delirium and cracked ribs."

"Never mind his ribs," Cingualan cut in as he approached, stick in hand. "Look what that bloody woman did to my head."

"Could have been worse," Maredudd threw out. "If you'd had hair, she'd have pulled it out."

"This is no laughing matter," Rhodri Gadno ground out, "it won't be when you start counting the cost – Caradog's honour price, bloodying his nose, peace-breaking, Cingualan's head…."

"You're missing the pith of all this," Maredudd interposed. "Why d'you think Tanwen is so determined to stop anyone entering them woods?"

"I told you," Caradog spat, "there's nothing in there but traps." He directed a finger at Maredudd. "As for you, you bastard, I'm going in there myself and don't try to stop me."

"That's exactly what I want you to do," said Maredudd. "Now move."

Caradog led off, followed by Maredudd who was himself flanked by Rhodri Gadno and Cingualan the Bald. "A waste of time," Cingualan remarked, "but at lease it shows Caradog's willingness to comply with what you want."

"He hasn't got much choice," Maredudd returned, "not when there's upwards of a dozen men heading for them woods. Me, I'd say he's only going there to obstruct." Raising an arm, he signalled to Owain to deter Morgan from entering the woods.

"Maredudd doesn't want you involved," said Owain, his hand closing on Morgan's arm. Morgan gave Owain a look that made it plain he did not take kindly to being manhandled. '*If you can't get some youth to do what you want,*' Owain recalled Maredudd saying, '*then sidetrack him.*' Owain relinquished his grip, saying, as he offered a hand in friendship, "I'm beholden to you for what you did back there. If you hadn't jumped on Gronw's back, he would have had me."

Slow to respond, Morgan gripped Owain's forearm. "I'm beholden to you, too, for supporting my pleading."

Banwen beamed; Anona was so pleased that she hugged Owain's arm – but one woman, Tanwen, bustled about the woods, shouting at men, her language atrocious – far worse than the dismissive retorts of those preoccupied in locating and springing traps, scuffing through dead leaves, searching the crevices of trees. When a youth knelt to probe between exposed roots, Tanwen fell upon him, dragging him away by the hair. Several men moved to restrain her; one of them quickly disengaged to hop about, clutching his manhood.

Then Caradog charged in support of his wife, grabbing a man by the tunic, hauling him back, only to reverse into Maredudd, who propelled him towards thickets where he lost balance, collapsing amongst offshoots. Maredudd's right hand closed over his sword hilt; almost immediately both Rhodri and Cingualan prevented him from withdrawing the blade. At the same time, Caradog's kinsman, Gruffudd Goch, took up a defensive stance over his fallen relative, spear at the ready. A heated exchange followed, one in which Maredudd alone remained calm.

Another altercation took place only a few paces away, one in which Tanwen was beside herself with rage, her screechy voice drowning out much of what was exchanged. Then Owain Is-coed rose from where a youth had been grubbing until Tanwen had dragged him away. In his hands Owain Is-coed held a bundle of cloth, which he proceeded to unravel. "Look at this," he exclaimed. "Jewellery – and coins, lots of them. Maredudd, here, take a look at this."

"So who does the jewellery belong to?" Rhodri Gadno demanded.

"Tanwen," Cingualan the Bald volunteered, and turning to Caradog, "Damn you! You've brought shame on your kin. You've lied, you've committed perjury, and I'll see you rot in hell afore you get any support from me."

"Now hold on," Caradog countered as he struggled to his feet. "You've got no right to assume that I hid the jewellery."

"Then who did?" Cingualan the Bald demanded.

"I dunno. Morgan, I suppose. Maybe he intended to come back for it later."

"And what about the coins?" Cingualan asked. "You said nothing of them."

"They're not mine, they gotta be Morgan's. He must have picked them up at Abertawe."

"That doesn't explain," said Maredudd, "why you and Tanwen made such a fuss about keeping everyone out of these woods. Seems to me, you both knew what was here."

"Not true," Caradog bit back. "Gruffudd, have I ever said anything to you about coins?"

"Don't bring me into this," Gruffudd Goch retorted. "I stood by you, I did so because we're of kin, but I can see now you misled me into believing that Morgan is a thief."

"Looks like you're on your own, Caradog," said Maredudd, "and since you say the coins are not yours, the *Rhaglaw* can claim them as the treasure trove of Lord Rhydderch."

"I'll take the jewellery too," said the *Rhaglaw*, making his presence known. "As for you, Caradog, you've got three days to procure sureties and prepare your defence against making a false accusation."

Grim-faced, Caradog stared, the scar above his left eye twitching. "You stupid bitch," he said to Tanwen.

"Don't you call me stupid. I'll tear you bloody eyes out." Tanwen sprang, taking Caradog by surprise. The ferocity of her attack was such that, when he tried to restrain her, she still kicked and clawed until several kinsmen hustled her away.

In the clearing, Banwen had been listening to the commotion that reigned within the woods. Unsettling though the raised voices were, she still felt elated, knowing that Morgan had won his cause – and more, beyond her wildest dreams, Maredudd had used his sword to drive Caradog and his supporters from the field. She focused on the leper, who stood some distance away, wondering why he should have led everyone to the woods. Then a youth came out from among the trees, shouting. "We've found the jewellery. Caradog was lying from the start."

Morgan spun round, staring at Banwen. "You hear that?" he said, his face enlivened by the revelation. "No one can call me a thief now."

"I never did," said Banwen.

"No – no, you stood by me. If it wasn't for you, I'd have been banished. And that's what Caradog can expect now that he's been found out. Isn't that right, Old One?"

"Yes, if it can be established that he hid the jewellery. Then he can expect whatever punishment would have been awarded to you. Aye, and I dare say the Church will proceed against him for perjury"

"Gronw and Tanwen," said Banwen, "what about them?"

"Nothing," the Old One replied. "Gronw made no false accusations, so no action can be taken against him unless, of course, Owain wishes to file a plaint for the knife attack, though Gronw will no doubt claim he was provoked. As to Tanwen, it will be said she acted while under her husband's domination. I tell you, the brothers are from a bad lineage. Their father was a vindictive man. Aye, and their father's brother was once a priest until defrocked for something unpleasant. Then the wretched man came back here, only to die a few years later. I heard it said that his old cassock still hangs from a peg in that hall yonder, though why anyone would want to keep that in memory of a miscreant is beyond me."

CHAPTER 22

REVELATIONS

"Now there's a man who'll tire himself out thinking." Maredudd threw out as entered the hall in the company of Rhydderch's steward, Sulien. He approached a table. "So what's on your mind now?"

Rhydderch straighten up in a chair. "Caleb," he replied, "been gone four weeks and still no word from him."

"I reckon Rhain will get lucky this time," said Maredudd, taking a chair opposite his foster brother. "So why this council?"

"We've a few things to thrash out, they concern *you* and they're long overdue."

A grin distorted Maredudd's beard; he looked at Sulien who was about to join him at the table.

"What's the joke?" Rhydderch asked.

"You tell him, Sulien."

"They've found Caradog's horse, grazing on the moorland above Ynys Ammon, and there was blood on the saddle. Looks suspicious – explains why he didn't turn up at the *Rhaglaw*'s court yesterday."

"Na," Maredudd laughed, "Caradog has absconded and it's good riddance, I say."

"You would," said Sulien, "you don't have to pay his honour price now, nor pay him for bloodying his nose."

Maredudd considered Rhydderch. "Looks like I'm in the clear again."

"You breached my peace," said Rhydderch. "I could have you fined twelve kine."

"You wouldn't do that – not to me."

"Don't count on it. And like I said, you shouldn't have attended Morgan's trial. You're supposed to be suffering from delirium and cracked ribs, which means you can't ride anywhere."

While Rhydderch spoke, Maredudd pulled out his skene; with a piece of whetstone he began sharpening the blade, saying, "Yes, yes, so what's the problem?"

"*You*. It's likely that by now de Turberville knows about the affray. So, tomorrow, you go on your second pilgrimage – and take your time,

Maredudd. I don't want you back too soon, not like the last occasion."

"What, don't you want me here for Easter?"

"No, you'll cause too much trouble and, furthermore, you don't do as you're told."

"I'm not one of your officers, remember? I'm free to do as I like."

"Wrong. I stand surety for you and it's time you gave thought to your defence."

"Hah! My only defence is to object to de Viles assuming the role of plaintiff."

"Yes," said Sulien, "but if de Londres were to return, you wouldn't be able to object to *him* as the plaintiff, not when it was *his* castle you burnt."

"Doesn't change anything. I've no defence against the men who saw me at Ystum Llymarch, and who'll no doubt testify to seeing me lord it over others."

"You'll still have to appear at court," said Sulien, "otherwise de Turberville will take action against us."

"Oh! I see. I get tried and hanged so you don't fall foul with de Turberville. That's good, I like that – I don't think." Maredudd paused, running his thumb over his blade, then continued to sharpen it, saying, "Na, a trial by combat, it's the only way, and you both know it. All I got to do is hit de Viles on the head and he's dead."

"And you can do that, can you?" said Rhydderch. "Without practice?"

"Who needs practice?"

"*You.* I know all about you, sloping off with Owain Is-coed."

Maredudd looked askance at Sulien, who blurted out, "Don't look at me, I've said nothing."

"Two maces," said Rhydderch, "two helmets and two French shields, all missing from the armoury. Need I say more?"

"So I practise a little, no harm in that."

"Except that Owain Is-coed doesn't have the same proficiency as de Viles."

"My lord," said Rhydderch's doorward, striking his staff of office, "your brother-in-law, Rhain ap Rhodri, has returned from his travels and is anxious to speak to you."

Rhain had no sooner entered than he approached the table, saying, in French, *"I've found Caleb, he's alive and well and sends his regards. Same goes for my brother and young Tewdrig."*

"There, what did I tell you?" said Maredudd. "That should make life easier for you and me where Gwenllian is concerned."

"Somehow I don't think so," said Rhydderch. He waited for his brother-in-law to be seated, then said, in French, *"So where has my son been all this time?"*

"Caerfyrddin," said Rhain, his voice barely audible. *"He and his two companions went there, posing as drovers, selling cattle."*

"Stolen cattle, were they?" Maredudd asked.

"Probably – *and after they'd sold out they stayed in the town, making out* Tewdrig *was sick, when really they were there to discover how best to breach the castle. Now I didn't know about this till yesterday. You see, I went straight to* Gruffudd ap Rhys's *camp, only he wasn't there. So his wife told me that, if I wanted answers, then I should go to* Caerfyrddin, *and that's what I was about when I ran into* Gruffudd *and his rebels,* Caleb *among them. And do you know what? They'd burnt* Caerfyrddin, *both the town and the bailey.*"

Maredudd laughed. "Caerfyrddin *belongs to the King; he's not going to like that.*"

"*He'll like it even less when he finds out that the only man killed was the one who had charge of its keeping.*" Rhain paused, regarding Rhydderch. "You're kinsman, Lord Owain of Gwynllwg – I regret having to tell you this – he's dead."

Rhydderch nodded, his expression showing no sign of remorse for a kinsman who, like Iorwerth, collaborated with the French. "So," he said, thinking aloud, "*we have four lords, each keeping the castle for two weeks at a time, and the attack took place when* Lord Owain *had custody. Was that* Caleb's *doing?*"

Rhain nodded. "*He said they'd struck up a rapport with some of* Owain's *men while drinking in a tavern. Seems the men had a grievance against* Owain, *something to do with him being hostile towards* Gruffudd ap Rhys *and – well, the attack took place at night and, like I said, the only man to get killed was* Owain. *His men deserted him, left him in the bailey, while they took refuge in the tower.*"

While Rhain spoke, Maredudd sliced a sliver from the edge of the table, an act that did not go unnoticed by Rhydderch, who met Maredudd's gaze.

"*Seems to me,*" said Maredudd, grinning, "Caleb *has done well for himself. You should be proud of him.*"

Rhydderch continued to stare. "*So he's proved himself less of a hothead than I would have thought. Trouble is, an attack like that means he'll stay with* Gruffudd ap Rhys. *Am I right, Rhain?*"

"I'm afraid so – and there's something else. Gruffudd ap Rhys *told me to tell you, his invitation to join him still stands.*"

Rhydderch wried a smile. "*The rebellion is doomed, the soothsayer said so; that's good enough for me, even if I don't like it.*"

"Come now," said Maredudd, "*it's doomed because you won't take up arms. Aye, and what's more we're not going to get another chance like this. The King is in France, we know that – probably been gone two weeks or more.*"

"Do you think I don't wrestle with that?" said Rhydderch. "I know what the situation is, I know what'll happen if it all goes wrong."

"Yes, but the alternative is to go on accepting things as they are."

"It may be, but my instinct says *no*."

Maredudd embedded his blade in the table, leaned forward and said, "And mine says *yes* – though why I came back here to help you I don't know."

"Help me! You're never here half the time."

"Yes, well, I've been busy," said Maredudd, wrenching his blade from the table. "And it won't be long afore I can tell you who the informer is."

"Is that so?" said Rhydderch.

"Yes, I've been around, asking questions, keeping my eyes open, and I find there's quite a few suspects, all of whom have strong links. First, there's our inquisitive blacksmith. Now Bledri's brother is a priest, right? And on the night the bards were here, Bledri sloped off because his priestly brother was supposed to be sick."

"Now hold on, Maredudd," said Sulien. "Bledri's brother was at death's door. I know that for sure because...."

"Wait, let me finish. If Bledri was at St. Teilo's Church, then he should have been the first to see Gruffudd's rebels cross the nearby ford – but does he inform us? No, he says that, because he'd been up all night, he fell asleep and didn't see anything."

"And you're saying he did," said Sulien, "and went off to warn the garrison."

"Wearing his sick brother's cassock, no doubt," said Rhain.

"No, Bledri is a good man," Sulien countered. "He wouldn't do that, and from the description you gave us, Maredudd, I'd say the priest who warned the garrison was Iorwerth's."

"Yes, but if it was Iorwerth's priest," Maredudd countered, "he could only be a messenger for the simple reason that he is in no position to know what goes on here. So let's forget about Iorwerth's priest and consider Caradog, Tanwen and Gronw. Now the day the bards arrived here, Tanwen was at St. Teilo's Church, tending to her sick brother, the priest, and not only was she there, but Gronw was there too. Then later, when the bards were at play, Tanwen sends Gronw here to tell our blacksmith that his priestly brother is sick. So off goes Bledri and he knowing that the bards were the harbingers of Gruffudd ap Rhys. Now it's my guess Bledri told Gronw all he knew about the bards, and what does Gronw do after he arrives back at the church? He goes home to tell his brother all that he's heard. Then Caradog turns up at the church to question Bledri for more information. Then Caradog rides off to warn the garrison, only he's not wearing the sick priest's cassock. No, if you remember, his father's brother had been a priest until he was defrocked, right? Aye, and that brother came home only to die a few years later. So it's my guess Caradog has been wearing his uncle's old cassock each and every time he had something to pass on to de Viles. And that, gentlemen, would account for all them coins we found with Tanwen's jewellery."

"So what about Bledri, Gronw and Tanwen?" Rhain asked. "What exactly is their part in all this?"

"They're all in it together," Maredudd replied, slicing a large sliver from the edge of the table. "Now what d'you think of that, eh?"

You've got imagination as well as gall," said Rhydderch, "and I'll remind you that Gwenllian hasn't forgotten what you said about her priest."

"What, Piro," said Sulien. "Surely you don't suspect him?"

"Consider this," said Maredudd, tapping the side of his nose. "On the day the bards arrived her, Piro was in retreat at St. Cyfelach's Monastery, right? But it seems he was never there half the time. In fact, the day afore the attack he missed one prayer service and was late for another."

"Yes, but we all know," said Sulien, "Piro has a habit of wandering about in woods. It's his way of getting close to God."

"That's as maybe, but to have missed one prayer service and be late for another, that's not like him. And d'you know what he said when I questioned him about it? He said he hadn't realized how long he'd been wandering about because he'd been wrestling with his conscience. Now why would he be doing that, eh? Was it to do with them Saxons who were at risk at Abertawe? I mean, he did know the castle was about to be attacked – Huw ran into him on his way to inform me that Caleb had gone missing. Then, when Huw found me, along comes this priest to warn the garrison."

"Ah! Come now, Maredudd," said Sulien, "you're talking about a man who's been faithful to this household for, what, fifteen years?"

"To the extent," said Rhydderch, "that I consider him trustworthy enough to be a member of my inner council."

"All I'm saying is – well, you know how Piro is about Saxons."

"Na," said Sulien, "I know what you're thinking, Maredudd, but Piro's concern for Saxons is stretching it bit far."

"I agree," said Rhydderch, "the whole idea is absurd."

Rhain had, by then, perceived that his company knew something about Piro that he did not. "What's absurd?" he asked, eyeing everyone in turn. "And why should Piro be concerned about Saxons?"

Maredudd looked Rhydderch in the eye. "Do we tell him?"

"You tell him, only make sure it's the truth."

"*Don't go, repeating this,*" Maredudd said in French, "*but* Piro *is a* Saxon *by birth.*"

Rhain looked about, suspicious that those present were amusing themselves at his expense. "Maredudd, is this another of your *tales*? Everyone knows that Darren is Piro's father – his foster father, anyway."

"His foster father, yes, and everyone knows that Darren was footloose for years." Maredudd lowered the tone of his voice, saying, "Well, he hadn't gone wandering long when he took part in a raid on some Saxon village. Piro's parents were among those killed, and Piro, who was only a child at the time – well, Darren found him in the surrounding fields and didn't have the heart to kill him. So he decided to sell him as a slave, only he was a bit slow in getting round to doing that – so slow that he got attached to him. Then, when Darren finally came home, he declared he had fostered a son and that his name was Piro. No one suspected that Piro was a Saxon because he'd been brought up in the care of a slave, and she a Countrywoman. So he was able to speak our tongue. Well, don't look so suspicious, what I've said is true."

"That's right, it is," said Sulien. "You remember how, at Death's Acres, Piro nearly got himself killed, trying to save that Saxon rearguard? Well, now you know why."

Still wary, Rhain turned to Rhydderch. "Does Gwenllian know about this?"

"Yes, Piro told her the day she asked him to be her priest. Then, when she told me, I saw no reason to object. I knew Piro – we'd served together in Lord Rhys's retinue. Maredudd and I used to give him hell for his godly ways. Then he left Rhys's retinue afore we did and became a priest."

"What we don't know," said Maredudd, "is whether Piro is still a Saxon at heart, and if he is – well, there's many a Saxon at Abertawe. Could be, he took it upon himself to save them like he did that rearguard."

"Na," said Sulien, "if Piro had done that, he'd have said so rather than live a lie."

"I agree," said Rhydderch. "The thought of him doing anything behind my back is absurd."

Maredudd leaned back in his chair, grinning. Then in walked Piro. "Talk of the devil," Maredudd muttered.

Fair-skinned and sombre in his appearance, Piro approached the table, throwing back the hood of his grey cassock to reveal the tonsure of a Countryman priest: his forehead tonsured to a line extending from ear to ear, beyond which his flaxen hair fell to the back of his neck. "I apologize for being late, my lord, some small matter that I had to attend to."

Piro sat down, acknowledging Rhain, then cast his eye upon all four men in turn. Rhydderch cleared his throat, Sulien shifted uneasily in his chair, Maredudd looked up at the roof and Rhain quaffed ale. "I don't know why," said Piro, "but I've a feeling someone's been talking about me."

"We were just discussing," said Rhydderch, "who the informer might be."

"I trust no one suspects me."

"There's none of us here would dream of it," said Maredudd. "I wouldn't, anyway."

Piro frowned. "In my opinion the informer is no priest, but someone with a grudge against you, Maredudd, for your aggravating ways."

"That could be anyone," said Sulien.

"Or it could be Ammon," said Maredudd.

Sulien laughed, "Can you image Ammon in a cassock? You'd still recognize him by his shear size."

"That's as maybe," said Maredudd, "but he could still pass on information, he knows a lot about what goes on here." He fixed his gaze on Rhydderch. "That's because you still take him into your confidence, and you use him as a messenger whenever it suits. It was you who sent him to Hereford to find out if the priest who taught us all to speak French was still alive. '*Dead*,' Ammon said, and we've only got his word for that."

"If Ammon can't be trusted," Rhydderch returned, "then tell me, how do you link him with a priest when we all know he has little or no time for the Church?"

"That's no longer true, my lord," Piro interposed. "One of the brethren at St. Cyfelach's was telling me that, of late, Ammon has been spending time at the monastery. A priest who is convalescing there has become his soul companion."

"And this priest," said Maredudd, leaning forward, "go on, tell them who it is."

Piro hesitated before saying, "Bledri's brother."

"Right," said Maredudd, proceeding to slice a wedge from the edge of the table, "and there's more to be said about Bledri's brother. You see, he may well be convalescing, but I know he's able to get about, able to wander into the surrounding woods for instance. Now the monastery is close to the border, right? A short walk and you're on French land. What I'm saying is, someone, de Viles for instance, could well be waiting for him there."

"Makes sense," said Rhain. "Might be as well to post a few men in those woods."

"Aye," said Maredudd, raising his skene, "and when de Viles turns up" – he plunged his blade into the table – "it's got you, you bastard." His eyes rose to meet Rhydderch's. "My table."

"It *was*," Rhydderch returned, "when you were captain of guard."

"It will be again when I'm reinstated."

"Who said you'll be reinstated?"

"Stands to reason, you've not appointed someone in my stead."

"I don't have to, the two Owains are doing well enough without you. And you damage this table again and you'll pay for it."

Maredudd swept a hand over the damaged edge. "It's not that bad, it still stands."

"No thanks to you. And on the subject of the monastery, I'll have you know that the Abbot was saying to me, only yesterday, that he thinks it's time you were married."

"Me, married!"

"Yes, *you*. While he appreciates the time you've spent at the monastery lately, he's concerned about your friendliness towards his monks, particularly when, on a number of occasions, he's seen you follow them into the woods. Now I'm warning you, you cause any more trouble at the monastery and I'll have you chained to a pillar."

CHAPTER 23

INHERITANCE

Morgan held the reins of two horses while Maredudd sauntered towards him, enquiring after his health, adding, as he took charge of his bay, "And how is Banwen this morning?"

"Cheerful and as busy as ever, my Lord Captain."

"You've got a good woman there."

"No one knows that better than me. I try to do what's right, but it's not easy."

"No, I don't suppose it is," said Maredudd, gaining the saddle.

They rode out through the gates together. It had come as a surprise to Morgan that, with his trial past, Maredudd should still seek his company. During the eleven days that Maredudd had been away on his second pilgrimage he had missed the company of a man who had been almost a father to him. '*Eleven days.*' He thought, and wondered whether the rumour was true, that Maredudd had spent time with Caleb and Gruffudd ap Rhys. The rumour had it's origin in the fact that, unlike the first pilgrimage, which took only five days, Maredudd had been away eleven days, during which time open rebellion had broken out in the west. Curiosity compelled him to say, "They say the rebels have attacked another castle, my Lord Captain."

"That's right, Blaen Porth in southern Ceredigion. I heard it said the fighting there went on all day, and yet the rebels failed to take the tower."

"Blaen Porth – is that near St. David's?"

"Near, yes, about half a day's ride to the north – near enough to pick up what'll soon be common knowledge, that three lords in Ceredigion have thrown in their lot with Gruffudd ap Rhys, all of them of kin to him."

"Well, let's hope Caleb is still in one piece."

"He is; now you and me, we're going to a meeting at St. Cyfelach's – clan business, usual thing after they leave church – and we're going to have a word with your father in the presence of Rhodri Gadno and the rest of our kinsmen."

"I'd rather we didn't. I don't want anything to do with my father."

"You will when you find out what it's about." Maredudd reined in, outside the forge. "Hey! Bledri, I got something for you."

His muscular arms bare, the blacksmith placed a hammer on an anvil and, wiping his hands in an apron, made towards them, ducking under the low roof as he came out from the forge, a sullen expression on his face.

"See this, my buckler, it's got a dint in the rim. Can you fix it?"

"Some dint," said Bledri, examining the rim. "How did it come about?"

"I dropped it at St. David's, right in front of the Bishop, and it rolled all the way down the aisle and out the door."

"Looks to me as if it was done by a battle-axe."

"Shouldn't think so, the Bishop wasn't carrying an axe when I saw him. No, he just preached to me about the danger in placing one's trust in men – men who'd inform on you as easy as breaking wind."

His face set, Bledri glared. "Some," he said, "make the mistake of taking men into their confidence. Then, when they realize their mistake...."

"Yes, go on, say it."

"Nothing. You're the clever one, you think it out."

"Oh! I will. Then I'll dint someone's head."

Bledri continued to match Maredudd's gaze until, turning away, he growled "When d'you want this buckler back?"

"Tonight," Maredudd returned, reining away. "I might want to attack Abertawe in the morning."

Morgan caught up with him. "Is he the informer, my Lord Captain?"

"Could be."

"Then why doesn't Lord Rhydderch get rid of him."

"Without proof!" Maredudd shook his head. "That would only upset Bledri's kinsmen and we can do without that. Now where was I? Oh! Yes, you see all the land round here, it belongs to Lord Rhydderch, right? Well, there's a lot more that Lord Rhydderch and I share, what we inherited from our father. Now you, when you've completed your seven years in our lord's bodyguard, you'll have a right to a share in your kindred's *resting-place*. That's not just because Ammon is your father, but because you spent more than a year and day under his roof. Now me, when my father died, I stood to inherit half his wealth. Lord Rhydderch inherited the other half because he spent more than a year and a day under my father's roof."

As they approached a hamlet of churls the track became increasingly muddy. The smell of pigs' muck caused Morgan to screw up his nose, his face expressive of the contempt that he had for the unfree, those who held their land in return for labour obligations to whoever owned the land on which they lived.

"I'm not one," Maredudd continued, "to be bothered about rearing cattle and the like. So Lord Rhydderch and I, we got Sulien to oversee our combined inheritance; that is until ten years ago when Lord Rhydderch appointed Edwin to be his *rhaglaw* and, as such, Edwin not only attends to the legal affairs of this commote, but he also has charge of all those churl hamlets that belong to Lord Rhydderch. I tell you, Lord Rhydderch is the wealthiest man in the commote. Me, I'm fairly wealthy myself – got a lot of land, a lot of livestock and I've got churls to work the land for me."

"We had churls until the French drove us from our lands in the Peninsula. Aye, and slaves too."

"Yes, I know all about that," said Maredudd in a manner that was intended to deter Morgan from bragging about how things were. As they drew near to the first of several long-houses, he noticed two girls, their clothes ragged, tittering in the porchway. He also caught the disdain on Morgan's face, the way *he* gestured to the girls to get inside. "My problem is, when I die, I've got no heir to inherit what's mine. Some of it will, therefore, revert to the clan; some of it will escheat to Lord Rhydderch. D'you understand what I'm saying?"

"Yes. What I don't understand is why you're telling me."

"Let's just say I'm sharing with you my dilemma."

A churl woman, her face dirty, moved to one side of the track, bowing while Maredudd nodded, uttering her name. The woman appeared pleased that Maredudd should have acknowledged her. She eyed him flirtatiously as he passed by.

"Good day to you, Docal," Maredudd said to the dung-bailiff as he came out of a hut. "How's that grand-daughter of yours?"

"None too good, my lord. The priest could do nothing for her."

Reining in, Maredudd dug in his girdle. "There's a physician residing at court for a day or two. Take your grand-daughter to him and tell him I sent you." He pulled out two coins, throwing them to the man. "If he wants more, tell him I'll settle with him when I get back."

"Thank you, my lord, I'll do that."

Morgan drew abreast of Maredudd as he moved off. "That was two silver pennies you gave him."

"My pennies, I can do with them as I like. What I can't do is take them with me when I die."

"Yes, but you gave them to a churl – they're beneath us."

"From the point of wealth and status *you* are beneath me, but I don't look down on you for it. And as for Docal, his appointment as the dung-bailiff makes him a free man, which means his status as a court office makes him above you. D'you understand?"

Morgan shook his head. "All your wealth, it came easy to you, didn't it?"

"That's right, it did, and some would say I'm a lazy good-for-nothing, but *that* is my privilege, as it is to treat people as I see fit."

Morgan bit his lip, believing that he had displeased Maredudd. He wanted to put things right. '*But how?*' he wondered. When he made to say something it was too late: Maredudd had descended a muddy slope; when he caught up with him in the river, splashing water made speech pointless. After gaining the far bank they began ascending a wooded slope, Morgan trailing behind, expecting Maredudd to turn and correct him, but Maredudd did no such thing.

"What is it you're telling me, my Lord Captain? That all men are equal?"

"They're not equal, not in wealth, status or in their abilities, but that doesn't give one man the right to walk all over another – or a woman for that matter. *You*, you looked down on Banwen, but in the end she proved her worth. As for them churls, they're Countrymen, they fought for these lands and I dare say they'll do so again."

"My father always said they were scum."

"Was a time when your father thought he was someone special, stood to inherit some of the best land there is. Then the French marched in and took it for themselves. Since then he's been aggrieved because he doesn't have the wealth and status that *he* says should be due to him, and that what he's got he's had to work hard for. Could be, his lot is not entirely his fault, but the same can be said for them churls."

Morgan bit his lip again: all too often, when they rode together, he experienced another side to Maredudd, one which he found difficult to understand. Head down, he kept silent until Maredudd turned to him, at which point he recognized a grin that made it plain they were still as one.

"My father never bothered to explain much to me. It was always *do this, don't do that*. The only time he came near me was to give me a thrashing. That's why I don't want to talk to him, we've got nothing to say."

"I'm not expecting you to say anything to your father. It's simply a matter of me putting my affairs in order. You see, de Viles will have finished his castle guard three days ago and must be well on the way to Warwick by now. When he gets back he'll have something written on parchment that says I'm to stand trial for my part in the attack on Ystum Llymarch, if not Abertawe as well. If it's according to our law, I'll lose. If I go for a trial by combat, then my chances of winning won't be that much better, not if I'm up against the likes of de Viles."

"Na, you'll beat him, everyone says so."

Maredudd laughed. "He's the best, the Earl's champion, never lost a fight, so I'm told, and while it's true someone did scar his head, the man didn't live long enough to gloat over it."

"Na, you'll beat him, I know you will."

"Whatever; now let's talk about your father. Eighteen years ago your father and I were serving in Lord Rhys's bodyguard. Well, your mother, Hawys, was there at the court too, a handmaiden to Lord Rhys's wife. She was a beautiful woman, your mother. At the time I was grieving because the woman I loved had been betrothed to someone else. So I found comfort in your mother's arms. What I didn't know was that Hawys had been betrothed to your father – and he came upon us in the long grass, which is why he and I have always been at odds."

Morgan knitted his brow. "I – I'm not sure I understand."

"Well, put it this way. When your father and I fought some weeks ago, he said something to me that made me think – something about you."

"Me! What did he say?"

"That you're not his son; that you're mine."

Morgan stared, agape. "I don't understand," he stuttered. "Are you saying that you're my real father?"

"That's what Ammon thinks," Maredudd returned rather than state the truth, that there had been several men involved with the woman in question. "And I must admit he could well be right. I did lay with your mother in the long grass."

"But – but I don't have red hair."

"No, you take after your mother. She was as dark as her brother, Iago Du. You can, of course, dismiss what I've said because neither Ammon nor I can swear to it. All we can do is swear that it could be so. So, if you don't accept.... "

"No! No, you're word is good enough for me; it's the best thing I've ever been told."

"Why – because you'll end up wealthy?"

"No, because you're my father, and if you don't believe me, then you ask Banwen what I've said about you."

Maredudd reined closer, his right hand on Morgan's neck, drawing him closer so that the youth's head rested on his side. Morgan threw an arm around Maredudd's waist. The horses soon forced them to separate. Maredudd laughed. "Life isn't going to be any easier for you. I'll expect you to do well in whatever is required of you; now you see that dead tree over there? I'm going to spear it; you're going to put an arrow in it."

Maredudd spurred, the hooves of his bay spattering mud, his cloak billowing above the beast's hindquarters. Leaning to the right, he roared, casting his spear into the dead tree, then galloped on. Morgan followed in his wake, his bow trained on the tree until an arrow embedded itself in the bark. Reining in, Morgan wheeled, shouting, "I'll get your spear and the arrow."

They repeated the move a second time, targeting the same dead tree. When they reverted to a leisurely pace, Morgan said, "Will you teach me how to handle a sword?"

"Why should I do that?"

"Because you're the best swordsman there is, everyone says so."

"Men say I handle most weapons well. So what does that mean? That I can kill a man with ease? That's not what my father taught me. I learned these skills because that's what I wanted to do, but I tell you this, there's more to life than killing. Cadog – now he had his mind set on doing what my father would have wanted me to do. So you could say that, in one sense, I let my father down, which brings me back to the pith of all this, that an inheritance carries responsibilities, and whatever men may say of me, I never squandered mine – my salary and all my perquisites maybe, but that's it. I expect no less from you."

"I won't, I promise you, you don't know what this means to me, you being my father. I'll do whatever you say."

"And you don't abuse your churls, right?"

"Right, you have my word on it."

"Good. You just remember that wealth carries influence. And you keep your nose clean and you could end up as clan chieftain."

"Na, I'm not clever like other men."

"All you lack is a good teacher, which is why, when we get back, you'll take up lodgings with the *Rhaglaw*. He'll be your teacher, and from him you'll learn all about cropping and the like, how to organize the work of churls, how to sit in judgement fairly when they do wrong. Learn well, Morgan, because a fool and his inheritance are soon parted. And who knows? You could be appointed *rhaglaw* yourself one day; if not, you will at least know how to value your inheritance."

Morgan nodded. "When I go, will that mean I won't see much of you?"

"You'll see me, of that you can be sure."

"What about Banwen?"

"I'm glad you've not forgotten her. I see no reason why she shouldn't join you, keep your nose pointing in the right direction; now follow me, I want to show you something."

They reined off the track, skirting a ploughed field until they came to a place overgrown with nettles and thorns. Maredudd dismounted and led through the thick growth until he came to a large stone. "This is it," he said, "the jewel of my inheritance, a fireback stone. It marks the spot where my father's winter hall stood – and me, being younger than Lord Rhydderch, I inherited it. Unfortunately, I was still in Lord Rhys's bodyguard at the time of my father's death, and when I left I settled at Y Faerdref; that's the manor that Lord Rhys gave Lord Rhydderch when he reached full manhood at twenty-one. Neither Lord Rhydderch or I have forgotten this place, it's a place full of memories. Oh! It's overgrown, yes, but that's how we wanted it. We believed that all this brush would keep those memories safe. Remember it well, Morgan, this is your ancestral home, the place where I was raised by a man like no other. One day you may want to settle here."

"Was he a good man, your father?"

"The very best. He had time for us, Lord Rhydderch and I." Maredudd moved to one side, trampling undergrowth, then dropped to his haunches. "It was about here that he used to sit in the evenings, telling us stories, making us laugh, letting us know that we were all the world to him."

"My father – Ammon – he never did anything like that, not to me, anyway." Morgan dropped down beside Maredudd. "I think my real mother cared for me. It's just that I don't remember much about her. What was your mother like?"

"Don't know, she died afore I could walk – after that my father became a man of vows. He always talked highly of her."

"He was clan chieftain, wasn't he?"

"He was. Maredudd Hir they called him. He was a giant of a man in more ways than one. Everyone respected him." Maredudd placed a hand on Morgan's shoulder. "The monastery, d'you still want to go there and have it out with Ammon?"

"Yes," Morgan replied, his tone betraying a reluctance to encounter the man who overawed him.

"You needn't worry about Ammon. I'll just remind him of what he said the day he and I fought. I doubt very much whether he'll deny it, he's practically disowned you as it is. Come, I'll tell you more about your grandfather along the way."

CHAPTER 24

WRITS

Payn de Turberville sat in his resurrected hall, skimming through accounts that itemized the cost of rebuilding the castle bailey. He leaned back in his chair, resigned to the fact that he could no longer apply himself to the task, as several matters robbed him of his concentration. The thought of de Viles alone plagued him. Eight days ago the madman had finished his forty-day castle guard; he must surely be at Warwick Castle now, complaining to the Earl about the way Maredudd Goch's trial had thrice been postponed.

The fact that he had sent a message to the Earl, explaining why the postponements had been necessary, was no guarantee that Beaumont would view the delays as expedient. Beaumont had always considered Rhydderch's allegiance to be suspect. Such a view would undoubtedly be reinforced by de Viles, who had only to amplify the words of the priest – whom he had taken with him – and Beaumont would issue a writ for Maredudd's trial to proceed without further delay.

Equally disturbing was the unholy alliance between de Viles and William de Londres, Lord of Ogwr and holder of the castle at Ystum Llymarch. The evening before de Viles finished his forty-day castle guard, Lord William had turned up at Abertawe, insisting that action be taken over Ystum Llymarch, being unwilling to consider delaying proceedings until the rebellion in Ceredigion had been quashed. Then de Viles had burst into the hall, demanding an escort as far as Caerdydd, which he had refused in the hope that someone might *ambuscade* him. And lo! Lord William offered to provide the madman with protection to wherever he so wished. It had hitherto been inconceivable that these two Frenchmen could work towards a common goal. Both men hated each other, but both had also sworn to avenge themselves against Rhydderch for the humiliation he had inflicted on them ten years ago; now the one was at Warwick and the other had taken steps to ensure that he got there.

More worrying still were the reports that, in the west, Gruffudd ap Rhys had not only attacked the castle at Blaen Porth with the aid of four lords who were of kin to him, but the Countrymen of Ceredigion were up in arms, plundering and burning the homes of Saxon settlers. There was even an unconfirmed report that a castle at Ystrad Peithyll, in northern Ceredigion, had been burnt outright. And goddammit! The French and Flemish lords of that land were reported to have taken refuge in the remaining castles, unable to quell the violence that threatened to spread throughout the Southern Lands.

De Turberville gulped wine, then slammed his goblet on the table. *'Frenchmen,'* he thought, *'they're all the same, all they think about is Normandy. And the King, he should have appointed someone to take charge of the situation, someone who could order the French and Flemish lords in these Southern Lands to take to the field.'*

Wine dribbling from his fleshy lips, he pondered on what bothered him most: whether Rhydderch would join the rebels. The man was a wily bastard, and to have had the gall to trick him into believing that the informer was *his* man was yet another example of *his* confounded trickery. The man was also a serious a threat, more so than Gruffudd ap Rhys, more influential too: one word from *him* and several lords of *his* kind would be at *his* side; one word from *him* and the tribesmen throughout Gower would be up in arms. French and Saxon Gower would then be laid waste, the colonists slaughtered in their beds.

A voice drew his attention to the cleric who sat at the far end of the table, recording supplies that were being stockpiled as a preparation against siege. "Tell me, Master Thomas, would you say I've got an *idée fixe* about Rhydderch ap Cadifor?"

The cleric, a thin-faced, balding man, stared. "Why would I say that, monsieur?"

"Because the more thought I give to him the more I'm convinced he's up to something. Take Cae Castell. When he built that castle he told me it was to counter the threat of having a madman on his border, and I believed him, but according to the informer he built it so his men could practise storming a castle. So what castle does he have in mind? This one?"

"I wouldn't know, monsieur, I'm not knowledgeable about such matters."

"Then forget I asked. I only wanted to know if I'm going mad." De Turberville caught the grin of a man-at-arms who, eight days ago, had taken over castle guard from de Viles; the man was counting sacks of grain. "Did I say something to amuse, monsieur?"

"No, Monsieur la Steward, you're not mad, no more than the rest of us."

De Turberville withheld comment: the man, Elgar the Saxon, was one of few to whom he would allow liberties. He considered the man, focusing on the tight-fitting tunic that emphasized his broad shoulders. His long auburn hair, parted in the centre, and a heavy moustache made him appear older than his twenty-eight years.

Hooves disturbed the gravelly surface outside. A harsh voice carried, one that had everyone look to de Turberville. Elgar made for the door, pausing in the porchway, then came back, saying, "It's de Viles, back from Warwick."

"Back," de Turberville exclaimed. "The man's only been gone eight days. What did he do, ride day and night?"

"Driven by hate, I'd say," said Master Thomas. "May God have mercy on us."

"I think it best," said Elgar, "that I stay here, near the table."

A man came in, a smoked carcass on his shoulder. De Viles followed him in, pushing him so that he stumbled, almost dropping the carcass. Then de Viles stood in the doorway, hands on hips, feet apart, ranting, "*The Lord bringeth the council of the heathen to nought. He maketh the devices of the people to none effect.*"

"Enough of your psalm-singing," de Turberville rasped. "Just get to the point of your unwelcome visit."

Striding towards the table, de Viles threw back his cloak to reveal that he wore no armour, just a tunic and breeches dirtied by mud. He stopped short at a bench, removing from a leather satchel a scroll, which he threw onto the table. "A writ, monsieur, read it."

Unrolling the scroll, de Turberville read instructions for Maredudd Goch's trial to proceed without further delay. He looked askance at de Viles, whose hollowed, tired eyes made him appear all the more intimidating.

"That," de Viles snarled, "puts an end to the arrangement you have with Rhydderch ap Cadifor."

"It does no such thing. What it says is, that Maredudd Goch is to be tried without further delay, and the question as to whether it will be according to Countryman Law or combat will be his choice."

"Either way, I shall be the one to bring him low."

"You! It's Lord William of Ogwr who's the plaintiff, not you."

"That's right, he is," said de Viles, bending so that, hands upon the table, he could look de Turberville straight in the eye, "but should Maredudd Goch opt for a trial by combat, then Lord William has agreed that I shall be his champion. And not only that, if it's to be a trial by Countryman Law, then I will be Lord William's pleader."

"Huh! You may be invincible with a mace and shield, but in a trial by Countryman Law you'll never get the pleading right. You'll foul up because you're nothing more than an ignoramus."

De Viles straightened up to stand, hands on hips, looking down on de Turberville with contempt. "That's what you would have everyone believe, but like you I speak three tongues. What's more, I can quote the psalms word for word, and word for word I know exactly what Lord William wants me to plead. So you see, Pagan, no matter what course of action Maredudd Goch may take, I will be the one to bring him low. And you, you'll see to it that a writ is sent to him – and you'll do so *today*."

"My bailiffs are away, attending to other matters. So it'll have to wait."

"Liar! I just saw that drunken slob, Baldred, out there, in the courtyard." De Viles paused, curling his lip. As he leaned forward, slamming a fist on the table, he caught Elgar's advance. He straightened up, his right hand circling for the dagger in his belt.

"No, wait," de Turberville snapped, a hand raised to caution Elgar, but the Saxon had already anticipated trouble, his dagger drawn. "I'm warning you, de Viles, you engage this man and I'll see to it that you loose your fief."

"You wouldn't dare."

"Wouldn't I? The Earl left instructions to that effect ten years ago, and I'll take great pleasure in carrying them out; now get out, wait by the drawbridge."

De Viles expanded his chest, his ireful expression giving way to an evil grimace as he produced a second scroll, throwing it onto the table. "Read it, Pagan."

De Turberville ran his eye over the second writ. "The Devil's hoof!"

"That's right, the names of eight other men who were here when this castle was attacked, including Rhydderch ap Cadifor's two sons."

"You bloody ignoramus! The witnesses who saw these men here are either women or children, none of whom are competent to testify against a man."

"That's as maybe, but three of those men, including the edling, were with Maredudd Goch at Ystum Llymarch and I have competent witnesses who'll testify to their presence there. The problem is, all three men have been absent from this lordship for seven weeks. So you, you'll proceed against those three men today, and again on two other occasion. And when those men don't respond you'll outlaw them.

"It's all a waste of time – my time! And what's more, I'll not be pushed into doing things when you say so."

An evil grimace appeared on de Viles's face again. "I knew you'd say that, Pagan. That's why the Earl, in his wisdom, ordered two men to accompany me from Warwick to report on what action you take to enforce his will." He pricked up his ears, hearing hoof beats outside. "Ah-ha! Those men are here."

Two men entered, their faces sullen as a result of journeying in the company of a madman. When de Viles said, to them, "Declare yourselves, messieurs, and your purpose," they both gave him a look that showed their disdain for him.

"Monsieur la Steward," said the older man, "I am Maurice de Bohun; this is Arnulf fitzGilbert. Our purpose here is to deliver this writ to you personally, and to report on how you put into effect the instructions therein. I will add that you remain close-mouthed about the contents of this writ. You'll understand why when you read it."

De Turberville unrolled the scroll and read hurriedly. The first few lines came as a surprise; what followed made him groan within.

"Well, what does it say?" de Viles demanded.

"You heard what the man said, I remain close-mouthed."

"No, we've all taken oaths to be the Earl's men. I demand that you read it aloud."

"Demand! You don't demand anything from me; now get out. Out, I say. Master Thomas, call out the guard and have them remove this ignoramus by whatever means is necessary."

The cleric had no sooner risen than de Viles backed towards the door, intending to obstruct, only to be forcibly pushed by Elgar. As de Viles staggered back, stiff and tired from travelling, Elgar pushed him again so that he fell back onto sacks of grain. In a flash Elgar was upon him, a dagger at his throat, his right forearm held in a vice-like grip that prevented him from drawing his own dagger. The two men from Warwick looked to de Turberville, but a gesture from him proved sufficient to have them refrain from any involvement.

"Master Thomas," said Elgar, "the guard, bring them in here."

"*How long will ye imagine mischief against a man?*" de Viles rasped. "*Ye shall be slain, all of you.*" He was still threatening the wrath of God when three men-at-arms entered.

"Take his sword," said Elgar, "and escort him beyond the drawbridge."

"No, don't touch it," de Viles spat, his free hand closing on his sword hilt as one man made to remove the blade, "for *the Lord will hear me when I call unto him.*"

"If you want to retain your sword," de Turberville shouted, "then swear by God you'll go peaceably. Well, what's it to be, psalm-singer?"

"I swear to what you say, Pagan." Free of Elgar's hold, de Viles straightened up, pointing a finger at de Turberville. "That last writ, you'll see that it's contents are put into effect." Then, throwing an arm in the air to keep those near him at bay, he went out the door, chanting psalms.

His voice could still be heard when de Turberville said, "I apologize for the upset, messieurs. Monsieur de Viles brings out the worse in a man."

"No need to apologize, Monsieur la Steward," said de Bohun. "We've had his company all way from Warwick."

"Aye, and if he wasn't chanting psalms," said fitzGilbert, "he was demanding to know the contents of that writ. I could have killed him willingly."

"So what exactly does he know?" de Turberville asked.

"Nothing," replied de Bohun. "The contents of that writ have been kept from him because the Earl considers him – how shall I say – unstable? Just indulge him with a few trials while you, monsieur, attend to those other matters. In the meantime," he said, drawing attention to his dress.

"Pierre," said de Turberville, addressing his retainer, "escort our guests to the bath house and provide them with wine and clean clothes, anything they so wish. I will see you later, messieurs."

The two Warwick men had no sooner left than Elgar approached the table, saying, "What exactly does that last writ contain?"

"Later. Right now you'll escort my bailiff, Baldred, to Y Faerdref so he can deliver four writs, which Master Thomas will prepare while your horse is saddled. What I want *you* to do is appease Lord Rhydderch, assure him that no action will be taken against the five who were seen only at Abertawe – you know why. And tell him I strongly advise Maredudd to go for a trial by combat. Oh! Yes, and Maredudd will have to change his sureties because the men I want will have to remain here, at Abertawe, till the trial is over. As for the three who where seen at Ystum Llymarch, tell Lord Rhydderch we can accommodate one another on that matter, but they'll have to appear afore me, if not on the day of Maredudd's trial, then in response to my second or third summons. That'll give him time to get his house in order. Oh! And – er – not one word about this last writ. You understand?"

. . . . . .

Elgar approached Y Faerdref, pained that he should be the bearer of ill tidings. Yet he reasoned that doing a superior's bidding was a facet of life. As a boy he had aspired to enter the Church, but his father had made other arrangements and he, being a dutiful son, had spent seven years as a retainer to one Odo fitzStephen, the man who, when he was seventeen, gave him the ceremonial slap across the face that elevated him to the rank of a man-at-arms.

That slap had led to his participation in a savage campaign here, in Gower, enforcing the Earl's right of conquest. He had been rewarded with a fief for his service, but with that fief went obligations, all at de Turberville's bidding.

He considered the young man who accompanied him, his former retainer, William, once a snotty-nosed rascal; now a fine young man whom he had himself slapped on the face. William should have left to seek his fortune in the Earl's service, but in a province where it was difficult to find a replacement, William had elected to stay until the summer, not as a retainer, but as a friend.

A loud belch served as a reminder that, trailing behind, the bailiff, Baldred, quaffed ale. A Saxon, podgy and in need of a shave, Baldred appeared gnome-like in his phrygian bonnet, his beady eyes betraying his fear of travelling beyond the bounds of French and Saxon Gower.

"We're almost there, Baldred," William threw out, "and still in one piece."

"Won't stay that way if we spend the night among them Welsh."

"What choice do we have? If we refuse their hospitality, they'll be offended."

"You may laugh, but I know these people. It don't take much to get them vexed."

"Well, thank the Lord," William returned, "it's not me whose carrying them writs."

Amused by William's banter, Elgar dismounted within Y Faerdref's walls, to be escorted to the hall where a doorward announced his arrival. There were several men in the hall who, he suspected, had assembled after his approach had been observed. Rhydderch made towards him, welcoming him in French, offering a hand in friendship. He responded to a handshake, saying, "I'm afraid your hospitality may wane, my friend, once you know the purpose of my visit."

"Not so," said Rhydderch, prompting him towards a table. "Baldred's presence tells me all I need know. Come, sit yourself down. We'll attend to what needs to be said over a horn of ale. William, Baldred, come, join us, you're both my guests."

While Elgar gave an account of de Viles's return, Baldred guzzled ale, sure that Lord Rhydderch would be vexed when informed of the summons for his eldest son. '*What then*?' he wondered. '*Raised voices*? *Knives drawn*?' Elgar and William might be fooled by the present calm, but not him. He determined to get so pixilated that, when knives *were* drawn, he would be oblivious to the touch of cold steel. He had no sooner drained his horn than a youth offered to refill his empty vessel. He belched loudly, proffering the horn, then proceeded to wipe froth from his lips with his woollen sleeve. As he looked about it occurred to him that he may have missed something. Then Lord Rhydderch spoke.

"What you've said, Elgar, comes as no surprise, but I must confess that none of the men named in those writs are here right now, though Maredudd may turn up shortly. As to the revised requirement for sureties, I'll agree to that, and two men will accompany you on your return journey. However, you're going to have to tell Monsieur la Steward that, if he wants the accused to turn up on Monday, then he will have to hold court outside the bailey."

"I've a feeling he won't like that."

"I'm sure he won't, but I'm not prepared to put members of my household at risk when de Viles could quite easily provoke a blood bath. And that, I think, concludes what needs to be said. So tell me about yourself. I heard you were sick recently."

"I told you," said William, nudging the bailiff's arm, "there'd be no trouble."

"It's not over yet, you young devil. Wait till these Welsh get ale inside them. They'll get quarrelsome and there'll be blood all over the place, you mark my words."

The youth returned with a replenished horn, from which Baldred took a large gulp, then belched again. He felt slightly inebriated, though no less determined to resist being taken in by the pleasantries concerning Elgar, William's future and the whereabouts of another former retainer by the name of Mark. He was halfway through his second horn when a voice carried from the doorway.

"Elgar!"

"God's Hooks!" Baldred spluttered. 'It's 'im, Maredudd Goch."

Maredudd approached the table to slap a hand on both Elgar and William. "So what brings you two here, eh? A writ! What for? A trial – on Monday! Baldred!" Maredudd plunged his skene into the table, hissing, in the bailiff's face, "Is this your doing, Baldred? No! Who's then? De Viles! Then I've no quarrel with you."

Maredudd had no sooner sat on the far side of Elgar than William whispered, over his shoulder, "You did well there, Baldred. You calmed him down with hardly a word."

"It's not over yet," Baldred returned , his hand shaking as he raised his horn to his mouth. "I told you knives would be drawn. Aye, and if I know that miscreant, he's sure to cause trouble."

The company settled down, men talked, they laughed, and there arose an exchange between Elgar and Maredudd. Baldred tried to eavesdrop on the conversation, something about a big, Flemish grey, which Maredudd claimed to have won in a wager on his second pilgrimage. Elgar expressed his reluctance to buy. *'As likely as not,'* Baldred thought, *'because he knows the horse to be stolen.'*

"It really is a fine grey," said Maredudd, rising from the table. "Come, see for yourself."

Both men were absent long enough for Baldred to begin his third horn of ale. Then a youth entered the hall, shouting, his words translated by Rhydderch.

"It's a fight," said William, "between Elgar and Maredudd – near the stables."

"God's hooks! It's started," Baldred groaned, "the blood-letting has started." He raised his horn. *Glug, glug, glug* – by the time he had drained his horn he found himself alone.

Near the stables two men peered over the rims of French shields. The broad-shouldered contestant appeared content to watch and wait, barely shifting his ground, whereas his red-haired opponent made feints to confound and catch him unawares. In one such feint Maredudd directed his mace at the lower half of his opponent's shield, then swiftly struck at the top, hoping to get Elgar to obscure his vision by raising his shield, but Elgar reacted unexpectedly, swinging his mace at his opponent's shield with such force that Maredudd reeled, then staggered back under successive blows until he fell to the ground.

Elgar stood over him, his mace poised. "You've had more than a week to practise what I taught and you still haven't got it right."

"More than a week, eh," said Rhydderch, looking down at Maredudd. "So, you've spent time at Elgar's abode, being drilled by him."

"It was you who put the idea into my head," said Maredudd, regaining his feet. "Take your time on your second pilgrimage, you said. So I spent two days at Elgar's abode afore he left to take up castle guard."

"And you told him to say nothing about it, right? Well, now I'll tell him something about you. Elgar, that grey, I wouldn't buy it if I were you. It's got staggers like he has when he's drunk."

When everyone returned to the hall, Baldred, who had helped himself to two more horns of ale, was surprised to find that Elgar and William were still alive. He whispered, in William's ear, "If zere's any more twubble, yew leave 'em to me. I'll zort the bastards zout," but Baldred passed out long before the evening drew to a close.

. . . . . .

The following morning, somewhat the worse for drink, Elgar and William left Y Faerdref, taking with them two court officers – Sulien and Father Piro – both of whom were to stand surety for Maredudd. Trailing behind them, his head sore, his complexion a ghastly grey, Baldred refused to accept that the cut above his left eye was due to a fall, insisting that it had come about as a result of struggling with several youths – after he had toppled from a bench.

CHAPTER 25

ENTRAPMENT

At daybreak, darkness still reigned in the chamber even though, from narrow windows, pale light penetrated sackcloth coverings. Gwenllian turned restlessly between woollen blankets, thinking of Caleb. She had derived little comfort from the knowledge that Maredudd, after receiving absolution, had caught up with Caleb in Ceredigion, finding him, her brother and young Tewdrig in good health. All three had been in high spirits until the attack on the castle at Blaen Porth, which Maredudd described as an ill-planned and disorderly affair.

What had since heightened her fears was not so much news that two more castles had been attacked, but her recollection of a series of dreams. In each dream she had a clear picture of a castle upon a low hill. Other aspects of the dreams were not so clear, or even the same, but she could recall seeing, at the foot of the hill, French archers shooting at Countrymen on the far side of a river, infuriating many of them to charge across a wooden bridge. The archers had then fled in disarray, heading back for the castle, the Countrymen in hot pursuit, when suddenly French horse had appeared on one side of the hill, silhouetted on the skyline, advancing at the trot, a long line of them, their chain-mail glittering, pennants fluttering below flashing lance heads. The rumble of hooves had grown louder, as did the shouts of Countrymen when panic made them turn tail and run.

She recalled, somewhat vaguely, that the Countrymen who had remained by the bridge could only watch in horror as their doomed companions ran until they fell to the horsemen's lances. The nightmarish part came when, in one dream, she saw a youth sprinting, terror written across his face until he was decapitated by a horseman's sword – at which point she had woken up, screaming, '*Caleb!*'

She retrieved that Rhydderch had said the French referred to such action as *stratagem*, which he defined as entrapment; it was a means of engagement at which he had proved himself a past master. Then she remembered, albeit vaguely, that Rhydderch had been present in two of her most recent dreams – he being prey to the horsemen who rode out of the bailey at Abertawe to charge down a slope, their lances aligned on him as he wheeled to ride for dear life.

He stirred, prompting her to peer through the shadows to discern that he lay on his side, facing her. Why she had been ill-disposed towards him she would never know. Only the worry associated with Caleb's absence could be said in her defence, though even that did not warrant prolonging the agony for two weeks before making amends. Now she was concerned for him: Abertawe was one place she had always associated with entrapment and he would be there today to witness Maredudd's trial. She snuggled up to him, her right arm across his shoulder.

"Another sleepless night?" he whispered.

"Yes – you were there, in my dream. I saw you at Abertawe in the open space outside the castle. It's a trap, Rhydderch, I know it is."

"Yes, you said so yesterday. That's why I sent word to de Turberville – there'd be no trial unless it takes place near the church west of the castle."

"Is that any safer than on the northern highway?"

"It is insofar as I'll have a better chance of escape. And if de Turberville is prepared to hold court near the church, as I believe he will, there'll be a stream between him and me, and the ground on either side of that stream is boggy enough to slow any horsemen who attempt to across it."

"Is there a bridge across that stream?"

"Yes, only I won't cross it."

"But Maredudd and Rhain will."

"That doesn't mean they'll meet with drawn swords. We simply don't know what the High Steward's intentions are. It may be that he'll stand by the arrangements we've made. If not, then be assured I've taken all the precautions I can think of. That's why I've called the men of Uwch-coed to arms; that's why this court will be abandoned today; and that's why you'll leave and take refuge in Cantref Bychan."

. . . . . .

De Viles stood outside the church at Abertawe, inhaling the morning air after spending a night in prayer. He felt animated: it was Monday, the one Monday in the month when the landowners of French and Saxon Gower were obliged to do suit at court as jurors. He would not be among them on this occasion because Lord William of Ogwr had appointed him to be the pleader of his cause.

A bowshot away, on a knoll to the north-east, stood the bailey within which the landowning jurors had spent the night. He threw a hand in the air, shouting, as though the jurors could hear him, "Attend to my cry, fools, for I am the Earl's servant, here to do his bidding, while you, you shall learn from me, for *God shall let me see my desires upon my enemies.*"

Wilfred emerged from a nearby tithe barn, resentful that he had been denied an evening in the bailey, drinking with his peers. "The horses, monsieur, d'you want...?"

"Never mind them; follow me." His jaw fixed, de Viles set off, ascending the southern slope of the knoll. His intention was to enter the bailey by the south gates and seek out the High Steward, but as he approached the drawbridge he paused to survey the rebuilt township. Some distance from the drawbridge, longhouses straddled a highway that led to the estuary. Similar houses also stood on the low ground between the knoll and the river. It was down there, on the low ground, that he caught sight of horses ranged on the landward side of buildings, unobservable to anyone on the far side of the river. He no sooner reasoned that the horses belonged to the garrison men-at-arms and their retainers than he set off, striding downhill.

"Now we know what all the noise was about at dawn," he ground out, recalling the clatter of hooves on the bailey drawbridge. "So what does it mean, Wilfred? Could it be that a trap has been set for Rhydderch ap Cadifor? If it has, then why hasn't de Turberville informed me – me of all people?"

As he approached a longhouse known as Sweyn's Hall, a hooded priest appeared to view, having made his approach from the river. The priest's appearance took him by surprise, causing him to stop and stare as the priest passed close to a gable end of Sweyn's Hall. Dark thoughts flittered through his mind: the priest was one who ministered to Countrymen, a disciple no less that of the Devil. Moving to obstruct, he snarled, "It's the Devil that's sent you. I know. So tell me what he requires of you?"

"I have a message for the High Steward," the priest countered, "it's no concern of yours." As the priest made to push past, de Viles grabbed him by the cassock so that his hood fell to his shoulders.

"You," de Viles snarled, recognizing the man as Iorwerth's priest, "You're here to spy, aren't you?"

"In the name of God unhand me!" The priest shook free, desperate to distance himself from one he knew to be mad. De Viles fell upon him from behind, a hand closing on his mouth, drawing his head back so that, close up, he felt the madman's breath upon his cheek. Suddenly a dagger appeared directly in front of his face, causing him to stare, wide-eyed, as fear gripped him. "No, no," he mumbled, refusing to accept that he was about to die.

"Ah-ha! *You cry, but there is none to save you, even unto the Lord, but He answers you not.*"

The priest felt the dagger puncture his windpipe. He choked, warm blood dribbling from his mouth. His eyes rolled heavenward, the sky appearing as an endless expanse of pale grey. *'No-no, it's not happening to me,'* he thought as the hand over his mouth relaxed, allowing him to collapse, face down.

De Viles rubbed both his blade and his hands on the priest's cassock, smearing it with blood. Close by, Wilfred stood rooted to the spot, staring at the corpse. "Well, don't just stand there. Cover him up. Use that straw there."

Leaving Wilfred to conceal the corpse, de Viles approached the corner of Sweyn's Hall to see horses ranged along the length of the building. Several retainers were among the horses; none showed any sign that they were aware of what he had done. "You," he demanded, advancing on two retainers, "what are you doing here?"

First one, then the other retainer shrank from him; one ran off. Moving swiftly, de Viles seized the nearest retainer, at which point he caught the approach of two men-at-arms, one of them shouting, "Unhand that retainer." Recognizing Elgar's voice, it took only a moment for him to realize that the Saxon must have observed his descent to the township, for he could see, on the landward side of a second longhouse, a score of men looked on. "What's going on? Why are these men here? Tell me!"

"You were told yesterday," Elgar returned, "to stay away from the castle and the town; now get back to the church and wait."

"You haven't answered my question, Saxon!"

"Nor am I going to. I warn you, my orders are to remove you by whatever means is necessary."

Curling his lip, de Viles turned on his heels, ranting, as he walked away, *"Princes have persecuted me without cause, but my heart standeth in awe of the Lord...."* When level with the end wall of Sweyn's Hall he shouted, "Wilfred, let's be gone from here, you Saxon whelp."

"To horse, William," said Elgar. "He'll make for the castle next."

As he rode past the gable end of Sweyn's Hall Elgar looked to the shoreline where, amongst reeds, he caught sight of a small boat made of withies and covered in hides. "That curragh, it belongs to Iorwerth's priest. Rally those retainers, William, and go find him, then bring him up to the castle." Elgar spurred, thinking, *'Madman,'* as he followed de Viles uphill. *'you'll have reasoned that those men-at-arms are there to capture Rhydderch – or kill him if he tries to escape.'*

It pained him to think of Rhydderch dead, so much so that he considered warning him of the danger – but how? Then it dawned on him that Iorwerth's priest must have seen what was going on in the town. *'He could warn Rhydderch?'* he thought, then muttered, under his breath, "Damn! He'll not do that, not if William finds him."

He was about to overtake de Viles when the madman turned, snarling, *"Let them be confounded and confused that are adversaries of my soul; let them be covered with reproach and dishonour that seek my hurt."*

"Enough of your rancour. And you attempt to enter the castle and you'll have me to contend with." Elgar cantered on, ignoring the abuse that fell from de Viles's lips. The hooves of his bay clattered on the drawbridge. When he reached the gateway he wheeled, drawing his sword in the hope that it would deter the madman from entering the bailey. It was then, amongst the bailey buildings, that he caught sight of archers, all lounging about.

He shook his head: it was not enough that men-at-arms were in position to swoop down on Rhydderch; garrison archers were also ready to man the palisade so that, at close range, they could not fail to target Rhydderch. *'A necessary precaution,'* de Turberville had said. *'We've been told that Rhydderch has summoned his tribesmen to arms; that means he could turn up here with more men than we bargained for.'*

And there was more. A mixed force of Frenchmen, Saxons and Countrymen had already set out from Morgannwg with orders to cross the River Tawe at Upper Ford and cut off any retreat to the north. It had also been arranged that, from the west, Lord William of Ogwr, the High Steward of Cydweli and Carnwyllion, would cross the Llwch Dwr and descend on Abertawe from the north-west; if that were not enough, then one John de Penrhys, a man-at-arms who held land in the Peninsula, would lead Saxon levies towards Abertawe from the west.

'If, against all odds,' Elgar thought, *'Rhydderch escapes entrapment here, then he and his men will be cut to pieces when they try to break out of the encirclement.'*

De Viles came over the crest, shouting, *"The Lord shall send the rod of His strength out of Zion. He shall fill this place with dead bodies. Therefore, shall I see my desires upon them that hate me."*

Elgar waited until it became apparent that de Viles would return to the church. Then he made for the hall where he found de Turberville standing proud, a retainer pouching his red, ceremonial tunic over the belt beneath his paunch. "It's de Viles, Monsieur la Steward, he's seen what's going on in the town."

"Has he now? Well, he's hardly going to warn Rhydderch."

"No, but I suspect Iorwerth's priest will. I saw a curragh beached by the reeds."

"Well, why aren't you down there, apprehending him?"

"I've got William directing a search."

"He'd better find him. That priest is here because Iorwerth sent him and I wouldn't put it past Iorwerth to warn his kinsman. And you, you should have had a man watching the estuary."

"I did. It's my guess he crossed up river, then paddled down beside the reeds."

"I don't give a damn what he did, I want him caught." De Turberville threw a hand in the air, snapping, at his retainer, "That's enough pouching, Pierre. Get my over-tunic." He heaved a sigh, his gaze on Elgar. "I've gone to great lengths to lay hold of Rhydderch and one chance is all I'll have."

"One! You'll have men at him from all directions. And the archers – what part will they have in all this?"

"I told you, they're a precaution against attack."

"Then why are they gathered where the palisade overlooks the church?"

"The Devil's hoof! We're up against a man renowned for his trickery. We can't afford to take chances, not when he's called his tribesmen to arms."

"With respect, Monsieur la Steward, he's summoned his men because he feels threatened. He's hardly going to march them here to…."

"Don't try to reason with me. That Countryman who turned up yesterday made it plain his master is spoiling for a fight. I can't afford to ignore that. And even if it were not so, it's still the Earl's wish that he's apprehended; now get out and apprehend Iorwerth's priest."

Elgar had almost reached the door when de Turberville relented, saying, "Elgar, wait. Look, I know you regard Rhydderch as a friend and – well, there's things you know nothing about, things that weren't written in the last writ. You see – Pierre, get out. Come back when I call you." He waited for his retainer to leave. "Elgar, the Earl wants Rhydderch alive; that's why I put *you* in command of the men-at-arms. So is that not proof enough that I also want him alive?"

"Very well, have it your way, but I still say the idea that Rhydderch will come here to assail this castle is absurd – it's not his way of fighting."

De Turberville shook his head, his fleshy cheeks quivering. "Then concentrate on the wider issue. That last writ, for instance, it makes it plain that the King's son, along with two Countryman lords from the north, will enter Cantref Mawr to flush out Gruffudd ap Rhys and his rebels and drive them south. If the rebels try to enter Ceredigion, they'll find the fords closed by Gilbert fitzRichard's men; if they try to take refuge in Cantref Bychan, they'll find the fords closed by Richard fitzPons' men. So they'll have to retreat south into the arms of those of us who'll be waiting to finish them off. There'll be Gerald de Windsor and the Flemings from Cantref Rhos, William de Londres from Cydweli, you and me with men from Gower and

Morgannwg. It'll be like driving fish into a net. Simple, isn't it? Except the moment we leave this lordship, we leave it open to attack. Can't do that; that's why we have to capture Rhydderch."

"With respect, Monsieur la Steward, Rhydderch is hardly going to involve himself in rebellion when the rebels have all been put to flight."

"Agh! You underestimate the man. Me, I'm a Breton, I know how he thinks, and I know what that priest had to say of him because I spoke to the treacherous bastard on a number of occasion afore he accompanied de Viles to Warwick. All things considered, yes, Rhydderch wants Gower free, but he knows that if he drives us out, then it's only a matter of time afore we retake it – it is after all only a small lordship. So what does he do, eh? He widens his horizon; he plots rebellion with other like-minded lords, something the informer said has been going on for years. You understand what I'm saying?"

"Yes, and what you say may well be true, but the fact remains, he didn't throw in his lot with Gruffudd ap Rhys."

"Yes, and you know why? Gruffudd may have a claim to be King of these Southern Lands, but he's not a man eminent in arms. And now that he's lost credibility Rhydderch can step in and have everything done his way. Aye, and right now he's doing what he does best, he's waiting to catch us at a disadvantage. So, when we march westwards, that's when he'll make his move. First thing he'll do is take this castle, and he's quite capable of doing so. I tell you, a success like that would inspire others of his kind to do much the same elsewhere. Then he'll rally them into a force to be reckoned with. Well, I intend to put a stop to all that."

"If you believe all that, then you really do have an *idée fixe* about the man."

"Aye, and for good reason. It's what the Earl foresaw ten years ago." A long moment passed. Then de Turberville asked, "Well, have you nothing to say?"

"What is there to say? You have it all worked out."

"Well, maybe I've overlooked something."

"Yes, you have. You said there were things that I know nothing about, things that were not written in that last writ. Then you changed the subject. So what exactly are you keeping from me?"

Averting his gaze, de Turberville poured wine into a goblet. "Those two Warwick men, I spoke to them in private. You know what they said? They said that de Viles has made allegations to the Earl about you and I. *You* have been accused of passing on information to Rhydderch. Me – de Viles claims that while I've been administering this lordship I've been feathering my own nest."

"And have you?"

"If I have, it's no more than what any other man would do – with the exception of you, that is."

"I see – and you paid those Warwick men to loosen their tongues. Am I right?"

"What if I did? The point is, we're both suspect, but if we take Rhydderch, that could put us in good stead. I mean, you don't want to loose your fief, do you?"

"Nor you your office."

"I've got a lordship to fall back on, you haven't, but let's not quibble. At the appointed time *you* will lead the garrison men-at-arms against Rhydderch. You can take him, capture him, do what you want. *That* I'll leave in your capable hands; now I can't be fairer than that, can I?"

"Except that when Rhydderch sees me top the ridge he's not going to yield. He'll run and if I corner him, he'll put up a fight, which means I may have to kill him. And what about you? Will you order our archers to shoot afore I get anywhere near him?"

"Come now, Elgar, if I wanted Rhydderch dead, I'd have archers out there, in the woods and in the dunes, where they couldn't fail to target him; now trust me."

CHAPTER 26

TRIAL BY COMBAT

On his approach to Abertawe, Rhydderch's doorward, Llywelyn, rode down the northern highway, supervising the six youths who skirted the tree-line on either side. At intervals a youth dismounted on Llywelyn's instructions to check that no danger lurked in the surrounding woods. A spear's throw behind Llywelyn, Rhydderch travelled in the company of eight others, wary of entrapment; conscious too that his escape route might be in jeopardy.

Earlier he had met one of Iorwerth's men at St. Cyfelach's. The man had been waiting for him with a message that his master had reason to believe that men from Morgannwg were marching on Gower, apparently on the King's instructions, as it was rumoured that moves were afoot to flush out the rebels in Cantref Mawr. The inference, however, was that those Morgannwg men could be used against him. If they crossed at Upper Ford, they could turn south and cut off his escape route, thereby dispersing the men that he had mustered to cover his retreat.

At Abertawe, Llywelyn left the highway, directing his six youths to check the woods west of the castle. Rhydderch followed at a distance, at one point instructing his huntsman to take up a position that would enable him to keep watch on the western highway, as well as the bailey's northern gates from which French horse might sally forth and attack his little band.

Rhydderch continued to skirt the western tree-line, his eyes roving until they came to rest on the two hooded clerics who observed his progress from the bailey. The clerics were too far away for him to discern who they were. So he switched his attention to the church, south of the bailey, beyond which was the low ground where the High Steward would preside over Maredudd's trial. He was distracted by his doorward, waving a spear to signal that no danger lurked in the woods to the west, nor in the sandy wasteland to the south.

Wheeling, he made for the stream that separated him from the church. South of the church a low bridge spanned the stream, beyond which the High Steward sat in a chair, a pavilion behind him; on either side of de Turberville stood the landowning jurors of French and Saxon Gower. Further south, horses grazed under the eye of retainers. The horses undoubtedly belonged to the jurors; that they were saddled and ready to ride was cause for concern.

He switched his attention leftwards. The two hooded clerics had moved to the bailey's southern drawbridge, presumably to obtain a better view of his approach. Now he could identify one of them as a Countryman priest by his grey cassock, whereas the other wore the black garb of a Benedictine monk. Then he caught sight of two mailed horsemen as they appeared on the skyline behind the High Steward's pavilion.

He turned to the two volunteers who would accompany Maredudd over the bridge. "Rhain, Elidir, listen to me. When Maredudd stands afore the High Steward, you keep your eyes on the crest near that drawbridge. If horsemen are to descend on us, that's where they'll come from; that's when you get out fast. Elidir, you don't dismount; you keep the horses close to Maredudd and Rhain." Rhydderch drew rein. "And now, gentlemen, this is as far as I go. May God be with you from hereon."

While he watched the two men-at-arms on the skyline begin their descent towards the High Steward's pavilion, Rhydderch listened to Maredudd attempt to dispel Morgan's fears. Morgan had wanted to be with Maredudd, to take charge of the horses, but as a father Maredudd had said *no* as, indeed, he had said *no* to Owain accompanying him beyond St. Cyfelach's. In his case he had stressed both his concern and the fact that, in the event of mishap to himself and Caleb, Uwch-coed's continued existence would depend on the survival of a son in whom he was well pleased. Maredudd, on the other hand, had compromised, allowing Morgan to come this far, but selecting a volunteer such as Elidir to accompany him over the bridge.

As Maredudd rode forward he turned to Rhydderch, saying, "If I get killed, I'll be coming back to haunt you."

A faint smile became discernable beneath Rhydderch's moustache. "What for?" he asked. "So you can plague me about your lost salary?" He watched the trio ride towards the bridge. All three were at risk with little chance of escape, but they were not the only ones. Near the church stood his steward, Sulien, and Father Piro. Neither of those two men could have foreseen what they had let themselves in for when they agreed to stand surety for Maredudd, but the fifteen men who had come with him today knew they might be captured or killed. Yet they had come willingly; now they had time to reflect on their isolation, and none more so than his huntsman, Huw, he being three hundred paces away and close to the bailey.

As to the four men around him, Morgan's first concern was Maredudd. Awst, on the other hand, would die for him, he being both a kinsman and a companion from an early age. By contrast, the blacksmith, Bledri, was a newcomer, his loyalty suspect; it was as well that Morgan had been told to keep an eye on him. The fourth man in his presence was Gruffudd ap Meilyr, an Is-coed man who knew the terrain around Abertawe better than most. Gruffudd was the man to lead them to safety over *the Mountain* that lay to the north; he had no reason to doubt him.

The trio were no sooner riding across the low bridge than Rhydderch became aware that the sky had darkened, threatening rain. Then, as he ran his eye over the slope south of the castle, he noticed that the two clerics had removed themselves from the drawbridge and were making their way down the slope to where scattered groups of townsmen stood within earshot of the court proceedings. The Countryman priest progressed with apparent confidence, whereas the Benedictine monk seemed fearful about straying too far from the castle.

"Black clouds," said Awst, airing his superstitions. "It's an omen. I don't like it."

"No more do I," said Rhydderch. "Signal Huw to come, join us quickly. Then get Llywelyn to call in his youths."

Awst separated from his company to wave a spear in the air. Huw responded immediately, but it would take time for Llywelyn to call in his scattered youths, and having misconceived Awst's signal, Llywelyn would then make the mistake of leading his youths towards Rhydderch.

Meanwhile, on the far side of the bridge, Maredudd and Rhain had reined in to take up a position below and to the left of the High Steward. To their right stood a dozen male witnesses from Ystum Llymarch, but neither the plaintiff nor the pleader were with them.

"I don't see de Londres or de Viles," Maredudd threw out, alighting from his bay. "I'd have thought they'd have been anxious to get things moving."

"Maybe they're in the church," Rhain joked, "praying for guidance."

"Hah! I can't imagine those two knelt together like a pair of saints, but I tell you, that they're not here makes me suspicious."

Maredudd fixed his gaze on the two mailed horsemen who had descended the knoll to draw rein near the High Steward's pavilion. One of the men-at-arms had dismounted to become lost to view behind a line of land-holding jurors. The man reappeared to view when close to de Turberville, who turned in his chair, growling, "What, in God's name, are you doing here?"

"I've decided to exercise my right as a juror," Elgar returned. "So I've handed command of the men-at-arms back to de Dreues, which means I don't have to put up with him undermining my position anymore."

"That won't keep Rhydderch alive. I told you, de Dreues will have no qualms about running him through."

"Nor will his men. I overheard several of them wager on who would lance Rhydderch first."

"Are you suggesting that I am responsible for their inclinations?"

"No, what I'm saying is, I'll have no control over those men once they break into the gallop. So what's the point of me leading them?"

"*Fie!* You disappoint me. I was relying on you to capture Rhydderch, though why I should trouble myself about him is beyond me. Look at him – he knows something is up. Someone's put him on his guard. Iorwerth's priest most likely."

"Iorwerth's priest is dead. William found his body near Sweyn's Hall. He'd been stabbed in the throat – by de Viles, I'm sure, because I confronted him only paces away from where the body lay."

"I'll deal with that in due course. Right now my immediate concern is Rhydderch."

"On the contrary, monsieur, your immediate concern is coming this way."

De Turberville followed Elgar's gaze to see de Viles in full chain-mail, striding from the tithe barn near the church. He stared aghast when, further back, he saw Wilfred leading his master's battle charger. "Now what's he up to?"

"He knows the men-at-arms are in the township," said Elgar, "and the moment they come over the crest he'll mount up and go for Rhydderch himself. So what would you have me do? Take charge of his horse?"

De Turberville did not answer, but rolled his eyes upwards as thunder rumbled across the heavens, promising rain. It occurred to him that a downpour would delay proceedings, give more time for armed men to close on Abertawe and cut off any attempt at escape. He was distracted by de Viles as he drew closer, striding as though his role as pleader made him the most important man on the field.

'*You ignoramus,*' de Turberville thought. '*As if Lord William has any regard for you or this trial. It's Rhydderch he wants and right now he's on his way with many men, whereas you, you have no purpose.*'

De Viles strode past Maredudd and his supporters to take his place in front of the witnesses from Ystum Llymarch. Then the madman turned to stand, arms folded, bellowing, "I am the pleader of Lord William of Ogwr. I demand to know where he is so that I can confer with him."

Even as the madman spoke so the first heavy drops of rain fell. De Turberville looked up, threw a hand in the air and shouted, "That's it, I call a recess."

"You haven't answered me," de Viles snarled. "I demand that you do so now."

De Turberville ignored the demand as, head down, he hurried into the pavilion. His bemused retainer stood near an opening in the opposing wall, a coloured piece of cloth in each hand – a yellow one to signal archers to action; a red one to summon horsemen from the town. "No, Pierre, not yet," he snapped and, turning, looked out, between the flaps, to see men scattering under a deluge of rain. Most men took shelter in the church; some raced to the tithe barn beyond, but several men stayed where they were, de Viles being one of them. A short distance away, Maredudd and Rhain had not strayed from the horses. Though lashed and bedraggled by torrential rain, they were both apparently amused.

"Laugh, miscreants," de Viles thundered as he advanced towards them, "but the Lord, *He shall judge among the heathen. He hath also prepared for* you *the instrument of death. He ordaineth his arrows against the persecutors. He will wet His sword*, and *as the horse rusheth into battle, He shall fill this place with dead bodies*. None shall escape, for *an horse is a vain thing for safety....*"

De Turberville groaned: the madman was disclosing his stratagem, provoked by Maredudd Goch and the bard who stood by him. Then he witnessed Elgar, sword half drawn, move to meet the madman's advance. Elgar's unexpected appearance proved reason for de Viles to think twice about engaging three men.

De Viles looked to the ridge, wondering why the Breton had not signalled the garrison men-at-arms to action. His jaw set, he glowered at the three men who confronted him, thinking only of reasons why they deserved to die. The Saxon had confronted him many times, only days ago pinning him down over sacks of grain – but above all it was Maredudd Goch who deserved to die first, for not only did the miscreant mock him each time they met, but he was the one who, with Devil's aid, had brought about his capture ten years ago. Both men had to die, but how?

"Give me a sign, O Lord," he muttered through dripping lips, "so that I may know." His gaze fell upon the tithe barn beyond the church. Dark thoughts flittered through his mind. He saw himself enter the barn, mount up, then ride out, mace poised, to bear down on the two men who had caused him grief.

"Wilfred, let us take shelter in the barn, away from these miscreants, and bring my horse." He strode forward, his right arm swinging, his left hand resting upon his sword hilt. His adversaries gave way to his passing. One of them mocked him. '*Soon*,' he thought, '*you will laugh no more, nor will the Saxon stand and stare. Then I'll be free to turn on Rhydderch ap Cadifor.*' As he approached the eastern end of the church his gaze fell upon a niche in the end wall where three men sheltered from the rain. The bailiff, Baldred, he ignored; Rhydderch's steward, Sulien, was of no import – but the priest, Father Piro, captured his attention.

Something about the priest, the church, the torrential rain – they evoked memories of the monastery where, ten years ago, he had instigated the massacre of thirty men, women and children. He had himself bludgeoned several of those lost souls until the head of his mace had been covered in blood and bits of hair. It had to be done: it was the Lord's wish that the children of the damned be laid low; it had been *his* wish that the massacre would have drawn Rhydderch ap Cadifor into a close fight.

Still focused on Piro, he had a clear picture of the priest he had killed earlier. Dispatching Piro would be just as easy, except there were witnesses at hand. Yet he could not resist casting a furtive glance over his shoulder. Maredudd Goch and his company had not moved; he gave no thought to the whereabouts of the Saxon. He turned his head towards the church. It was plain that his approach troubled those sheltering in the niche, the more so when, moving closer to his horse, he reached for his shield and removed it from the high frame of his saddle. The unease that emanated from the niche made him mindful of the fear he had witnessed in Iorwerth's priest. Such fear he found gratifying. It prompted him to reach for his mace.

The first to react was Sulien. "Piro," he said, drawing his sword, "get behind me. Baldred, look to your spear."

"Not me," Baldred returned, lowering a pigskin of ale from his mouth. "I'm not standing up to 'im. I'm off."

Moving out into the rain, Sulien crouched, his sword held ready to engage. De Viles rushed him, using his shield to deflect the sword, then directing his mace at the man's forehead. The handle of his mace struck Sulien's raised forearm, fracturing bone. Sulien staggered back, agonized and fearing that a second blow would mean certain death. De Viles had no sooner moved in for the kill than the flat side of a blade struck his shoulder. He spun round.

At first, de Viles saw only a face encased in a chain-mail hood, the features distorted in part by his own blurred vision, and in part by the eyes that he discerned were half-closed as a protection against heavy rain. Not that the identity of the mailed man mattered to him. The fact that, sword drawn, the man backed away only drove him to direct a blow at his opponent's head. The handle of his mace jarred against his opponent's raised blade. Unable to prevent his mace being forcefully swept aside, he tilted his shield sharply, the rim striking the man's left shin, causing obvious pain. Pressing home his advantage, he advanced, forcing his opponent to retreat until, loosing balance, the man fell to the ground, a raised foot against his shield. As he drew back to deliver a blow that would smash the man's leg he recognized him as Elgar.

An instant later he caught the approach of a horseman whom he presumed to be William, who came at him, lance couched, hooves sending sods flying in the air. He turned sharply, angling his shield so that William's lance glanced off the surface. He staggered back as William galloped by, bespattering him with muddy water.

His eyes fixed on Elgar as he struggled up, he sprang, determined to lay his mace on the Saxon's back, at which point Piro fell upon him from behind, an arm about his neck, grappling for his mace. He turned sharply, driving the rim of his shield into Piro's ribs, then directing the flat, leather-bound surface into Piro's face, the impact bloodying Piro's nose and knocking him off his feet.

Eyes screwed against the rain, he squared up to Elgar, who had regained his feet. On his right, Maredudd and Rhain were running towards him, their swords drawn, their feet splashing water. He let his shield fall, allowing it to dangle from his neck by a strap, and pounced on Piro, grabbing him by the hair. "Stand back," he bawled, his mace poised above Piro's head, "or I'll kill him." His adversaries checked themselves. He watched them closely, more so Elgar as he circled round towards Maredudd. "*Be not far from me*, O Lord," he chanted, "*for dogs have compassed me; the assembly of the wicked have enclosed me.*"

"Maredudd, listen to me," said Elgar, his words almost drowned out by the madman's chanting. "You're about to be entrapped, you and Rhydderch. So get away from here quickly."

"What and leave him...."

"I'll see to him, just keep him occupied till I'm ready, then go."

As Elgar moved away, Maredudd shouted, "Remember this, psalmsinger?" He let fall his sword, the blade landing crosswise on his inclined right foot.

Elgar, meanwhile, as he moved further to the right, shouted, "William, get my horse so I can lay hold of my mace and shield."

De Viles half-turned to see William had his lance aligned on him, but could not – or would not – charge due to the close proximity of the three men who confronted him and the hapless priest about his legs. The moment he saw William canter away, towards the Saxon's horse, he turned to face his adversaries, chanting, "*All that hate me whisper together against me; against me do they devise my hurt. They image a mischievous device which they are not able to perform.*"

Desperate to offer an alternative distraction, Maredudd jerked his sword upwards, catching it by the handle, then twirling it about in the air, at the same time calling on Rhain to circle leftwards. To his right, Elgar backed away from de Viles, making it possible, on William's return, for him to get close to his horse and remove his shield in safety.

De Viles, believing that Elgar would mount up, shouted, "Wilfred, to me, bring my horse."

Unnerved by his master's violence and threatened by William's close proximity, Wilfred did not respond.

"Wilfred, *why hast thou forsaken me? Thou hast known my reproach, my shame and my dishonour; mine enemies are all afore thee!*"

"You're on your own, de Viles," Elgar shouted as, armed with mace and shield, he reappeared from behind his horse. "Now fight me, man to man, you as Lord William's champion, me as the champion of Maredudd Goch. If I lose, he's guilty."

De Viles cast a suspicious glance at Maredudd.

"If you're fearful of him," Elgar shouted, "I'll tell him to remove himself to the far side of the bridge."

To Elgar's surprise, de Viles suddenly made towards his horse, dragging Piro by the hair, his mace still poised above the priest's head. Elgar moved in the same direction, at which point Piro struggled up, then drove a heel at the madman's toes. De Viles agonized; he raised his mace, but found the priest too close for him to deliver a mortal blow. He drove a knee into Piro's ribs; as hair came away in his hand so Piro threw himself towards Elgar and rolled. Elgar sprang, forcing de Viles to choose between killing the priest or defending himself. De Viles chose to regain a hold on his shield, and did so quickly, taking advantage of the priest's position at Elgar's feet.

"*Blessed be the Lord, my strength, which teacheth by hands to war and my fingers to fight. My goodness, my....*"

Elgar had no sooner signalled to Maredudd to leave than de Viles attacked, striking his shield, the impact jarring his arm, reminding him that the madman was as strong as an ox. A rapid succession of blows, battering his shield, forced him to retreat until de Viles charged, shield first, almost knocking him off his feet. Unable to see, not daring to peer beyond the rim, Elgar broke away, darting rightwards, leaving the madman carried forward by his momentum. Elgar squared to his opponent, unnerved by the realization that the madman was a formidable adversary, known to dispatch men swiftly by battering them to confusion and catching them unawares by a succession of dirty tricks. If he was to survive, then he needed to keep his distance, weathering the attacks until the madman tired.

In the meantime, Rhain had knelt beside Sulien, enquiring about his injury, only to be told, "My arm – broken, I think – but you, get away from here. Something's up, a trap, I'd say. No, never mind me, I'm going nowhere, my arm's too painful; now go."

A similar warning had been conveyed to Maredudd by Piro, who likewise considered himself in no condition to ride, nor had he any wish to abandon Sulien. If Maredudd held back out of loyalty to those he considered friends, he soon found himself considering yet another threat. Men were leaving both the church and the tithe barn to witness de Viles in action; those from Ystum Llymarch had an eye on him as well as the fight.

De Viles, meanwhile, had paused. It seemed inconceivable that the Saxon had survived his savage onslaughts. No man had ever done that, not even the man who had scarred his bald head. "Lord," he gasped, "*my heart panteth, my strength faileth me* – but no, *in God I have put my trust. I shall not die, but live and declare the works of the Lord.*" He advanced, determined that he would have the Saxon this time. Shields clashed, the Saxon gave way, moving to one side. He stumbled forward, carried by his momentum, and caught the Saxon's arm swinging towards him. '*No!*' he thought, raising his shield. '*It can't be.*' A mace struck hard the top of his shield, driving the rim against his mailed hood, numbing his brain. His senses reeled. He collapsed to his knees; he slumped forward, aware only of water and wet grass in contact with his face – then nothing.

By then, Rhain had prevailed upon Maredudd to leave. Both men mounted up to wheel round and gallop towards the bridge, scattering those who tried to stop them. They were watched by Rhydderch, whose view of what had been going on had been partially obstructed by the church. Then, as suddenly as it had started, the heavy rain eased off.

"Pierre," de Turberville shouted over his shoulder, "signal with both cloths."

CHAPTER 27

FLIGHT

A retainer pushed through the rear flaps of the pavilion, waving two cloths – one red, one yellow – prompting a man near the bailey drawbridge to sound a horn. The first to respond were the forty horsemen who, soaked to the skin, advanced towards the crest, their wet pennants drooping at the top of their upright lances. In the bailey the captain of archers bustled about, bellowing at his men as they spilled from buildings where they had taken shelter from the rain.

Maredudd, Rhain and Elidir were galloping over the bridge when Rhydderch reined about, shouting, "Let's go. Spread out and ride hard." His men responded, tugging on reins, except the blacksmith, who continued to stare at the low ground south of knoll, where two clerics were running towards a stream known as the Cadle. "Bledri," he bawled, "are you with me or not?" Only then did the blacksmith wheel.

Galloping towards a trackway that led to the western highway, Rhydderch's company spread out so as not to be a concentration for French archers. Behind and gaining on them fast, Maredudd signalled to Rhain and Elidir to spread out, then glanced about in search of Morgan, but with Llywelyn's six youths among those heading westwards he failed to identify his son.

Snatching a glance over his shoulder, Maredudd witnessed horsemen careering down the slope between the bailey and the church. He faced his front, his thoughts on Elgar, wondering whether he had survived the madman's savage onslaught. He felt exposed, expecting arrows to pierce his back, being unaware that French archers had not yet manned the palisade; nor was he aware that the blacksmith was now heading south for the sandy wasteland, pursued by Morgan.

Rhydderch rode hard on the heels of his guide, Gruffudd, heading for a woodland track that led to the western highway. He had no doubts about outrunning heavily armed horsemen. What bothered him was that it would soon be necessary for his men to converge on him so that, should they meet opposition, they could charge their opposers as one. Spurring hard, he caught up with Gruffudd, signalling to him to rein in. Then turning in the saddle, he observed that his pursuers were ploughing through the stream, but were still some distance away; better still, he judged himself to be beyond the range of French archers. As his men closed on him, drawing rein, he caught sight of two of them heading for the sandy wasteland to the south. He cursed: nothing could be done about their detachment now – French horsemen were approaching fast.

"Let's ride!"

Spurring, he followed Gruffudd along the woodland track that led to the western highway. Maredudd appeared abreast of him, cloak billowing in the wind. By shouts and gestures, Maredudd made it plain that Morgan had headed south in pursuit of the blacksmith. Rhydderch threw a hand in the air as if to say *there's nothing can be done about Morgan now*. He felt a pang of guilt, knowing how he would have felt had Owain been the one to pursue Bledri.

Ahead, the track merged with the western highway, beyond which lay *the Mountain* that his guide knew well. In Gruffudd's wake he rode out onto the western highway, turning left as he did so, to see, more than a bowshot away, a column of men marching towards him – men who unbeknown to him had marched from the Peninsula to cut off any escape to the west. Then Gruffudd veered right, off the highway, heading north into woodland where the ground rose sharply, causing him to slow, hooves scuffing ground cover as he weaved between tall, upright trees. For a little while it appeared that his pursuers would catch up until they, too, lost their momentum. The lower slopes of *the Mountain* grew increasingly steep, so steep that it became a struggle to continue upwards. Soon men were dismounting to lead, even pull their horses on, hooves and feet slipping on wet soil.

Below, the French were finding the going harder, encumbered as they were by chain-mail and heavy weaponry. They were dispersed, most of them dismounted and they were losing ground. Yet they struggled on, searching for footholds in the wet soil, their leader, de Dreues, exhorting the dispirited to keep going.

Where the steepness of the slope eased, Rhydderch paused to take stock of the situation. His men were exhilarated by the plight of their pursuers. Youths shot at them with their bows; officers mocked them for their inability to catch up.

"If this slope doesn't tire them out," said Gruffudd, "then the higher ones will."

"That's it they keep coming," Rhydderch returned. "They may turn back and circumvent to the northern highway."

"And if they do that," Maredudd threw out, "they could cut off our escape."

"They don't know where we'll leave *the Mountain*," Gruffudd retorted. "Only I know that."

"Just so long as it's above where the northern highway meets the highway to St. Cyfelach's," said Maredudd. "We don't want to run into those Morgannwg men."

"It'll be well to the north," Gruffudd replied. "And now, my lord, you'll want to be away from here."

"Not yet," said Rhydderch.

Gruffudd appeared bemused. "I thought you wanted to clear *the Mountain* in haste, my lord."

"I do, but if we move too soon, those Frenchmen down there will give up and circumvent."

"And that's not what we want," said Maredudd. "We want them them behind us so we'll know exactly where they are."

Gruffudd shook his head, laughing, "I've heard it said you both know what the other thinks; now I know why."

When he set off towards the crest, Rhydderch did so at a brisk pace. The delay had served its purpose; now he was anxious to join forces with his tribesmen, and quickly, before de Turberville learned of their whereabouts. And the man most likely to pass on that information was Bledri.

. . . . . .

In the tidal waters of the bay into which the River Tawe flowed, Morgan impelled his mount forward, the current strong, his determination to catch the blacksmith even stronger. He would prove his worth, show everyone that Maredudd's trust in him was not misplaced, that he was as dependable and resourceful as any man. Yet rein and kick as he might, he had to concede that the traitor had proved himself to be the better horseman, firstly by fording with comparative ease a stream known as the Cadle, then outrunning him over sandy wasteland. It had come as a surprise to him that Bledri had not sought safety in the town, but had made straight for the river, bent on catching a ferryboat.

That ferry the traitor had missed, as had three men from the town, the boat leaving with only the ferryman and two churchmen as passengers. The three men on foot had returned to the town in haste, whereas the traitor had ridden off to ford shallower waters to the south; now he was in those waters, fearful and struggling against the current, while his quarry had made it to the far bank.

Distracted by shouts to his rear, Morgan turned in the saddle to see several horsemen had entered the shallow waters of the bay. His immediate thoughts were that the men were after him. In fear he began to swear – at the horse, his predicament, that he had fouled up yet again. He stopped swearing when he recalled Maredudd saying, as he pointed to his mouth, '*Instead of using this, try using what's between your ears.*'

'*But what's there to think about?*' he thought. '*Those men are after me, me and Bledri. They must have seen us ride away from the others. That's why three of them cut us off from the boat.*' Then he remembered: the three men who had turned back to the town had shown little interest in Bledri as he approached at speed, but were more concerned in catching the ferry – either that, or the two churchmen who were in it, the same who had long since made it to the far bank. Then it dawned on him: if those men had no interest in Bedri, then they were not after him; it was the two churchmen they were after.

· · · · · ·

In the sandy wasteland on the far side of the bay a breathless Gronw dropped to his knees, his black Benedictine garb wet through and covered in sand. "For St. Teilo's sake," he gasped, "stop. Let me get my breath."

Caradog turned back, breathing heavily. "Useless, that's what you are."

"Not me. It was you who got us into this mess. I wish to God I hadn't come to warn you about the call to arms. I should have stayed at our father's hall, but, no, I had to come and you, you had to talk me into staying."

"It was for your own good. I told you there was no point in you going home just to get killed in the service of Lord Rhydderch – he's finished. Even if he escapes entrapment, he'll have Frenchmen at him from all directions."

"Yes, but what about us? What about de Viles? He could be dead...."

"Forget him. When things settle down I'll go back, come to an arrangement with de Turberville. He's already said he can use someone like me."

"That's not going to help us now. We should have stayed in the castle, but you, you had to hear what was going on at that trial."

"That's as maybe, but how was I to know Iorwerth ap Meirchion would try to take us when it rained. It's as well I saw him coming, him and his henchmen; now you've got your breath let's go." Caradog pricked up his ears; when his brother made to speak, he snapped, "Shut up, someone's coming." He ducked into the brush, followed by Gronw, crawling on all fours. "Shh!" he whispered, a finger near his lips, a skene in his right hand. He peered through foliage to see the legs of a horse, its hooves thumping the wet sand as it progressed towards him. The horse came to a standstill.

"I know you're in there, Caradog, you and your rat-faced brother. I'm going to kill you both."

Caradog turned his skene around, concealing it in the sleeve of his cassock, the blade aligned on his wrist. "Bledri, wait," he said, coming to his feet, "You can't kill us, we're of kin. And me, I'm married to your sister."

Fearsome in his appearance, more so due to the peculiar way he held his spear near the butt, the shaft almost an extension of his bare, muscular arm, Bledri snarled, "You treacherous bastard, I took you into my confidence and everything I said, you passed on to de Viles; that means I betrayed my lord and I'll hang for it."

"Na-na, you'll not hang," said Caradog, edging out of the brush, "not now that Lord Rhydd...." The tip of Bledri's spear touched his chest; he would have to get closer to use his skene. "Now hold on, Bledri. Lord Rhydderch is finished, whereas you and I, we can work this out. We can...."

"That's it, grovel, you bastard. I want to see you grovel afore I kill you."

"Yes, yes, we'll grovel. Gronw, get on your knees."

Gronw fell to his knees, crawling like a dog towards the horse's legs, blubbering for mercy. Bledri drew back, easing his spear from Caradog's chest, time for Caradog to knock the spear shaft aside and leap forward, directing his skene at Bledri's leg, but the blacksmith wheeled so as to thrash Caradog with his spear shaft. Caradog recoiled, covering his head, and forced his way between thickets. Unable to follow, Bledri made to circumvent the thickets until, seeing Gronw scurry away, he turned back, driving his spear into Gronw's thigh.

Gronw screamed, clutching his leg, while Bledri went in pursuit of Caradog, whom he observed zigzagging through the brush. He resisted the temptation to hurl his spear, fearing that, should he miss, his quarry would have a weapon that he was well able to use. Caradog disappeared to view beyond a small dune. By the time Bledri had circumvented to the dune, Caradog was nowhere in sight, but his footprints had left a clear trail in the wet sand.

Head down, back bent, Caradog zigzagged through several small dunes. Then descending in haste to a watercourse between sandy slopes, he fell back, his feet buried in the sand. He struggled up, turning fearfully to see his tell-tale footprints. In a state of panic he headed back towards the brush when, suddenly, a horseman appeared to view. He stood agape before turning back, but the horseman bore down on him, causing him to turn again, falling to his knees, gasping. "No, Morgan, wait. It's Bledri, he's right behind me. He'll kill us both. He's already killed Gronw."

"Gronw will have got what he deserved," Morgan spat, reining in. "Now I'm going to kill you, you damn liar, for saying I stole your wife's jewellery."

"Na, that was Gronw's doing. I only went along with it because he was my brother. You'd have done the same for one of your own, you know you would."

Morgan circled around his quarry, his bow aligned to loose an arrow at Caradog's chest. "You still betrayed Lord Rhydderch, you treacherous bastard."

"No-no, Bledri's the traitor," Caradog gasped, following him around on his knees. "He used my brother to pass on information to de Viles. I only got drawn into it because I had to flee from becoming a saleable thief. Now, you, you can do what you like with me, but then you're going to have take on Bledri by yourself. Better we go for him together – oh! No, look, there he is."

Silhouetted against the sky, Bledri came over the crest of a dune, directly above Caradog's footprints. His appearance caused Morgan to feel vulnerable. Bledri was known to be a formidable spearman, well able, with his muscular arms, to wield a spear with ease as some men would a sword.

"Morgan, listen to me," Caradog jerked out. "He's not going to admit he's a traitor, but that's what he is. If we kill him, we'll have done Lord Rhydderch a service, and I, I will have avenged my brother's death."

"Morgan," Bledri shouted as he descended to the watercourse, "whatever he's saying, don't believe a word of it. He's a liar is our Caradog."

"You believe that, you'll believe anything," Caradog croaked. "Kill him. You can do what you like with me afterwards, I've got no horse, I can't escape."

"Watch him, Morgan," Bledri warned, "he's got a skene."

"That's right, I have," Caradog spat, rising to his feet. "I'm not going to stand by while you kill me. And Morgan, are you going to kill him too?"

Bledri drew rein. "Take it easy, Morgan," he growled as, tight-lipped, Morgan raised his bow. "I got no quarrel with you. It's *him* I want, he's a traitor."

"Me," Caradog hurled back. "It's you who came to my father's house, telling us all you knew about Lord Rhydderch. Aye, and then you played on my brother's stupidity. You got him to pass on the information to de Viles."

"Liar! Anything I said, I said to you and your brother, and I said it in good faith. I was a fool, I know that now, but that's how it was."

"Don't listen to him, Morgan," Caradog spat, picking up a stone. "Let's kill him. Are you with me?"

Not knowing who to believe, Morgan cudgelled his brain as to what Maredudd would do in a situation such as this. All that came to mind was Maredudd's words, '*Think, Morgan, there's no point in putting yourself at risk when a few words could turn things round.*'

"Well, what are we waiting for?" Caradog demanded. "You shoot him; I'll stone him."

"You stone him," said Morgan. "I want to see *you* do something first."

Caradog darted forward, hurling the stone at Bledri, who deflected it with his shield. Caradog recoiled, dismayed that Morgan had not used his bow. "You didn't shoot him," he shouted, retreating with the intention of taking refuge behind Morgan's horse, but Morgan circled around him so that both men remained in front of him.

"I don't want to fight you, Morgan," Bledri ground out. "You just ride off and leave Caradog to me."

"You'd do better to let him live," said Morgan, "take him back to face trial, like I had to do. It's the only way you'll clear your name, if what you've said is true."

"It's true, but the fact remains that what he passed on to de Viles came from my mouth."

"Liar," Caradog spat, and turning to Morgan, "I never had any dealings with de Viles. So who do you believe – me or him?"

"All I know for sure," Morgan replied, "is the man who warned the garrison of attack was dressed in a grey cassock like the one you're wearing right now."

"Na-na, you don't understand. When I took refuge at Abertawe I was given a black cassock so no one would know who I was, only it didn't fit me. So I changed it for the one my brother was wearing – this one. If my brother was alive now, he'd say the same, only *he* silenced him, same as he'll silence me and you."

"I haven't silenced anyone," Bledri cut in. "Gronw is back there, bleeding like a pig. All I did was spear him in the back of the leg."

"So why," said Morgan, "don't we find Gronw and see what he has to say about Caradog laying the blame on him?"

"I'll agree to that – but first things first." Bledri advanced, his right arm raised, his spear poised as though he was about to lunge with a sword. "Caradog, either you throw down your skene, or I'll spear you."

Caradog retreated in fear, his face turned towards Morgan. "It's a trick, Morgan. All he's doing is trying to get close enough to kill us both."

"Then do what he says," said Morgan. "Drop the skene, or I'll kill you myself."

Caradog flung his skene to the sand. Bledri drew to a standstill, his spear head close to Caradog's chest. Then jerking his head for Caradog to move, Bledri growled, "Go, follow your footprints. I'll be right beside you all the way."

"Bledri, look," said Morgan, his gaze fixed on the crest of dunes where seven horsemen had appeared to view. "Those men, they followed me across the bay, and it's Caradog they're after."

"Yeah? Well, if it's him they want, they can have him dead." Bledri prodded Caradog with his spear. "On your knees, you." He turned to Morgan. "Get ready to run; make for the brush."

"No, let's talk first, now while they've drawn rein."

"Talk! You see that one in the costly clothes, it's Iorwerth ap Meirchion, a treacherous bastard if ever there was one, and he'll have no qualms about handing us over to the High Steward; that's if he takes us alive."

CHAPTER 28

PURSUIT

In woods close to the northern highway, Rhydderch drew rein in response to a signal from his guide, Gruffudd ap Meilyr. A halt before venturing out onto the highway would give his men time to catch up, to close on him. They were in no danger: the last he had seen of his pursuers had been on the far side of *the Mountain*. He assumed that his pursuers had given up, that they had returned to Abertawe. They would certainly not have had time to circumvent *the Mountain* to become a threat to him a second time.

On the open ground beyond the tree-line, Gruffudd signalled that it was safe to venture out onto the verge. Rhydderch led the way, weaving between partially hidden tree stumps. To the south the highway was deserted; to the north it appeared much the same except that, less than a bowshot away, part of the highway was lost to view in dead ground. On reaching the highway he waited for his men to join him, Maredudd counting them as they filed out onto the verge.

"My lord," Gruffudd shouted, "horsemen to the north."

At first Rhydderch saw only pennants at the top of upright lances, reason for Gruffudd to warn of horsemen. That they were French lances went without saying, as lances were for the most part the weapons of foreigners. With his intended escape route to the north now blocked, he wheeled, shouting, to those nearest him, "About face," and to those still traversing the verge, "To me, quickly. Maredudd, get everyone onto the highway."

The ground rumbled as his men cantered towards him, in which time he witnessed to the north the heads and shoulders of half a dozen horsemen appear to view. That the horsemen had seen him was evident by the speed in which they and others rose up from the hidden ground. He waited long enough to see the livery of the leading Frenchmen. Then spurring, he gave the order to ride.

Heading south down the highway, he focused his thoughts on the blue livery worn by the leading Frenchmen, the livery of his old adversary, William de Londres, Lord of Ogwr and High Steward of Cydweli and Carnwyllion. It was no coincidence, as far he was concerned, that de Londres and his Cydweli men were advancing on Abertawe at a time when men from

Morgannwg were conceivably doing much the same thing. He had no reason to doubt that the object of these invasive forces was to cut off any escape from de Turberville's entrapment. That the men from Cydweli had succeeded in blocking his escape to the north put him in a precarious position, for now he had to ride south, in the direction of Abertawe, thereby risking a clash with either the garrison horsemen under de Dreues, or the jurors whose horses he had seen grazing south of the church. On an open highway such as this his men would be no match for heavily armed horsemen. The best he could hope for was to make for the woods and, if necessary, continue his escape on foot.

Less than half a mile into the ride south, Gruffudd caught his attention, pointing to the left, as if seeking his approval to turn onto the highway to St. Cyfelach's. He nodded in agreement, conscious that there really was no alternative. As he slowed, intending to wheel onto the St. Cyfelach's highway, he was thankful that he had not encountered French horse from Abertawe.

The sharpness of the turn presented him with an opportunity to look back, to observe that his pursuers were some distance behind him, about thirty or forty of them. He also caught sight of one of his youths cutting across the verge, a dangerous move due to hidden tree stumps. Then it happened – something he had been dreading. Above the rumble of hooves he heard his huntsman shout, "Someone's down." The youth who had cut across the verge sprang to mind. He gritted his teeth, telling himself that he could not turn back. Whoever had fallen would have to see to his own safety: if he could run, or limp, he would have to make for the woods.

His thoughts on whoever had fallen soon passed, being pushed to the back of his mind by a more pressing problem: now that he rode the highway to St. Cyfelach's he risked running into the Morgannwg men. In many respects they were more of a threat than his pursuers, for not only were they likely to overwhelm him by sheer weight of numbers, but most of them would be Countrymen, well able to pursue him of foot should he make for the surrounding woods.

His gaze fell to the highway, rocky in places, otherwise a morass of mud, pools and innumerable indentations, far more than he could remember seeing on the northern highway. At the gallop it was impossible to scrutinize what he saw, or what he imagined he saw, on the verge as well as the highway – that many of the footprints were recent, made by men who had marched this way after the thunderstorm had passed. Were they the footprints of the Morgannwg men, of his own men, of travellers who had banded together for safety? Or were the more recent footprints a figment of his imagination, something in which he could place his trust? He dismissed such thoughts with a definitive, "*No!*" In truth, whatever lay ahead, the prospect of being killed or captured by the Morgannwg men did not daunt him. He felt exhilarated by the chase and by his belief that God was with him.

As he topped a rise he glanced back to see that the Cydweli men were still in hot pursuit, but had lost ground. In the intervening space one of his men trailed behind, in danger of being caught or killed. He could do no more than pray for the man.

On the far side of the rise the highway fell sharply to a stream known as the Burlais. In the distance there was no sign of the Morgannwg men, a good sign in that the closer he got to the Uwch-coed border, the better his chances of escape. The question, then, was what if he were to evade both the Morgannwg and Cydweli men? What would de Turberville do then? Would he march on Uwch-coed? If the High Steward were to do that, it would mean war – a war not of his choosing, one that he was not entirely prepared for, but one he would respond to nonetheless.

Before fording the stream he slowed, the rumble of hooves giving way to the sound of splashing water. The splashing grew louder as Maredudd drew abreast of him. "Who's that trailing behind?" he called out.

"Elidir," Maredudd returned. "He went back for Cadell, he being the one who fell when we turned onto this highway. They're riding two to a horse."

"They'll never keep up."

"That's as maybe, but Elidir is a good lad, he'll make for the woods afore the French catch up on him."

Beyond the stream the ground rose gently, making it difficult for Rhydderch to look back at his pursuers due to the men behind him, even though they were spread out to avoid flying mud. An opportunity to observe his pursuers came when, a quarter of a mile from the stream, he rounded a wide bend in the highway. Elidir and Cadell were nowhere in sight. His pursuers had fallen far behind; they had no hope of catching up.

Maredudd, his face and clothes flecked with mud, drew abreast of him again, calling upon him to slacken the pace, then shouting, breathlessly, "They'll soon give up. That'll spoil our surprise. Let's stop – make out your horse is lame."

"What – here, in the open?"

"Yes. All you've got to do is rein in and dismount."

Rhydderch continued to ride while he considered whether, after reining in, his men could spur to full gallop before their pursuers got too close. His own stallion had the strength; the mounts of his youths were less than thoroughbreds. He raised an arm, shouting, "Keep the youths moving." Then reining in, he dismounted, leaving Gruffudd to ride on alone, oblivious to the halt.

Maredudd wheeled, shouting and signalling to the youths to ride on.

In the meantime, Rhydderch called, to his huntsman, "Huw, check the footprints near the verge; see what you make of them." He regained the saddle, his head turned towards his pursuers who were still some distance away. Their speedy approach unnerved his officers. He warned Huw to be ready to move. Then, when he saw the first lances levelled, he gave the order to ride.

Not daring to look back, he rode his white stallion hard, hoping that he had not left it too late. Huw appeared on his left, shouting, "Them tracks – there's many of them fresh – all leading to Abertawe."

After signalling acknowledgement, he focused his thoughts on whether the Morgannwg men had already passed this way; if they were no longer a threat, then he would be free to deal with the Cydweli horsemen, whom he believed were led by William de Londres, the Frenchman accredited with the conquest of Is-coed on the Earl's behalf. It had to be de Londres, he reasoned, because any other man would have given up the chase after the first mile, as had de Dreues on *the Mountain*.

It seemed odd, almost fitting that de Londres should be the one to lead the pursuit because they were passing through a locality where, ten years previously, when the highway had been no more than a woodland track, he had inflicted several humiliating setbacks on the Frenchman. It had started with a bloody repulse at Upper Ford, two miles to the north-west, to be followed by a succession of woodland ambushes. It was no secret that de Londres still considered those setbacks as unfinished business; hence the man's determination to hound him to the Uwch-coed border, or even beyond.

The highway rose sharply; it would continue to do so for a mile until it traversed a rise on *the Little Mountain*, beyond which lay the border and a reception to cover his retreat. His pursuers were still with him, though some distance behind and, therefore, not an immediate threat in that he could outride them whenever he so wished. He could be confident, too, that there would be no encounter with the Morgannwg men, for had they dispersed his tribesmen he would have been warned of their approach by now.

Maredudd drew abreast of him, shouting, "Things could get bloody soon. So where do I fit in?" In response to Rhydderch's blank expression he added, "Am I reinstated as your captain of guard, or not?"

"I'll think about it."

"That's cutting it fine. I'll wager de Londres doesn't need time to think – he just keeps coming – makes me wonder if it really is him back there."

Rhydderch withheld comment to consider Maredudd's words. De Londres was certainly no fool: he would know better than any Frenchman that to enter the foothills to which they were heading was to invite trouble; if that were not enough, then the man must surely know by now that feigning a lamed horse had been no more than a trick to lure him into the foothills. So why did he keep coming? Did the man press on in the belief that the Morgannwg men would cut off his retreat? Or that a relentless pursuit would prevent him from attending to the defence of Uwch-coed? Or was it, as Maredudd had suggested, that his pursuers were led not by de Londres, but by someone out to prove himself?

As the rise that concealed the border came into view, so Rhydderch focused on the sobering thought that should his pursuers venture beyond the crest, then what would follow would put an end to the concord of the last ten years. There would be no more compromises, no more brinkmanship with the likes of de Turberville – it would be all-out war.

On his left one of his youngest youths ventured out from the tree-line, beckoning to him to leave the highway. "Hywel," he shouted as he cantered across the verge, "have the Morgannwg men passed this way?"

"Yes, my lord, they did so when the rain came. We took cover in the woods till it was safe to come out again."

"D'you know how many?"

"I heard it said they were two hundred strong, my lord."

On reaching the highest point of the rise, Rhydderch saw, on the low ground beyond, a line of felled trees and boughs – the trees relatively small – all laid out across the highway and the verge on either side, the topmost branches towards him. The trees were a form of defence known to the French as an *abatis*, a barrier designed to halt a charge by horsemen. Behind the *abatis* some seventy bowmen stood in line, arrows notched on their lowered bows. They were either youths of his retinue, or young men who had served in the bodyguard in the last ten years, all of them trained and practised bowmen. Beyond the bowmen were the older men, most of them high men, four of whom were the appointed leaders of kindred groups, his father-in-law, Rhodri Gadno, being one of them.

Rhydderch cantered down beside the tree-line, heading for a gap between the *abatis* and the woods. All eyes were upon him, every man keen for action, being warned of the approaching danger by the youths who had ridden ahead. He passed through the gap to circle round to the rear of the bowmen and drew rein beside his father-in-law. Too breathless to shout, he instructed Rhodri to repeat his words.

"Men of Uwch-coed," Rhodri shouted hoarsely, "your lord has been pursued by more than thirty French horse. Soon they'll come over the rise, and they'll do so because the concord is over. By an act of treachery they tried to kill our lord and those who were with him. So look to your bows; await my order to shoot."

A youth signalled from the tree-line on the rise. Everyone waited in silence, eyes fixed on the highway near the crest. The rumble of hooves suddenly grew louder as three horsemen appeared to view, silhouetted on the skyline, galloping hard, to be followed by others in ragged procession, the slope of the rise giving renewed impetus to their jaded horses.

The leading horseman seemed oblivious to the *abatis* until, raising his lance, he attempted to rein in, turning his head left and right as he searched for a way forward. He barely had time to raise his shield before a hoarse command sent a flight of arrows hissing towards him. Two arrows embedded in his shield; three sank deep in his horse's flesh so that, neighing loudly, the horse collapsed, throwing him to the muddy highway, oblivious to the carnage all around. Three more horses had collapsed, one of them crushing a wounded rider as it rolled. Two horses had stampeded onto the verge, one riderless and in pain, the other fighting against reins as a wounded man-at-arms struggled to control it. Only one horse passed him by, dragging a retainer by a stirrup, his lifeless body trailing behind like a rag doll.

The horsemen following behind barely had time to veer away from those already down. They had no time to retire beyond the rise, for even as they reined in to wheel about a second flight of feathered shafts rained upon them, piercing mail and flesh, bringing more men and horses to the ground. Several more horsemen were visible on the crest when yet another flight of arrows took to the air to descend upon them as they desperately tried to retire beyond the rise. Some fell, others made it to safety, leaving the skyline devoid of life.

The man-at-arms who had led the pursuit stirred, raising his head to see a slope strewn with the bodies of men and horses, as well as lances, helmets and shields. The only objects that stood anywhere near upright were the arrows that had missed their targets. His gaze drifted to the crest where several youths demonstrated their exuberance by shouting and jabbing their weapons in the air. The shouts of equally exuberant men drew his attention to one end of the *abatis* where Countrymen, both on foot and on horseback, were pouring through a gap near the tree-line. He struggled up, ignoring the pain in his knee, and fumbled for his sword, intending to defend himself against the horseman who cantered towards him. By the time he stood, feet apart, with both hands on the hilt, his blade levelled before him, the Countryman had dismounted. The man made no attempt to engage him, only manipulating his blade in the manner that was intended to impress. Then a spear shaft fell across his back, bringing him to his knees, his sword falling from his grasp. The pain in his knee caused him to pitch forward on all fours, staring at the untanned leather boots of the Countryman who stood in front of him.

"Good man, Iago; now let's see who he is."

Rough hands removed his chain-mail hood, regardless of the hurt it caused; removing his leather coif, the same hands gripped his hair, pulling his head back.

"Your name, monsieur?"

The man-at-arms gave no reply, but stared contemptuously at the red-haired, bearded man whose wolfskin coat prompted him to recall de Turberville's description of Rhydderch ap Cadifor's right-hand man, Maredudd Goch.

"Are you ashamed of your name, Frenchman?"

"Not me. I'm Maurice de Londres, eldest son of William, Lord of Ogmore."

"Agh! That would explain your reckless pursuit. I heard it said you're as headstrong as an ox, which means you've got the brain of an ox."

"Your insults I can ignore, miscreant, because soon – soon you and your Lord Rhydderch will be counted among either the vanquished, or the dead."

"Soon! How soon? Tomorrow? Next week?"

"Sooner than you think, miscreant: that's all I have to say."

"So, my Lord Rhydderch's days are about to end, but who will be the one to bring him low? Not de Turberville, that's for sure. That fox knows only treachery and he's had his chance. Then there's your father. He may talk of a day of reckoning, but that's all he's done in ten years – talk. So he sends an ox-head like you to do what he hasn't the courage to do himself. And look at you now, a prisoner. No, your father, he'll do what he's always done – he'll shy away from measuring his strength against my Lord Rhydderch."

"My father never shied away from anything – never! The only reason he's held back is because that's how the Earl of Warwick wanted it. But all that's changed; now the Earls wants your Lord Rhydderch where he can no longer plot rebellion, and that's the way it'll be."

"What, today?"

"Yes, today. Today is my father's day of reckoning, and anyone who stands by your Lord Rhydderch will live only to regret it."

"You hear that?" said Maredudd, turning to one of the horsemen who had gathered nearby. "We're in trouble and all because of you."

Ignoring the jibe, Rhydderch inclined towards his guide, Gruffudd, saying, "Does your offer to be of further service still stand? Then go back to where the two highways meet and watch all who pass by. Watch which way they go, count their number; above all I want to know how many of the garrison leave Abertawe. Send word if you can; if not, I'll meet you there later. Huw, pick out two youths and go with him." No sooner had the four men taken their leave than Rhydderch addressed the leading men around him. "Gentlemen, two days ago we talked; if your decision to fight still stands, this is what I would have you do. Get the men to gather up all arms and armour from the vanquished and place it in front of the *abatis* so those of us who can speak French can attire ourselves to look like Frenchmen, myself included. I'll want the Frenchmen's saddlery placed there as well, so we can complete our guise. And, gentlemen," he added as he wheeled to face the rise, "I'll want it done quickly so we can make good use of what remains of the day."

CHAPTER 29

DOUBTS

After passing on his father's instructions to the youths, Owain rode towards the *abatis*, wondering what his father's intentions were. Although the young men had responded with enthusiasm, that had not stopped them plaguing him with questions. He looked towards the crest where his father had dismounted to kneel and pray. No doubt all would be revealed in due course, but for the moment he would have some answers from the one man who knew his father better than any other.

Maredudd stood by the *abatis*, issuing orders to everyone in earshot. His doorward, Owain Is-coed, took from him whatever he disrobed. Close by, the lifeless body of a retainer – one who had been dragged by the only French horse still standing – was in the process of being disrobed in a rough and hurried manner.

"So what's the purpose of all this?" Owain asked as he dismounted.

"We're going to take Abertawe."

"What! I never heard my father say that. So when did he tell you?"

"He didn't. I just know how he thinks, though not in the way men say. You see, getting into a castle in the guise of Frenchmen is something your father and I have often talked about. So when he gave the orders he did, I knew exactly what he had in mind; now get yourself attired in that retainer's clothes."

Owain stared at the retainer, stripped naked except for his breeches, his wounds clearly visible, his skin covered in blood. Cadog sprang to mind. He felt sick.

"It's the reality of war," said Maredudd. "If you stand up to those who mean you harm, then it's either you or them; now take off your cloak, plaid, boots and tunic."

Still in a state of partial shock, Owain made to remove his cloak, but found himself hemmed in by several youths, all of them acting on Maredudd's instructions. "So you're my father's captain of guard again."

"Again! I've never been anything else in ten years."

Maredudd's response had no sooner registered in his mind than Owain wondered how much influence Maredudd had continued to exert on his father's youths when, a month previously, his father had put him in command of the bodyguard. He had it in mind to challenge Maredudd on the subject, but the thought passed when a youth, jabbering about Abertawe, motioned for him to raise his arms so that a tunic could be pulled over his head. The tunic reeked of stale sweat; it was wet through and stained with blood. Another youth placed a shoe upon his left foot that was obviously too big, while two other attempted to bind the lower half of his breeches with thongs. '*It's madness,*' he thought; the very idea of marching on Abertawe was typical of Maredudd, but surely his father had considered that, apart from a garrison of seventy men, there would be two hundred men from Morgannwg at Abertawe by now, to say nothing of an unknown number of Cydweli men. Then it struck him: the prisoner, Maurice de Londres, had said today is his *father's day of reckoning*, meaning, presumably, that every available man would march out from Abertawe to engage these Uwch-coed men who would, themselves, be marching in the opposite direction to take a castle in which, it was assumed, there would be few defenders.

"Maredudd, most of these men don't know what my father's intention are. So what happens if…."

"Don't trouble yourself about that. They'll be told soon enough, and when they are I'll wager there's not a man here who'll object. You know why? Because these men will follow your father to hell and back if need be."

Owain bit his lip, wondering why he should be the only one with doubts. None of the youths around him were anything other than enthusiastic, especially Meurig, who pressed him to raise his arms so that a protective jerkin could be pulled over his head. It proved a struggle to get the jerkin on, but once Meurig had succeeded in doing so, he examined what weighed heavily upon his chest and shoulders: a thigh-length, leather jerkin, to which were attached a fair number of overlapping iron plates. Several of the plates were missing, one near his heart. He put a finger in the gap to find a blood-stained hole in the leather jerkin. At first he told himself that the hole was of no import, that he never wore armour, so what difference did it make? Then he took a good look at the hauberk that Maredudd had on: the chain-mail covered Maredudd's body from the shoulders to his knees.

"So what's on your mind?" Maredudd asked.

"Nothing," Owain replied, somewhat irked by the oversized leather coif that had been placed on his head.

Maredudd grinned. "You look just like your father when something bothers him."

Two youths set about placing a blue tabard over Owain's head. The back of the tabard was covered in mud as a result of its former owner being dragged down the highway, whereas the front had two large blood-stains, one below his throat, the other near his heart. Stains such as these would surely capture the attention of someone at Abertawe.

"Meurig," Maredudd called out to the foremost youth attending to Owain's attire, "cover those stains with mud."

Meurig willingly obliged, smirking as he did so, causing other youths to laugh. Owain did not object, but entered into the spirit of the joke, even though Meurig's facial resemblance to Caleb prompted a recall of his brother's tendency to pick on him. If there was one thing he had learned over the past few weeks, it was that, as the edling, it was both necessary and rewarding to establish a rapport with his father's youths. He would grieve if any of them were to die.

While a youth placed a belt about his waist – attached to which was a short sword – Owain looked to the crest to see his father no longer knelt in prayer, but had re-mounted to rotate a spear above his head, a signal for the men of Uwch-coed to gather round. "Maredudd," he said, voicing his thoughts, "what does my father pray for? Is it victory?"

"Na, whenever I rib him about it, he always says he asks the Good Lord to be with him, come what may. I don't know why when he's got me."

"What I mean is, he's a Christian, right and – oh! I don't know."

"No more do I, but what you have to understand about your father is this. He's got three choices – he can submit, he can run, or he can fight back. As to these Uwch-coed men, they look to him for leadership; that's why he's their lord. And I can tell you this, it wouldn't do with these men if he was unwilling to draw his sword."

"He's still a Christian. Does that bother you?"

"Why should it? He's still my foster brother and my lord – and more, he's a man I respect like no other. So why all the questions?"

"I don't know. Is it wrong that I should have so much going on in my head?"

"No, it just shows you take after your father; now let's hear what he has to say."

Owain listened to his father outline his wishes and his intentions: that his tribesmen should remain behind to conduct a fighting withdrawal in the face of an enemy advance, while he marched on Abertawe with his retinue – his officers, his youths and the ten churls who were with him, in all some sixty men. His objective would be to take the castle by guile, then send word to de Turberville, warning him that, if his men did not return to Abertawe by nightfall, he would not only burn the town, but he would call upon the Is-coed tribesmen to rebel, an act that would inevitably lead to the annihilation of French settlement in the Peninsula. Only one man raised an objection – Morgan's father, Ammon – and he insisted that he should be with his lord as he had ten years before.

As to those who would march on Abertawe, they would avoid a clash with de Turberville's men simply by taking refuge in woods. Then, when the enemy had passed by, some thirty men, almost all of them youths, would pose as *prisoners*. The *prisoners* were to be escorted by five French-speakers wearing armour, Rhain and Awst included, as well as a dozen men and youths masquerading as Countrymen in the service of William de Londres. When the men of Uwch-coed were invited to speak, none raised any objections, none had any cause to: the tribesmen would be defending their lands; their lord and his retinue would be taking the war to the enemy, hitting the French where they least expected it.

"Right," said Maredudd, "let's mount up and make ready to march. I want the youths on the highway in two lines."

Owain mounted the only French horses to survive unscathed, then rode off, calling on youths to gather on the highway; there were thirty-four of them in all, each and every one of them armed with a bow equal to that of any French archer. Maredudd rode up and down the two lines of youths, singling out those who would masquerade as an armed escort, as well as the carriers of captured bows. The remaining youths were shown how they should march into the castle as if their hands had been tied behind their backs when, in fact, they would be holding their quivers concealed beneath their cloaks.

Owain looked on, amazed by the thought that Maredudd and his father had given to what lay ahead. Only occasionally did he turn his attention elsewhere, usually to the *abatis* where his father donned armour, assisted by his page and several tribesmen. What struck him about his father was that while he dressed he conversed with leading men. It was as if, like Maredudd, his father did not care to waste time, nor leave anything to chance. Little wonder that men said of his father and Maredudd that they were two men with one mind. He wondered whether he would ever be at one with them, or even be included in the fraternity of court officers, all of whom – with the exception of Hywel the Cook – appeared to know exactly what was expected of them.

Maredudd, meanwhile, had moved on, telling the youths that once they had entered the castle they would be given a signal to grab their bows and split into groups, each group following the lead by an officer, namely their Lord Captain, Awst, Rhain, Hywel the Cook and Owain ap Rhydderch. It came as a surprise to Owain to hear his name mentioned, he being the one to lead six youths to the hall, the object being to prevent any Frenchman venturing out into the courtyard.

When it became apparent that his father was all but ready to mount up, Owain watched Maredudd move to the rear of the column where ten churls stood with their laden packhorses. Evidently the churls had a part in the action, though what exactly that entailed was difficult to discern due to the chatter of exuberant youths. Then, on the far side of the youths, he saw his father ride towards the head of the column, his page, Gerwyn, falling in with the youths. Moments later, Maredudd broke away from the churls, making towards him.

"We can't leave anything to chance," said Maredudd as he passed by, "so get rid of Giff. Give her to one of our churls and get him to put a leash on her."

"What about the horses?"

"What about them?" said Maredudd, continuing on his way.

"Take a look at this French rouncy – its mane and tail have been cut short. The mane and tail of your bay are long; that could give the game away."

Maredudd reined in, turning in the saddle as he did so. "Ah! Yes, I was about to attend to that."

"You were? Somehow I don't believe a word you say."

"That's because you know me so well."

CHAPTER 30

COUNTER-MARCH

Rhydderch led off, Maredudd at his right-hand side, Rhain, Ammon and four officers at his heels. Owain rode behind them, at the head of thirty-five youths, a lance in one hand, a kite-shaped shield hanging at his side by a shoulder strap. He found it gratifying to assume the role of edling. Over the past five weeks it had proved a rewarding experience, one in which he found himself no longer a younger son lacking purpose and responsibility. True, his position as edling had been made tenable because he had the backing of older youths, as had Caleb when he assumed the same role. His father and Maredudd had given every indication that they were pleased with the way he had conducted himself, not because of what they may have seen, but because Owain Is-coed would have kept them informed of any occurrence worthy of mention.

There had been times when he wondered how Caleb would have handled certain situations, but one thing he could be sure about: Caleb would have wanted to be here, marching on Abertawe. Had Caleb returned of late, his new-found role may have come to an end, but he would gladly have accepted Caleb's presence as the brother and companion he had been on the day they had parted company.

Ammon intruded on his thoughts. "Owain, your father wants you up front."

Owain spurred onto the verge to circumvent officers and rein in on his father's left. Something struck him as odd about his father: it was not that he rode a bay, or that he wore armour, but that his moustache had been cut; only stubble remained.

"I wanted you here," said Rhydderch, "so we can talk."

"That's right," said Maredudd from Rhydderch's right, "you're one of us now."

"I am? Since when?"

"Since now," Maredudd returned. "It's no longer your father and me; it's your father, *you* and me."

Owain found himself speechless. Caleb had never been one of his father's inner circle of councillors let alone rank as one with his father and Maredudd. So why had he been favoured?

"Whether we go for the castle," said Rhydderch, "will depend of two things. The first is that de Turberville makes an advance on Uwch-coed with as many men as he can, leaving only a small garrison behind. The second is whether *you* can get us into the bailey."

"Me!"

"Yes, on our approach to the castle I would have you ride ahead and tell those at the gates that your Lord William of Ogwr has had a resounding success, capturing my retinue. Tell them that the prisoners are to be kept under guard so that those with you can return to the fight. Get them elated – tell them that it'll all be over soon; that the men of Uwch-coed are expected to submit or suffer the consequences."

"What about how I speak the Frenchman's tongue? They'll know I'm not French."

"Most men speak the Frenchman's tongue in the manner of their own tongue. De Turberville is a Breton and speaks it little different from us. De Viles, on the other hand, is – or was – a Norman and recognized as such by the way he spoke. Then there's the Saxons, to say nothing of the Flemings. So let's just say you're Arthur de Caerdydd, the son of a Breton nobleman, and that you serve Lord William of Ogwr."

"The man most likely to challenge you," Maredudd cut in, "is Olaf, the castle constable. He's a Dane; he speaks gruffly from here, in the throat. Or you may be challenged by de Chalus, the captain of archers; now he speaks like he's in a hurry. I heard it said it's because he's a Gascon from somewhere in France."

"The question is," said Rhydderch, "are you prepared to do what I ask?"

"I'll do it, father," Owain replied confidently. A moment later he wondered what he had let himself in for. Then, as he topped a rise in the undulating hillside, something caught his eye. On the lower slopes of the *Little Mountain*, two men had dismounted from one horse to take cover in woods.

"That's Elidir and Cadell," said Maredudd, and twisting round in the saddle, he barked, at his doorward, "Owain, get after those youths – they think we're Frenchmen."

Owain Is-coed had no sooner passed by than Maredudd moved forward, jerking a thumb over his shoulder, in response to which Rhydderch nodded as though he knew exactly what Maredudd's intentions were.

"He's going to make sure our youths know exactly what's expected of them," Rhydderch explained, "whereas I'm going to tell you what I would have *you* do once we're in the bailey. When you hear Maredudd whistle you spur straight for the entrance of the nearest hall; your six youths will be right behind you. It will be your task to stop anyone leaving that hall, but be warned, there'll be bowmen in there. Call upon them to yield if you must, but don't go inside. And don't forget the windows – we don't want anyone shooting at us through the windows. Any questions?"

"How will I know who's to follow me?"

"Maredudd will have already singled them out. When he gets back here, you'll drop back and talk things over with those youths. When you've done that, come forward again."

"So what's Maredudd's task?"

"To take the tower, him and Owain Is-coed; now there's something you need to know. If the bailey has been rebuilt as it was afore last March, there'll be two halls and there'll be a passageway between them. The hall you'll go for is the one used by French bowmen; the other stands behind it and is used by the garrison horsemen. I doubt if there'll be any horsemen there, but Hywel the Cook will make his way round to the entrance just in case. The reason I'm telling you this is because there'll come a time when you and Hywel will have to enter the halls. What I don't want is you both meeting in the passageway and exchanging blows."

As they drew closer to where Owain Is-coed had left his grey, so three men emerged from the woods, one of them leading a horse. The two youths waved, prompting Owain to respond, only to check himself once he realized that they had not recognized him. Both youths took their place in the column, their horse passing to churls.

"So that you know," said Rhydderch, resuming where he had left off, "Awst will seize the bailey's southern gateway. Then there's Rhain; he'll have the largest number of youths and all our churls because it'll fall to him to take prisoners from the north gates and wall, where at least some of the garrison will gather to watch our approach. Mark you, I said *take prisoners*. The same goes for you – take prisoners if you can, shoot only if you must. I don't want this escapade to end in a bloodbath."

"Where will you be in all this?"

"By the north gates in the company of Llywelyn and Ammon. That's where our first prisoners will be held by some of Rhain's followers."

At the foot of the *Little Mountain*, Maredudd reappeared on Rhydderch's right, saying, "I think it time we had a couple of horsemen ahead of us. I'll send Owain Is-coed and Llywelyn."

Rhydderch nodded in agreement, then said, to Owain, "You'd best get back there and speak to those youths who'll follow you to the hall. Don't be too long – the other officers will want to speak to their youths."

Owain reined aside to drop back and shout, "Who's with me?" He was delighted with the response; pleased, too, that his father had entrusted him with no mean task, one that could turn nasty if Frenchmen emerged from the hall before he reached the entrance. He had no need to generate enthusiasm: all six youths were already eager for the fray, though not necessarily attentive to his father's wishes. What they wanted to know was whether his father would call upon the heavens to rumble and pour forth heavy rain, as it was rumoured that he had done just that at Abertawe. It made Owain mindful of the fact that, ever since the day de Viles had been routed, men believed that his father could bring down blinding rain.

When he resumed his place at the head of the column, Owain found his father conversing with Rhain – time enough for him to reflect on when he came this way seven weeks earlier, along with Caleb. And Cadog! They had shared horses then; they had ridden at the canter; now they were travelling at the trot, the youths well able to keep pace. It occurred to him that, at the pace they were travelling, they might arrive at the castle before the High Steward rode out across the drawbridge.

The conversation with his father resumed, Owain asked, "What happens if the High Steward doesn't march north as you say?"

"Then we'll torch the bailey with fire arrows; he'll march north then." Rhydderch considered Owain, then said, "Is there anything else you're not sure about?"

"No, I've asked too many questions as it is. It just goes to show that I – well...."

"Think? I wouldn't want it any other way. If you don't think, if you don't ask questions, then you live in ignorance. When Maredudd and I have something that demands our attention, we raise questions and we each say what's on our mind."

"Has he said anything to you about Morgan riding off the way he did?"

"No, but then I wouldn't expect him to. Why d'you ask?"

"I find him close-mouthed about someone who is now his son."

"That only shows the depth of his concern. He'll go looking for Morgan soon enough." In the silence that followed, Rhydderch considered the heavens. "Looks like we can expect rain."

A half-mile into the ride below the foothills the rise beyond the Burlais stream came into view, the scouts barely visible on the crest. Both scouts turned back to gallop downhill towards the Burlais, soon to be followed by a third rider. Owain turned to his father to hear him say, "That's it; they're coming."

Maredudd twisted round in the saddle, shouting, "Off the highway; into the woods quickly."

The column fell into disarray as men broke ranks and made for the woods. Near the tree-line, Owain dismounted to find Elidir taking charge of his horse, and Meurig relieving him of his lance as though he were his arms bearer. No sooner had he pushed in, under the trees, than he heard the pit-a-pat of rain on the canopy of foliage above his head. Elidir turned to him, saying, "Your father, he's called down rain just like he did at Abertawe."

Owain nodded, not caring to disillusion Elidir by stating that his father had no control over the clouds. Then another youth approached, telling him that his father wanted him at his side. He followed the youth until he came upon his father, who sat upon a low branch of a crooked tree. Unable to locate Maredudd among the officers nearby, Owain caught sight of him, returning to the edge of the woods in the company of several youths. Owain knew exactly what Maredudd's intentions were: to position the youths in pairs close to the tree-line, where they would count the High Steward's men as they passed by. One youth in each pair would count up to ten, at which point his companion placed a twig on a bare patch of earth, and so the counting in tens went on. It mattered not if the count was accurate, only that it gave a fair indication of what they were up against.

Owain had no sooner sat upon an exposed root of the crooked tree than his father turned to him, saying, "You know those youths will count the number of horse and foot, but what else will they count?"

"The men wearing the red livery of Warwick."

"Why would they do that?"

"So we'll know how many of the garrison have left Abertawe."

"That's good. Already you are of one mind with Maredudd and myself."

They both pricked up their ears. Above the pitter-patter on foliage the rumble of hooves grew louder until, reining in, three men entered the woods. One of them, a youth led by Maredudd, made towards them.

"My lord, Huw sent me to tell you the French are on the march. We saw them as they made towards the place where the two highways meet."

"D'you know how many?"

"No, my lord, only that they are many."

The youth moved on, Maredudd wandered about and soon the woods became silent except for the pit-a-pat of rain and the incessant drips from wet leaves. As time passed, so Owain became oblivious to the cold, to wet clothes and to the fleas that he imagined were at home in his coif, being totally absorbed in his thoughts of Anona. '*Where is she now?*' he wondered. Certainly not at Ynys Ammon, but somewhere far to the north on her way to Cantref Bychan. Two days ago, his father had sent word for everyone in the commote to bring in their herds and flocks, to bury or hide their chattels, and begin trekking to safety beyond Uwch-coed's borders. Some had headed east, crossing the River Tawe to find shelter in the wooded hills of Nedd; others had traversed the high moorlands to the north to escape into the wilds of Brycheiniog and Cantref Bychan. Anona would have left Ynys Ammon in the company of the men, women and children of her *resting-place*. Ammon would have been with her until such time as he, like every other able-bodied man, had turned back to muster at the Monastery of St. Cyfelach.

Now Anona, along with the women and children of her *resting-place*, would be without the help and protection of kinsmen, defenceless against man and beast. He visualized her, driving her father's cattle, stick in hand, over windswept moorland, through streams, stumbling over stony ground. His image of her put him in mind of Heledd, sister of Cynddylan, *the clear-mind and wise* Lord of Powys. Long ago, according to the bards, at a time when Saxon hosts were laying claim to the land of England, Cynddylan had been the bright buttress of the borderland. No Saxon *trod on Cynddylan's domain*, for *he would not yield a foot* – but one day Cynddylan, the *chain-clad, steadfast* Lord of Powys, was slain, his court on the Severn burnt in a surprise attack.

Heledd, his sister, had made good her escape into the mountains, there to survive with but her cattle and a blanket that was *the hide of a tough goat*; there to lament Cynddylan and his brothers, *all slain at one stroke*. A similar fate of poverty and grief might await Anona. And if by nightfall Y Faerdref crackled to the fierce tongues of flame, then halls throughout Uwch-coed would also burn brightly, devoid of life. Uwch-coed might never be the same after the invaders had returned home. '*What then?*' he wondered.

Still, there were a few thoughts that gave him small comfort. His mother, his sister and the women of his father's court would be making for Cantref Bychan, though they would not be herding cattle, nor would they travel on foot. They might meet up with Anona at some ford; if they did, they would not find her barefooted, but wearing his mother's untanned leather boots. Two days ago, those boots his mother had given him at his request; those same boots he had given to Elidir before he, like so many other youths, had set out to pass on his father's instructions to move and muster. Anona would be wearing those boots to protect her feet from coarse grass and stones. They would keep her feet dry when fording streams; they would be something by which she might remember him.

His thoughts fled when Maredudd poked him in the back, saying, "No more thoughts for loved ones."

Raising his head, he looked to his father, still sat on a low branch of the crooked tree. "They're gone," his father said. "The rain has stopped; it's time we moved."

It came as no surprise to Owain that everyone left the woods in haste, eager for what lay ahead. Even as men gathered on the highway he could hear Maredudd shouting not only at youths, but directing officers to take their allotted places in the column; it was as if Maredudd knew exactly where each man should be. The to-ing and fro-ing continued even when Gruffudd, Huw and another youth rode up to the head of the column. What these late comers had to say only confirmed what Owain had already been told: that over three hundred men were marching northwards, the garrison horsemen included, as well as fief-holders from the Peninsula, each with their own small accompaniment of men; better still, as Huw pointed out, none of the opposition had hived off where the two highways met, so there would be no two-pronged advance on Uwch-coed.

When the column set off, heading for the Burlais stream, Owain took note that only two officers rode behind his father – Rhain and Awst – both of them in armour. Maredudd did not join them as expected, but remained rearwards, directing the three late comers to take up positions flanking the column so that they, along with two other officers and seven youths, would masquerade as an escort of Countrymen from distant parts. Two other officers – Ammon and Llywelyn – were now marching as prisoners, as both men were likely to be recognized by the castle constable as past and present doorwards of his father. It was not difficult to discern that anything Maredudd had to say to these two men was received by Llywelyn in good part, whereas curt responses from Ammon demonstrated that he still harboured ill will.

Owain's deliberation as to whether the ill will might cause problems was cut short by his father, saying, "It's a fair assumption that we'll find the castle held only by garrison bowmen, thirty men at most. Chances are, many of them will be in the hall, warming themselves by a fire."

Owain nodded. "Don't you ever have doubts about what you do?"

"Always, but when you lead you have to keep them to yourself, otherwise others will pick up on them. Believe me, those doubts will pass when we get to Abertawe. Then we'll know only what needs to be done."

"I just hope I don't falter like I did with the boar."

"You won't. It wasn't far from here that I met you last March, returning from Abertawe. You stood firm then; you didn't run."

Beyond the Burlais stream, Owain gave thought to whether Maredudd would ever return to the van so that all three might be as one; only Maredudd's voice travelled forward. At one point he heard Maredudd tell the youths who posed as prisoners to hand over their bows to whoever marched alongside them as their escort; once that had been done, Maredudd directed the same youths to conceal their quivers beneath their cloaks, encouraging each and every one of them to check the concealment of whoever marched in front of them.

At the place where the two highways met, the column veered left and, with only half a mile to go, Owain knew that he would soon be riding ahead on his own.

"There's one thing we haven't discussed," his father said, "though whether you'll give due consideration to it is entirely up to you."

Even as his father spoke, Owain knew instinctively what those first words were leading up to; his mother had raised the subject many times.

"Men say I can confound the French whenever I so wish; that I have command of the clouds; that I can do other things as well. None of these things are true. At best I can think, but where each stratagem comes from is beyond me; nor can I make my stratagems work. Maredudd and I, we may work at them, each of us in our own way, but the rest is all down to Someone I saw crossing the Kedron. My father spoke of that Someone more times than I can remember, but Maredudd and I, we were young and his words fell upon deaf ears. Then, when our father died, we turned our backs on all that he had said, and that's how things were until ten years ago. At the time all my stratagems had come to nought; I had no inner strength. Then your mother made me realize there was another way forward. All I had to do was accept who that Someone was. You know what I'm saying?"

Owain nodded, not caring to be drawn into a discussion about God.

"As I said, the choice is yours, but should you find yourself faced with some insurmountable problem, or even death, then don't hesitate to call on the One who made me what I am."

Owain watched his father transfer a lance to his left hand. He was distracted by the appearance of Maredudd – not on his father's right, but on *his* left so that he rode between the two men. His father extended his right arm towards him and, transferring his lance to his other hand, he gripped his father's right forearm

"May God go with you, my son."

"Until I see you in the bailey," said Maredudd, proffering his right hand. "Now go, do what needs to be done."

Gripping both his spear and shield firmly, Owain spurred, heading for the castle directly ahead. He gave a thought to his father's last words, then dismissed them, unable to reconcile the things that his mother had said with his mission to lie his way into the bailey and perhaps kill. Besides, he needed to be focused. If he failed, this march on Abertawe would come to nought; those left behind would suffer the consequences.

As he remembered it, the bailey had been surrounded by a palisade about the height of a man and backed by an earthen bank for defenders to stand on, but the rebuilt palisade was reported to be higher with openings in it, which the French called embrasures. The rebuilt palisade was as yet barely discernable, being overshadowed by the buildings immediately behind it. What stood out, silhouetted against a leaden sky, was the tower crowning the motte. It appeared daunting, just as it had in the pale light of dawn some months earlier.

Still focused he tried to recall the names of those likely to challenge him. Olaf, the castle constable, he had heard of many times, but the other, the captain of archers – he could recall only that he was a Gascon. *'What matter?'* he thought. *'I know exactly what I'll do. I'll act jubilant; I'll be brash.'* He raised his lance, jabbing it in the air so that he might get the action right.

Directly ahead the north gates stood tall between two timber frames, above which there appeared to be an embattled platform. There were no archers looking down at him from the platform, but there were several men watching him from the embrasures to the right of the gates. He was sure he could hear someone shouting, causing him to wonder whether that someone was summoning the whole garrison to the palisade so that bows would be trained on him.

His father's words pricked him; he dismissed them again. He would survive. If threatened, he could raise his shield, thereby protecting himself from the shoulders to his left knee. He also felt confident about his plate armour, until he became conscious of the hole where a plate had been lost. He raised his shield slightly to cover the hole.

With the drawbridge only a short distance away he began jabbing his spear in the air, undeterred by the fact that there were perhaps a dozen men in the embrasures to the right of the gates. He reined in, shouting, in French, "Open the gates. My Lord William of Ogwr has captured the retinue of Rhydderch ap Cadifor and wants them handed over to Olaf, the castle constable, so that we can return to the fight. So come, open the gates quickly."

The man in the first embrasure to the right of the gates replied, hastily, "I'll open the gates when I'm satisfied I know who you are. So declare your name."

"Arthur de Caerdydd, the son of a Breton, and I serve my Lord William of Ogwr."

"You sound like a Countryman."

"So does your High Steward, whereas you, you're a Gascon, and if you moved your feet as fast as your tongue, I could be with my master afore nightfall."

"Enough of your insolence, Breton. I don't jump to the words of a retainer."

Owain spurred onto the drawbridge, the hooves of his mount drumming the wooded beams as he shouted, "Tomorrow I will have won my spurs. Then I'll be your equal, Gascon." Raising his lance, he pounded the gates with the butt end. "Now open the gates so that I might speak to Olaf the Constable."

A torrent of abuse fell from the Gascon's lips, causing Owain to wonder if his overweening manner had been ill conceived. The abuse was cut short by a man in the second embrasure right of the gates, one who appeared better dressed and who spoke gruffly. "So how many prisoners do you have?"

"Thirty-three, monsieur. My Lord William took them by surprise, almost without a fight."

"And what of Rhydderch ap Cadifor?"

"He's as good as finished, monsieur. His tribesmen are expected to submit by tomorrow and when they do so, my Lord William will have exalted himself."

"In my opinion he exalts himself enough as it is. And what's more, I'll have you know I don't take kindly to him giving me orders."

The man Owain suspected to be Olaf withdrew from the embrasure, growling, "This castle is my responsibility – mine, not some Frenchman with a ten-year-old grievance."

Owain's face fell: he was sure he had succeeded in convincing those behind the palisade that they had nothing to fear from him, yet the constable had turned his back on him. He twisted round in the saddle to see that his father had almost reached the drawbridge and the gates were still shut. "Lord," he said in a moment of desperation, "help me now," but the rumble of hooves on the drawbridge drowned out his words. Then he heard a bar being raised and the gates creaked open.

CHAPTER 31

THE BAILEY

Unrecognizable in a chain-mail hood, Rhydderch rode through the gateway towards Olaf, the castle constable, who stood some distance away, facing the gates, in the company of two archers. Rhydderch had no sooner reined in than the two archers moved to direct the column to wheel rightwards, as rightwards led to the only available space where the column could remain as one. The space made it possible for Rhain's followers to hem in the archers who stood with their backs to the palisade.

"Monsieur, I take it Arthur here has informed you about the prisoners."

Rhydderch paused, having detected suspicion in Olaf's eyes. For the briefest of moments he wondered whether the suspicion was due to the manner in which he spoke, but this he dismissed: Olaf was a Dane, his French course, his ability to distinguish one manner of speech from another limited. Then it dawned on him: Olaf had his eye on Maredudd, who was himself surveying the tower to his left.

"Monsieur, would you do me the service of having someone attend to my retainer?"

"Why, what's wrong with him?"

Rhydderch turned in the saddle, directing Olaf's attention to Awst who, slumped in the saddle, held a position to the rear. "He's hors de combat," he said, casting his eyes on the last of his churls as they came through the gateway, leading packhorses.

"Get some of your men to carry him into the hall, monsieur," said Olaf. "We've a Countryman priest in there who's well able to attend to wounds."

A disturbance at the head of the column caught the attention of both men. The two archers, after bringing the column to a halt, had pushed through the escort to humiliate Ammon on account of his size. In response, Ammon did no more than look to Rhydderch, who nodded, then gave Maredudd a pre-arranged signal. A whistle caused pandemonium. Ammon removed his hands from behind his back to grasp the archers' heads and bang them together with a deadening *thud*. The majority of Countrymen took off in different directions. Several churls quickly overpowered two archers at the gates. Others aligned their bows on the seven archers lined up against the palisade,

251

threatening them with death if they did not yield. It all happened so fast that Olaf had time only to face Rhydderch, expressing surprise, when the tip of Rhydderch's lance touched his chest, forcing him to retreat.

"Yield, Olaf! It is I, Rhydderch ap Cadifor! If you and your men yield, then no one need be hurt!"

Even before his father had spoken, Owain had spurred, galloping towards the hall where two archers had emerged from the porch, one of them aligning an arrow on him as, lance couched, he cried, "No, Lord, don't let anything stop me now." He sensed rather than saw, the arrow speed towards him, its tip destined to penetrate his flesh, but where that arrow went was a mystery to him. He bore down on the archer, saw him break away to take shelter in the porch, to be followed by an equally fearful companion. As he reined aside to avoid colliding with the porch he wheeled a tight circle, fearful that the companion would reappear to shoot him in the back.

The companion had, indeed, re-emerged from the porch, only to retire, howling, when an arrow, loosed by Meurig, grazed his hip. Owain circled round, shouting at his followers to stand back from the entrance. Raising his lance as he approached the porch, he drove it into the thatched roof, jabbing it about in the hope of forcing the archers to retire into the hall.

A youth sprang, loosing an arrow into the darkened entrance, causing Owain to damn him for his recklessness. A door was heard to slam shut. Then the reckless youth shouted, "Owain, look, they've gone inside."

Retrieving his lance, Owain urged his mount round to where his six followers had their bows trained on the dark interior of the porch. Further afield he could see his father had dismounted to stand with his back to a horse, a French shield to his front and a doorward on either side, both of them ready to die in his stead should arrows fly. The word *windows* sprang to mind.

"Elidir, Guto, Maredudd, move down, under the eaves, and cover any windows with your cloaks – jam them between the roof and the wall. Then get back here quickly."

Once dismounted, Owain removed his own cloak, saying, to his three remaining followers, "When they get back, you do the same further on. And use my cloak as well." He cast a glance down the side of the hall. Two youths were returning, but Guto appeared to have difficulty in hanging his cloak above a window. "Guto, hurry yourself up," he rasped, surprising himself with the harshness of his words. "I don't want anyone shooting at my father through the windows."

Maredudd, meanwhile, had his own problems. After whistling, he had galloped straight for the walkway to the tower where, on the embattled roof, one man observed his approach. By the time he reined in at the foot of the walkway the man had laid an arrow to his bow and taken aim. An instant later a narrow lodged in the high frame of Maredudd's saddle. He leaned forward, gripping the saddle, then attempted to dismount only to find his hauberk a hindrance to his legs.

Close by, Owain Is-coed had leapt from the saddle, calling on youths to shoot at the archer on the tower, but the man had retired from view. Owain switched his attention to Maredudd, who appeared to be sliding towards the ground, and rushed to his aid. Owain struggled to get Maredudd on his feet; together they hurried onto the walkway. Maredudd led, his kite-shaped shield held aslant above his head, Owain hard on his heels. The archer reappeared to let fly an arrow that lodged, quivering, in Maredudd's shield. They kept going, trusting to youths to neutralize the archer.

Moving unsteadily over the *swaying section*, one hand on a rope that served as a handrail, Maredudd felt confident that his youths had succeeded in neutralizing the archer as no more arrows came his way. Then it struck him: the archer may have left the roof to descend three floors in a bid to close the gate at the top of the walkway – if not him, then someone else.

Stepping onto a platform beyond the *swaying section*, he forced himself to ascend, as quickly as he could, that part of the walkway that led up to the gate. Sweating profusely in his leather coif and jerkin, the skirt of his hauberk a hindrance to his legs, he pressed on, up and up, keeping a wary eye on the embrasures in the palisade surrounding the tower. A few paces from the gate he considered drawing his sword, but had to accept there could be no time for that. Then he caught sight of the archer, hurrying past the embrasures. The gate swung shut. He threw himself at it, shield first, to fall in the gap between the gate and the gate frame.

Owain Is-coed stepped into the breech, a shoulder to the gate, a foot pressed hard against the gate frame. Suddenly the gate gave way, the archer retreating to disappear around a corner. Owain went after him to find that the man had entered the tower, a door swinging shut. He jammed his shield against the door frame; the door jarred against the shield. Growls and curses fell from the lips of both men as each strained against the door.

Maredudd appeared on the scene, sword drawn, to take up a position beside Owain Is-coed. They shouldered the door together so that it sprang open and hand's breadth before closing again. They were about to shoulder the door a second time when they heard the archer shout, in French, "*Maurice, get up the stairs quickly.*" As shoulders closed with the door again so the door burst open. Maredudd led into the interior to see the archer toppling a butcher's block as he made for a stairway adjoining the far wall. A youth had already ascended halfway up the stairway. A third man – a cleric

– recoiled from the butcher's block as it crashed to the straw-covered floor, sending knives and choppers all over the place.

Maredudd made to circumvent the butcher's block, whereas the archer, one foot on the stairway, drew a dagger from his belt and hurled it at Maredudd's chest. The blade struck Maredudd full in the chest, the point hitting chain-mail, the impact absorbed by the padded-leather jerkin that lay beneath the iron rings. He recoiled as the dagger fell to the floor. Then he looked down at his chest, a hand searching for signs of a wound.

Owain Is-coed pushed past Maredudd to meet a hail of arrows, which the archer threw at him after snatching them from his quiver. By the time Owain had recovered from the shock the archer had all but disappeared from view. Undeterred, Owain made for the stairway. He put one foot on the bottom step and a stool came tumbling towards him, forcing him to leap aside.

"Fools," the archer shouted in the Countryman's tongue. "Come and get me now. I've got another bow."

"He's lying," said Maredudd, rubbing his chest.

"I think not," said Owain Is-coed. "This room is both an armoury and a pantry. Could be the same in the chamber above."

Maredudd turned to the Benedictine monk who stood rooted to the spot. "*Master Thomas,*" he said in French, "*is there an armoury up there?*"

The monk shook his head. "*Just scrolls, wine and other victuals.*"

"*There's two men up there. Are they both archers?*" Maredudd levelled his blade at the monk's face. "*Come, Master Thomas, loosen your tongue; don't try my patience.*"

"*There's only one archer up there. He's a Breton, loyal to Monsieur la Steward above all others; that's why Monsieur la Steward appoints him guardian of the tower whenever he leaves this castle. It's his task to stop others from pilfering what's up there.*"

"*And the other man?*"

"*A mere fifteen-year-old.*"

"*Call them down. Tell them this castle has fallen to my Lord Rhydderch ap Cadifor.*"

"*They won't listen to me.*"

"*They won't?*" said Maredudd questioningly as two youths entered the room. He sheathed his sword, saying, "Dewi, get me that rushlight. Take care you don't drop it in the straw." He inclined his head upwards, saying, loudly for those above to hear, "*And now, Master Thomas, pay heed to what I say. This tower is mine, though whether it stands or burns makes little difference to me. So I shall leave you, and the last thing I'll do afore I close the door is to throw this rushlight to the floor.*" He took hold of the rushlight, waving it so as to cause shadows to move on the wall above the stairway. "Everyone out," he shouted in the Countryman's tongue. "Let's leave them to burn in hell."

"No, wait, don't go," Master Thomas blurted out before making for the stairway. "Brian, *Maurice, you both heard what he said. The man means it – he's evil. So come down quickly."*

"What, so he can kill us," the archer returned.

Master Thomas looked to Maredudd questioningly.

"There's a loophole up there," Maredudd shouted in his mother tongue. "Look to the bailey. You'll see there's no slaughter taking place down there; nor will there be any killing here – providing you come down unarmed, and with your hands upon your heads."

Footsteps were heard as someone made for the loophole in the upper room; words were exchanged. Then the archer shouted down, "I still don't trust you."

"Why not?" said Maredudd. "You have my word, the word of a good Christian."

"Brian, *listen to me,"* Master Thomas interposed. *"You must do what's best for Maurice. Monsieur la Steward entrusted you with his life."*

"Maurice," said Maredudd questioningly. *"You mean* Meurig, *Monsieur la Steward's youngest son*? Ah-ha," he laughed, looking up, "now the word ransom comes to mind. I'm sure the High Steward will pay handsomely for both a son and a loyal supporter – just so long as you're both still alive."

· · · · · ·

Meanwhile, in the bailey, Rhydderch made his way to the entrance of the first hall, accompanied by his two doorwards and the castle constable. "You'll be pleased to know," he said to Owain, "I've received word from Awst that he's taken the south gates with little more than an exchange of hot words. Hywel holds the entrance to the other hall, Maredudd has taken the tower, and Rhain has cleared the walls and searched all the buildings with the exception of the two halls. Thankfully, there's been only a few injuries and, as far as I know, no deaths. All we have to do now is clear these two halls. So, if it were down to you, how would you go about doing that – bearing in mind that Sulien and Father Piro are in there?"

"How many archers have been taken prisoner?"

"Fourteen," Rhydderch replied, "if we include de Chalus."

"Elidir, Meurig," Owain shouted, "among the prisoners there's a man with a shiny helmet. Bring him here, but don't lay a hand on him."

The two youths had no sooner made for the gathering near the north gates than Maredudd approached, easily identified now that he had removed his chain-mail hood. "I tell you," he said, "that tower was full of surprises. There's enough provisions up there for twenty men to hold out for a month. Aye, and more wine than you've ever seen. It's good wine, too – I drank some to make sure it wasn't poisoned. And now, the best surprise of all is this young man here, Meurig, youngest son of – guess who?"

"Payn de Turberville," said Rhydderch, grinning.

"You only know that because Dewi told you when he came to tell you I'd taken the tower. Well, now I'll tell you something you don't know. De Viles, he's down there in the church. According to Master Thomas, he's neither living nor dead. He breathes, grunts and farts, but that's all. It seems de Turberville wanted him dumped in the tithe barn where Wilfred could minister to him. The trouble was, Wilfred couldn't be found. It seems he'd had enough of de Viles and took off. So a priest had de Viles's body taken into the church where it now lies afore the alter."

"And?" said Rhydderch.

"I was thinking, it's not right that a man should be somewhere between two worlds. So why don't I go down there and push him into the world where he belongs?"

The two men regarded each other, the one with a raised eyebrow, the other grinning. Owain, on the other hand, considered the well-attired Meurig de Turberville, who obviously resented being a prisoner. He felt inclined to enquire about Meurig's betrothal to Elinor ferch Iorwerth, but dismissed the idea when he caught the approach of the captain of archers, who walked right up to Rhydderch, saying, "*You sent for me, monsieur.*"

"*No,*" said Rhydderch, "*he did.*"

"*How many archers are in the hall?*" Owain demanded.

"*That's for you to find out,*" de Chalus retorted.

"*As you wish,*" said Owain, looking the Gascon straight in the eye. "*Now, either I set fire to the hall, or you call them out of there. So that you know I mean what I say I shall send two of my father's retainers to find rushlights.*"

The castle constable protested, only to be cut short by Rhydderch, saying, "*What I said, Olaf, is that if your men yield, then no one need be hurt.*"

"*Do as he says,*" Olaf growled at de Chalus. "*Your men have a right to choose whether they live or die.*"

De Chalus strode boldly into the porch to pound on the door, shouting, "*It is I, Robert de Chalus. You have a choice – either you come out, unarmed, or you'll burn when they torch this hall.*"

Owain gestured for everyone to retire from the porch, then directed his six youths to train their bows on the entrance. Shield raised, his short sword drawn, he waited for de Chalus to persuade his men to yield. Then the door opened and, one by one, thirteen men came out, hands upon their heads, as well as three women.

"*Satisfied?*" de Chalus spat.

"*Not quite*," Owain returned. "*Lead in. I want to see for myself there's no one else in there.*" Indicating for his youths to accompany him, he followed de Chalus as he strode into the hall. In the tawny light of rush candles the interior was awash with shadows. His instincts made him wary, but for the sake of his equally chary companions he adopted the dauntless manner of the Gascon who, hands on hips, taunted him, saying, "*You're no Breton. You're a liar and, if it were not for* Olaf, *you would never have gained entry into this castle.*"

Ignoring the jibe, Owain barked, "Elidir, Meurig, take a candle each and a companion and go, search the side aisles, starting that end."

De Chalus watched the youths until it became apparent to him what their intentions were. "*Why don't you check the dark corners yourself, deceiver?*"

"*Because I would prefer to keep my eye on you.*"

De Chalus laughed. "*I'll say one thing in your favour, you've got resolve.*"

"*I could say the same about you*," said Owain. "*Now move to the passageway.*"

Before venturing into the dark passageway, de Chalus took the precaution of shouting his name. He then proceeded on his way, shouting, "*Don't shoot – I'm coming through.*" At the far end of the passageway he stopped. "Godwin, Osbern," he said to two archers, "*lay down your bows. This castle has fallen to* Rhydderch ap Cadifor; *there's no point to further resistance.*"

Once de Chalus had moved out of the way, Owain peered into the hall to witness two archers place their bows onto a table. Two men sat at the far end of the table; a third stood over them, a spear in his hands. "Baldred," he shouted, "*put up your spear and go, open the door.*"

Baldred wasted no time in doing as he had been told. One of the men seated – his arm in a sling – rose from the table, saying, "Owain – Owain, is that you?"

"Yes, Sulien, I'm here because you've been neglecting my father's estate."

. . . . . .

Reunion followed reunion, both within and without the second hall. A reunion also took place when Sulien and Piro met up with Rhydderch and those with him. At the last reunion, Owain sensed that something had been going on during his absence, that his father was anxious to get things moving.

257

It was apparent that his father had already spoken to his churls and, no doubt, his officers as well. Whatever his father's intentions were, they evidently involved de Chalus, as his father had sent word that he desired the Gascon's presence. His father wasted no time in coming straight to the point.

"Robert de Chalus, I've heard that, for all your blustering, you're a man who has the well-being of his men at heart. If that is so, then you'll understand my concern for my own. So, I give you your freedom; in exchange I want you to take a message to Monsieur la Steward and do so with all haste."

"You mean try, monsieur. I could be ambuscaded once I enter your lordship."

"You could, which is why you'll leave here in the company of a priest and two youths. You will not be their prisoner; they will be your protection against my men. Once you find Monsieur la Steward they will leave you."

"What about my men?" said de Chalus. *"My family?"*

"If you mean, will I do them harm, then the answer is no. I didn't come here to slaughter, only to prevent the slaughter of my own; that said, the fate of your men will depend on what Monsieur la Steward does when he gets back here, because where I am so will your men be, and his son will be at my side no matter what. As to your family, if they are among the women and children gathered near the north gates, then they will all leave here shortly and, with the townspeople, make their way to Ystum Llymarch. *If you prefer some other arrangement with regard to your family, then say so."*

"Let's hear your message first."

"It is that you tell Monsieur la Steward what's happened here, and you warn him that if he and his men are not back here afore nightfall – and I mean all three hundred and thirty of them – then I will burn both the castle and the town. When he gets here, I will expect him to array his men about half a bowshot from the north gates. If his men proceed beyond where I've said, or if any of them attempt to make their way down beside the river, then I will assume the worse; I will not hesitate to call the men of Is-coed to arms, so that everything that is French in the Peninsula will be laid waste. That is my message. Will you take it?"

"I will on two conditions. One is that I choose four of my archers to accompany my family, and that all four will be armed. My reason for wanting this is that there are few men in the town – most of them marched with Monsieur la Steward."

"Then I will agree to that condition, providing you don't choose the Breton, Brian, *and that your four men do not return here to take action against me."*

"The second condition is that I have my sword returned to me."

"Agreed, providing you don't use it against those who ride with you; now, afore you swear, I will add one last condition, that you will ride with all haste – and mark you, I will know how you ride because your escort will be witness to what you do; now, do we have an agreement?"

. . . . . .

Mounted and ready to ride in the company of Father Piro and two youths, de Chalus waited at the north gates. As the gates opened he said, *"I'll not forget you, Owain ap Rhydderch, neither your name nor your face,"* then rode off, hooves clattering on the drawbridge.

"What was that about?" Rhydderch asked.

"He resents that I deceived him."

"That will be as nothing when compared with de Turberville's response to what's happened here. Question is, what will he do about it? If he returns here with over three hundred men, he could surround the castle and attack; that being so, there's no point to us all getting killed or captured. So, in a little while you'll leave with my youths, whereas I will remain here with my officers and my churls, all of whom have agreed to stay of their own free will."

"A score of men won't hold this castle."

"No more will sixty, whereas forty youths could do well in the defence of Uwch-coed."

Silence reigned between them until Rhydderch said, "Owain, understand this. If we all die here, then Uwch-coed is finished. It will have no lord; it will have no young men to carry on the fight. That's why you must leave, and should anything happen to me, then you will be lord in my stead until such time as Caleb returns."

"Am I up to it?"

"I have no doubt that you are – you've proved that today – but you'll need officers, which is why Maredudd and Sulien will go with you."

"When will I go – now ?"

"No, not for a while. I don't want the prisoners, nor the townspeople, to see you leave. Right now, Master Thomas is in the town, telling everyone that no action will be taken against them if they make their way to Ystum Llymarch. The women and children who are here will go with them. So we'll wait until they're out of sight on the western highway. Until then, there's several things that need to be done. The first is that you take half my youths to the kitchen; when they've had their fill, take the other half and eat something yourself. There's no telling when you'll eat again. Oh! And get rid of the armour; now go."

Rhydderch made to where the prisoners were gathered. "Gentlemen," he said to his officers, "I want the women and children to leave by the south gates. As to the men prisoners – with the exception of the High Steward's son, I want them lodged in that hall there, and the porch blocked up. Docal," he said, placing a hand on the dung-bailiff's shoulder, "take your men round to the far hall quickly and block up the passageway at that end; when you've done that, send half your men to feed."

. . . . . .

Rhydderch stood by an embrasure, following Owain's departure. He was glad that his son was no longer present in a castle that could prove a death trap; glad, too, for those who were with him. Most of all he took comfort in the knowledge that Owain had turned out to be all that he had hoped for in a son. *'Perhaps one day,'* he thought, *'he and Caleb will be as one, just like Maredudd and me.'*

In the distance he visualized the foothills and mountains of an empty land, save for those tribesmen who were preparing to thwart an enemy advance. Those tribesmen would be lying in wait, thinking of their loved ones, as he thought of his – his wife, his daughter, the Old One and many more. Taking the castle had given him small satisfaction. There was no telling whether his stratagem would work, whether de Turberville would return, or whether the man would agree to terms. Possibly the High Steward would do all these things, if only to secure the release of his son. William de Londres, on the other hand, might not give a second thought to his son, Maurice. Yet none of these nagging thoughts compared with the one that weighed heaviest on his mind.

"I don't like it, my lord," said Gruffudd ap Meilyr, his arms resting in an embrasure.

"Don't like what?"

"Well, for a start, there's only nineteen of us here to hold this castle, and half that number stands guard on some forty prisoners."

"Soon it'll be seventeen when you and Owain Is-coed leave to find a place on *the Mountain* where you can keep watch on this castle. As I said afore, I'll have a fire lit and, if the worst comes to the worst, I'll have wet straw put on the fire. When you see the smoke, you both ride hard and call the men of Is-coed to arms. Mark you, what I don't want is them laying waste French and Saxon Gower because, one, if they do that, there will be no turning back and, two, there'll be no time for such things. I want the men of Is-coed to gather at Penllergaer by noon tomorrow, where I will tell them what I would have them do. Tell them if they waste time burning and plundering, then I won't wait for them; they will have to fend for themselves."

"As you wish, my lord," said Gruffudd with little enthusiasm.

"What troubles you now, Gruffudd?"

"I'd rather not say, my lord."

"Then I'll say it for you. If things go wrong, then it's the men of Is-coed who'll suffer most. That's because the Peninsula is like this castle – there'll be no escape once the fighting starts, and your kinsmen, they could end up fighting with the sea at their backs. All this I know and, believe me, it weighs heavy on my mind. There's a part of me that say, *no, this is my fight; it doesn't concern the men of Is-coed*. Maybe that's how it should be. Maybe it's as well you don't call those men to arms."

Gruffudd stared: he had been surprised that the man he looked upon as his lord could have read his thoughts; now, as he looked at him, back arched, hands resting in an embrasure, he wondered if the same man had lost his resolve.

Rhydderch straightened up to put a hand on Gruffudd's shoulder. "The worst thing a man can do is await what he dreads most, because then he ponders and, if he's not strong, he begins to doubt. I learned that at Upper Ford ten years ago; now, what I have to hold onto is this. I came here with a clear stratagem as to how I would take this castle, but the rest – the rest is a little vague because I have no power over what men will, or will not do. I know only that I believed my stratagem would confound de Turberville's march. I have to stand by that stratagem, come what may, because I handed it over to the One up there. I think it time I stopped dwelling on doubts and spent time in prayer."

Rhydderch walked away, passing the horses that were lined up ready for a possible break out, and drew level with his dung-bailiff, who stood guard on the entrance to the hall. "Have your men taken all the captured bows and quivers up to the tower, Docal?"

"Yes, my lord, there's enough up there to hold back an army."

"Good. Have two of your men light a fire in the open space there, and have them place wet straw beside it. And, Docal, if anyone wants me, I shall be in one of the buildings beyond this hall."

Chapter 32

Moment of Truth

Near a gap in the rubble wall that enclosed the Monastery of St. Cyfelach, Payn de Turberville pondered on the wisdom of continuing his *anabasis*. Already he was cold and wet through, as were his men, horses and baggage; already the rear of the column had been *ambuscaded*; now he had been told that the monastery was deserted, save for the Abbot – a clear indication that the men of Uwch-coed had abandoned their abodes and sent their families migrating north.

He cast his eye over the monastery, its thatched buildings forlorn, eaves dripping, the ground awash with pools of rainwater. He focused on his long-standing associate, William de Londres, Lord of Ogwr, as he rode from the church towards him, several foot soldiers at his heels. Even in full chain-mail it was plain that William had once again been consumed with rage. Only a short while ago, on the reverse slope of a rise, William had come upon seventeen of his men, their bodies scattered before an *abatis*, five of them stripped naked, their flesh pecked by scavenging birds; at the sight of such carnage William had fumed.

"D'you know what the Abbot told me?" William ground out. "He said three of my men were brought here to be ministered to, but their wounds were so bad nothing could be done for them."

"What about your son, Maurice?"

"Not here, damn it!"

"That's good news surely. It means he could still be alive."

De Londres gave no reply, being more concerned in manoeuvring his bay alongside de Turberville – time for Payn to reflect on his youngest and most favoured son, Meurig. He had intended to bring Meurig on this *anabasis*, but that Rhydderch had escaped entrapment had been reason for him to change his mind, to have Meurig remain at Abertawe in the care of Brian the Breton.

"Well, what are we waiting for, Payn?"

De Turberville jerked his spurs into the flanks of his grey, resentful that his neighbour of twenty years standing was pressing him again, and would continue to do so until this ill-fated *anabasis* came to an end. Much as he empathized with William's loss, the man was proving to be a source of irritation, always grinding his teeth about something or other, usually Rhydderch ap Cadifor.

Distracted by the rumble of hooves and men shouting, de Turberville cast a glance over his shoulder. The approaching horseman he recognized as the captain of archers, Robert de Chalus, by his shiny helmet. Then he caught sight of a man-at-arms following in the Gascon's wake; that man he recognized as John de Penrhys, the most influential of the Gower fief-holders, a man formerly known as John de Burgh. He presumed that de Chalus had said something to de Penrhys as he passed by; whatever had been said must have prompted de Penrhys to ride forward.

De Chalus reined in so as to kept pace with de Turberville. "Monsieur la Steward," he gasped, "the castle at Abertawe has been taken by Rhydderch ap Cadifor. He took it by guile, along with sixty of his men."

"What! William, halt the column – halt it now!" De Turberville fixed his gaze on de Chalus, his fury evident by his reddening face. "I knew that wily bastard was up to something; now explain!"

"He and several of his men approached the gates in the guise of men-at-arms," de Chalus explained. "His son, Owain, came first, telling us Lord William had captured the retinue of Rhydderch ap Cadifor. I knew something was wrong...."

"You knew! Then why in God's name did you let them in?"

"Not me, monsieur. Olaf gave the order to open the gates."

"So it's Olaf's fault now, is it? And what about my son?"

"He's alive and well, monsieur."

"It's as well he is, and as to whose at fault, I'll find out the truth, believe me."

"Payn, it matters not whose at fault," de Londres interposed. "That this man is still alive shows *he* yielded without a fight. Is that not so, Gascon?"

Ignoring the barb, de Chalus said. "I've a message, Monsieur la Steward, from Rhydderch himself. It is, that if you and your men are not back at Abertawe afore nightfall, he will burn both the castle and the town; what's more, should you return, then you will array all these men half a bowshot from the north gates. If anyone approaches the castle other than by the northern highway, he will assume the approach to be hostile and won't hesitate to summon the men of Is-coed to arms."

"He's got a damn nerve," de Londres thundered. "He's doing exactly what he did ten years ago. I'll see him dead afore I have any part of it."

"If you want him dead, monsieur," said Elgar the Saxon from a position ahead of de Londres, "then you'll have to return to Abertawe because that's where he is."

"Who gave you leave to state the obvious, Saxon?"

"I'll state whatever I so wish when it concerns me," Elgar returned, "which is, if the men of Is-coed are called to arms, then my tenants and I will suffer loss."

"That goes for me too," de Penrhys ground out, "and for every fief-holder back there. There's none of us want our lands laid waste, certainly not so *you* can settle a ten-year-old grievance. I will return, with or without you, Messieurs, and I'll take with me all those fief-holders back there."

While de Penrhys reined about, so de Londres ground out, "You're not going to let him go, Payn, he's got obligations to fulfil."

"So have I," de Turberville retorted. "I've got lands in the Peninsula of my own, and I've got a son back there at Abertawe; what's more, I've a writ that says I'm to rendezvous on the River Tywi in four days time. I can't do that if the Countrymen of this lordship are up in arms. And you, you're to rendezvous there yourself."

"I'll be there," de Londres bit back. "Once I've laid waste these lands I'll pass on through Cantref Bychan. Then we'll settle with the pretender, Gruffudd ap Rhys."

"No," de Turberville snapped, "I forbid you to go any further with this *anabasis*."

"Forbid! What are you going to do, Payn? Turn your men against me? No, you'll not do that; it would serve no purpose. So, I have a solution. The fief-holders return to safeguard their interests. And you, you return to Abertawe to appease Rhydderch ap Cadifor while I lay waste his lands. He's not going to burn that castle while he's in it. So all you've got to do is keep him hemmed in until I join you. Then we'll take the castle together. That way we can deal with him and half his men in one stroke."

"Elgar," said de Turberville, "you have an opinion about most things. So what d'you make of all this?"

"As I see it," said Elgar, "if we don't return to Abertawe, Rhydderch will certainly burn both the castle and the town. Then he'll head into the Peninsula where he'll do one of two things. Either he'll lay waste all that is ours to show that whatever we do to him, he can do to us, or he'll lead the men of Is-coed into this wilderness where he can *ambuscade* us in woods that best suit his manner of fighting."

"Makes sense," said de Turberville, "but if I were to return with my men, I have only to surround the castle and he'll be caught in a trap of his making."

"With respect, monsieur la Steward," said Elgar, "we don't know he's there. All we know for certain is that he wants *us* there, all of us, that is."

"And he knows," de Chalus interposed, "exactly how many men left Abertawe."

De Turberville threw a hand in the air in despair. "Agh! I've no time for all this. De Dreues, get these men of mine moving. I'll catch up with you as soon as I can." He faced de Londres. "William, I can understand your desire to settle an old score, but the man you want is back there at Abertawe, or somewhere nearby. So what's the point of continuing with this *anabasis*?"

"Without these lands," de Londres ground out, "he's finished; his people will starve. That's why he settled for terms ten years ago; now he's got your son and probably mine, and he'll use them to exact terms. I'll not see him do that again."

"May God give me strength," de Turberville exclaimed. "Elgar, you are forever inflicting your reasoning on me. So inflict it on him; make him see sense."

De Londres loured, then ground out, "There's nothing the Saxon can say that will deter me from my purpose."

"No! Then consider this," said de Turberville. "You and I, William, have been friends and neighbours for twenty years. For the sake of that friendship I urge you to listen to what this man has to say. If you choose not to heed his words, then so be it, but at least listen to him because I desire it."

"Very well," said de Londres, his gaze on Elgar, "say what you have to say, Saxon."

"Monsieur, ten years ago I marched with de Viles. From the moment we set out it rained, just as it has today. We endured *ambuscades*, time and again – it was like we had disturbed a nest of wasps. So far we've been hit once, again nothing more than a sting, but the attacks will continue and then, in his own time, Rhydderch will catch you out. And he will, monsieur."

"Will," de Londres exclaimed. "How can he do that when he's at Abertawe?"

"As I said," Elgar replied, "we don't know that he is. All we know for certain is that he wants *us* there. It could be that his stratagem is to get Monsieur la Steward to return so he can deal with you. Now what you have to consider is this. De Viles had eight score fighting men when he started out. You have only five. What de Viles had to contend with were tribesmen armed with little more than slingstones and darts. What you'll be up against are bowmen, probably the best in these Southern Lands. Those men who fell at the *abatis* back there are testimony to that. In short, monsieur, you've got less chance of succeeding than de Viles ever had."

"Have you finished?" de Londres demanded.

"Not quite," Elgar replied. "We both know that Rhydderch has dealings with others of his kind, and it wouldn't surprise me if some of those lords were to join him – his kinsmen, Maredudd of Cantref Bychan, being one of them. You could find yourself outnumbered by two, three or four to one. What then?" When no answer was forthcoming, Elgar turned in the saddle to address the handful of men who had converged to witness what was going on. They were some of de Londres's leading tenants, all of them Countrymen whose men formed the vanguard. "Have you understood what's been said? Your Lord William seeks to measure his strength against Rhydderch ap Cadifor. You'll all end up dead like those men back there...."

"That's enough," de Londres ground out. "Anything you have to say, you say to me, not my men; now go, both of you."

With a sigh de Turberville wheeled; when Elgar appeared at his side he said, "I was hoping you'd get him to return."

"He will," said Elgar, grinning. "Those Countrymen of his, didn't you see the look on their faces? They've all heard of Rhydderch's exploits, both here in Gower and in Cantref Bychan. I wouldn't be surprised if they get him to reconsider his position. They might even get him to return to Abertawe."

. . . . . .

At Abertawe, Payn de Turberville arrayed his forces so the men of Gower, Morgannwg and Cydweli straddled the highway some distance from the north gates. Then, in the company of Elgar and William de Londres, he advanced towards the drawbridge. It galled him to think that, ten years previously, a similar gathering of forces had taken place north of the castle. The difference then was that it had been Rhydderch who had advanced toward the castle where, outside the bailey ditch, the Earl of Warwick had arrayed his forces. He had not been present on that occasion, but Elgar and de Londres had both witnessed the event – Elgar as Rhydderch's prisoner; de Londres as the Earl's advisor. Elgar showed no sign of resentment at being present at this situation in reverse, but de Londres fumed – so much so that it had taken all his powers of persuasion to get the man to agree to listen to what Rhydderch had to say before launching an all-out attack.

"This is as far as we need go, Messieurs," said de Turberville, reining in, "Now, first things first, I want to be assured about the well-being of my son."

"Monsieur de Gower," Elgar shouted, addressing Rhydderch by his French nomenclature, "Monsieur la Steward seeks to be assured about his son."

Behind the palisade, the bard, Rhain, rose from counting sticks, saying, "I make them three hundred and thirty-two."

"I've counted three hundred and twenty-one," said Awst.

Rhydderch nodded, then indicated for Meurig de Turberville to appear in an embrasure, where the youth shouted, "Father, he's only got...."

Ammon pulled Meurig away, his huge right hand covering the youth's mouth.

"I'm warning you," de Turberville snarled, "you harm my son and you'll get no quarter from me."

"Only your actions will put him at risk, Monsieur la Steward," Rhydderch shouted back. "So pay heed to what I have to say. Today you tried to entrap me, presumably on the Earl's instructions, and he acting on the word of a madman. Then, when you failed to entrap me, you marched against me, presumably at the insistence of a man with a ten-year-old grievance; now the concord is broken; now we all stand to lose, with the exception, that is, of Monsieur de Londres, who seems to have no regard for his possessions in the Peninsula. The concord could, of course, be restored if you and I were to come to an arrangement, but for that to be so I would require your oath that you will take no further action against me. For my part I will swear to take no action against you; that means, when you march westwards according to the King's will, I will do nothing that will undermine your authority; nor will I take action against the fief-holders of this lordship. In short, monsieur, I will not call the men of Is-coed to arms."

"*Fie*," de Londres spat. "He seeks only to divert us from our purpose; what's more, he seeks to divide us by appeasing the fief-holders." Distracted by the approach of a horseman, he turned to see John de Penrhys rein in behind de Turberville.

"If that's what he seeks," said de Penrhys, "then he has succeeded as far as I'm concerned."

"Then you're a fool, monsieur."

"No fool," de Penrhys bit back. "When I first came here I had no love for these Countrymen, but now that I've learned to live with them I'm all for having the concord restored so that what I have at Penrhys will not be tarnished by blood and ash."

"Messieurs, enough" de Turberville blurted out. "Let's not squabble amongst ourselves. Elgar, tell Monsieur de Gower to finish what he has to say."

In response, Rhydderch shouted, "On its own, Monsieur la Steward, your oath won't allay my fears. So, until I no longer feel threatened, I will not respond to any summons to this castle. If it is necessary for you and I to meet for whatever reason, then we will do so on the highway near the Monastery of St. Cyfelach. Should you agree to this, monsieur, then I for my part will not torch this castle, nor the town."

"What he's saying, Payn," said de Londres, "is that your oath is of little worth."

"As to the attack on Ystum Llymarch, Monsieur la Steward," Rhydderch shouted, "any further proceedings against members of my household will only...."

"Ystum Llymarch belongs to me," de Londres bellowed, "and I will have full restitution, or, so help me, I'll see you dead."

"As I was saying, Monsieur la Steward," Rhydderch continued, ignoring de Londres, "in the case of Maredudd Goch, the plaint that Monsieur de Londres brought against him was settled here today when Elgar struck...."

"Don't speak to him," de Londres bawled, pointing at de Turberville, "speak to me, you damn miscreant."

"Elgar," Rhydderch shouted, "inform Monsieur de Londres that if he wishes to bring a plaint for loss against me, or members of my household, then so be it, but such a plaint can never be dealt with until peace prevails in this Lordship of Gower."

"Monsieur de Londres," said Elgar, "Monsieur de Gower says...."

"I heard what he said, Saxon," de Londres spat, "I'm not deaf! And you, don't take me for a fool."

"Calm yourself, William," said de Turberville. "I understand your frustration, but right now I want to hear what he has to say about my son."

"So, Monsieur la Steward," Rhydderch shouted, "you have heard what I had to say. The question now is, are you prepared to swear to no further hostilities? To agree to meet near the monastery? And to put off further proceedings?"

"Elgar," said de Turberville, "tell him I want to know what he intends to do with my son."

"The fate of your son, Monsieur la Steward, depends on whether we can come to some arrangement on what I have said."

"I knew it," de Turberville ground out. "He seeks to use my son to force my hand. Well, he seeks what I cannot give. Elgar, tell him that, with regards to taking no further action against him, I have no authority to enter into such an arrangement. Only the Earl can decide on such matters."

Elgar had no sooner repeated de Turberville's words than Rhydderch shouted, "Then let the Earl decide. Send someone to Warwick Castle, someone who the Earl will listen to, someone who is neither mad, nor consumed with a grievance, someone who is not partial to you, me or de Londres, someone such as Monsieur de Penrhys – but until he gets back we neither of us take action against the other."

"If that's what it takes to keep the peace," said de Penrhys, "then I will go. The Earl will listen to me. I've known him longer than any other man in this lordship."

De Turberville stared, pondering on what had been proposed, until Elgar said, "As to meeting him at the monastery, Monsieur la Steward, you are at liberty to attend to the affairs of this lordship wherever you so wish."

"I still want to know what he intends to do with my son."

"Monsieur de Gower," Elgar called, "what are your intentions with regard to Maurice de Turberville?"

"Monsieur la Steward, it should take no more than a month for Monsieur de Penrhys to get back from Warwick. If you agree to stand by what I've said, then one month from now I will release your son without any demand for ransom."

"That's an offer you cannot refuse, Monsieur la Steward," said Elgar.

De Turberville did no more than stare, causing de Londres to growl, "Payn – Payn, you can't agree to what he says. If you do, then what has existed between us all these years is at an end."

"That I would regret, William," said de Turberville, "but if that is what it takes to get my son back, then so be it."

"No – no, I'll not be bound by anything you agree to," de Londres snarled. Then, turning to Rhydderch, he shouted, "You still have me to contend with, miscreant, and I won't rest until I settle with you once and for all."

"You, monsieur, are of no import," Rhydderch shouted back, "and if you ever march against me again, I will not only oppose you, but I will march my men to Ogwr, where I will lay waste all that is yours."

"You wouldn't dare. I hold Ogwr of the King. Despoil it and you'll incur the King's wrath."

"I'm not impressed," Rhydderch returned. "If you despoil all that I have, then what can the King do to me? Nothing – whereas I can take refuge in the mountains of Morgannwg, where I will raise men so that I can descend on Ogwr time and again until it becomes a desert. As for your son, monsieur, for whom you obviously have no concern, I will send him to a place where you'll never find him. In short, monsieur, you may never see your son again." Rhydderch focused on de Turberville. "And now, Monsieur la Steward, are you prepared to swear to what has been agreed?"

"And my son," de Turberville shouted in return, "will you swear to release him one month from now, no matter what the Earl's reply may be?"

"I will swear to that.

"Then so be it."

Rhydderch leaned forward, hands resting in the embrasure, to check that Master Thomas still stood on the drawbridge, a holy relic in his hands. "Come forward on foot, Monsieur la Steward," he shouted, "and bring with you Messieurs Elgar and de Penrhys as witnesses, and I will meet you on the drawbridge with two witnesses of my own."

Once oaths had been sworn, Rhydderch said, to de Turberville, "For me to leave this castle I will require that you have your men withdraw to the western highway so that a bowshot separates your men from mine."

"Agreed," de Turberville replied, "but I would have it that I wait beside the northern highway so that I may see my son ride past."

"Where you wish to wait is entirely up to you, Monsieur la Steward, but Monsieur de Londres must withdraw with his men. Should he object, or should he have a mind to pursue me, then impress upon him that no quarry is worth pursuit unless it has a head start. If he still refuses to withdraw, then I will not come out until he does."

Nodding, his face grim, de Turberville turned and walked away, accompanied by his two witnesses. Rhydderch watched them go, then said, "I thank you, Master Thomas, for your trouble, but there is one more thing I require of you; it is that you ride out with me the distance of a bowshot. After that you will be free to return."

Once the gates had been closed, Rhydderch returned to his place in an embrasure where, for a while, he watched the men of Gower, Morgannwg and Cydweli withdraw down the western highway. Apart from his own departure, his stratagem to take the castle and compel de Turberville to call off his *anabasis* had reached fruition. His men were evidently elated. He could hear them laughing as they ran about congratulating one another. Even Ammon showned signs – faint though they were – of satisfaction. Yet it was the response of his churls that affected him most. He had a clear recall of Docal's expression when he had returned through the gates. It had been an expression not so much of elation, but one that he interpreted as humble appreciation for allowing him – a churl – to have a part in all that had happened since the ambush at the *abatis*. It was, to some extent, a reflection of his own appreciation for what could only have come from above, from the One he had visualized crossing the Kedron. It made him feel humble as well as grateful.

He turned away from the embrasure to descend a bank, shouting, "Mount up; let's be away from here."

Twelve men responded, several of them crowding the prisoner, Meurig de Turberville, to deny him any opportunity of escape. Once mounted, Rhydderch wheeled towards the northern gateway, shouting, at two churls,

"Docal, Gwgan, open the gates, then mount up quickly." He trotted round the east end of the nearest hall, his eye on the two churls as the scooted for their horses. Then he lead his men towards the southern gateway where Awst and Hywel the Cook had thrown open the gates, each of them mounting their steeds in haste. Hooves clattered on the southern drawbridge. Then, spurring, he galloped down a highway, passing newly-built halls as he made for the estuary where mud flats had been exposed by an ebb tide.

Meanwhile, some distance from the north gates, de Turberville waited – and waited.

. . . . . .

After a hard ride through the Lordship of Cilfái, Rhydderch crossed the River Tawe at Upper Ford. He assumed that his tribesmen would be at the monastery and, with less than a two miles to go, he sent Rhain ahead to declare the good news. A while later he observed the approach of two horsemen, one of whom he recognized as Maredudd. The identity of the accompanying horseman – a youth – did not become apparent until the distance between them had closed to within fifty paces. Evidently, Maredudd had come to present him with the return of his son, Morgan.

"I heard de Turberville agreed to terms," said Maredudd, outstretching his right arm as he drew close. "Well, now I've got news for you." He gripped Rhydderch's forearm. "As you can see, Morgan made it back, and with him came Bledri, Caradog and Gronw." He indicated for Morgan to take up a position on Rhydderch's left. "I don't know what to make of Bledri, but the other two were definitely de Viles's informers."

"I'm impressed," said Rhydderch, his eye on Morgan as he manoeuvred leftwards, ready to move off. "I congratulate you for taking all three of them."

"Er – no, my lord, not me. Bledri took Gronw and we both took Caradog."

Aware that Morgan had cast a furtive glance at Maredudd, Rhydderch then witnessed Maredudd jerk his head, an indication that they should continue their converse out of earshot of those who followed behind. He spurred.

"It's thanks to Morgan that we got all three of them," said Maredudd, trotting beside Rhydderch. "He talked Bledri into turning himself in. Then, when they were overtaken by Iorwerth ap Meirchion, he spoke again with the result that Iorwerth had his men escort them to Upper Ford. What I don't understand is why Iorwerth should have done us a favour. I'd like to think he did it to safeguard his own interests rather than find himself on the wrong side of a uprising, but the truth is, he couldn't have known about us taking

Abertawe because Morgan turned up at the monastery afore I did. Whatever his reasons, what needs to be said is that Iorwerth wants few to know of his involvement, the fewer the better."

"So how many know about his involvement?" Rhydderch asked.

"You, me, Morgan and the three prisoners. Everyone else knows only that Morgan made it back with Bledri's help."

"So tell me about Bledri?" Rhydderch asked, turning to Morgan.

"He saw two men in cassocks, wandering about at Abertawe, my lord, and guessed they were Caradog and Gronw. So he went after them to kill them because he says anything he said to them, they passed on to de Viles."

"So he's admitted to passing on information, has he?"

"Yes, my lord. He said he'd done it in good faith, foolish though it was, but Caradog claims they were all in it together."

"And who do you believe?" Rhydderch asked

"Not Caradog, that's for sure. And I'll say this, my lord, Bledri never tried to harm me, though there were times when he could have done so."

Rhydderch pondered until Maredudd said, "So what's on your mind?"

"Prisoners. We don't know whether de Londres will march this way again. So it's no time to be burdened with five prisoners, all of whom may try to escape."

"I thought you were sending de Londres's son to you-know-who in Brycheiniog."

"That still leaves four to be watched night and day."

"Agh! Just tie them up and have them trail behind us whenever we move."

"I would prefer not to do that with Meurig de Turberville. He's done nothing to deserve rough treatment, and as I see it, it might go better for us if Payn de Turberville had him back without him complaining of ill treatment."

"Why worry about Payn? If you ask me, I'd say his days as High Steward are numbered."

"I'd say so too, but the question then, is who will be High Steward in his stead? If it's John de Penrhys, then our troubles will be over soon enough. If it's William de Londres, then they've only just begun."

. . . . . .

After a jubilant reception at the monastery, Rhydderch sent for his blacksmith. Escorted by two men, Bledri came to him and immediately went down on one knee, saying, "My lord, I have failed you by my heedless talk, and for that I am guilty of treason, but afore I hang let me be a tongue man against Caradog and Gronw, so that everyone will know them for their treachery."

"So you admit that you betrayed me by saying things that would have been best left unsaid?"

"Yes, my lord, my talk was idle, but that changes nothing, nor does it excuse me for deserting you at Abertawe."

Rhydderch considered Bledri's response, then said, "For the next few days most of us will remain here, ready to counter de Londres, should he march this way again, and while we're here I will hold court. In a little while, you, Caradog and Gronw will each be given three days to prepare your defence, the charge being treason. None of you will be allowed to leave this place. So there will be no requirement for sureties. If you require advocates or witnesses, then you will find them from among the men gathered here. Caradog will be tried first, then Gronw; you last. That way you'll have the opportunity to be a tongue man against both Caradog and Gronw. However, first things first, tomorrow, Caradog will stand trial for his wrongful accusations against Morgan ap Maredudd."

CHAPTER 33

THE HIGH SUMMIT

Nine days after the cessation of hostilities, Gwenllian forded the River Amman to ascend the wooded slopes that led to the moorlands surrounding the High Summit, the loftiest peak in all Uwch-coed. The previous day she had left Myddfai, the court of her husband's kinsman, Lord Maredudd of Cantref Bychan; now she was back in the commote of her birth, riding in the company of her daughter and several members of Y Faerdref household, as well as the six men whom Lord Maredudd had assigned to her as an escort. She was glad to be going home, back to Y Faerdref, for although Lord Maredudd had been lavish with his hospitality, her stay at Myddfai had been blighted by anxiety for those she had left behind, and by the fact that Lord Maredudd had told her there were moves afoot to entrap Gruffudd ap Rhys in Cantref Mawr. The anxiety relating to the situation in Gower had abated with the arrival of her brother, Rhain, telling her of Rhydderch's exploits; that both her son, Owain, and her father, Rhodri Gadno, were alive and well.

Gwenllian raised the hood of her mantle. The wind had become increasingly biting as she ascended the open slopes of the High Summit, but fair weather clouds in an otherwise blue sky seemed to welcome her return, promising both a joyful homecoming and a return to normality. What hindered her progress was the track: it was unbelievably muddy, abounding in dung, much of it submerged beneath extensive pools of rainwater; above all it was clogged with people and animals, all slowly trekking home. In the lower wooded slopes through which she had already passed, her doorward, Cadwgan, had done his best to clear the track, riding ahead, truncheon in hand, shouting and waving at everyone to get their livestock out of the way. On the higher moorlands he had found it easier to clear the track, but even then there were occasions when he considered it expedient to make wide sweeps, circumventing herds and flocks, because most people travelled in kindred groups, thereby occupying lengthy stretches of the track.

Close to the High Summit, Gwenllian approached a herd of cattle that had been driven to one side of the track by two men and a woman. The men were some distance away, making it difficult to identify them. She could only presume that they were some of the many men who, according to Rhain, her husband had released to assist with the return of their kindred's stock. The woman – who held a position at the tail end of the herd – appeared to be both young and fair; stick in hand, she seemed well able to herd cattle, whistling as loudly as any man.

Something about the young woman prompted Gwenllian to think of Anona. She felt tempted to have the young woman brought to her, but her attention was diverted by Rhain, saying, "Gwen, our escort beckons. I'll drop back; see what they want."

As she directed her attention back to the young woman, so her handmaiden said, "My lady, it's the Old One, something's wrong."

Gwenllian wheeled round to where the Old One sat motionless on his horse, his head bowed. "Merfyn, what ails you?"

"Just tired, my lady," said Merfyn, raising his head. "I need to rest a little."

"Mother," said Cadi, Gwenllian's eleven-year-old daughter, "he's been so quiet I knew something was wrong. What can we do for him? We must do something."

"We will, Cadi, we will, believe me." Gwenllian looked back to where Rhain conversed with her escort. Until he returned she had to do something: the Old One looked deathly pale, worn out by the long ride from Myddfai. She cast her eye about the hillside until her gaze came to rest on a rocky hollow surrounded by brush. "Arwena, Eswen," she said to her handmaiden and her sewer, "rein in close to Merfyn; keep him safe while I lead his horse to that hollow yonder."

Taking the reins of the Old One's horse, Gwenllian led towards the rocky hollow and had not gone far when, turning her head rightwards, she saw that the young woman, the herd and the two men had moved on, all heading towards the south-west to follow a track that she knew would take them to the Dulais Valley. She felt sure, then, that the young woman had, indeed, been Anona.

"What's wrong with Merfyn, Gwen?" said Rhain, appearing at her side.

"He needs to rest out of this wind. If we take him to that hollow…." Gwenllian paused: Rhain had turned his back on her to whistle, then wave his spear, a signal for Cadwgan to return quickly. "Something's wrong. What is it?"

"There's men back there, maybe a dozen or more. They're herding cattle and they've overtaken those of our kindred whom we passed on the lower slopes."

"And?"

"Well, they may not be a threat to us. Our escort are of a mind they're Lord Maredudd's men, assisting our *Rhaglaw* with the return of Rhydderch's cattle. Still, it might be as well we press on, just in case."

"And leave Merfyn?"

"Gwen, no one loves the Old One more than I, and he wouldn't want anything untoward to happen to you, or any of us here. I'll stay; you go."

"What, and leave my brother?"

Rhain shook his head. "I somehow didn't think you'd leave."

On reaching the hollow, Rhain alighted and, removing his cloak, searched for a place among the rocks to prepare a bed. He was joined by Cadwgan, who likewise removed his cloak. Both men lowered the Old One from his horse, carrying him to the cloaks where they laid him down, wrapping him in the woollen garments on which he lay.

"I'll go, light a fire," said Cadwgan.

"Might as well," said Rhain. "Whoever those men are back there, they must know we're here."

When the approaching strangers drew near, the eight men in Gwenllian's company formed a line some distance below the hollow. Gwenllian stood closer to the hollow, from which she observed the strangers halt on the track, allowing their cattle to graze on the surrounding grassland. One of the strangers rode forward, a young man, but her view of him soon became obscured by the eight men to her front. She saw Rhain go forward to speak to the young man, but their words were carried away by the wind. Then the young man rode past her protectors. He appeared dirty, his hair unkempt, his jawline covered by some semblance of a beard. She discerned a pleasurable smile on his face. Then she recognized him.

"Caleb," she cried, darting towards him.

Alighting quickly, Caleb rushed towards her so that they fell to an embrace. She hugged him dearly, taking pleasure in having him close, in telling him how glad she was that he had at last returned. When she stood back, holding his arms, she considered him. Yes, he was tall, he was handsome, and more, he was a man. She would have told him so, but her daughter's appearance distracted her.

Cadi held back, unsure how her brother would react, but when he faced her, arms open wide, she threw herself at him. He lifted her off her feet, hugging her, laughingly referring to her as *my little sister*. Gwenllian stared in amazement: the two of them were usually at odds, the one teasing, the other expressing displeasure; now their sibling rivalry had given way to brotherly and sisterly love. She warmed to them both. Then a thought struck her like a bolt out of the blue.

"My brother, Einion, where is he?"

"He's back there, mother. Rhain has gone to greet him. They may be a while, you know what they're like."

"And who are all those men over there?" Cadi asked.

"They're all Gower men, and like me they're returning home."

"Are you their leader?"

"Yes, Cadi, and it's been my pleasure to have them as companions." Caleb faced Gwenllian. "So tell me, mother, what's this I hear about my father taking Abertawe?"

"You know about that!" said Gwenllian.

"Everyone knows about *that*. We'd have come sooner, only we were forced to turn aside for several reasons."

"We've had to turn aside," said Cadi, determined to hold her brother's attention.

"Oh! And why is that?"

"It's the Old One, we've had to take him to the rocks back there so he can rest."

"Then, let's go, see him, shall we?" Holding Cadi in one arm, Caleb placed his other arm around Gwenllian's shoulders and, together, they made for the hollow. "So tell me, Cadi, how is Owain? Is he well?"

"Yes-yes, he is. And d'you know what?" He was the one who got them to open the gates at Abertawe. He was dressed like a Frenchman, and when they opened the gates he trapped half of them in the hall."

"Good for him. I only wish I'd been there."

"Yes, and he's the edling now."

"Is he now?"

"It's only a temporary thing," said Gwenllian, feeling the need to explain, "until you got back."

"Don't misunderstand me, mother, I'm pleased with all I hear. I was hoping Owain and I would be as one, share responsibilities."

"Oh! He'll want that, believe me," said Gwenllian, and drawing closer, she whispered, "I love you, Caleb."

"And I love you too, mother."

When they reached the rocky hollow they found that the Old One not only lay, covered in cloaks, but that Eswen lay beside him so that her body gave warmth to his. Caleb knelt beside the old bard who had been his teacher and companion for as long as he could remember. He kissed the Old One's forehead. A moment later, Gwenllian heard a familiar voice and, leaving her son and daughter, rushed into the arms of her brother, Einion. "Oh! Einion, why didn't you return sooner."

"We would have, Gwen, only we were delayed for several reasons. You see, Tewdrig got hit by an arrow at Aberystwyth. So we took him to the monastery at Llanbadarn Fawr so monks could tend to his wound. We were there only a day when we got word the French were out for revenge for all that we'd done in Ceredigion. So we crossed into Cantref Mawr where we found a hermit to look after him. I tell you, Gwen, Tewdrig was in a bad way, but Caleb wouldn't leave him, no more would the rest of us. Well, Tewdrig got worse – his jaw became fixed tight and he kept arching his back upwards. He died in Caleb's arms."

While her brother spoke, Gwenllian had given thought to Tewdrig, the son of a prominent Is-coed landowner who, six years earlier, had commended his son to serve in Rhydderch's bodyguard. Tewdrig had been singled out to be one of Caleb's chosen companions. She had approved their companionship and, being three years older than her son, Tewdrig had proved himself a stabling influence. Little wonder that Caleb had stayed with him to the end; she felt saddened by his eternal departure.

"That was three days ago," Einion continued. "We then headed south, intending to ford the Tywi at Llandeilo Fawr, but made slow progress because of all the cattle and spoil we'd taken in Ceredigion; worse still, Cantref Mawr was in turmoil because two Countryman lords from the north were hunting for Gruffudd ap Rhys. Well, we'd almost made it to Llandeilo Fawr only to be told the ford there had been closed on the orders of the King's son. So there was nothing we could do except take refuge in woods. Then the night afore last we were told the fords were no longer closed. So we forded the Tywi yesterday morning and have since made our way here."

"And Tewdrig," she said, "did you bury him where he died?"

"No, Caleb wanted his body brought back for burial in his *resting-place*. We were all of the same mind because we knew, if anything happened to us, Caleb wouldn't abandon us. I tell you, Gwen, those of us who have been with him these past two months think highly of Caleb. His father should be proud of him."

"I'm proud of him," said Gwenllian, tears welling in her eyes, "of both my sons." Einion put his arms around her; she sobbed, "Oh! Einion, I'm happy and I'm sad. Happy about Caleb and the way he's turned out, about the way everything has turned out, and then there's Tewdrig – and Merfyn."

"Ah! Yes, Merfyn. Rhain said he was none too good. Maybe we should go, see how he is."

"No, you go," she said, separating. "I need to be on my own for a while."

As she waked away, Einion called after her, "Don't go too far, Gwen, not so we can't keep an eye on you."

Sheltered from the wind by a large stone, Gwenllian knelt, crossed herself and gave thanks for Caleb's return, for Einion's return, for Rhydderch's success, for Owain; she prayed for Tewdrig's soul and for Merfyn's recovery.

When she stood up she looked south, beyond the stone, and said, "Rhydderch, I know you'll hear what I say when my words carry on the wind. I've just prayed for Merfyn, but that doesn't mean we do nothing for him ourselves. So what do we do? How do we get him down from the High Summit?"

Walking back to the others, Gwenllian noticed that almost everyone either sat or stood near the hollow, sharing whatever food they had. Cadi hovered about Caleb while he and Einion appeared to be at work on what looked like a *car llusg* – a sledge, consisting of two lengthy poles, cross-pieces, cow hide and rope. One end of the *car llusg* had been attached to Merfyn's horse. Cadi turned to her as she drew closer.

"What do you think, mother?" said Cadi, drawing her attention to the *car llusg*. "It's a bier to get Merfyn home."

"It looks more like a *car llusg* to me, and if that's what it is, it'll mean dragging him through mud and the rough ground will go hard on him."

"No, mother," said Caleb, "he won't be dragged over stony ground. The horse will carry the front end; two men will carry the rear."

"So where did it come from?"

"Ceredigion," Cadi volunteered. "'They've just tied a clean cow hide to it."

"What Cadi doesn't know," said Einion, "is that Caleb made it when we were at Llanbadarn Fawr. That's how we were able to get Tewdrig about the county when he was alive and when he was dead."

"Don't look so surprised, mother," said Caleb. "It's not as if I've never made a bier afore. You see, back in February my father insisted that I made one for Giff. Well, no one believed that I'd put my hands to work, but I did; that's when I first had a mind to make something like this."

"So, in a way your father had something to do with it."

"In a way, yes. He said that one day I might have to make one for a companion; that turned out to be Tewdrig; now we'll use if to get the Old One home."

CHAPTER 34

THE PROPHECY

After a memorable descent from the High Summit, Caleb's homecoming was marked by an unusual event in that Y Faerdref hall became crowded to the extent that tables had to be removed, for not only did the men of his father's household assemble there, as did the fourteen men who had served with him in Ceredigion, but the women and children of the court gathered there too. Almost everyone sat on the straw-covered floor; almost everyone had something to say of their experiences in Gower, Cantref Bychan or Ceredigion. From the converse Caleb learned of all that had happened during his absence; he learned, too, that de Turberville had arrived back at Abertawe the previous day to disband his forces shortly after his return. So the likelihood of further hostilities in Gower had, therefore, passed.

Among the many occurrence that affected Caleb most was the welcome that he received from his father – no admonishment, just expressions of joy at his return – whereas Maredudd's response had been predictably hearty. Any doubts that he had about his reunion with Owain were dispelled by his brother's unreserved embrace. It was, on reflection, unsurprising that he should experience a new-found relationship with his brother: they had parted company on good terms at Abertawe. Morgan, on the other hand, was full of surprises: first and foremost he was now accepted as Maredudd's son; secondly, he exhibited none of his usual bluster, nor did he brag about his pursuit of Bledri; he was certainly content with his marriage to Banwen.

When, eventually, Caleb settled down in a side-aisle in the early hours, he reflected on the change he had discerned in Owain, as well as the reason why that change had come about. Everyone was of the opinion that he had himself changed because of his experiences in Cantref Mawr and Ceredigion, which he accepted in part as true, but he knew that what had wrought the change in him was the experience of leadership. In the hall he had said little of that experience, preferring to keep it to himself, and although Einion had sung his praise, he knew the truth to be that he had remembered the things that his father had said to him.

'*When you share bread with men who may be dead on the morrow, you don't just lord it over them. You consult with them, and more, you get down off your horse and you eat, sleep and march with them, so that when there is loss you experience that loss; and when there is gain you will be moved to be a part of their rejoicing.'* All that he had done. Einion had been witness to it; his father had been pleased.

. . . . . .

The following morning the court became a hive of activity. The unsettled state of affairs had completely disrupted the seasonal migration from valley homesteads to fresh pastures on higher ground. Under normal circumstances the move had to be undertaken between the first and ninth of May; now, on the tenth of May, Y Faerdref household would soon be on the move again, this time to the summer camp on Tor Clawdd, some three miles to the north, a place that he and his mother had passed through during their descent from the High Summit.

Caleb took no part in the preparations, being otherwise engaged in the share-out of spoil between his men. Then he set off in the company of Einion and those returning to the Peninsula, taking with him the bier on which Tewdrig's body lay. When he returned to the summer camp two days later he learned that his father had received word from Cantref Bychan that Gruffudd ap Rhys had not only escaped entrapment, but that the campaign against him had ended in disaster. It was said that one of the Countryman lords in the service of the King had been killed when his men clashed with several hundred Flemings in the vicinity of Caerfyrddin. Gruffudd was, therefore, still at large; the French had suffered humiliation at their own hand.

Although everyone at court had received the news with joy, Caleb's response was less than enthusiastic, he being ambivalent about Gruffudd ap Rhys. Much as he liked the man, he had to concede that his father had been right: Gruffudd lacked leadership. The campaign in Ceredigion had been one of utter confusion, no more so than on the day the rebellion failed. On the fateful day Gruffudd's followers and the rebellious men of Ceredigion had marched on the castle at Aberystwyth, so it was said, like *a furious rabble without a ruler over them.* Most of the day had been wasted because Gruffudd and his leading men had stood by a bridge, dithering over how best to attack the castle. Then the French put an end to the inactivity by sending archers to the bridge to provoke a response, which resulted in Tewdrig being hit by an arrow. Many of Gruffudd's infuriated followers had charged over the bridge in pursuit of the archers as they retreated uphill, back to the castle. Then French horse appeared, silhouetted on the side of the hill, to descend on Gruffudd's men. For what seemed an age, Gruffudd had watched in horror while the French massacred his men. Then he departed, his disillusioned followers deserting him as he headed back for the wilds of Cantref Mawr.

That, Caleb mused, was the last he had seen of Gruffudd; that was when he took Tewdrig to the monastery at Llanbadern Fawr. Maybe one day he would meet Gruffudd again, but the prospect of doing so did not enthuse him.

. . . . . .

On the morning after his return from Tewdrig's *resting-place*, Caleb made ready his bier to journey yet again, this time to Y Faerdref where the Old One had been left to rest and recover. It was hoped that the Old One would be well enough to travel; if not, Caleb would be content to converse with him, tell him that all he had taught had not fallen on deaf ears. The visit would also give him the opportunity to converse with Morgan who, with his wife, Banwen, and others had remained at Y Faerdref to care for the Old One.

Assisted by his companion, Dewi, Caleb set about securing his bier to the Old One's horse. While he worked, Caleb took in his surroundings. The summer camp occupied a fairly level plateau, the northern half of which was protected by steep slopes that were overlooked by a palisade. There were no defences to the south, but with ten miles of difficult terrain separating the camp from Abertawe it was nigh on impossible for the French to launch a surprise attack, as his father's court and cattle would be long gone before the attackers got within striking distance. Even if the French set out from Cantref Bychan to the north, they faced a gruelling five-mile march, most of it uphill, to be confronted by the steep slopes beyond the palisade. Close to a gateway in the palisade stood the court, defended by a ring of paling and a shallow ditch. Other buildings could be seen scattered about the grassy plateau, which served as an ideal place to keep cattle and horses at night. His father could not have chosen a better summer campsite in all Uwch-coed.

When the bier was all but ready, Caleb was joined by Owain and his two companions, Elidir and Meurig, and also the High Steward's son, Meurig de Turberville, whom Owain had been made responsible for. Although resentful about his status as a hostage during the first few days following his capture, it was now evident that Meurig de Turberville had settled in among the youths of the bodyguard, confident that he would be released in eighteen days. The last to join the company was Maredudd, who immediately bantered with Owain about his forthcoming betrothal to Anona.

The seven set off; a short distance from the court enclosure they approached the forge to see the blacksmith wave to them, a gesture that prompted Caleb to be mindful of Morgan. The brothers Caradog and Gronw had been found guilty of treason on the testimonies of both Bledri and

Morgan – Morgan being witness to what Caradog had said when cornered in dunes. Consequently, the brothers had been hanged, whereas Bledri had been pardoned – subject to a fine – on the testimony of Morgan. There were those who questioned his father's leniency on the ground that Bledri could not be trusted, but it had to be said that the blacksmith seemed more amiable than as Caleb remembered him. The one thing that everyone was in agreement with was that Morgan had earned respect.

· · · · · ·

In Morgan's abode on the outskirts of Y Faerdref estate, Merfyn lay upon straw in a side-aisle, covered by a blanket. A sporadic cough played havoc with the old bard's chest, but he took comfort from Banwen's presence. During the past three days Banwen had spent most of her time tending to his needs: washing him, spoon-feeding him broth, or just talking to him; as a result his health had improved – but today he felt poorly, unable or unwilling to find the strength to get to his feet.

"Do you want to sleep, Old One?" Banwen asked.

"No, no," Merfyn croaked, placing a hand on Banwen's forearm, "but tell me, my child, what is that I hear outside?"

"It's Morgan, he's chopping wood."

"Ah! Always busy."

"I know, I'm so proud of him, and it's all down to you."

"No, not me. You – you were the one to stand by him from the first."

"But it was you I came to for help. If I ever have a son, I will call him Merfyn after you. I'm sure Morgan will agree to it if I...." Banwen paused. Morgan had stopped chopping wood; she could hear voices carrying from afar. She rose, saying, "I think someone's coming this way. I'll go, see who it is."

Merfyn watched her as she made for the door, mindful of what she had said about naming a son after him. The thought evoked memories, the same memories that had haunted him time and again over the past few days. Some fifty years ago he had stood over his young wife as she lay in a side-aisle, much as Banwen had stood over him of late, except that his wife no longer breathed. There had been voices, there had been wailing, but the sound that had demanded his attention was the cry of a new-born babe. The child was his, one small, consoling life in exchange for the tender love of another. Holding the child in his arms, he could see that she was so like her mother. He could almost feel the child's warmth. Yet the chilling hand of death was soon to take his daughter too.

'*How old would she have been now, had she lived?*' he wondered. '*Old enough to have had children of her own – grandchildren too.*'

That Banwen should show such concern for him, be so willing to attend to his every need, made it possible for him to experience what it would have been like to have had a loving daughter.

Outside, Banwen found Morgan involved in a hearty reunion, from which Maredudd was the first to break away and greet her, to inquire after her health, then ask about the Old One. It pleased her to have Maredudd visit her abode, not so much as her father-in-law, more someone she could look up to, someone she could depend on, someone who paid her the compliment of respect. She led him in through the porch, telling him how Merfyn had improved until this morning.

When he reached the low-roofed side-aisle Maredudd crouched, saying, "Awake, Old One, it's me, Maredudd."

"Yes, I know, I have been expecting trouble."

"Does that mean you're pleased to see me?"

"Only if I have your word that I will not have to suffer your atrocious verse."

"Then I shall tell you something amusing that happened yesterday."

What Maredudd had to say soon brought a smile to Merfyn's lips, at which point seven youths entered. Maredudd withdrew from the side-aisle to allow Caleb and Owain to kneel beside the one who had been their teacher and companion for as long as they could remember. Merfyn was evidently pleased to see them, the more so because they were as one. Maredudd looked on, wondering whether the brothers realized that the Old One was dying. When the old man breathed no more the brothers would grieve, as would the whole court, though none more so than Gwenllian, Rhydderch and himself.

He had been fourteen years old when he first came to know Merfyn as the household bard of Rhys, Lord of Gower. Both himself and Rhydderch had been drawn to the man, though each for different reasons. He had been intrigued by the bard's metered verse, especially the haunting epics of old, as well as the lively tunes that set feet moving. His attempts to emulate the old bard may have failed, but his recollections of the man's rhythmic verse had been of use because, as captain of guard, he was comptroller of all music in the hall.

Rhydderch, on the other hand, had not been captivated by Merfyn's verse, but by his knowledge and his wisdom. For his part the old bard must have recognized in Rhydderch those qualities that set him apart from other men because, when Rhydderch reached full maturity at twenty-one and became possessed of Y Faerdref, the Old One had relinquished his honoured position in Lord Rhys's court to become Rhydderch's bard and the teacher of his children. Rhydderch had, therefore, benefited from both the Old One's talent and his wisdom, he being one the inner circle of councillors.

Gwenllian, of course, had her own reasons for holding Merfyn in high esteem. For her, his presence had been her refuge at Rhys's court, the more so during those occasions when Rhydderch had been away on forays at the Lord Rhys's bidding. That she continued to take pleasure in the Old One's company would be reason for her to be deeply affected by his passing. Indeed, the soothsayer had failed to impart the fullness of her prophecy when she said, to Rhydderch, that the attack on Abertawe would mean *sorrow too because someone close to you will die*. The Old One's passing would mean sorrow for all who had been close to him.

Maredudd leaned against a roof support, content to let Merfyn enjoy the company of seven youths and the young woman whom he had come to regard as his daughter. He listened to their converse, their laughter, until movement in the porchway caused him to turn and see the dung-bailiff beckon to him from the doorway. He sauntered to the doorway, saying, "Yes, Docal, what is it?"

"There's two men from Abertawe outside, one of them the Saxon who was here two weeks ago. I think they've come with a message for Lord Rhydderch. So I thought maybe they'd best see you first."

Maredudd ducked out of the porch to see two mounted men-at-arms, whom he rcognized as Elgar and William. He extended an arm in friendship to both men, exchanging pleasantries, then said, "So what brings you two here?"

"We've news," said William, grinning. "Some good, some bad. What do you want to hear first?"

"The good – it'll take the sting out of the bad."

William turned to Elgar, who said, "Monsieur John de Penrhys arrived back from Warwick last eventide. We were both there when he told Monsieur de Turberville that he had informed the Earl of recent events and that much of what he had to say had been confirmed by the two Warwick men who were with him. Monsieur de Penrhys then produced a writ that says he's the new High Steward, and as such he's sent us to inform Rhydderch of the change and to tell him that the concord is to be upheld. Monsieur de Penrhys also requests that he and Rhydderch meet at the monastery in three days time to settle any uncertainties."

"That is good news," said Maredudd. "So how did de Turberville take it?"

"He was none too pleased, though not surprised. He's still at Abertawe, partly to assist with the changeover, and partly because – well, he's asked me to pass on a message to Rhydderch. He says that as he's kept the peace and is no longer in a position to take action against Rhydderch, he requests that his son be set free when Rhydderch meets Monsieur de Penrhys at the monastery.

"Seems reasonable to me, but it's for Rhydderch to decide."

"And now for the bad news," said William.

"It's de Viles," said Elgar, "he's back on his feet, and that's put Messieurs de Penrhys and de Turberville in a quandary. You see, everyone is of the opinion that de Viles killed Iorwerth's priest. The problem is there's no witnesses. So de Turberville suggested the matter should be decided in a trial by combat while the madman is still in a weakened state, but there's a problem with that too because de Viles is claiming sanctuary, and will continue to do so until he gets his strength back. Then no one will stand up to him, including myself because once is enough to take on that madman."

"In the meantime," said William, looking Maredudd straight in the eye, "he swears he'll have his revenge on all them that hate him. And you – you'll be the first to stand in awe against him."

Maredudd laughed, "I wouldn't want it any other way."

GLOSSARY

abatis – a barrier of felled trees intended to halt a frontal attack by horsemen

Absalom – a son of the biblical King David. He was slain by an enemy after his hair got tangled in a tree

anabasis – a military expedition, especially one from the coast to the interior

ap/ab – Welsh, meaning 'son of'

bailey – the outer ward of a castle, within which were domestic buildings

baldric – a belt for a sword, worn over one shoulder and reaching down to the opposite hip

bard – a poet or minstrel

cantref – meaning 'one hundred households', a territorial division comprising of two or more commotes

castle guard – a feudal obligation, one whereby men-at-arms held their fiefs on the understanding that they would serve their lord in a military capacity for a period of 40 days each year

churl – an unfree Countryman, his status similar to that of a serf

commote – Welsh *cymwd*, a district (similar to an English hundred) in which free Countrymen/Welshmen worked together for the purpose of upholding law and order and the collection of whatever was due to their lord

compurgator – someone who swears that, in his opinion, a defendant's denial is true

Countryman – from Welsh *Cymro* , meaning 'fellow countryman'

dart – a short throwing spear

doorward – a bodyguard whose duties included announcing visitors

embrasure – an opening in a palisade to allow an archer to loose off his arrows

ferch – Welsh, meaning 'daughter of'

French (the) – what the Countrymen/Welsh called the Norman invaders who conquered England in 1066 and who later established themselves in the lowland areas of Wales fief – a landed estate given by a lord to a man in return for military service as a heavily armed horseman (knight); this often took the form of a forty-day castle guard obligation each year

harbinger – someone who announces the approach of an important person

hauberk – a knee-length, chain-mail tunic worn by French men-at-arms

high man – (Welsh *uchelwr*) a Countryman who owned ancestral land and who was head of a household that included his wife, children, grandchildren, servants, tenants and slaves

Is-coed – one of two commotes within the Lordship of Gower. It comprised mainly of the Gower Peninsula, the southern coastline of which formed part of French and Saxon Gower

kine – cows collectively. In the early 12th century a cow was worth 60 old (pre-1971) pence, equivalent to 25 modern pence

Marcher lords – foreign lords who held extensive territory in the lowland areas of Wales

man-at-arms – a heavily armed horseman, to all intents and purposes a knight, but not one holding the title of 'sir'

miscreant – a person who behaves badly or unlawfully

motte – a pudding-shaped mound surmounted by a wooden tower

nod man – from Latin *notus*, meaning man of distinction

palisade/paling – a fence of stakes for protection against attack

pence (old, pre-decimalization) – 2.4 old pence is equivalent to 1 modern penny. There were 240 old pence in a pound

plaid – a long piece of tartan material worn over the shoulder in the manner of a Scottish clansman

plaintiff – a person who brings a legal action against another

resting-place – for the purpose of this story, land occupied by a group of related Countrymen

retainer – a youth in the service of an important person

rhaglaw – an officer responsible for the legal affairs of a commote; he also had overall charge of his lord's churls (serfs)

rushlight – a candle made by dipping rushes in tallow

settle – a wooden bench with a high back

skene – a long, single-edged knife used by Countrymen

Southern Lands – from Welsh *Deheubarth* – a kingdom comprising of modern Pembrokeshire, Cardiganshire and Carmarthenshire, plus what was once the Lordship of Gower

steward – a person employed to manage an estate and attend to legalities

surety – a person who takes on the responsibility of ensuring that someone else abides by law

tunic – a voluminous, below-the-knee shirt with long sleeves

Uwch-coed – one of two commotes within the Lordship of Gower; its southern boundary lay somewhere between modern-day Loughor and Morriston

Welsh – from Anglo-Saxon *Welisc* or *Wealh*, meaning 'foreigner'

Ystum Llymarch – Welsh for Oystermouth

HISTORICAL CHARACTERS

Beaumont, Henry de, alias Henry de Newburgh, Earl of Warwick; also Lord of Gower after its conquest in or soon after 1106

Gruffudd ap Rhys – much of what has been written of him in the text follows what has been recorded of him in *The Chronicle of the Princes*.

Londres, William de, Lord of Ogwr (Ogmore), believed to have been Steward of the Lordships of Cydweli (Kidwelly) and Carnwyllion (the Llanelli area) on behalf of the Bishop of Salisbury; also believed to have held Ystum Llymarch (Oystermouth). Died c1126

Londres, Maurice de – son and heir of William, depicted by the 12th century writer, Gerald of Wales, as both cruel and stupid

Maredudd ap Rhydderch, Lord of Cantref Bychan – mentioned in both the Peniarth and Hergest versions of *The Chronicle of the Princes*; he appears among the entries for the years 1109 and 1116

Rhys ap Caradog – the names appears in Iolo Morgannwg's Aberpergwm/Gwentian version of *The Chronicle of the Princes*, which record that he was slain at Penrice by Henry de Beaumont's invasive forces

Rhydderch Fawr – in his *Morganniae Archaiographia*, published 1574-5, Rice Merrick referred to him as the last Lord of Gower before its conquest by the Strangers (the French)

Turberville (d'Urberville), Payn de, Lord of Coety. Active in Gower c1131. Died sometime after 1131

Turberville, Meurig/Maurice de – third son of Payn.

290

Part One of the Trilogy

The Last Lord of Gower
—
A Prophecy Unfolds

ISBN 0-9546544-2-0
203 pp. Maps and plans. Card cover
Draisey Publishing, 2005 £9.95

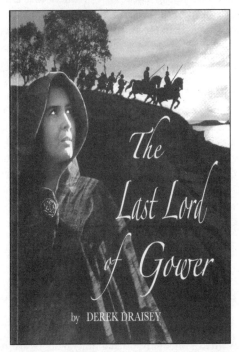

Set in twelfth-century Gower, the heart of this sinewy tale is based on the cameraderie shared by two foster brothers in their struggle to remain free from foreign rule. Running parallel to scenes of bloody conflict is an eternal triangle; when the foster brothers were youths it was Maredudd who first won Gwenllian's affection; at her father's insistence she marries Rhydderch with whom she finds a different, more mature relationship – but the embers of her love for Maredudd still smoulder. The invasion of Gower is led by two Norman-French knights; the resolute William de Londres and the brutal theomaniac, Henry de Viles, each seeking to outdo the other in terrorizing the native population into submission – but they have, first, to contend with Rhydderch's uncle, Rhys, Lord of Gower, and while he takes steps to offer battle, the foster-brothers confound the invaders in several well-placed ambushes.

By the Same Author

The People of Gower

ISBN 0-9546544-0-4. 136 pp. Illustrated. Card cover
Draisey Publishing, 2003 £9.95

This book tells the story of man's presence in the Gower Peninsula and its upland extension between the Tawe and Loughor rivers. What happened in this unique area, where man's past achievements in earth and stone abound, is a reflection, albeit on a smaller scale, of the rise and fall of successive cultures that existed in Wales and, indeed, mainland Britain from Stone Age times to c.1400.

The people who spearheaded these intrusive, often invasive cultures settled, initially, in relatively small numbers in the coastal lowlands where they coexisted with, and eventually imposed much of their cultural identities on the indigenous inhabitants, leaving the natives in the upland areas to carry on in their time-honoured ways for centuries until they, too, became absorbed into the intrusive cultures.

Some newcomers, like those who initiated the Neolithic period, introduced farming, and in the remains of their megalithic tombs the bones of their dead show them to be the ancestors of the short, swarthy Welshmen of historic times. Others, such as the Celts, appear to have established themselves as a warrior aristocracy, bringing with them a language which, although subject to change, has survived to the present day. Above all it was the Anglo-Saxons and later Norman-dominated English who imposed an overwhelming cultural identity on mainland Britain and, in doing so in Wales, shaped the Gower landscape that we know today.

Women in Welsh History

ISBN 0-9546544-1-. 205 pp. Illustrated. Card cover
Draisey Publishing, 2004 £9.95

The names and achievements of many outstanding women are to be found within these pages — and more: this is the story of women throughout the ages, both rich and poor, of courtship, marriage, childbearing, abortion, crime, employment, dress, and a host of other issues that were, and continue to be, relevant to the women of Wales.

For the most part the women of Wales have been burdened by poverty, hard work and repeated pregnancies. Yet despite these difficulties they have proved themselves no more subservient, no less spirited that they are today. They have shown themselves to be passionate about the things that mattered to them, supportive to their husbands and families in times of adversity, stoic in times of tragedy. They were, and still are, admirable women.